ON A
DARK TIDE

A BRETT BUCHANAN MYSTERY

VALERIE GEARY

**BROKEN
BRANCH**

ON A DARK TIDE
Copyright © 2021 by Valerie Geary
Broken Branch Books
Portland, OR

Firs edition April 2021

ISBN 978-1-954815-00-1

www.valeriegeary.com

For Nathan.
He knows what he did.

ON A
DARK TIDE

CHAPTER 1

Brett hadn't seen any signs of rats in the four months she'd been living with her grandmother in the big house overlooking Sculpin Bay, but Amma insisted she heard them. They were keeping her awake at night, she said. Furry little bastards would chew apart the attic if someone didn't stop them. And by someone, she meant Brett.

Amma was afraid of the ladder that unfolded from the ceiling, worried that if she tried to climb the narrow rungs, she would fall, break her hip, and lie for days in agony until someone found her. If someone found her. A woman who lives alone dies alone, Amma liked to say with a bitter twist of her coral-tinted lips. But she wasn't alone anymore, Brett reminded her nearly every day.

In June, Brett had uprooted her entire life to come and live with Amma in Crestwood, a salt-encrusted fleck of nowhere town in Washington, less than an hour's drive from the Canadian border. Part of their arrangement was that Brett could stay on rent-free indefinitely as long as she helped out with the things Pop used to do. Like raking leaves, and cleaning gutters, and climbing into the attic on her day off to set traps for imaginary rats.

As far as Brett could tell, no one had been in the attic since Pop died of a heart attack five years ago. A thick layer of dust covered the beams and eaves and boxes stacked underneath. She wiggled a trap into the narrow space between an old wardrobe and the wall. Once all the traps were in place, she worked her way back toward the open hatch, weaving through the cluttered odds-and-ends her grandparents had accumulated during their sixty years together. At some point, she and Amma would have to go through it all and decide what was worth saving.

Downstairs, a door slammed. Brett startled at the sound and bumped into a stack of boxes. The top one fell, and the lid opened. Cameras, film canisters, and stacks of curled, faded photographs spilled across the attic floor.

Brett sat a minute listening, in case Amma needed help. She'd been losing her balance recently, tripping over uneven thresholds and her own feet. *It's nothing*, she'd say, waving away Brett's concern. *I'm getting clumsy in my old age, that's all.*

When no other sounds came from downstairs, Brett assumed everything was fine.

During the summer months, Amma took her breakfast of black coffee and toast onto the back patio, where she would watch cormorants glide across the glinting surface of Sculpin Bay and scan the horizon for whales. Though it was mid-October now, and most mornings were too cold to sit out on the porch for long, Amma would sometimes wrap herself in a sweater and do it anyway. According to her, the murmur of water against the pebbled beach calmed her nerves.

Brett returned her focus to cleaning up the mess she'd made. She put the cameras and lenses back into the box without much thought but took her time with the photographs.

Many were black-and-white, abstract glimpses of light and shapes, her grandfather dabbling with his artistic side. She took a minute flipping through a small stack of pictures where the subjects were people rather than buildings and landscapes. Pictures of Amma and Pop together and impossibly young. A baby in Amma's lap grinning toothless, followed by more photos of the same baby in a frilly, white dress. Then in a diaper, crawling across the dock. Then in a sailboat with Pop. Then sitting in the grass outside this very house that hadn't changed much over the years with its wrap-around porch, Victorian turret, and wind vane shaped like a whale. The baby in these pictures was Brett's mother. The cowlick curl over her forehead was the same cowlick Brett had been trying to tame her whole life. In a later picture, her mother's cowlick had disappeared, her hair turned honey-blond and soft, her eyes mischievous. The resemblance to Brett's older sister was startling enough, she did a double-take. She had never realized how much Margot looked like their mother.

As girls, Brett and Margot spent every summer from the Fourth of July to Labor Day in Crestwood with their grandparents. Wild days, golden days, she remembered them as glinting and saturated bright, until the summer of 1964 when their lives shattered. Brett hadn't thought she would ever return to Crestwood after what happened that summer. Yet here she was twenty years later, and though her heart was no less broken than the day they found Margot's body, she had at least gotten better at pretending.

The smell of burning toast wafted into the attic.

"Amma?" Brett called down. "Is everything okay?"

When she received no response, Brett abandoned the rest of the mess to pick up later. She climbed down the ladder and went into the kitchen, where gray smoke billowed from the toaster. Brett fumbled with the handle until the damn thing finally popped. She pinched a corner of the charred toast and tossed it into the sink. A flush of water and the smoke dissipated, though the stench of it hung thick in the air.

"Amma?" Brett called out again.

From the small radio on the counter, two pundits discussed

tomorrow's second presidential debate between Reagan and Mondale. A mug beside it had been filled to the brim with coffee and left to go cold. Brett flicked off the radio.

The double french doors leading out to the back porch hung wide open. A cool breeze blew through. Brett slipped on a pair of rain boots, grabbed Amma's favorite sky-blue cardigan from its hook beside the door, and went outside. She stepped off the porch and walked across the backyard that sloped to a pebbled beach.

Amma, a petite silhouette against a damp gray October sky, stood on the beach a few steps from the dock and a small boathouse, painted the same cheerful yellow as the main house. A fourteen-foot sailboat bobbed in the water, tugging against the ropes that kept it lashed to the dock. Amma's back was to Brett, but she wasn't looking out over the bay. Her head was tilted, and she was staring at her feet. Not at her feet, Brett realized as she walked closer, but at a pile of wet clothes. She quickened her pace. Even this far away, she could tell that what had washed up this morning was more than rags.

She stepped off the lawn. Pebbles crunched underfoot.

Without looking up, Amma flapped her hand and said, "Don't come any closer, Brett, dear. This isn't something you need to see."

Brett grabbed Amma and pulled her away from the body.

Small waves rocked the man gently. He was on his stomach, face pressed into the rocks, his arms trapped beneath him. The skin of his neck, visible above his shirt collar, was bloated and splotched purple. Working as a sheriff's deputy for the past ten years, and now as a detective, Brett had seen enough bodies to know without needing to bend close or check his pulse that this man was unmistakably dead.

She swung her gaze along the beach and out across the water, looking for a wrecked boat or something else to explain how he'd come to wash up on this particular shore. There was nothing out of the ordinary. An empty stretch of sand and stone, the soft pull of the tide, a seagull eyeing them from the roof of the boathouse.

Brett turned her attention back to Amma, who was shivering so hard her teeth chattered. She had been out here only a few minutes, but the thin linen pants and short-sleeved blouse she was wearing did little to protect her from the mist and light breeze coming off the water. They were close enough to the shoreline that waves rolled over her bare feet. The cuffs of her pants were soaked past the ankle.

Brett spread the cardigan over Amma's shoulders. "What are you even doing out here?"

"I was going to take the boat out for a jaunt." Amma wrapped the cardigan tight around herself.

"You don't have any shoes on."

Amma looked at her feet, confusion rippling across her face, then she blinked and straightened her shoulders. A frown tugged at the corners of her mouth. "A man is dead, Brett. I hardly think now is the time to hassle me about my choice of attire."

"I wasn't trying to hassle you. I just—"

"I'm going to call the police." Amma spun away from her and marched up the hill toward the house. The long hem of her cardigan a fluttering scrap of sky against the gray mist and steel-colored clouds.

CHAPTER 2

"Clara Louise, are you listening to me?"

Clara blinked and returned her full attention to her mother. She'd been staring out the plate glass window of Crumbles and Cakes, the coffee shop downtown where they shared breakfast every Saturday with few exceptions. Sculpin Bay glinted in the distance, a dark thread against a vast sky, the horizon bleeding gray into the clouds. Orcas and San Juan islands, normally visible from almost any high point in Crestwood, were shrouded in fog today. A light mist coated the window and dripped from the eaves.

Geana Pearce shifted in her chair, the antique wood creaking under her weight. "What's wrong with you today?" She sipped her milky coffee and ate a bite of a chocolate croissant.

"What do you mean?" Clara reached for her own coffee, hot and black.

"You seem..." Geana fluttered her hand, a trio of bangles on her wrist clattering together. "I don't know, distracted, I guess."

"Just a little tired. I could use a refill." She started to get out of her chair, but before she could get far, Mary appeared, coffee carafe in hand.

"You two ladies doing okay?" Mary Andress, the owner of

Crumbles and Cakes, smiled at them. Her plump cheeks were dusted in flour, as was the apron tied around her waist. Her auburn hair, turning silver at the roots, was pulled into a thick braid, the tail draped over one shoulder.

"As always, your croissants are too divine, my dear," Geana said.

Mary poured coffee into each of their cups, then set fresh creamer on the table in front of Geana and a small pink pastry box in front of Clara. "Treats for Marshall and Elizabeth."

"Mary, you don't have to." Clara started to push the box away, but Mary covered her hand, stopping her with a quick squeeze.

"Full bellies, happy hearts." She offered a soft smile before returning to the front counter.

"So you'll think about it?" Geana asked when Mary was gone, returning Clara's attention to the conversation they'd been having about the upcoming Halloween festival before Clara got distracted by the distant clouds. "A couple of hours, that's all I'm asking. Please, Clara, I need you there."

She sighed. "You did fine last year without me."

Geana laughed. "Two kids twisted their ankles, one woman got knocked over by a man dressed as Gumby who couldn't see where he was going, and Linda released the balloons an hour early. It was an unmitigated disaster."

"Disaster might be a bit of an exaggeration, don't you think, Mother? I'm just saying, there are plenty of people in this town willing to help you."

Before Geana could respond, three police cars screamed past the café, sirens blaring and lights flashing as they sped down Main Street toward the bay.

"What in the world?" Geana craned her neck as the cars turned a corner. She rose from her chair. The legs scraped loudly across the linoleum.

"Mama, don't," Clara protested, but Geana was already grabbing her hand and pulling her toward the door. Clara barely had time to snatch the pink pastry box off the table.

It was a ten-minute brisk walk from the café in historic downtown Crestwood to Bayshore Drive, where the town's wealthiest citizens lived on private beaches in generous mansions with unobstructed views of the ocean. Clara and Geana were the first to arrive at the police barrier. More people gathered by the minute, drawn by the sirens and lights and possibility of tragedy. Crestwood wasn't so small a town that nothing interesting ever happened, but small enough that everyone came out to watch when it did.

The three cop cars that had blazed past Crumbles and Cakes were parked at angles blocking the street. Eli Miller, dressed in a crisp navy uniform and shiny leather boots, unrolled a spool of yellow tape in front of the sidewalk to keep onlookers from stepping into the yard of a three-story, cedar shake, gabled house. Clara had known Eli since elementary school. Eli and her husband, Marshall, had been best friends for even longer than that. He'd been with the Crestwood Police Department for over ten years, but she didn't think she'd ever get used to seeing him with a badge, carrying a gun on his hip like it weighed nothing. He waved when he saw her, finished tying the yellow tape around a signpost, and came over to where she and her mother stood.

"What's going on?" Geana asked.

They were about one hundred yards from the beach where another officer crouched beside a dark lump near the water's edge. It was impossible to tell what the lump was from this distance.

Eli leaned close and lowered his voice, so only Clara and her mother could hear. "A body washed up early this morning."

Geana gasped and pressed her hands to her mouth. "Oh, dear. A body? Like a person?"

"Is that for me?" Eli grinned and reached for the pink pastry box in Clara's hand. "You shouldn't have."

She pulled it away. "Do they know who it is?"

"Oh, Clare Bear," Eli said, using a nickname from high school that he knew she hated but for some reason insisted on resurrecting. "You know I couldn't tell you that even if I knew. Don't be mad," he teased, dimples creasing his cheeks. "You'll find out soon enough. I'm sure Arlo's on his way. Surprised he's not already here actually."

Arlo Savage was the long-time editor of the *Crestwood Tribune*, the town's daily newspaper. He was a man who might easily be as old as the town itself and who, like her mother, made it his business to know everyone else's business.

Another uniformed officer, younger than Eli, walked up to the yellow tape. He held a clipboard in one hand. He tipped his head toward the house's back deck, where Detective Irving Winters stood talking with another man.

Except for three years when she attended the University of Washington in Seattle, Clara had lived her entire life in Crestwood. While she wasn't friends with everyone, between volunteering at her daughter's school, her husband's realty job, and her mother's love of gossip, she knew a lot of people. Eli had introduced her to Irving Winters several years ago. Even without that connection, Irving was a man she would have noticed and remembered on her own. In a town where most people could trace their lineage to England or France or some ruddy group of Vikings, Irving was African-American. His dark brown skin contrasted starkly with the sea of pale faces that surrounded him. The bird ties he always wore, no matter the occasion, made him stand out even more.

"Detective Winters wants you looking for this car." The younger officer slipped Eli a torn piece of paper. "Medical examiner's on his way. I'll take over here."

Eli frowned at the slip of paper before tucking it in his pocket. He flicked a glance at Clara, showing off his dimples again, and gave her a playful wink. "Duty calls. See you and Marshall tomorrow?"

She nodded, waving him off.

He pumped his fist in the air. "Go Hawks!"

He took his time walking along Bayshore Drive, checking license plates, zigzagging from one side to the other, before finally disappearing down a smaller side street. The officer standing in front of the perimeter tape widened his stance and stared into the distance, ignoring Clara, her mother, and the rest of the gathered crowd.

Geana bumped her shoulder against Clara's, her voice filled with reproach. "Aren't I always telling you not to swim in the bay? I guarantee you that's not the only body floating around out there."

"Mom," Clara warned.

"What? You know I'm right. That water's deep. Who knows what else—or who else—could be hiding down there. At the very least, you shouldn't be swimming alone."

Clara sighed and said, "I'm going, Mom. Thanks for the coffee."

"You're not leaving with all of this going on, are you?"

Officers were setting up a tent on the beach. The medical examiner's van drove up and parked along the curb.

"Elizabeth's soccer game is starting soon." Clara turned from the commotion.

If she hurried, she could make it to the school in time for kickoff.

A shrill whistle echoed across the field. White and red-striped Crestwood jerseys darted and wove through purple Anacortes jerseys. Freshman and sophomore girls with long ponytails and stilt legs shoved and feinted, twirled and spun, as they kicked the soccer ball back and forth, trying to gain ground against the other team. Seated in folding beach chairs and a set of metal bleachers, parents cheered from the sidelines.

Clara stood a moment apart from everything and watched her daughter play. Elizabeth waited in the goal box, half-crouched with her hands spread and her quads tense. Her focus stayed on the ball, her whole being alert to every shift and twitch. She had been playing soccer since she could walk and was the best player on the Junior Varsity team, her skills far surpassing that of the other girls. Clara thought she should be playing Varsity, but Marshall and Coach Lansing disagreed.

The Anacortes team took possession of the ball and moved it down the field with sloppy, uncoordinated kicks. They didn't stand a chance. With a playful swat, Elizabeth knocked the ball out of the goal. An easy kick like that she could have blocked with her eyes closed, hands tied behind her back. Her teammates swarmed and guided the ball around the Anacortes defenders to the other end of the field.

Clara found Marshall where she always found Marshall during Elizabeth's games—pacing the sidelines. So invested was he in each play, he couldn't sit still. A few times in past years, Elizabeth's coaches had threatened to ban him from games for being too competitive. He'd since settled into a habit of pacing and muttering under his breath, only shouting when a goal was made or deflected.

He scooped Clara into a quick hug, pecking her on the cheek before releasing her and returning to his pacing. She stayed in one spot, watching the ball fly between the players' feet. When Marshall reached her a second time, he paused to ask about her mother.

"She's fine." Clara waved the pastry box at him. "Mary says hello."

He took a muffin, then turned and paced the opposite direction, eating as he walked.

When he returned to her a third time, she told him about the dead body on the beach.

He stopped in his tracks, and for the first time that she could remember since Elizabeth had joined soccer, he wasn't paying attention to the game.

"Jesus," he exhaled, then asked, "Was Eli there?"

She nodded.

"What did he say?"

"Not much." She started to explain how it was too soon to know many details, but a chill ran through her, and she gave herself over to it, her whole body shuddering.

"Hey." He gathered her up, tucking her against his chest. "Are you all right?"

She loved it when he held her like this. Loved that she fit so neatly under his chin, how he could wrap his arms fully around her, envelope her in a way that felt protected and forever. He kissed the top of her head, made small circles with his hand over her back. They'd been married fifteen years, had been dating over twenty, since her sophomore year of high school, and she never tired of his tenderness, the way he took care of her. From the very beginning, he had been it for her. The only man she'd ever loved.

"It's going to be okay," he whispered.

She leaned into his platitudes, allowing them to crush the fear rising in her chest. Allowing herself to get swept away by the rhythm of his steady heartbeat.

"It's probably a fisherman. Or an overdose. No one we know. Don't worry, baby." He kissed the top of her head again.

She nodded against his chest, folding his words into herself until she believed them. *Don't worry, don't worry.*

A whistle blew. The bleachers roared.

Marshall turned his head toward the field and shouted, "That's my girl!" as Elizabeth deflected another goal.

The sound reverberated against Clara's cheek. She hadn't known it was possible to love someone so much and to feel such love in return. She didn't deserve it, a love this steady and good, but whenever she tried to tell Marshall that, he would laugh and say no one would love anyone if it came down to deserving.

He stayed close to her, holding her hand until the final whistle blew and the game ended. It was a blowout—seven to zero.

The teams high-fived and trotted off the field to their respective benches to gather their gear and water bottles. A few girls wandered over to the bleachers to meet up with their parents. Elizabeth talked with her coach a minute and exchanged a quick hug with her best friend, June. Then she tugged off her cleats and shin guards and stuffed everything into a duffel bag.

Clara and Marshall started to cross the field to meet her. Before they got halfway, a boy wearing tight, acid-washed jeans and a black leather jacket approached Elizabeth from the other direction. He said something, and she smiled bashfully at him, ducking her head, making her ponytail bounce. He sat on the bench facing her, close enough he might have been leaning in for a kiss. She nodded at something he said. Marshall cleared his throat loud enough for Elizabeth to hear. She stiffened and looked over at them, then flashed the boy a quick wave, stood, grabbed her duffel and the rest of her gear, and left him sitting on the bench.

Head lowered, she walked past Clara and Marshall toward the parking lot behind the gymnasium.

"Who was that?" Clara asked, following her.

"No one, a kid from school."

"He looks too old to be in high school," Clara pushed.

Marshall tugged on her hand and gave her a warning look, but Clara persisted. "What's his name?"

"He's no one, I told you. He's a senior. I don't even know him that well."

"He has a name, though, right?"

"Zach, okay? His name is Zach." She threw up a hand in frustration. "He's friends with June's older sister or something. He was congratulating me on the win. No big deal."

Clara caught Marshall's eye, trying to gauge how he felt about his fourteen-year-old daughter hanging around a senior boy who looked like he could be the lead singer in a British punk band. Marshall shook his head. *Let it go.*

When they reached the car, Elizabeth flopped into the backseat. Marshall drove. As they pulled away from the school, Clara twisted in her seat and passed the pastry box to Elizabeth. "There's a Danish in here with your name on it."

Elizabeth frowned, but she took the box.

"You did great out there today, sweetheart." Marshall smiled at her in the rearview mirror. "We're so proud of you."

She relaxed against her seat and smiled back at him. She was her father's daughter in every way, with her high cheekbones and chestnut hair, a broad forehead, and sharp chin. When she smiled, she smiled with her whole self, the same as Marshall. She would be tall like him someday too. The only thing she got from Clara were her eyes, which were turquoise and bright as the summer sea most days, shifting to gray whenever she was upset or the weather turned dreary. They were Caribbean blue as she took the Danish from the box and bit into it, smearing sugar and jam in the corners of her mouth.

"You've got a little something..." Clara pulled a crumpled tissue from her purse and passed it back to her.

Elizabeth rolled her eyes as she took the napkin.

"So," Clara said, facing forward again. "About this boy."

"Mom." Her voice pitched into a whine.

Marshall laid a hand on Clara's knee, a clear signal telling her to stop pushing. Clara shook her head and turned to stare out the window. She didn't see how wanting to know what was going on in her daughter's life and who she was hanging out with was intrusive, but apparently, now it was.

Recently Clara had been trying to give Elizabeth more space. Because she asked for it, and because Marshall kept insisting it was the right thing to do. Elizabeth was old enough now to make some decisions on her own and test her burgeoning independence. She would succeed at some things and fail at others. Either way, it was good for her to try, wasn't it? How else would she learn resilience? How else would she grow into a strong woman like Clara? These were the arguments Marshall used, and Clara could say little in response. *Remember when you were a teenager?* He'd whisper in the dark of their bedroom, their bodies curled together. *Remember how much freedom you had?*

And that was the problem, wasn't it? Left to do whatever the hell they wanted, children grew into monsters.

CHAPTER 3

There were more seagulls on the beach than crime scene technicians, and more birds flying in each minute. Brett watched them as she waited for the on duty detective to find her. Several birds paddled in the waves, bobbing like bits of white Styrofoam. Others floated like kites overhead. A few huddled on the boathouse roof, muttering to one another. They eyed the body, which was now covered by a small pop-up tent for privacy and protection against impending rain. Protection against the birds, too, she thought. One of the techs, who was bent looking at something on the ground, stood suddenly. A dozen birds near the tent perimeter flapped away, screaming their indignation.

Brett was so focused on the seagulls, she didn't notice Detective Irving Winters' arrival until he was standing right beside her.

"Voracious scavengers." He fixed his gaze on the birds. "Dead or alive, they don't care. If it looks like food, they'll try and eat it."

He wore a long gray coat over a suit. His tie was decorated with a pair of fancy pheasants. After a few seconds of watching the seagulls settle again, Irving took a spiral notebook from his pocket and jotted something down. "Mostly herring today, but there are a few ring-billeds mixed in."

He tucked the notebook away before finally turning to look at her. Mist clung to the gray hairs dusting his temples. His expression was guarded.

Brett had transferred to the Crestwood Police Department only four months ago. It had taken her less than a day to understand Irving Winters was a man who kept to himself. He was the sole African-American officer in a relatively small department. He'd worked his entire twenty-some-odd-year career in the same precinct and seemed to have carved out a place for himself as a man who could be counted on to do his job well, which Brett knew couldn't have been easy. She hadn't spent enough time with him yet to know his full story, but she did know what it was like being an outsider, having to work twice as hard to get half as far.

Brett didn't fit the mold of a typical police officer any more than Irving did. She could try and hide beneath bulky shirts and mannish jackets all she wanted; it would make no difference. She would never be a tall, broad-shouldered, white man with a neat military haircut, muscular arms, and an arrogant smirk. No matter how many cases she solved, how many criminals she brought to justice, how much she did right her first ten years, and how much she continued to prove herself capable in the next ten, there would always be people—officers and civilians alike—who thought she belonged in an apron, holding a spatula. Not in a uniform, carrying a loaded gun. She wondered if it was similar for Irving. If people looked at him the way they looked at her—as a liability rather than a hero.

"You were the one who found him?" Irving asked her.

"Technically, my grandmother did," she answered.

Irving nodded once, then laced his hands behind his back and marched toward the tent. Brett hurried to keep up with his long strides. As he walked, he threw questions over his shoulder, barely allowing her time to answer before rushing to the next.

"How long was she alone with him?"

"Less than ten minutes."

"Did she touch anything?"

"I don't think so."

"Did you?"

"Of course not." Her voice was sharp with annoyance that he thought her stupid or rookie enough to mess with a possible crime scene.

"I'll need to talk to your grandmother as well," Irving said.

Brett glanced at the house. After the first car had arrived on scene, she'd left the body with the uniformed officer to go check on Amma. She'd found her grandmother in the kitchen, already changed into dry clothes, and scooping fresh grounds into the coffee maker.

"They're going to want something warm to drink when they're done out there," she'd explained.

"You don't have to do that," Brett had told her.

Amma pulled several mugs out of the cupboard anyway, arranging them in a neat line on the counter beside the coffee maker and sugar canister. She smiled at Brett. "You want those men to like you, don't you?"

"I want them to respect me," Brett said.

"No reason you can't have both, is there?" Amma's blue eyes were so pale they were almost gray.

She turned eight-four this year but looked a decade younger thanks to good genes and a fondness for wide-brimmed hats. She claimed living next to the ocean kept her young, too. There was something about the salt air, she said, that was as good for the skin as it was for the soul.

If someone had asked Brett six months ago, she would have told them she was perfectly happy living in the Willamette Valley, working as a deputy for the Marion County Sheriff's office. She'd just returned to regular duty after spending several months assigned to a special unit hunting serial-murderer Archer French, a psychopath who, over the last decade, tortured and killed eleven women across the Pacific Northwest. It had been a challenging case, and though she played more of a supporting role, she'd learned a lot. Her hope was that her work with the unit might finally lead to a promotion, and she was preparing to talk to her sergeant about what came next for her when Henry Bascom called.

Henry was an old friend of Amma and Pop. He also happened to be the chief of the Crestwood Police Department. When Henry called at the end of May, he'd sounded worried but not panicked. *When was the last time you talked to your grandmother?*

Brett tried to call Amma at least once a month. It seemed even more important now that Pop was gone, but sometimes Brett got too busy with work and forgot. Talking to Henry, she realized she hadn't spoken to her grandmother since February. Brett hadn't noticed anything concerning during that phone call, but according to Henry, Amma had called him several times in the past few months, looking for Frank. Frank, Amma's husband and Brett's grandfather, had been dead for five years.

There was more, Henry said. When he went over to the house to check on her, he discovered the garbage hadn't been taken out for weeks, and there was no food in the fridge except a moldy block of cheese and an unopened jar of pickles. The explanation Amma had given Henry for the garbage was that it had been Frank's job to take out the trash. As for the food, she'd said she simply couldn't find the time to go to the store, though what she'd been doing instead Henry didn't know.

I don't think it's a good idea for her to be alone anymore, Henry said.

Brett was the only family Amma had left, so the responsibility fell to her.

At first, Brett wanted to hire someone to check on Amma a couple of times a week and help with the chores. Then Henry mentioned something about a detective position opening up in the department. He said he would rush the hiring process for her if she wanted it. She hesitated only a minute before saying yes.

Brett had never imagined herself returning to the town where her older sister was murdered, let alone living there. But in June, after confirming her plans with Amma and making sure the transfer paperwork had gone through, she packed up everything she owned in her ruby red VW Beetle and left Oregon for Washington. She'd been in Crestwood four months now, working as a detective for four months, which so far had been mostly burglaries and smash and grabs. She'd also been filing a lot of paperwork, learning how the department worked, and figuring out where she would fit in.

With this body washed up on the morning tide, she had a chance to carve out a space for herself in the department, but she didn't want to come across as insensitive by appearing too eager. She tried for a nonchalant tone when she asked Irving, "Do you know who he is yet?"

They were standing just outside the tent. Where an hour ago there had been little to no stench, it was overwhelming now. Brett swallowed down rising nausea and forced herself to breathe shallowly through her mouth. She'd handled her share of death calls over the years, but it never got any easier.

Irving took a handkerchief from his pocket and pressed it to his nose before answering her. "His name is Nathan Andress."

The name was familiar. She hoped it wasn't who she thought it was, though the likelihood of two Nathan Andress' living in Crestwood was small enough to be impossible.

An older man wearing a navy blue windbreaker and khaki

pants, with a crown of frizzy white hair and wire-rimmed glasses perched on his nose, crouched beside the body. Glancing up at Irving, he shook his head. "Don't even ask, Irv. You'll know the cause of death when I know, and right now, I don't know. He was in the water long enough to make this case a pain in my ass, I'll tell you that much. Anything I say right now would be little more than a guess, and you know I don't like guessing. Send an officer over to me on Monday. We'll cut into him and see what's what."

"Charlie, this is Detective Buchanan," Irving said. "I don't think you two have had the pleasure of meeting yet. This is Charles Hadley, our county medical examiner."

"The only person allowed to call me Charles is my wife after I've left the toilet seat up." He offered a wide grin and gestured to the younger man standing next to him, taking copious notes. "This is Kevin Park. He's the cub they hired to replace me. Joke's on them, though, I'm never leaving."

Kevin pushed at thick black glasses and smiled shyly at Brett.

She smiled back. He was about her age, early thirties, with delicate features and no facial hair, good-looking in a bookish, nerdy way, his dark hair slicked back with gel. Like Irving, he was overdressed for this kind of work in a brown suit and matching brown and gold-striped tie. Everyone else working the scene wore long-sleeved shirts and jeans, with windbreakers and rain jackets to keep warm. Kevin turned a page in his notebook and went back to writing.

"He had a wallet on him, but that's about it." Charlie handed Irving a paper bag.

Irving put on a pair of latex gloves, then handed a second pair to Brett.

The picture on his driver's license wasn't great but confirmed what she already knew in her gut, what she hadn't wanted to be true. Muddy brown eyes, unsettled and unsettling. Lips twisted to a scowl, his skin pale, his beard thick, a glint of the flashbulb off the dome of his forehead where his hair was beginning to thin though he was barely thirty-two. The Nathan Andress found dead on her grandmother's beach was the same Nathan Andress she'd shared a beer with at the Pickled Onion, a local dive bar, a month ago. And the same Nathan Andress who'd left a message on her phone not even twenty-four hours ago.

I have some information you might be interested in. It's about your sister.

She waited over an hour for him last night at the Blue Whale Diner, but he never showed.

She returned the wallet to the bag and handed it back to Irving. "I know him."

Irving hummed in acknowledgment. "Small town. It's hard not to know people."

"No, I mean..." But Irving had stopped listening to her.

"Did my guys already get pictures?" he asked Charlie.

Charlie nodded. His knees cracked as he rose to his feet. "An Officer O'Reilly, or something equally as Irish, took a whole roll's worth."

He flapped his hand at the officers and other crime scene techs wandering the beach, searching the pebbles and shallow water for evidence. Some walked the dock. Some searched the yard and around the house. A handful of yellow markers were scattered over the ground, but fewer than Brett expected at a scene like this one. Someone inside the boathouse snapped pictures, the camera's flash a bright explosion through the single small window overlooking the bay.

"If you don't need anything else," the medical examiner said, "we'll go ahead and wrap him up and put him on ice."

"Do your thing, Charlie." Irving looked glad to be done with it and hurriedly walked away from the body, moving toward the dock and boathouse.

Brett followed him. "Irving, there's something I need to tell you about the victim."

"The deceased."

"Excuse me?"

"We don't know he's a victim of anything yet but cruel fate." He stopped where the beach met the lawn, squinted at the boathouse, then out across the water, then spun around and looked at the main house before turning back to the water.

The number of seagulls had doubled and were becoming even more raucous and aggressive. Two left the water and landed on the beach, hopping right up to the tent. Kevin swatted at them with his notebook.

"It could have been an accident," Irving said. "Nathan works for a fishing charter. He's on boats all day long. He could have slipped, lost his footing, hit his head on the way down. Or maybe he was out drinking with his buddies. Drinking and boating make for a terrible combination. Or maybe he was taking a late-night walk along the cliffs." He gestured to the north, where the shoreline changed gradually from a flat beach to sandstone cliffs. "It's too early to sign on the dotted line, don't you think?" He narrowed his gaze on her. "Remind me again? You and your grandmother found the body around...?"

"Nine-thirty, give or take."

"And then?"

"She went up to the house to call the police," she said. "I stayed with the body. No one else came anywhere near the beach until Officer Miller arrived to secure the scene properly."

As if he was hovering nearby waiting for someone to say his name, Officer Eli Miller appeared at her elbow. He was wearing a patrol uniform and an easy grin. Most of the squad's uniformed officers buzzed their hair short, but Eli kept his longer on top. It was puffed up like he'd been running his fingers through it.

In one hand, he gripped a slip of notebook paper.

"Find it?" Irving asked.

Eli shook his head. "No, sir. I went all up and down this main stretch and even checked a few of the side roads. His car's not anywhere around here."

Irving was quiet a minute, scanning the property and bay beyond. He tugged on the flaps of his coat and asked Brett, "Have you had any trouble with trespassers recently? Any disturbances? Strange cars parked outside your house?"

"It's been quiet," she said. "Nothing stands out."

Even in summer, when the town was flooded with tourists, this beach was usually frequented by people living or renting houses along Bayshore Drive. Everyone else went to the public beaches and docks a few miles to the south. Since moving in, Brett occasionally saw neighbors, older folks like Amma, taking slow strolls with their poodles or paddling their kayaks close to shore. But in October, because of mist and rain and colder temperatures, the beach was empty most of the time.

"Whatever happened to him," Irving said. "I don't think it happened here. Eli, we need a BOLO for his vehicle."

"Already done, sir."

Irving nodded. "Good. We'll do one more sweep so we can say we crossed our t's. But I doubt we'll find anything useful. We should be able to release the scene by this afternoon." He scratched at his chin. "Someone needs to contact next of kin. The sooner, the better."

Though it was Saturday and technically still her day off, Brett volunteered.

Irving shook his head. "I need you somewhere else if you're up for it. I was on my way to follow up on a complaint that came in overnight when your call came in. I know you're not on duty today, but I could use the help. I'll get the sergeant to sign off on overtime."

"Sure." She wasn't about to turn down a little extra money. "Where am I headed?"

"You know Lincoln Byrne's place? Out near Lake Chastain?"

She thought for a moment and said, "No, but I'm sure I can find it."

"Call says there were a bunch of ATVs driving through the woods, tearing things up. There was loud music and shouting, maybe a fight. A couple of shots were fired."

"No one went out there last night? When it was in progress?"

A scowl furrowed Irving's brow. "Of course we sent an officer. We might be small town, but we're not stupid. The forest was empty by the time he showed up. There were tire tracks and crushed vegetation, though, and some signs of blood. Poor Billy's been sitting up there in his car half the night making sure no one disturbs anything, waiting for one of us to come have a look." He started to walk away, calling over his shoulder. "Take Eli with you. He knows the place."

"Irving, wait! About Nathan—"

"There will be a briefing on Monday morning," he called back. "Don't be late."

Brett watched him walk down to the beach where Charlie and Kevin were loading the body onto a stretcher. Then she turned and started toward the house to grab her gear and tell Amma where she was headed and for how long. Eli followed her.

"I don't need a babysitter," she said.

"What do you know about Lincoln Byrne?" Eli asked.

The name didn't ring a bell. She shook her head.

"He's married to Danny Cyrus' sister."

She stopped walking. "Shit."

"Danny's been living in a trailer on their property for a few years, ever since the packing plant shut down and he lost his job." Eli waited a minute, and when she didn't fill the silence, he added,

"So, look, I get it. If you want me to get lost, I can. Like Detective Winters said, Billy's up there, and he might be a rookie, but he's still good police. He can help you work over the scene and get what you need to write up a decent report. He'll watch your back, too. You don't need me. But..."

"But," she echoed, turning to face him.

Twenty years had passed since that terrible summer, but Eli Miller still looked so much like his seventeen-year-old self. Brett remembered one afternoon at the country club, one in particular that stuck in her memory even though every afternoon that summer was spent at the country club. Margot, with her oversized sunglasses, a fashion magazine spread over her bronzed, flat belly, sitting up and asking Brett to put more sunscreen on her back, jerking her chin toward a group of boys doing cannonballs in the deep end of the pool. *The one with lips like James Dean*, she whispered, *I think he has a crush on you*. Of course, he didn't. They all loved Margot—beautiful, seventeen-year-old, gold-trimmed Margot. But Brett had blushed anyway, suddenly unable to catch her breath. The boy looked over at them, smiled with twin dimples crinkling his summer-tanned cheeks, then tucked his legs into his chest and hurled himself into the water. It was the last time Brett and Margot were at the pool together that summer. The day before she went missing, the last good day before everything went so wrong.

"We're driving separately." Brett turned her back on Eli and resumed her march toward the house.

Chapter 4

Brett followed Eli's police cruiser south and east, rolling a few miles through town before turning on to a highway that eventually ended somewhere in the North Cascades. Buildings thinned and gave way to farms and sprawling acreage, with trailers and cabins tucked in among tall stands of second-growth fir trees. They drove past Lake Chastain, a freshwater lake tucked beneath the foothills, popular with water-skiers and fishermen, and large enough to accommodate both. Eli made a sharp turn on to an unmarked, single-lane, paved road that quickly narrowed and turned to hard-packed gravel. With every jostling pothole, Brett's VW Beetle shuddered, but she wasn't worried—the old girl was as tough as they come.

The clouds from this morning had burned away. Sunbeams pierced the canopy, turning the shadows to burnished copper, the color of geese flying south, of warm days and cool nights, of red and spinning leaves. It almost looked inviting. As a child, Brett loved spending her summers in the northern reaches of Washington. The forest here had always seemed more remote and treacherous than the woods by her childhood home in Corvallis.

For nearly ten summers, she ran like a wild thing beneath these towering giants, chasing down tangled paths, the sound of her sister's laughter echoing close by. As a child, Brett had felt ferocious among the trees, infinite, as if the roots and canopy and everything in-between were hers to command.

But that was before. When she didn't know any better.

It felt claustrophobic now, the trees choking the light, the air through her half-open window damp and tinged with autumn rot. Now all she saw was danger lurking in every shadow, pockets of darkness where evil hid. Now all she thought about when she entered these trees was her sister dying.

The search for Margot lasted four days and three nights. For half a week, they searched the beaches and bay because she loved the water; then the industrial part of town because someone claimed they saw her smoking a cigarette behind Tadd's Frozen Foods; then and finally, the woods surrounding Lake Chastain because someone said they saw her parked on Lover's Lookout with Danny Cyrus.

They found her body on a too-bright Saturday morning, twelve days before Brett's fourteenth birthday.

At the time, no one told Brett much. Two officers came to Amma's house to give her parents the news. Brett stayed upstairs, hiding out of sight around the corner, listening to their soft murmurs at the front door. Her mother wailed, a sound so terrible it had stuck in Brett's chest, formed a knot so tight it hurt to swallow, to breathe. Her father shouted and began to weep, a strangled sound. She had never seen her father cry, not before or since.

Her grandparents stayed quiet the entire time.

Later that night, Brett had come downstairs to find Amma sitting at the kitchen table in the dark, her fingers wrapped around a cup of tea, silent tears streaming down her face. Pop stood stoic, with both hands resting on her shoulders as if the very force of him could hold her together.

The next morning they sat Brett down with a box of tissues and puffed red faces and told her what the police had told them the night before, what Brett already knew.

Your sister is dead.

There would be an investigation. The police would ask questions. Don't be scared, they told her. Just tell the truth.

But she was scared, scared that whoever had killed Margot would come for her next. So when the police arrived, she didn't tell them much more than what she had already told them when Amma and Pop first filed the missing person's report. The last time she saw Margot was Tuesday morning at Amma's house, out on the dock where they were playing. Margot went to get something from the house and never came back. And after that? Brett read a book in the boathouse until Amma called her for dinner, and they realized Margot was missing.

There was more she didn't tell. She and Margot had fought.

Brett wanted to go swimming at the country club the way they always did, but Margot said she couldn't take her today because she was meeting up with a friend. When Brett asked who, Margot said none of your business. When Brett asked where they were going, Margot called her an obnoxious gnat and told her to bug off.

Fine, go! Brett had screamed at her. *I don't care! Go, and never come back!* She didn't tell anyone that she'd said those things, not even the police, because she hadn't meant it. She didn't want them to know what a horrible sister she'd been. Telling them wouldn't bring Margot back anyway.

Her birthday that year was a sad affair. Her mother refused to get out of bed. When Brett tried to wake her, she threw an empty wine bottle at her head and screamed at her to leave. Brett had no idea where her father was. Amma made her a cake, though. Chocolate with strawberries. A larger-than-normal slice with extra berries and a flickering candle stuck in the top. The dim light illuminated the sad lines in her grandparents' faces as they sang "Happy Birthday" in two-part harmony. Amma and Pop gave her a beautiful wrist watch that year, a thin gold strap with a mother-of-pearl dial. The bezel was decorated in a ring of tiny diamonds. An expensive watch for a fourteen-year-old, but they said they trusted her not to lose or break it.

Brett kept the watch, wore it now for luck, for comfort, as a reminder that time hadn't stopped when Margot died. She brushed her fingers over it as she pulled her VW off to one side of the fire road behind Eli's police cruiser.

Another cruiser was parked a few feet up ahead. Billy climbed out of the driver's side, arching his back and stretching. He had a baby face, soft and round, bright apple cheeks, and glittering blue eyes. He looked like he was still in high school, playing dress-up in his daddy's clothes. Brett had met him at the chief's Fourth of July barbecue, where she learned he was twenty-one, barely, and fresh out of the academy.

As she and Eli approached, Billy nodded at them both. "I was starting to think you all had forgotten about me."

Eli slapped Billy on the shoulder in greeting. "Anything interesting happen overnight?"

"A family of skunks came for a visit." Billy hitched his pants higher around his waist, turned, and started walking along the fire road.

"After you." Eli swept his hand in the air, letting Brett go ahead.

"Spot's through here a little ways." Billy veered left, stepping over a clump of ferns and pushing aside a large branch, leaving the road and leading them into a tangled understory.

There was a path, but it wasn't much wider than an animal trail and was hard to follow. The deeper they pushed in, the denser the foliage became, thick with clawing branches. Just when it seemed Billy had led them the wrong way, and they would get stuck in the tangle, they broke through the brush into a large clearing. Billy stopped at the edge and folded his arms over his chest. He nodded toward the center of the clearing. There wasn't much to look at but trampled grass.

"Blood's over there," he said. "A few splotches, but not much to worry about. And there are tire tracks up that way." He gestured to the other side, where the underbrush appeared to have been crushed. "Those meet up with another dirt road a few yards in that direction." He shifted his arm about ninety degrees east from the hole in the forest and said, "The neighbor who called it in lives less than a half-mile in that direction. Said they heard engines revving for a while, then shouting, like people were really getting into it. That lasted for an hour or two. They called after they heard the gunshots."

"How many?" Brett asked.

"Two. One right after the other. Pop, pop."

"Could someone have been hunting?" Brett asked.

Billy shrugged. "Doubt it. It's illegal to hunt at night."

Though they all knew there were certain types of people in this world who didn't care whether something was illegal or not. If they wanted to do something, they'd do it.

Eli walked toward the center of the clearing, checking the grass before putting his feet down so he didn't step on anything that might help them figure out what the hell had happened last night. Brett followed but veered slightly to the left, angling a more sweeping arc before moving toward the center. Billy went right. They worked silently, a search team of three, looking for blood, shell casings, disturbed areas, anything that didn't belong in this natural space.

Twenty years ago, searchers had found Margot near a clearing similar to this one. At the time, Brett knew very little about Margot's case. Her parents refused to talk about it. Her grandparents told her only what the news reported, which was vague and unhelpful. For many years what Brett knew about her sister's murder couldn't even fill a single sheet of notebook paper: Margot's body had been found in a wooded area; there was evidence her body had been moved; police were investigating it as a homicide and asking for the public's help and for witnesses to come forward with information that might be relevant.

Sometimes, in those early years, Brett woke sweating, heart slamming in her chest, convinced that it was her fault. If she'd gone after Margot, if she hadn't stayed in the boathouse so long, if she'd told someone sooner, her sister would still be alive. It was only later as an adult that she had a chance to read through the case notes herself and learned the truth. Based on decomposition, the medical examiner determined Margot had been killed some time on Tuesday. Amma and Pop hadn't called the police until Wednesday morning.

Margot was dead before they even started looking for her.

Brett knew reading her sister's file might compromise a future trial if they ever found Margot's killer. But her need to know was compulsive, as if in the details—every single gory one—she might finally understand and find some sort of absolution.

When the search teams found Margot, she had been stripped of everything but her bra and underwear and posed on a bed of pine boughs. The pictures in the file showed a half-naked Margot lying on her back, feet crossed at the ankles, arms over her chest, a deceptive repose. Her golden hair was fanned around her face and tangled in ferns and leaves. Her hands clutched a bouquet of dried wildflower husks, and her mouth hung halfway open as if she were about to break into song. It might have been lovely, a princess waiting for her prince, if not for the lividity, her flesh peeling away, chunks missing where animals had scavenged. If not for her tongue carved out with a knife.

The investigation into Margot's murder had lasted only a few months before it was pushed aside for other cases. According to the notes in the file, the investigating officer, Stan Harcourt, liked Danny Cyrus as a suspect. There was no physical evidence linking him to the scene, though, only rumors of a summer fling, a heated argument, and a break-up. When asked about his whereabouts on Tuesday morning, the last time anyone saw Margot alive, Danny said he was home alone. He claimed he hadn't seen or spoken to Margot in several days. He denied they were even in a romantic relationship. They were just friends, he told the detective, just hanging out. He said he had no reason to be angry with her, no motive to wanting her dead.

Lacking strong physical evidence and good witnesses, the police were left with their suspicions, their incompetence, and a dead girl who wasn't talking. Unsolved, the case was shoved into a box and filed in the basement for over a decade where it might have stayed for another decade, if Brett hadn't pushed for answers.

Growling engines pulled her from her thoughts. Two ATVs roared into the clearing through a gap in the trees and stopped at the meadow's edge. The drivers, both men, weren't wearing helmets. They shut off their engines and swung down to the ground. One man was older and fit, muscles bulging beneath a long-sleeved shirt. The younger man was pudgy with a thin mustache and wearing overalls.

Before Brett had a chance to tell them to stay put, they walked straight across the meadow toward Eli. Brett retraced her steps over the section she'd already searched to reach Eli at the same time.

"You all are trespassing," the older man said in a gruff voice.

His head was shaved close to the scalp. His hands were bear paws and bruised at the knuckles, the fingernails stained with what looked like motor oil.

Billy spoke first, moving to join the group, "We got a call from one of your neighbors last night, Lincoln. Said they heard gunshots."

The older man cocked one eyebrow. "Is that so? Well, that still doesn't explain what you're doing trampling around on my property. Because as far as I know, none of you asked my permission. Did they ask your permission, Danny?"

The younger man turned and spat a wad of chew into the grass. "No, sir, they did not."

Brett hadn't recognized him at first but could see now the faint outline of the hard-edged boy she remembered beneath the forty or so extra pounds he'd packed on. He was rounder, softer through the middle, but his chin still jutted out defiantly, and his copper eyes glinted mean. If he recognized her as Margot's kid sister, he didn't show it.

"We're not looking for trouble, Lincoln," Eli said, trying to break the tension.

Lincoln's eyes dipped, examining Eli's uniform, the utility belt around his waist, the gun and baton at his hip. "Even if you were here looking for mushrooms, you still have to ask my permission."

"We're allowed to enter a property if we're concerned about someone's safety," Brett said.

Lincoln's lips twisted in an amused smirk as his gaze skimmed the length of her. She moved aside her jacket so he could see her badge and the gun in its holster, but this only made him laugh. "Well, I'll be damned if they aren't letting anyone be cops nowadays."

"Your neighbor seemed to think there was some trouble over here last night," she said. "A lot of engines revving, loud music. People shouting. Like Officer Jones said, they heard gunshots."

"Look," Lincoln said with a shrug. "Everyone around here knows there's no love lost between me and my neighbors. If you'd checked your records before you came all this way, you would-a seen so yourself. Rich motherfuckers think they own these woods, and they're always coming up with reasons to call the cops on me. If they heard gunshots, it wasn't coming from my property. But I get it, you have a job to do, gotta make sure everyone's safe."

He leaned hard on the word, mocking her.

Brett darted a glance at the grass around his feet. They were close to the spot Billy had indicated he'd seen blood splatter the night before. If there had been blood, it was minimal and mixed in with the dirt now, trampled by Lincoln's heavy boots. They'd worked most of the rest of the clearing before Lincoln and Danny showed up and hadn't found anything interesting. She'd check in with the neighbors to make sure nothing of theirs was damaged. Not much else she could do without evidence of a crime.

She hitched her shoulders back and offered Lincoln a stiff smile. "We appreciate your cooperation, Mr. Byrne. Thanks for letting us take a look."

"Next time, come knock on my front door first. A fine lady such as yourself deserves nothing short of the grand tour." Lincoln grinned, exposing a gap where he was missing a front tooth.

Brett opened the trunk of her Beetle and leaned inside, pretending to look for something. She needed a moment alone, a second to press down the anger rising in her chest. She hadn't thought that seeing Danny Cyrus would have such an effect on her. For over a decade, he'd been the prime suspect in Margot's murder—the only suspect. Brett had spent ten years of her life alternately fearing him and wanting him dead. Even after the somewhat tenuous connection between Archer French and Margot was made, Brett still couldn't shake the feeling that Danny had been involved, that he was lying about something. He'd sworn up and down he had nothing to do with Margot's death, but then again, Archer French swore the same.

After a few deep breaths, Brett straightened and slammed the trunk shut. She was startled to find Eli leaning against her car, watching her with concern.

"Everything okay?"

She grimaced and gestured to nothing. "Looking for a jacket."

His eyebrows arched as he stared pointedly at the windbreaker she was already wearing. She cleared her throat and moved around him to get to the driver's door.

"I hear the Blue Whale Diner makes a killer bowl of clam chowder," he said. "Best in the state, if you believe the news clippings the owner hangs on the walls. Will cure anything that ails you, apparently."

She fumbled the keys in her hand and shook her head. "I can't. I'm sorry."

She had told Amma she'd be back in time for lunch.

Eli backed away from her car so she could get in. "Rain check, then?"

"Yeah, sure." She gave a non-committal smile and shrug, hoping he'd forget about it later.

Once in the car, she pulled a U-turn and drove away. In the rearview mirror, the forest loomed dark and sinister.

Brett wanted to be done with her grief and get on with her life. The evidence was there, and everyone else who saw it drew the same conclusion: Archer French killed her sister. Most likely, Margot had been his first victim. But all Brett saw were missing pieces and loose ends. All she felt was doubt. If only Archer French would confess, perhaps she would be able to finally move on, but he kept saying it wasn't him. So always in the back of her mind, Brett wondered if not Archer, then who? She felt she owed Margot this at the very least: certainty of what had happened that day in the woods, the ending to a story she never had a chance to tell.

CHAPTER 5

Clara brought two cold beers into the living room along with a plate of potato skins hot from the oven. Marshall took the beers from her and passed one to Eli. She set the potato skins on the coffee table next to a bowl of peanut M&Ms.

"I mean, right now, yes, we're considering it a drowning," Eli said. "But honestly, we won't really know much of anything until the autopsy report comes in."

"And when do you think that will happen?" Marshall asked.

They were still talking about Nathan Andress. The body on the beach. His name on everyone's tongue, the only thing anyone wanted to talk about at church this morning was Nathan. The terribleness of it. The shock. All the things they didn't yet know.

"Thanks, Clare Bear." Eli tipped the can at her and took a swig.

She cuddled up on the couch next to Marshall and laid her hand on his knee. He put his arm around her shoulder. On the television, the Seahawks were beating the Packers. The entire first half of the game between plays, Eli and Marshall had talked about the investigation. Eli didn't know much more than what the *Tribune* had printed in this morning's Sunday Edition:

LOCAL MAN FOUND DEAD, POLICE INVESTIGATE POSSIBLE DROWNING.

All the rest was pure speculation.

"I'm sure Eli's tired of talking about work. Aren't you, Eli?" Clara smiled at him.

He took another drink. "I don't mind."

"What else is there to talk about, though?" Marshall said. "Nothing interesting happens in this town, and when something finally does—"

"It's not interesting," she interrupted him. "It's a tragedy. Poor Mary."

"We should send flowers," Marshall suggested.

"I thought you said flowers were the worst things to get after someone dies? Remember how many we got?" Everyone sent lilies like they thought they were so clever sending flowers that shared a name with their dead daughter. "Remember how they all started dying at once?"

Marshall frowned at his beer.

"We couldn't get the smell out of the house for weeks," she finished.

"A casserole then?" Marshall said with less enthusiasm.

"We still have a stack of uneaten ones in the freezer from a year ago." She shifted, pulling out from under his arm. "We could give her one of those."

It came out sounding meaner than she intended, and when he gave her a dejected look, she curled into him again, leaning her head on his shoulder.

"I'm sorry," she said. "I know I sound callous. It's just, people think they're doing something nice for you, bringing you flowers or food or whatever, but you end up having to throw it all out. Then you feel guilty on top of your grief, and it's just...it's complicated."

He kissed the top of her head. "We should send her something anyway. Let her know we're thinking of her."

"Someone gave us a ficus after Grandma Miller died," Eli said.

"That was maybe seven years ago, and it's still alive."

The football game resumed, and for a few minutes, their focus was on the television. Then the Packers called a timeout, and the station cut to commercials.

"So, Eli." Marshall took a drink before continuing, "Have you asked her out yet?"

Clara perked up. Eli had been engaged a few years back to a woman his parents set him up with. The daughter of a friend of a friend, some well-to-do, high-ranking Seattle politician. The woman's name was Bridgette, and that was all Clara needed to know about her to decide she was a terrible match for Eli. He'd tried to make it work, though. Bridgette was beautiful and rich, and Helen, Eli's mother, liked her. But Bridgette broke it off in the end. She said she was looking for someone with a little more ambition. Meaning someone more interested in climbing the corporate ladder rather than dedicating himself to public service. And good riddance. Eli was a good-looking man, a hard worker, loyal, kept a neat house, and made a mean chicken cordon bleu. He deserved a woman who would love and appreciate him for everything he had to offer, not just his last name and inheritance.

Since the break-up, he'd had a few dates here and there, but nothing serious. No one worth talking about. The fact that Eli had brought her up at all meant that this new woman was more than his usual, casual fling.

"Ask who out?" Clara said.

"No one." Eli blushed and pretended his beer was the most interesting thing in the room.

"Brett Buchanan," Marshall answered for him.

"But you two work together," Clara said.

"Which is great." Marshall's grin widened. "Finally, a woman who understands the long hours and stress of police work. And she's tough. She won't put up with any of his bullshit."

Eli's cheeks flamed bright red, but a smile tugged on the corners of his mouth. "I asked her out to lunch yesterday."

Marshall lifted his beer in a celebratory manner, but Eli shook his head. "She turned me down. Well, I mean, she said she couldn't right then, but it did feel open-ended, so maybe…"

"What exactly did she say?" Marshall asked.

"We were following up on a disturbance call—"

"You were working?"

Eli nodded and explained how she'd looked upset, so he'd offered to take her to the Blue Whale Diner for a bowl of chowder. "You know how that soup can work miracles."

Marshall barked a laugh. "Well, no wonder she turned you down. She probably had no idea you were even asking her out."

"What do you mean?"

"You were too subtle. Both of you on the job, being all professional, and it was around lunchtime anyway, right?"

Eli nodded again.

"She probably thought you were just being nice to the new guy. Cops grab lunch together all the time, don't they? You have to make it more obvious than that. Go to her front door, bring her flowers. Don't wear your gun." Marshall took Clara's hand and squeezed it. "Women like to feel special."

"What's she even doing back here anyway?" Clara asked.

Both men looked at her, confusion wrinkling their brows.

"I mean, after what happened to her sister, why would she ever want to come back?"

Eli shifted his gaze to the floor, then tipped the beer can to his mouth.

"She has family here," Marshall said, squeezing her hand again, firmer this time, the way he did when he wanted her to be a good wife and stop talking.

She pulled free of his grasp and scooted half an inch away from him, crossing her arms over her chest. "I think that Eli could do better. I mean, if she's anything like her sister—"

"Clara, don't." Marshall's voice was a low warning.

"You're going to sit here and tell me you want that kind of drama back in our lives?"

"It's not our life, it's Eli's."

"Guys, it's okay, I don't—" Eli tried to interrupt, but they talked over him.

"Well, if they started dating," Clara said. "We'd have to see her eventually, wouldn't we?"

"And that would be so terrible?"

"Yes."

"You don't even know her," Marshall argued.

"Neither do you."

He sighed and stood up from the couch, shaking his empty beer can at Eli. "Want another?"

"Yeah, sure," Eli mumbled with a shrug.

Marshall walked into the kitchen. Clara excused herself and followed him.

He tossed the empty cans into the trash, opened the fridge, pulled two beers from the top shelf, and let the door swing shut again.

"I don't like it when you say things like that," he said without turning to look at Clara.

"Like what?"

"You know what." He turned, and his hazel eyes sparked with anger. "I don't like it when you talk about Margot like she was some kind of..."

He let the sentence trail off.

"Slut?" Clara suggested.

His grip tightened around the beer cans. His jaw tightened too.

"She tried to break us up, Marshall."

"That was a lifetime ago." His voice softened. "And I'm here with you now, aren't I? I'm right here. I've always been here." He set the beers on the counter and gathered her in his arms. "So what if Eli asks Brett out on a couple of dates? And so what if we eventually have to see her? If Eli's happy, then we should be happy for him. We put up with Bridgette, didn't we?"

Clara closed her eyes and relaxed against him, jealousy leaving her. The old, familiar hurt effervescing like so many bubbles.

At that moment, Elizabeth burst through the door that connected the kitchen to the garage. She stopped short like she was startled to see her parents hugging, even though Marshall and Clara were often affectionate in front of her. They parted. Clara smiled and took a step toward her daughter. Elizabeth had slept over at June's last night. Usually, when that happened, she didn't come home until later in the afternoon, sometimes even after dinner.

"You're home early," Clara said.

Elizabeth's mouth opened and closed like a fish gasping for air. She was wearing dark green sweatpants Clara had never seen before. The pants looked big on her, sagging at the waist, the cuffs dragging across the floor. Her hair was pulled back in a neat ponytail and looked damp. She carried her backpack over one shoulder.

She gave a reluctant shrug. "I didn't feel good."

Clara reached to put her hand on Elizabeth's forehead, but Elizabeth ducked away.

"I'm fine. I just want to lie down."

She rushed upstairs. A few seconds later, her bedroom door slammed shut. Marshall started to go after her, but Clara reached for his elbow. "I'll go."

He looked worried, but she waved him back into the living room to keep Eli company.

"I'm sure it's nothing."

Clara tapped lightly on the bedroom door, then let herself in without waiting for a response. Elizabeth was in bed, curled under a blanket. She flinched when Clara sat next to her and reached to rub her shoulder.

"I'm fine." She curled herself tighter, drawing her knees to her chest, as small as she could possibly make herself.

"What happened, sweetheart? Did you and June get in a fight?"

"No. I told you. I don't feel good."

The walls in Elizabeth's bedroom were painted bubblegum pink, a color that three-year-old Elizabeth had chosen. Most of that pink was now covered in posters of girl bands like Madonna, Heart, and The Go-Gos alongside pictures of Elizabeth and June at various ages. At soccer camp, at the beach, dressed up for Halloween. Soccer trophies and ribbons were proudly displayed on the top of her dresser and desk. Stuffed animals lay scattered around a purple bean bag on the floor. Clara picked up a tattered bear with one eye missing. She held it in her lap, smoothing down the rough fur, tugging on the ears to make them stand straight again.

"You don't feel good, how? Is it cramps?" she asked. "Because that's an easy fix. I can get the heating pad."

Elizabeth groaned.

"There's no reason to be embarrassed. Every woman goes through this, Bits. Think of it as a rite of passage."

"Please don't call me that."

"What? Bits? Why not?" They'd been calling her Bits from the very beginning when they brought her home from the hospital, and Clara's mother had cooed, *Isn't she a bitsy little thing?*

"It's a stupid baby name," Elizabeth said.

"Okay then, Elizabeth." Clara stretched out each syllable. "If it's not your period bothering you, why don't you tell me what is wrong so I can help you fix it?"

She groaned again, louder and burrowed deeper under the blanket. "Please, Mom, I'm fine. I just want to be alone, okay?"

Clara returned the stuffed bear to the floor, propping it against the bean bag. She paused in the doorway. "You can talk to me about anything. Whatever it is, I won't be upset."

She waited another minute, hoping, but Elizabeth's only response was silence.

Clara retreated downstairs in time to see the Seahawks score another three points against the Packers, the game nearly over now. She sank onto the couch beside Marshall. He gave her a questioning look, and she patted his knee, saying, "She's just tired. She'll be all right."

The words soured on her tongue, and she tasted them for the lies they were. Her daughter, who used to tell her everything, was pushing her away a little more every day. Eli was interested in a woman who would never be good enough for him, whose return to Crestwood could only mean trouble. And a man was dead. She could say the words a million times, but there was no way any of them would be all right now.

CHAPTER 6

Brett wasn't on duty Sunday, but that didn't stop her from walking the three-mile stretch of beach between Amma's house and
Deadman's Point. A patrol officer had found Nathan's car the
night before, seemingly abandoned, parked near the bathrooms.
There were a dozen empty beer cans in the passenger seat, and
the door was hanging open. It looked as though Nathan might
have been drinking at Deadman's Point, then stumbled out to
take a piss, lost his footing in the dark, and fell into the ocean.
It was a likely-enough scenario. Brett walked the length of the
beach anyway, but the waves revealed nothing interesting.

After dinner, she called her friend Jimmy Eagan, a reporter
with the *Oregonian* and the only person she missed from her old
life. "It's good to hear your voice."

"Don't tell me you're lonely already?" Pans clattered in the
background. His words rumbled soothing and familiar, growing
distant before coming close again. "You've been there, what?
Three? Four months? I thought you would have made a few friends
by now, no?" He chuckled warmly. "I'm afraid you're going to have
to try a little harder, Bretty."

He was the only one who could call her that without getting smacked upside the head.

"What am I always telling you? You've got to be nicer to people. Sugar and spice and sweet as apple pie." In the background, a dog barked. "I hear you, Trixie. Hold on, here you go. Good girl." To Brett, he said, "Sorry, you caught us at dinnertime. You know, if you can't make friends, you could always get a dog. That's what I did, and it's working out fine so far, I think."

"Hello to Trixie," Brett said.

"Hello to Trixie," Jimmy repeated with the phone pulled away from his mouth. Then he was talking to Brett again, "She would say hello back, but her mouth is full of kibble."

She laughed and relaxed against her grandfather's leather chair, which smelled faintly of her grandfather's favorite pipe tobacco. There were two phones in the house. One in the kitchen and one in her grandfather's study, which was located at the top of the turret, facing the ocean. The office phone was the one Brett used when she wanted privacy. She left the door open a crack so she could hear if Amma needed her, but kept the lights off to gaze out the large picture window at the moon reflecting off dark water.

"How's the writing going?" She tucked her feet up, curling her body against the armrest.

Jimmy groaned. "It's shit. Thanks for reminding me."

"And what am I always telling you, Jimmy?"

"You can't edit a blank page," he replied in a mocking tone, then changed the subject. "How's Amma?"

Besides Henry, Jimmy was the only person who knew that one of the reasons Brett had moved to Crestwood was to take care of her grandmother. During their weekly phone calls, she filled him in on her latest antics and complained about their frequent arguments. Everything with Amma these days ended in a battle.

"She left the car in the church parking lot this morning," Brett said. "Walked all the way home, and when I asked her what she was thinking, she told me she couldn't drive without her sunglasses. But the sunglasses were right there on her face the whole time. When I pointed that out to her, she stormed off to her room, and I haven't seen her since."

"What did the doctor say?"

After several weeks of pleading, bribing, and arguing, Brett had finally convinced Amma to make an appointment. The doctor performed a general physical, then asked Amma a series of questions to test her memory. She got several of the questions wrong, including a question about who was the current president of the United States. *Nixon*, she'd said with startling confidence.

"I thought for sure he would recommend further tests or an appointment with a neurologist," Brett told Jimmy. "But he said he wasn't concerned. People start forgetting things as they age. That's what he said. And then he sent her away with a recommendation to take more walks and add a daily vitamin to her morning routine."

"Jesus."

She knew Jimmy well enough to know he was rolling his eyes over this.

"Of course, Amma felt completely vindicated," Brett continued. "The entire car ride home, she kept saying, 'I told you so. I told you this would be a waste of time. I'm absolutely fine.' She doesn't seem to think it's a big deal for her to forget little things from time to time. But that's the problem, isn't it? It's not just little things. The other day she came downstairs dressed in a blazer and slacks, holding a briefcase. I don't know where she found that old thing. When I asked her, she said she was going to work."

Amma used to keep the books for Pop's fish packing plant, which had shut down shortly after Pop's death five years ago. Except for an empty warehouse at the end of a decrepit pier they were thinking about selling, there was nowhere for her to go even if she had work to do.

"And it's not from time to time, either," Brett said. "It's every damn day."

"So, what are you going to do? Take her to a different doctor? Get a second opinion?"

"That would be ideal, but the more I push her, the more upset she gets. I guess, for now, I'll just do my best to keep an eye on her and make sure she doesn't get into too much trouble. Maybe the doctor's right? Maybe it's just old age, and this won't get any worse."

"It's something to hope for," Jimmy said.

"I've got a whole other issue I'm dealing with right now anyway." Brett shifted in her chair. Her right foot was falling asleep. "Do you remember Archer French's cousin?"

"Sure. Nathan Andress."

"Right," she said. "Well. He turned up dead yesterday morning."

Jimmy made a choking sound. "Please tell me you're kidding."

"Not kidding. His body washed up on our beach. Amma found him." The moon's reflection rippled as, somewhere in the dark, a boat passed. "We don't know very much yet about what happened to him. The autopsy is tomorrow. So maybe it was just an accident. That's what the lead detective is thinking right now. Except what's bothering me about that theory is that I was supposed to meet up with Nathan on Friday night at a local diner. He said he had information about Margot. He never showed."

Silence again, but this time it was heavy and tangled with unspoken words.

"Jimmy? You still there?"

"I'm processing." There was a muffled sound in the background, a door closing, and his tone shifted to his reporter's voice. "Let me get a pen."

"You don't need to write it down."

"I write everything down."

She heard a pen scratching over paper, then Jimmy said, "What do you mean he had information about Margot?"

"I don't know. He left a message, said he wanted to talk to me, but that was it. He didn't give any details."

Brett thought about how Nathan's voice sounded in his message—hurried and out of breath as though he'd been running.

"What are you thinking?" Jimmy asked.

"You know what I'm thinking."

"Probably, but I want to hear it from you anyway."

"When you were here interviewing him and Mary, he said he didn't know anything about what happened to Margot, right? That summer he was what? Twelve or something? Spent all his time in a peewee football league?"

"He was doing his best to stay out of his cousin's way," Jimmy confirmed.

"Cut to last week, and he suddenly remembers something about that summer? A few years? That's all it took to jog his memory?"

"You think he found out something new between then and now?"

"If only he'd shown up on Friday night, then maybe I'd know the answer to that." She tugged on the phone cord, wrapping it around her index finger, then letting it unwind again. "I talked to his mother, to Mary Andress, a couple of months ago. Right after I got here."

"Brett, you didn't." Whenever Jimmy used her real name, it always made her feel like a kid in trouble.

"I know, I shouldn't have, but Jimmy—"

"But nothing," he interrupted her. "Your sister's case is technically still open."

"Yeah, and no one's working it."

"Because they all know, we all know, who killed her. There may not have been enough evidence to bring it to trial, but we still know."

"I don't know. Not for sure."

"Don't do this to yourself, Brett. You were the one who first connected the dots between Margot's death and Archer's other victims."

"I noticed the similarities between how she was posed, not how she was killed," she argued.

Like Margot, French's victims had been found posed after death, arranged like woodland goddesses with flowers in their hair, their arms crossed over their chests. Each one had her tongue cut from her mouth. But where Margot had died from blunt force trauma, French's victims, the eleven women he admitted to killing anyway, had been strangled. They had also been found completely naked, and there was evidence of sexual violence and semen left behind by the killer. Margot had been spared that horror at least.

"Archer says he didn't kill her," Brett argued.

"Since when did you start believing psychopaths?"

"Jimmy, she wasn't with the others."

When Archer French was finally arrested, they found rows of canning jars in one of the bedrooms. Eleven jars, eleven tongues, and none of them belonged to Margot. This was the reason Margot's case was technically still open. There'd been no tongue and no confession and no other real physical evidence linking Archer to Margot. The bodies had been posed the same, and that was it; the connection was there, but it was too weak, too circumstantial to build a case, let alone gain a conviction.

Jimmy was quiet a moment, then said, "There could be a million reasons for that. He might have kept it somewhere else, or lost it. Or I don't know. Archer was in Crestwood that summer. He had opportunity. She was posed exactly like his other victims. A dozen different detectives say he did it. I'm saying he did it, and you know this case has been my life for nearly as long as I've been a reporter."

"Yeah, well, I'm saying he didn't do it," Brett cut him off.

This wasn't the first time she and Jimmy had argued about whether or not Archer French killed Margot.

Even before the police acknowledged there was a serial murderer killing women in the Pacific Northwest, Jimmy Eagan was writing their stories. He tracked missing persons' cases and Jane Does from the beginning, looking for connections. He wrote articles that got pushed to the back of the paper and almost no one read. He kept searching for answers long after the local cops had stopped, and he didn't give up until he found enough evidence to convince them to open a proper investigation.

Even after the special unit was formed and detectives took over, Jimmy stuck around to help. The entire time the police hunted French, Jimmy was there. He knew French better than anyone except perhaps Archer French himself. He knew Margot's case, too. Because of Brett, because after they'd gotten to know each other better—after she realized what he knew and what he had access to—she had asked for his help.

Jimmy was the one who had obtained Margot's file and let Brett read it. After agreeing there were disturbing similarities, he had returned to Crestwood to interview people who might remember. He was the one who came up with a name: Archer French. Mary Andress' nephew, a creepy young man, who clung to shadows and stole fish heads and hooks from the boat he worked on the summer Margot was killed. It was Jimmy who tracked down French. Jimmy who almost got himself killed in the process. He was writing a book about the entire ordeal, for Christ's sake. If anyone knew exactly what Archer French was capable of, if anyone knew how the cases were connected, it was Jimmy. So if Jimmy said French killed Margot, Brett should believe him.

Except Archer French swore up and down that he had nothing to do with Margot's death. He'd been denying it since his arrest. The detective who interviewed French asked about each of the eleven women he'd killed. With each name, French smiled and said, "Yes, she was mine. Yes, I took good care of her." But when the officer asked about Margot Buchanan, he turned serious and shook his head. "Not that one. Not her. I didn't hurt her." A smirk crept onto his face, and he winked at the camera filming the entire interview. "I would have, though, if someone hadn't gotten to her before me."

It shouldn't have mattered whether French admitted to killing Margot or not. He admitted to being in Crestwood that summer and talking with Margot once outside the movie theater. He even admitted to following her a few times. Plus, his signature was all over the crime scene—the flowers and crossed arms, the missing tongue, and carefully arranged hair. Everyone who worked on the French case said, yes, he killed Margot. Of course, he did. Most likely, she was his first, whether he confessed or not. He had been convicted for the deaths of eleven other women and was now sitting on death row. He could deny his involvement all the way to the electric chair, but Margot would still get justice, they said.

But to Brett, without a confession, without hearing the whole story, it was a hollow justice that left her feeling unsettled. Because why would French admit to killing eleven women, but not Margot? What was one more confession? One more life sentence?

"Mary didn't have anything new to tell me anyway," Brett said, remembering how Nathan's mother had been surprised to hear from her but willing to talk. "She said she told you and the detectives everything she remembered, and even if there was something new, it happened so long ago, she wouldn't trust her memory of it."

"And then you tracked down Nathan?"

"No," she said. "Yes. Well, sort of. Mary told me that she hadn't spoken to Archer in a long time, but that since he'd been in prison, Nathan had started writing him letters, and so maybe Nathan would know something."

There had been kindness in the older woman's eyes and pity, too. As she was leaving, Mary had said, "I know it does you no good now to hear it, but I'm sorry. If I'd had any idea the kind of things he was capable of..." She shook her head. "He's my sister's boy. I never thought. Well. I'm sorry, anyway. I truly am."

"I met Nathan at a bar sometime last month," Brett told Jimmy. "We didn't really talk much about Margot or Archer. I tried bringing it up, but he kept changing the subject. I thought it was a dead-end too, but I gave him my business card anyway. Just in case. And then, Friday morning, I get a message from him."

"And then, Saturday morning, he turns up dead," Jimmy finished.

"It could be a coincidence," Brett said.

Jimmy snorted a laugh. "Sure it could. So what are you thinking? What's your plan here?"

"I don't know. Wait for the autopsy. Let the lead detective work his case, but stick close. Keep my eyes and ears open for anything interesting."

"Does your new boss know you've been poking around like this?" Jimmy asked.

"I talked to him about it when I first got here."

"And what did he say?"

"He told me to leave it alone."

Jimmy's silence spoke volumes.

"I can't live the rest of my life with this seed of doubt," Brett said. "It's going to drive me crazy. I need to be sure it was French. But if it wasn't French, I need to be sure of that, too."

"No loose ends."

"No loose ends," she repeated.

Jimmy sighed. "I know you, Brett. You're going to do what you're going to do, no matter what I say. But be careful, okay? Officially your sister's case is still open. Which means, if you're right about French—"

"I think I am."

"If you're right," he repeated, "then your involvement in tracking down a new suspect could hurt a future criminal trial. Any defense attorney worth their salt would jump all over that demanding a mistrial. It would be a shame to lose a case like that on a technicality, right? Look. I've got a few vacation days piled up. Do you want me to come up there? I can be on the first flight out of Portland tomorrow. I'm happy to snoop around a bit if you think it'll do any good."

Jimmy was a badger of a reporter. He dug up answers where others found dead-ends. If she asked, he would drop everything and help her, but she already felt like she owed him too many favors.

She shifted her tone, wanting to lighten the mood and return them to a place that didn't feel so suffocated with grief. "I've got my hands full enough already without having to come up with ways to keep you entertained."

He laughed.

"Well, if you change your mind, you know where to find me." He added, "I miss you, Brett."

His words hung heavy in the silence between them.

It had been five months since he'd kissed her in the dark on his tiny apartment balcony, the lights of downtown Portland reflecting off the Willamette River. She remembered the taste of him, sweet from the wine, bitter from the cigar they'd shared. They were celebrating the sale of his book to a major publisher, and how all he had to do now was write it. She blamed the wine, the way it made her feel loose and happy. She blamed the tiny balcony, which was barely big enough for one person, their bodies brushing together, arms, hands, legs, and then his lips on hers. She kissed him back, and for a minute, she thought he could be everything. Then he pulled away, apologizing. She'd gone inside for a glass of water, and when she came back, she told him they couldn't start something, not when she was moving to Crestwood for who knew how long. He agreed and laughed it off. Said it was the excitement of the book deal, the wine, the lights on the water. He got carried away, that's all. She gave him a peck on the cheek, squeezed his hand, and left, stumbling home a little too tipsy that night, trying to convince herself she'd made the right choice.

She touched her fingers to her mouth now, missing him suddenly and painfully. It would be nice to sit with him and share a drink again. To accidentally brush feet under the table. To watch his hands move as he talked, how excited he got when he spoke about his work. To look into his dark blue eyes and see herself reflected back. It would be nice to be with someone who knew her entire history, more than what was on her résumé. Jimmy was comfortable, like a well-worn pair of shoes, a favorite blanket, like a hot cup of coffee in the morning. But his friendship was too important to her. She didn't want to complicate it with sex and inevitable heartbreak.

"Jimmy," she started to say but was interrupted by the chime of the doorbell. Amma's hurried footsteps crossed the foyer, and her muffled voice rose up the stairs.

"Listen, Jimmy, I gotta go," Brett said. "Someone's here."

She glanced at her watch, surprised to see it was nearing 8:00 PM, wondering who would drop in this late in the evening. Amma met her on the stairs coming down. Her smile widened mischievously, and she reached to pat Brett's arm. "There's a very nice young man waiting for you in the sitting room." She leaned closer and, in a hushed voice, said, "He's the mayor's son, you know. Quite a catch."

With a wink, she let go of Brett and continued up the stairs. "I'll be in my bedroom if you need anything, dear." There was a brightness in her voice, a hint of play. Their fight from earlier in the day, apparently forgotten now.

She fluttered her hand at Brett and disappeared into her bedroom.

Brett continued down the stairs where she found Eli Miller in the living room, studying a watercolor painting that hung above the fireplace. It was one Amma had painted years ago. Pop's sailboat tied to the dock, floating on a rippled surface. The colors made it seem as if the boat was gently rocking. Eli turned away from it when Brett entered the room.

He smiled at her and held up his hands, showing off a six-pack of beers in one and a white take-out bag in the other. "Thought I'd take you up on that rain check."

"What?" She blinked at him, baffled.

He rattled the paper bag. "Clam chowder. Best in the state."

Her cheeks warmed as she crossed her arms over her chest, trying to hide the fact that she wasn't wearing a bra. Along with her loose-fitting, torn-sleeved shirt, she was wearing ratty sweatpants that hadn't been washed in she didn't know how long. Her hair was tousled, probably sticking up in places, the cowlick kinked.

Eli was dressed in plain clothes, but nice ones. Fitted jeans and a black knit sweater that formed around well-defined muscles. His hair was combed back but not gelled down the way he wore it at work. It looked softer. All of him looked more relaxed, inviting, and she found herself warming to the dimples folding his cheeks. But it was late, and she was dressed for bed, and Jimmy's voice was still curled against her neck, *I miss you, Brett.*

She shook her head. "Did something happen with the Andress case?"

It was the only reason she could think that he would be here now in her grandmother's sitting room. A new lead, new information, something so big it couldn't wait until tomorrow's briefing. The soup and beers were to make up for the fact that he hadn't called first.

But, "No," he said, his smile faltering. "I thought you might be hungry, and I thought we could, you know, talk. Get to know each other a little better?"

Without thinking, her hand moved to smooth her cowlick. "I'm sorry, I—"

Shouting from upstairs interrupted her.

"I'm going to kill every one of you little bastards!"

There came a loud squeaking sound and a thump—noises Brett recognized as the attic ladder being pulled from the ceiling.

Eli took a step toward the stairs. Brett grabbed his arm.

"It's all right," she said. "I'll take care of it."

"You better run!" Amma shouted. "I'm coming up! I'll give you to the count of five!"

Brett pushed Eli out the front door as nicely as she could. His silhouette visible through the etched sidelight windows, he stooped to leave the beers and chowder on the porch.

Brett turned and took the stairs two at a time. She found Amma standing beneath the attic trapdoor with her head tilted back, Pop's old BB gun pointed into the gaping, dark hole.

"Amma! Give me that!" She pulled the BB gun from Amma's grip.

"It's those damned rats again." Amma put her hands on her hips and scowled up into the attic. "They're going to chew right through the floorboards."

"I'm sure they won't," Brett said.

Amma lowered her gaze to the gun now in Brett's hands. "Where did you get that? You know you're not supposed to touch your grandfather's things."

She tried to take the BB gun from Brett.

Brett moved it out of reach of her grasping fingers. "You were the one who brought it out, Amma. Don't you remember? A few seconds ago, you were pointing it into the attic, threatening the rats."

Amma laughed. "Don't be ridiculous. I don't even like guns."

Brett stared at her. She looked small in her oversized nightgown. Her sharp bones jutted through the thin fabric. Her silver hair, usually neatly combed, was tangled and flying in all directions. Brett didn't want to do this with her again, talk in circles, arguing until they were both exhausted and saying things that couldn't be unsaid.

"I'll put the gun away, Amma," she said. "I'll take care of the rats, too. But first, let's get you ready for bed."

She tried to take her grandmother's elbow and guide her toward the bedroom, but Amma pushed her away. "I'm not an invalid, Brett. You don't need to be fussing after me so much. Honestly, it's tiresome."

She shuffled into her bedroom and slammed the door.

Brett stood a moment beneath the open attic hatch, listening for the rats Amma swore were going to tear the house to pieces. She heard nothing but the distant hiss of the ocean against a pebbled beach. She climbed up the ladder to check the traps. All four were empty, the bait untouched.

CHAPTER 7

Brett checked her watch again. On any other Monday, the morning briefing would already be over. Crestwood PD usually handled simpler cases—either same day open and shut, or lacking any good leads, they were worked only a few days before being filed away in dusty boxes unsolved. Roll call usually lasted no more than an hour, and sometimes five minutes was all they needed. This one was dragging into hour two. And sure, the Andress case was complicated, but considering they didn't know much more than what they knew on Saturday, it seemed they should be spending their time tracking down leads and interviewing potential witnesses, not listening to their detective sergeant tell a tired story about the time a fisherman found a detached leg floating in Sculpin Bay.

He'd told this story three times in the four months since Brett had been working here. She didn't want to know how many times the other officers who had been with the department longer had heard it.

Brett wasn't impressed by Stan Harcourt. He insisted on wearing suits that were several sizes too big—the fabric always wrinkled and loose like he was a snake in the middle of shedding season. The earth tones he chose—browns and tans and taupes—

washed out his already pale skin. His bad comb-over did little to hide the fact of his balding. As he talked, his jaw worked over a piece of gum, his lips smacking with each word. Twenty years ago, he'd been the lead detective on her sister's case. He'd since been promoted, but his philosophy about the job hadn't appeared to change much: do the bare minimum and no more.

He reached the end of his story, the part where it turns out the leg was from a cadaver the local hospital had lost after one of their vans drove off a bridge in a freak accident. When he laughed, he tilted his head back, and his Adam's apple jutted like a knife from his skeleton-thin neck. A few officers laughed politely along with him, but most sat like Brett, slouched and staring at the floor, waiting to be given a task and released to work.

Nathan Andress' car had been towed to the police impound two days ago. The techs were taking a closer look at it this morning. Irving Winters, the detective leading the investigation, had talked to Mary Andress, Nathan's mother, on Saturday afternoon. She confirmed Nathan got home from work on Friday around five and that they ate dinner together around six. He'd left shortly after that saying he was meeting up with a friend at the Blue Whale Diner. Mary went to bed around ten. Nathan never came home.

Someone still needed to interview Nathan's boss and coworkers. Talk to his friends. Canvass the area around Deadman's Point to see if anyone witnessed anything strange the night he died. Attend the autopsy. Check into his financials. At some point, Brett needed to tell Irving that she was the friend Nathan was supposed to be meeting at the diner.

She glanced at her watch again. She usually called Amma around this time to make sure she was awake and had gotten herself dressed and eaten breakfast.

Last night had been rough for them both. Amma kept getting up and wandering into Brett's room to ask where Margot was.

The first few times, Brett told her the truth. Margot died twenty years ago. But that news sent Amma spiraling into despair, making it nearly impossible for Brett to settle her down and get her back to bed. Exhausted, annoyed at being pulled once again from sleep, Brett finally told Amma that Margot was staying at a friend's house. The answer seemed to satisfy her. She shuffled off to bed and stayed there for the rest of the night. Of course, by then, it was almost three in the morning, and any chance Brett had at a decent night's sleep was gone.

The yawn caught Brett by surprise. She quickly tried to stifle it, but she wasn't fast enough.

"I'm sorry, Buchanan, am I boring you?" The Detective Sergeant fixed his gaze on her. His lips pulled into a smirk as he crossed his arms over his chest. "Is there somewhere more important you need to be right now?"

"Just eager to get to work, sir," she said.

Stifled laughter erupted. Stan's face pinched, and his cheeks turned bright red as he swept a menacing glare around the room. The laughter stopped.

"Don't let me stop you," he said. "The medical examiner is starting his autopsy in a half hour. I know you're new in town, but I trust you won't have any problems finding the morgue."

"Sir," Irving protested. He was standing at the front of the room with the detective sergeant waiting for him to finish his story so he could pass out assignments. "I was going to send Officer Miller."

Eli shifted in his chair and shot her a quick glance from across the room.

On the way into the conference room this morning, Brett had pulled him aside. "I'm sorry about last night," she'd said. "Bad timing."

"Everything okay?" he asked.

The question was a land mine. Little by little, her grandmother was forgetting pieces of herself, and Brett had no idea how to help her because she didn't want help. Because she insisted there was nothing wrong. So, no, everything was not okay. Or maybe it was, and Brett was just overreacting. Either way, that was her personal life, and this was her professional life, and she tried not to mix the two.

"We've got rats in the attic," she told Eli. "Amma hates rats."

He nodded a little too eagerly. "I'd be happy to come by and set some traps."

"I already took care of it," she said, and then quickly added, "Thanks, though. And thanks for the food, too. I don't know if it's the best chowder I've ever had, but it was pretty damn good." She'd brought it in from where he'd left it on the front porch, microwaved a cup for herself, and ate it in front of the television after Amma had gone to sleep.

He smiled at her, said he was glad she'd enjoyed it, and she thought, maybe Eli was someone she could be friends with, her ally in the department. Once one person liked you, it was easier to get the rest on-board. But that wouldn't work if they were going to continue being pitted against one another like this.

Eli had been with the department long enough to be on the list for a promotion, but detective spots didn't come around often in a small force like Crestwood. And though Brett was well-qualified for this position, she knew part of the reason she was here was that the chief of police had pulled a few strings. Not everyone was happy about that. If Irving wanted to assign Eli extra tasks to ease some tension, Brett was fine with that. She didn't particularly like autopsies anyway. If Eli wanted to go, he should go. She was about to say as much when Stan spoke again.

"What's wrong, Irv? You don't think our little princess can handle an autopsy?" He cracked the gum he was chewing loudly between his teeth, looking pleased with himself.

On the other hand, Irving looked very uncomfortable, like he was being jabbed in the back with something sharp. He frowned into his Styrofoam cup of coffee. "No, sir, it's not that. It's just—"

Stan didn't let him finish.

"According to the chief, and I quote..." Here Stan lifted his fingers in the air. He curled them around invisible quotation marks and turned his voice mocking, "'Brett Buchanan is one of the best and brightest. She brings a unique expertise to our department, and we are very lucky to have her.' Do you hear that, Irv? We are lucky to have Princess Buchanan come down from her castle to help us work our very complicated cases. And seeing as how she's so much smarter and prettier than the rest of us, I think we should let her do some real police work. Don't you think we should let her do some real police work?"

Brett's cheeks were hot, her jaw clenched.

Chairs creaked. Someone coughed softly.

A rigidness crept through Irving's shoulders. Even from the back of the room, Brett could see a vein pulsing in his temple.

"Yes, sir," he finally responded. "Detective Buchanan can handle the autopsy."

"Good then." Stan put his hands on his waist, shoving his sharp hip points out. "The rest of you have your marching orders. Go, do, close this damn case."

Chairs screeched across the linoleum. Brett stayed in her seat as the other officers filed out. She kept her head up, her eyes facing forward. No one spoke to her. Even Irving brushed past without a word. He dropped a thin binder on the table in front of her as he left. When it was her and Stan alone in the room, the detective sergeant approached, bending so his breath was hot against her cheek. He reeked of onions and sweat.

"Truth is, sweetheart, some of us think the chief made a mistake hiring you. So." A small shrug. "Prove us wrong."

Brett gritted her teeth and said nothing.

When he was gone, she grabbed the binder off the table and followed Irving to his desk. "Irving, I don't think I should—"

He didn't let her finish.

"Everything you need is in the file." He picked up his desk phone and stared pointedly at her as he dialed. He tapped his wristwatch and mouthed, You need to go, before turning his back on her.

———————————

Twenty minutes later, Brett walked into the front lobby of Crestwood General Hospital. Kevin Park, the medical examiner's assistant, waited for her by the information desk.

"Charlie doesn't like to have people wandering into his morgue," Kevin said by way of explanation, giving her a tight-lipped smile and a half-shrug. He led her to the elevator that would take them down to the basement.

As the doors closed, she attempted small talk. "So, Kevin, what made you decide to become a medical examiner?"

"I like mysteries," he said, the corners of his mouth still twisted up in a polite smile. After a beat, he quickly added, "And my parents wanted me to be a doctor, but I have a hard time talking to people, so this seemed like a good fit."

"Because the dead don't talk."

His smile widened as he gave her a fleeting nod, then turned his gaze back to the panel lights flickering on and off as the elevator moved them closer to the basement. She waited for him to ask why she'd become a cop, but he stood quietly, saying nothing.

It was a question Brett got a lot. Why police work? And she answered differently depending on who was asking. Sometimes she told people she joined on a whim. Sometimes she said she failed out of law school. Sometimes the story was that her uncle was a cop, and he always made the job sound so interesting. These things were no less accurate than the real reason she joined the academy: because of Margot. Because Brett wanted to do better than the detectives who had mishandled her sister's case. Because she knew she could do better. She never wanted another family to suffer the way hers had. She'd been young when she signed up for the academy, barely twenty, and naïve, too, thinking a badge and a gun would be enough to fix the broken parts of this world.

As the elevator dinged and the doors began to slide open, Kevin smiled at her like they were both in on a secret. He said, "The work we do is good, Detective. There is honor in speaking for the dead."

He stepped from the elevator. Brett followed him as he led her through a maze of hallways to the medical examiner's office.

The air was chilled, the light dim except for a single bright lamp shining down on the metal autopsy table where Nathan Andress lay covered by a sheet.

Charlie was already there, prepping his tools. "Oh, good. I was just about to start. It's Brett, right?"

She nodded.

"Strange name for a girl." He pulled on gloves and walked to the table.

"My father liked Hemingway," she said.

The truth was her father wanted a boy, and so he'd given her a boy's name, but whenever she told people that version, they felt sorry for her. When she told them she was named after a character in a classic novel, they treated her like someone interesting.

Charlie tipped his head. "Can't say I ever much cared for Hemingway."

"You and me both," Brett said.

He nodded like he approved. "Shall we get on with it, then?"

Kevin offered Brett a gown, hair cap, and gloves, which she put on as Charlie pulled the sheet back from the body. "It was pretty obvious what happened once we got his clothes off."

He pointed to a large brown sack sitting on a nearby table. "You'll want to take those with you, though I doubt the lab will be able to do much with them. He was in the water long enough that even if there was any kind of usable evidence at one point, it's probably ruined now."

Nathan's body looked even worse than it had on the beach. His skin stretched tight around the bloating, discolored from decomposition. Across his chest and stomach were several deep and ragged puncture wounds.

Charlie pointed to these as he spoke, "He was stabbed over thirty times, though this cut here..." He pointed to a laceration on the left side of the neck below the jawline. "This is probably what killed him. Looks like the knife might have hit the carotid, which would have caused him to bleed out pretty quickly, within minutes. From the lack of defensive wounds..." He lifted one arm and pointed to a few small cuts on his forearm and hand. "It doesn't look like he put up much of a fight, which makes me think the carotid was hit early on, maybe even the first cut."

"So obviously, this wasn't a drowning." Brett's pulse quickened.

Charlie lowered Nathan's arm back onto the table and reached for a small electric saw waiting on a nearby tray. "We'll be able to confirm everything once we crack him open and examine the lungs and other organs, but yes. I'd bet you a thirty-year Glenfiddich and a steak dinner that Mr. Andress here was dead before he ever hit the water."

Chapter 8

Clara shimmied into her wetsuit, stretched a swim cap over her hair, and stood a moment at the end of the aging dock, staring down into steel-colored water. A light rain rippled the surface. In the distance, fishing boats motored through the channel, passing in front of round velvet islands, shadowed blue and hazy with fog. The horizon itself looked to be breathing with each cresting wave.

Typically when she swam at Deadman's Point, at least one other person was using the park, either fishing or walking a dog or drinking coffee on a bench. Monday morning, there was no one. A ribbon of yellow police tape fluttered in the breeze, and her mother's voice scolded her. *Never swim alone.* But Marshall didn't swim. Even if he did, he was at work right now. And Elizabeth was at school. And Clara didn't know anyone else who was a strong enough swimmer to brave the currents and waves and chill of the bay. Most of the women she knew paddled in the shallow end of the community pool, too afraid of getting their hair wet.

Clara had taken to the water slowly as a child, afraid of the way it slid over her skin, how it seemed to be a thing alive, wanting to devour her. Once she learned first how to keep her head above water, then how to hold her breath and tame her fear beneath the surface, she couldn't get enough. She'd been on the swim team in high school and her freshman year of college, and when that ended, she continued her thrice-weekly swims into adulthood. She swam even when she was pregnant. First, with Elizabeth and later with her second child, Lily. The water made her feel impossibly light, and the rhythmic nature helped her relax. She loved swimming in the bay best of all. Here the rest of the world disappeared. Here she could be alone with her body, her strength, the darkness swirling beneath.

She snapped her goggles in place and slid into the water, treading a moment before kicking out, taking a few strokes until she was well away from the dock. She sucked in a deep breath and dove. Down and down through that first icy, heat-sucking bite, the cold making her muscles clench. Deeper, until the cold was an afterthought, the water against her body warm again because of the suit. Even deeper, until the light from the surface faded to black. Through her goggles, she searched for shapes in the murky water and saw only her hands, bright twin stars pushing her into the dark. Down and down until her lungs began to scream. Still, she propelled herself deeper, fighting against the buoyancy of the wetsuit until the ache in her chest consumed her, and she was only pain, only her body. She twisted, kicked, and thrashed to the surface, breaking through the waves with a gasp.

That first suck of air spun her dizzy. She treaded water a moment, her eyes closed, breathing, just breathing, the terror of near-drowning leaving her body in a series of ecstatic tingles. Then she began to swim toward the no-wake buoy. Her body skimmed the surface, her legs and arms finding their rhythm quickly and propelling her across the bay in the direction of islands she would never reach. They were too far away for her to even think about swimming to.

When she reached the buoy, she turned parallel to the shore and swam until the land rose to cliffs, then she turned again and headed back to the dock.

Beneath her, the water seemed endless, a deep and unfathomable swirl of black and blue streaked with pale daylight. It was shallower than it appeared. Dive down twenty feet, less in some spots, and she'd touch bottom. Silt and sand, crabs and stones, discarded boots and cans, detritus of other people's lives, so many things forgotten, all of it swirling, shifting with the currents. She tried not to think about bodies floating beneath her in the dark.

Accelerating her stroke and returning her focus to her form—left, right, left, breathe—Clara reached the dock in record time.

Shivering, she peeled out of her wetsuit and tugged on sweatpants and a sweatshirt.

Above the dock, a seagull struggled to stay aloft in a sudden gust of wind. Head tucked, he beat his wings furiously for a few seconds, then turned and allowed himself to be blown inland. The rain was really coming down now, no longer a gentle mist, but a steady sheet of water that pelted Clara as she ran to her car.

―――――――――

Back home, Clara took her time under the hot spray of the showerhead, scrubbing the thin layer of bay water scum from her body. When she was clean, she stepped out of the shower and wiped steam from the mirror with a towel. Her narrow face was framed by damp, dirty-blond tresses. Her eyes swam gray today, swirled with blue. A new wrinkle was forming between her plucked eyebrows. She pressed it flat with her finger, but it sprang back.

She moved her hands to her soft belly, ran her fingers over her stretch marks. The twenty pounds she gained when she was pregnant with Lily clung to her even though Lily was gone. It didn't seem fair to have the weight, but no baby—nothing to show for the new shape her body had taken over the past year.

Lily had been a surprise, but one they were all excited about, unexpected but wanted, so very wanted. She and Marshall had tried years ago to have a second child with no success. So they stopped trying, deciding to simply be grateful for the child they did have, for Elizabeth, their perfect, beautiful Elizabeth. And then a miracle, a new baby, their entire lives changed. But just as they were starting to get used to her, she was gone.

Three months. They'd had three months of watching Lily sleep, feeding her in the middle of the night, stroking fingers down soft pudgy cheeks, three months of memories to cherish. Three months for Marshall and Elizabeth, but it was longer for Clara, who had carried her, nurtured her, given her life. Marshall tried to draw a silver lining around their grief, saying at least they had time together, however brief. But to Clara, no amount of time would have been enough, and she felt the loss as a hollow ache carved from the very center of her.

She dried and curled her hair, dressed in dark slacks and a lemon chiffon blouse, and went downstairs to make herself a cup of coffee.

She was alone in the house and grateful for the silence and space to breathe. Elizabeth was at school. Marshall was either working at his downtown office or out showing houses to clients.

His father had started Trudeau Realty over thirty years ago, and Marshall began working there as an agent shortly after he and Clara got married and moved back to Crestwood at the end of summer 1969. Clara was three months pregnant with Elizabeth at the time and madly in love, planning their happily ever after. Marshall was a natural at sales and quickly built up a healthy client list, earning the realty company more money than his father ever had. Robert Trudeau happily started working less and eventually retired completely. The transition from father to son was seamless, and to no one's surprise, the business continued to grow.

After Marshall took over Trudeau Realtors, he hired more agents and started listing commercial properties. He had yet to earn a commission on any of his commercial accounts, but Clara knew it would happen soon enough. Marshall was a striver. He always had been. In an earlier version of his life, he made other plans for himself, had bigger dreams, ideas of being a high-powered attorney on the East Coast. But Marshall was also a man who understood about responsibility and what it meant to put family first. So when Clara came to him fourteen years ago as he was packing his dorm room, preparing for a cross-country trip to start Harvard in the fall, when she came and told him she was pregnant, he changed his plans. For her, for Elizabeth.

All these years later, Marshall never said a word about what might have been. Because he was a good man, a good person, better than most. Better than her.

Clara carried her coffee into the living room and turned on the television. She flipped through channels until she found a local morning show broadcasting out of Seattle. A guest gave tips on decorating for Halloween. In the next segment, a columnist discussed the upcoming Presidential Election. The polls were still showing Reagan as the projected winner. He'd done well in last night's debate. There was nothing about Nathan Andress.

The phone rang. Clara flinched, spilling coffee over the edge of her cup and burning her fingers. She hurried into the kitchen, flicking her hand in the air, reaching for a towel and then the receiver. She'd barely gotten out the word hello before a woman's voice, prim and annoyed, said, "Mrs. Trudeau?"

"This is she."

"This is Ms. London over at Crestwood High."

Because Clara was trying to give Elizabeth more space, she hadn't been volunteering as much at the high school. Not the way she'd volunteered at Elizabeth's elementary and middle schools. Because of this, Clara didn't know the high school principal very well, despite having met her a few times in passing.

"I'm calling about Elizabeth," Ms. London said.

Clara's grip on the receiver tightened. She leaned against the counter to steady herself. "What happened? Is everything okay?"

Ever since last October, when she'd found Lily in her crib not breathing, Clara felt like she was teetering on the edge of a cliff, waiting for the next bad thing to happen.

"Elizabeth is fine," Ms. London said.

Clara released a rush of air.

"But we need you to come and get her."

"Is she sick?"

Elizabeth had been quiet at breakfast this morning, picking at her toast and eggs, hardly eating anything.

"She got into a fight," Ms. London said.

The words surprised Clara into silence. Not her sweet Elizabeth. Her straight-A student with perfect attendance, the girl who excelled at everything and had plenty of friends, and parents who loved her, and grandparents who doted, and no reason at all to get into fights.

"Mrs. Trudeau?"

"Yes," Clara said in a breathless rush. "I'll be right there."

The word 'fight' turned out to be a bit of an exaggeration. According to Ms. London, Elizabeth had dumped a can of soda over the head of a junior girl named Kimmy Darling. Upset about her expensive leather jacket probably being ruined, Kimmy had shoved Elizabeth. Elizabeth pushed back and then punched Kimmy in the nose. At least, Ms. London called it a punch, but nothing was broken. Kimmy's nose didn't even start bleeding. To Clara, the whole thing seemed to be more of a spat and certainly not justification for suspending her daughter.

"She deserved it," Elizabeth said as she buckled her seatbelt.

Clara steered the car from the school parking lot.

"Why don't you tell me what happened, then?" She tried to keep her voice calm. "Start from the beginning."

"It won't change anything," Elizabeth said. "I'm still suspended."

"For a day. It's not the end of the world." Clara gave her daughter what she hoped was a reassuring smile. "Besides, despite what Ms. London says, I believe there are two sides to every story. And I want to hear yours."

Elizabeth stared out the window. She was wearing her hair down today, brushed smooth, with soft fly-aways at her temples. A curtain of hair swung around her face, but it wasn't enough to hide the furtive brush of her fingers as she wiped away tears.

"Oh sweetheart," Clara whispered and reached to take her hand.

Elizabeth shifted in her seat, pressing her body against the door as far from her mother as she could get.

Whatever happened this morning between Elizabeth and Kimmy, Clara was sure it had been much more complicated than Ms. London implied. The principal blamed Elizabeth for the incident, claiming the initial act of pouring soda had been unprovoked, which, of course, was ridiculous. Elizabeth took after her father in personality, too, not just looks. Gentle souls, both of them. Marshall couldn't even smash a spider. Whenever he found one in the house, he trapped it in a jar and released it to the backyard. Elizabeth did the same. Unprovoked wasn't her style. So when Elizabeth said that Kimmy deserved to be doused in soda and punched in the nose, Clara believed her.

The rest of the ride home was a silent one. Once inside, Clara offered to make Elizabeth hot cocoa, hoping to extract more details of the fight. Elizabeth turned her down and retreated to her bedroom.

Clara called Marshall at the office. "I think you should come home," she said after telling him about what happened at school. "She'll talk to you."

———————————————

Even as a baby, Elizabeth had been a daddy's girl. If she was fussy and Clara picked her up, she would carry on with her screaming and thrashing. But if Marshall attended to her, Elizabeth settled into perfect contentment immediately. Magic powers, Clara used to tease him. As a toddler, too, whenever Elizabeth was hurt or scared, it was Marshall she ran to, Marshall who knew best how to kiss away boo-boos and scare monsters from under the bed.

Clara sat on the couch in the living room, her face tilted toward the ceiling, listening to the deep murmur of her husband's voice and the answering response of her daughter. She couldn't make out any of the words, but at least Elizabeth was finally talking to someone.

A long time passed. Clara went into the kitchen for a glass of water, then returned to the couch. She turned the television on, muted it, and flipped impatiently through the channels. Finally, she heard the bedroom door click shut. Marshall came down the stairs into the living room, sinking onto the couch beside her with a heavy sigh.

Clara turned off the television and leaned her knee against his. "Well?"

"Well, she didn't tell me much."

"You were up there talking for hours."

"It was twenty minutes." He rubbed the bridge of his nose. "Apparently she's been having trouble with this Kimmy girl and her friends since the beginning of the year."

"What does that mean, 'having trouble'?" Clara wrapped her hands around her water glass, stroking her thumb down the side.

"I guess they've been teasing her a lot. Leaving mean notes

in her locker, running into her on purpose, making her spill her lunch. Calling her names."

Her grip tightened on the glass, her thumb going still. "But why? How do they even know her? Kimmy's a junior."

"It's not that big of a school," Marshall said, smiling. "You know how it is."

Clara and Marshall had both graduated from Crestwood High, and Clara remembered all too well the claustrophobia of those narrow hallways and low ceilings. There had been mean girls in her class, also. Girls who teased her for being poor, or for not having a father, or not wearing the right clothes. All of that stopped when she and Marshall started dating, but she never forgot the way they treated her.

"Elizabeth claims she doesn't know why these girls are teasing her, that it started out of the blue, but I don't know, Clara." Marshall ran his hand through his hair. "Things like this, they usually come from something, don't they? It's usually a back and forth. Isn't it?"

Clara stared at the faint ripples she was creating by holding her water glass so tightly. "Sometimes girls are just mean because they know they can get away with it."

"That doesn't give her a right to do what she did, though, to retaliate like that. If she was being bullied, she should have gone to the principal. Or come to one of us."

"It was sugar, not acid," Clara said.

"She punched a girl in the face."

"Oh, she was fine. She didn't even need ice."

"That's not the point. Elizabeth knows better. She's a good girl, Clara. She doesn't act out like this."

"Which means she must have had a good reason to do what she did."

"Reason or no reason," Marshall said, "She's old enough to learn that actions have consequences."

When the glass in Clara's hand cracked, Marshall was the one who yelped in surprise. He sprang to his feet and ran into the kitchen. Clara stared at the jagged cut on her palm, the thin trickle of blood running down her wrist, wondering why it didn't hurt. Then the feeling came, sharp and stinging. Marshall pressed a towel to her palm, and the pain worsened, but Clara pretended it didn't bother her.

"There must have been a chip," she muttered and shook her head, returning the conversation to Elizabeth. "Don't you think her suspension is enough of a lesson?"

Without answering, Marshall pulled Clara to her feet and led her to the kitchen sink, where he removed the towel and forced her hand under the faucet.

The cold water burned. Clara hissed and tried to pull back, but Marshall held her there until the blood washed away. He lifted her hand, inspecting the cut as carefully as a surgeon might.

"I don't think it'll need stitches." He wrapped her hand in a clean towel and made her lift her arm over her head.

As they stood together, waiting for the bleeding to stop, a smile tugged on Marshall's mouth. "Poor you. Does it hurt?"

"A little."

He kissed her on the forehead. She lowered her head to his shoulder and closed her eyes. Her heart fluttered in her palm, a maddening pulse, pounding, pounding, the incessant rhythm of blood beneath her skin inescapable.

CHAPTER 9

Rain slashed sideways across the Beetle's windshield as Brett drove toward Deadman's Point. The wind howled through cracks in the door. It had taken Charlie over two hours to finish Nathan's autopsy, during which the mist that had started this morning escalated to a full-blown autumn storm.

Brett pulled the car into the empty parking lot, turned off the engine, and sat a moment watching waves lift from the raging ocean to smack hard against the shore.

During the autopsy, Charlie had confirmed that Nathan's carotid artery was severed and was most likely the cut that killed him. There were lacerations to his chest and abdomen as well and damage to the liver. But there was no water in his lungs, nothing at all to suggest drowning. Nathan Andress was dead because someone wanted him dead.

When Nathan's car was found here two nights ago on Saturday, officers had done a sweep of the area. They'd found empty beer cans, cigarette butts, and fast-food wrappers, nothing exciting. Nothing that would even come close to qualifying as a murder weapon. Of course, they weren't looking for a murder weapon at the time. There didn't appear to be any visible blood in the car itself either, but there might be trace amounts, droplets hidden beneath the floor mats or in the trunk, and if there were, the techs would find it. It was possible, Brett supposed, that Nathan had been killed somewhere else. The killer had then driven his body here and dumped it in the ocean. Or maybe he walked out to the end of the dock to meet his killer and only because of bad luck and a damning tide was his body discovered.

Whatever happened out here on Friday night, this case was officially a homicide. Everything they knew so far needed to be reexamined in that context. They needed to get a team out here as soon as possible to search again. Though Brett couldn't help but think that if there ever had been evidence in this parking lot, or in the tall shore grass, or out on that rickety-looking dock, it would be nearly impossible to find. The storm was washing it all away.

Someone needed to talk to Nathan's mother again, too.

It was late afternoon and nearing the end of Brett's shift. She should probably let Irving handle this because of her possible conflict of interest. It was his case, anyway, but with a homicide, the longer you waited to gather evidence, the faster it degraded. The longer you waited to talk to people, the more they forgot. It had been two days since Nathan's body washed ashore, and every minute they hesitated gave the killer more time to disappear.

———————————

It was one kind of horror to be told your son died in a tragic accident, another to be told he'd been murdered. Brett knocked on Mary Andress' front door and waited.

After speaking briefly with Irving over the radio, the lead detective had agreed to send officers to search Deadman's Point again. Then he asked Brett if she could go and talk to Mary. She should have told him then about the message Nathan had left her before he died, but it seemed too delicate a conversation to have over the radio. As soon as she got into the precinct tomorrow, she promised herself, as soon as she could get Irving alone, she would tell him everything. Mary Andress was about to get the worst news of her life. Brett didn't want to add to her pain by sending an inexperienced officer to her house, someone like Stan Harcourt, who knew nothing of this kind of loss or how it felt to have your whole life shatter in the span of a single sentence.

The rain was starting to let up a bit, but sheets of water still spilled from Mary's clogged gutters, turning the dirt around the foundation to mud. In one of the houses nearby, a dog was howling, lonely and mournful. It took a minute, but finally, the deadbolt clicked, and the door opened. Mary stood in the entryway, blinking at Brett in a way that reminded her of Amma. Like she didn't know where she was or who she'd become or how she'd even gotten here in the first place. Brett offered her a sympathetic smile. "Mrs. Andress? I'm sorry to bother you. I need to ask you a few more questions about Nathan. Is now a good time?"

Another slow blink, then she opened the door wider. "Yes, come in, dear. I'll make us some tea."

Mary's house was decorated with furniture that looked second-hand, but everything was tidied up and cozy. Lace doilies yellowed with age decorated side tables and pastoral paintings hung from beige walls. Mary brought a tea tray from the kitchen into the living room and, with a ragged sigh, sat down in a faded orange armchair as she lowered the tray to the coffee table. Brett sat on a floral print couch across from her. The older woman looked tired, pressed thin by her grief. When she reached to pour the tea, her hands shook so hard, the porcelain cups clattered. Tea splashed onto the carpet.

"I can do that." Brett took the pot and finished pouring as Mary settled into her chair.

"How is your grandmother these days?" Mary clutched her hands in her lap. "She used to come by the coffee shop every Thursday. Decaf with a splash of cream. And an almond croissant. Her favorite." She rubbed her knuckles. "But she hasn't been by in so long. I hope everything's all right?"

Brett stirred sugar and milk into her tea. Mary waved away both and said, "Just a little honey for me, that's good."

"Amma's doing fine, Mrs. Andress." She brushed away the question. "Just busy these days, I guess." She didn't come here to talk about herself or her grandmother.

"Please call me Mary, dear." She stared at the cup on the tray that Brett had poured for her, but she didn't reach to pick it up. The look in her eyes was distant and distracted.

Brett cleared her throat and said, "Mary, I know you already talked to another detective."

She nodded and finally reached for her teacup, taking a sip before saying, "Yes, Irving Winters came by Saturday. Such a sweet man. Did you know his wife used to babysit Nathan? A long time ago, when she was in high school, before she ever met Irving, of course. But Nathan took to her like a fly to honey. She was such a natural with him. Always knew the right thing to say and how to make him laugh. It was never that easy for me, but I did my best. I tried." She closed her eyes a minute, her hands tightening around her cup. When her eyes fluttered open again, they were damp with tears. She smiled sadly at Brett. "I keep thinking that he's going to walk through the front door. I keep thinking that he can't possibly be dead. It doesn't make sense. Wouldn't I have known? Wouldn't I have felt it?" She clutched one hand to her chest and shook her head, letting out a ragged sigh. "It doesn't make sense."

Brett shifted forward on the couch. She set the teacup back on the tray without drinking. "The questions I need to ask you, they're going to be difficult."

Mary brushed a finger under her eye and nodded. "Go ahead. I'll do my best to answer them. I just want to know how this happened."

"You told Detective Winters, Irving, you told him that Nathan was home for dinner and left again around eight to meet up with someone at the Blue Whale Diner?"

"Yes, that's what he told me anyway. I didn't press him on it. He lives with me, yes, but he's an adult. He comes and goes as he pleases. He has his own life."

"Had you noticed any recent changes in his behavior?"

"Like what?"

"Moodiness? Changes in appetite? Or how he was spending his time?"

Mary stared into her teacup a minute, a frown pulling at her mouth. "It's hard to say. He changed so much after the car accident."

"When was that?" Brett reached into her jacket pocket for a notepad and pencil.

"Oh, ages ago." Mary fluttered her hand in the air. "In college. He was going to Boise State on a football scholarship, but then one weekend, he was on his way home to visit, and this semi-truck crossed the median and crashed into him head-on. We almost lost him that day. But the Lord works miracles. He never fully recovered, though. His leg still bothers him from time to time."

Brett remembered Nathan walking into the bar last month to meet her, how he limped a little, a motion so slight she thought it was deliberate.

"He came to live with me after the accident, and I thought it would be temporary, for a few months, maybe a year, but he never could seem to pull himself out of his funk. Even after he found that fishing charter job, he just seemed to get sadder and meaner. I did what I could for him." She smoothed her hand over the fabric of her green pleated skirt. "He wasn't an easy boy to love. I was strict with him sometimes, I'll admit. But I did my best to make sure he knew he was loved, too. I was so worried he'd turn out like my sister's boy. And I didn't want that for him. I wanted—" She choked back a sob.

The cup in her hand rattled and splashed tea onto her lap. She leaned forward and set it on the tray, picked up a napkin instead, and dabbed at the wet spot. "I'm sorry. It's just, a mother never expects to outlive her children."

Brett gave Mary a minute to gather herself again, then pressed on with the questions. "What about girlfriends? Was Nathan dating anyone?"

Mary shook her head. "I don't think so. At least, not anyone here in town. Not anyone I knew about."

"Was there anyone you can think of who might have wanted to hurt Nathan? Anyone who was angry with him? Or held a grudge?"

"Why would you ask that?" Mary's eyes widened in surprise. "He drowned, didn't he? That's what Irving told me when he showed me that awful picture. But what now? Do you think someone did it on purpose? Pushed him in?"

"Mrs. Andress...Mary," Brett corrected herself. She leaned forward as if being closer to her would lessen the blow she was about to deliver. "Nathan didn't drown."

"You found him in the water, didn't you?"

"Yes, but he was killed before that."

"What? I don't understand." Mary clutched at her skirt. Her eyes searched the room as if the answers lay in the cracks and cobwebs.

"Mary, Nathan was stabbed to death. I'm sorry to tell you this. But someone killed him. Can you think of anyone who could have done that? Anyone who might have wanted him dead?"

Mary swallowed and swallowed. Her hands twisted her skirt. After a minute, the words finally sinking in, she whispered a single name, "Danny."

Brett sat up a little straighter. "Danny? Does Danny have a last name?"

"Danny Cyrus." Mary licked her lips. She reached for her tea-cup, took a sip, set it down again. "He came by the house a few weeks ago. Came roaring up on a motorcycle, waving a baseball bat, and screaming for Nathan to come out of the house and face him like a man. Well, Nathan wasn't home at the time, and I told him that. I told him I'd call the police if he didn't get the hell off my property. He left. But not before he broke the back window out of my car."

"Do you know what he wanted with Nathan?"

She shook her head. "Not then, I didn't, but later. He came around again last week. Tuesday, I remember, because I was making mini cheesecakes, and I make mini cheesecakes on Tuesdays. He came to the shop that time and brought a gun. Showed it to me right there at the front counter. Told me to tell Nathan that Danny Cyrus was looking for him. Said it just like that. His full name. Like I don't know who he is. Like I don't know who his mama is, either. Then he said that he was a patient man, but if Nathan didn't have the money by Friday, there was going to be trouble."

"Did you call the police that time?" Brett asked, though she already knew the answer. She'd checked the call log Saturday after leaving Lincoln Byrne's property. If there had been mention of Danny Cyrus at any point last week, she would have noted it.

Mary's shoulders straightened. "I'm not afraid of him."

But then she crumpled, and a tremor shook her body as she realized for herself the terrible timing.

"Oh, God." Her voice cracked around the words. "Did this happen because of me? Because I didn't? Did Danny—?" She pressed her hand to her mouth and gathered a shaking breath before continuing, "Nathan and I, we have coffee together every morning. We read the paper. We try to do the crossword, but we're both..." She laughed, a bitter sound. "We're both terrible at it." She shook her head as if trying to jar the memory loose. "When he didn't come home Friday night, I thought he might be crashing on a friend's couch. Saturday, he still wasn't home, and I didn't think...I just tried to do the crossword by myself." She pressed her fingers to her temple. "I couldn't even get one word on my own."

She blinked at Brett, fear and grief rolling shockwaves through her. "I should have called the police right away when he didn't come home that night. I should have done something. But honestly? I was glad." Another sharp laugh. "Can you believe that? I was happy that, for once, he wasn't home moping on the couch. For one night, I didn't have to listen to him complain about his sore muscles and aching leg, how he couldn't get the fish smell out of his clothes. I could watch my favorite TV shows in peace."

She buried her face in her hands, whispering, "What kind of mother does that? A monster. That's what I am. He needed me, and I wasn't there. I wasn't—" Her words broke apart as she started to cry.

"Mary. You can't blame yourself." Brett touched the older woman's knee, wanting to offer some small comfort, even though she knew it would never be enough to lessen the agony she was feeling. "This didn't happen because of you. Nathan's death isn't your fault."

"Isn't it, though?" She took a deep breath. When she lifted her face again, that familiar vacant look had settled in her eyes. "I'm supposed to take care of him. That's my entire purpose. To keep him safe. And I failed him." She rose abruptly from the chair, gathering the tea tray and carrying it to the kitchen. "You're not a mother. You have no idea."

Brett stood, too, shoving the notebook in her pocket. "I'd like to take a look at Nathan's room. If that's all right with you?"

"Fine, whatever you need. It's the second door on the left." Mary tipped her head toward the back of the house where the bedrooms were and disappeared into the kitchen. The porcelain cups rattled and clinked as she washed and put them away.

CHAPTER 10

On Tuesday morning, Clara entered her daughter's room to find Elizabeth still in bed with the covers pulled to her chin. Her alarm had gone off over an hour ago. She should have been dressed by now and headed out the door.

"The bus will be here in five minutes." Clara patted the lump under the blankets.

"I don't feel good," Elizabeth said.

Clara sank onto the edge of the bed and pulled back the covers. Dark circles from a sleepless night bruised Elizabeth's eyes. Red marks from the pillow creased her skin. Her cheeks were damp like she'd been crying.

"Oh, sweetheart." Clara smoothed her fingers over Elizabeth's hair and pressed the back of her hand to her forehead. "You're not running a fever."

"My stomach hurts, that's all."

Elizabeth had never been the kind of kid who pretended to be sick to get out of school. She got along with her teachers and liked learning.

Clara tucked the blanket over her shoulders again and sat with her hand resting on Elizabeth's back. "Is this about those girls who are being mean to you? That Kimmy girl and her friends?"

Elizabeth's lower lip trembled. Her eyelashes fluttered closed. She burrowed herself deeper into the blankets. "Can't I just not go this one time? June will tell me if I miss anything important."

Elizabeth was a good student. Two months into classes and she was already on track to get straight A's this semester. One day of skipped classes wouldn't ruin her life. She was already playing catch-up with the classes she missed yesterday; what were a few more?

Clara patted her hip and rose from the bed. "Just today, okay? We're not turning this into a habit."

Elizabeth nodded and whispered, "I'll go tomorrow, I promise. Thanks, Mom."

Clara went to the window and flicked open the curtains. Golden light poured into the room. The sky was a brilliant blue, the road dry as if yesterday's storm had never happened. She watched as the school bus rumbled past the house without stopping, then said, "How about I go get some doughnuts to cheer us up."

The shops along Main Street were starting to open for the day. Nearly all of them were decorated for the season. The doorways and sidewalks were festive with hay bales, scarecrows, pumpkins, and other colorful gourds. Signs advertising Saturday's Halloween festival hung from lampposts and in shop windows. There would be a bluegrass band, along with a costume contest and parade, hot apple cider, pumpkin carving, and a cookie decorating station, of which Clara, as of yesterday, was in charge.

Her mother had called in a panic, pleading with her to help. "Mary obviously can't possibly, not now," she'd said in a breathless rush, "not after," but she didn't finish, just rushed on, begging Clara, "Please, do this for me. The dough's already made. All I need you to do is show up on Saturday to babysit. You know, make sure people are only decorating the cookies they purchase and keeping everything organized and clean. Please, Clara. Please. I don't know who else to ask."

Maybe it was the stress from Elizabeth's fight at school, or the glass of wine she'd had with dinner, or the guilt she felt for not yet sending Mary any kind of condolences after Mary had been so kind to her and her family. Her yes had shocked Geana into silence. But yes, Clara had repeated, yes, she'd do it, if all she had to do was stand there and make sure everyone followed the rules, yes, she could handle that.

Crestwood would never be a premier tourist destination, but between the ferry terminal and the town's proximity to the Canadian border, they got plenty of tourists happy to spend money on hotels, food, and souvenirs, especially during the holiday season. Halloween was the beginning. As soon as November rolled around, the Christmas decorations would go up, and downtown would really start to get busy.

Right now, though, there were only a handful of people dotting the sidewalks. Postal workers, delivery personnel, a couple of well-dressed suits swinging by Crumbles and Cakes for their morning coffee, only to find it closed. Mary must be taking a few days off to grieve. Too bad because the doughnuts at Corky's weren't as good as the ones Mary made, but they would do in a pinch.

Clara bought a dozen and started to cross the street to get to Marshall's office building on the corner. She had every intention of popping in and dropping off a few doughnuts for him and the rest of the crew before heading home, but one step into the crosswalk, she stopped short.

Marshall was coming out of his office dressed in a suit and tie.

His head was tipped back mid-laugh. He held the door open for someone, and it took Clara a second to recognize the woman as Brett Buchanan. Marshall walked her to a cute VW Beetle parked on the corner. He opened the driver's door for her, closing it again after she climbed inside. Then he walked to where his car was parked a few feet away. Marshall drove off first, heading in the direction of the bay. Brett, in her Beetle, followed shortly after.

It was nothing, Clara told herself. It was business.

Marshall had been her husband for fifteen years, and she trusted him.

Yet her mind couldn't help but trace back to another day twenty years ago when she trusted him as she did now. Another car, another girl, a betrayal—Marshall threading his fingers through golden hair as he leaned in for a kiss.

The student parking lot behind the high school wasn't very big. Clara parked on the street and watched as groups of teens shuffled into the building for first period. She recognized a few faces— many of the kids had grown up with Elizabeth, sharing the same teachers and same classes since kindergarten.

Clara didn't have any idea what Kimmy Darling looked like. She wouldn't have been able to tell her apart from any of the other flouncy-haired, denim-wearing, jewelry-decorated girls walking into the high school but for a vanity license plate that spelled it out so clearly: **DARLING.**

The cherry red sports car with louvered back windows and a moonroof revved into the parking lot a few seconds before the bell rang. A girl with teased blond hair and flipped up bangs climbed out of the driver's seat. Her make-up was too heavy, her jeans tight and ripped at the knees. Her black T-shirt hugged her curves and had some sort of writing on the front, but Clara was too far away to see what it was.

Kimmy Darling tossed her hair, tugging on it to make it taller. She thrust her arms into a faded jean jacket, grabbed a hot pink backpack from her car, and trotted toward a group of similarly dressed girls. These girls crowded around their alpha, greeting her with air-kisses. Then, laughing like a pack of hyenas, they all walked into the school together.

Clara waited five more minutes before she walked across the parking lot with her keys gripped in her fist. It was the Kimmy Darlings of this world she couldn't stand. The shining girls, who never had to struggle for a single damn thing in their lives, who took what they wanted without thinking who it might hurt. The Kimmy Darlings who never thought about anyone but themselves. Selfish, spoiled brats.

Adjusting her grip, Clara pressed her key against the hood of Kimmy's car. The sharp metal teeth scratched effortlessly through the cherry red paint.

"Elizabeth! I'm home!" Clara's voice echoed through the house. "And I have doughnuts!"

She set the box on the kitchen counter and went upstairs to check on her daughter, but Elizabeth's room was empty. Her bed was made. Her desk tidied. Back downstairs, Clara called for Elizabeth again, but there was no answer. She wasn't in the living room watching television, wasn't in Marshall's office playing with his typewriter, wasn't in the backyard running drills. Her backpack, which she usually left by the front door, was missing.

For a moment, Clara stood in the kitchen with her hand clutched to her throat, unable to catch even the smallest breath of air. She was out of the house for less than an hour, but knew all too well that this was more than enough time for a life to implode. Inhaling deeply to keep her panic from spinning into a wild-eyed fury, she took a second to look around. That's when she noticed the bright pink note stuck to the refrigerator.

Changed my mind—Elizabeth had written in fat, happy-looking, bubble letters—*Went to school. See you after soccer practice.* A wobbly heart was scrawled in place of her signature.

Clara crumpled the note and leaned her head against the refrigerator, letting the smooth metal cool her flushed skin.

CHAPTER 11

"I'm glad you finally decided to grace us with your presence, Your Highness," Stan Harcourt said, interrupting the Tuesday morning briefing to make a point of Brett's lateness.

Ten minutes, not even. Eight-and-a-half. They probably hadn't even started talking about the Andress case yet. It should have been nothing. It would have been nothing if she'd been anybody else. Now everyone's heads were turned to stare at her. She was dressed in her usual work outfit—dark slacks, a pastel blouse, and an oversized blazer—but she felt suddenly exposed with her hair coiling loose around her face and her lips tinted pink from gloss she hadn't had time to wipe off.

She'd planned her morning to the minute. Wake up at five, go for a run, grab a coffee, meet the realtor at seven to talk about selling Pop's cannery, finish the walk-through by seven-thirty, go home and make sure Amma was awake and dressed and fed, arrive at the precinct by eight with time to spare before roll call started at eight-thirty. But when she got back to the house after her run, the kitchen had been ransacked, and Amma was sitting on the tile floor with a whisk in one hand and a cheese grater in the other. She had forgotten what she was looking for, just knew she was looking for something and was frustrated at not finding it—whatever it was. It took almost forty-five minutes to get Amma calmed down again and another ten to put the kitchen back together. Which meant Brett was late to meet Marshall Trudeau. The walk-through took longer than expected too. Marshall insisted on seeing every square-inch of the warehouse and all its outbuildings so he could set a fair list price. By the time they were finished, it was almost eight-thirty. There was no time to put up her hair, wipe off the lip gloss, or even grab a coffee. She drove over the speed limit and was still late.

"I'm sorry, sir. It won't happen again."

The only empty chair was at the front of the room. Brett slid into it. Irving, who was presenting again, gave her a sharp nod before continuing, "As I was saying, we're now investigating this case as a homicide. The victim was stabbed more than thirty times across his chest, neck, and abdomen. From the angle and placement of the wounds, we believe the attacker is right-handed. Additionally, since the victim was facing forward when the stabbing occurred, and given the level of rage indicated by the multiple stab wounds, we believe he may have known his attacker. There may have been some kind of personal relationship between the two, rather than a stranger-on-stranger attack."

He reached for a plastic evidence bag on the table in front of him. "We conducted a second search at Deadman's Point yesterday evening. Unfortunately, we didn't find much. No weapon. If there was blood evidence, the storm washed it away. We did find a fabric scrap stuck in between the dock boards." He held the evidence bag in the air. Inside was a thumbnail-sized shred of black cloth.

"It appears to match the clothing the deceased was wearing. We're sending it to the lab for confirmation, but it seems likely Nathan Andress was on this dock at some point, perhaps dragged or rolled into the water. The techs are working on his car, but initially, there doesn't appear to be enough blood to suggest he was inside or even near his vehicle when the stabbing occurred. They're running fingerprints, but a likely scenario is Nathan drove himself to Deadman's Point and met his attacker there. The stabbing might have taken place on or near the dock, and the attacker could have easily cleaned up whatever blood there was. We're working under the assumption that Nathan Andress' body was never meant to be found. And that our suspect did what he could to not leave behind evidence of his crimes. The rain certainly helped with that. I want as many officers as possible canvassing the area near Deadman's Point, finding out if anyone heard or saw anything unusual Friday night."

He named several officers, assigning them to the task, then looked at Brett. "Detective Buchanan interviewed Mary Andress again yesterday and also searched the deceased's room. If you'll update us about that, please?"

She rose from her chair and smoothed her hands down her blazer. Someone on the other side of the room whistled. Laughter rippled through the squad.

Irving silenced them with a glare, then he cleared his throat and adjusted his tie, which was decorated with a bald eagle against a navy blue background. "Go ahead, Brett."

She filled them in on her interview with Mary and the threats from Danny Cyrus. "As for the search, I didn't turn up much. There was a large amount of cash in a shoebox under his bed, about twenty-five-hundred dollars, along with a handgun that he purchased years ago, registered under his name. There were some pain pills in his dresser, but the prescription is his, and Mary confirmed he had an old injury that bothered him from time to time. Really, the most interesting things I found were three envelopes addressed to Nathan sent from a prisoner at the Oregon State Penitentiary."

"Just the envelopes?" Irving asked.

"I looked for letters but didn't find any," she said. "And Mary had no idea where Nathan might have put them. She did say he was in contact with his cousin, with Archer French, so the letters were likely from him."

"I don't really see how that's pertinent to this case," he countered.

"I'm not sure either. Call it a gut feeling," Brett said.

"I work my cases based on evidence, not feelings."

"Of course, but—"

"So it looks like Danny Cyrus is our best lead right now," he cut her off.

She sat back down as he passed out assignments. He sent one officer to follow up on Nathan's financials, another to check Mary's phone records, and another to interview friends and co-workers.

"Brett and I will go pick up Danny Cyrus," Irving said. "Any questions? Good. Let's get to work."

The conference room grew loud as the other officers rose to leave.

Irving gathered his notes and gestured for Brett to follow him to his desk, where he tucked the folders in a filing cabinet and grabbed his jacket off the back of his chair.

"You ready?" he asked. "The sooner we get Danny in here, the better."

"There's something you should know before we go," Brett said.

Irving arched his eyebrows.

In addition to the things mentioned during the briefing, Brett had also found her business card in Nathan's room, propped against the dresser mirror. She'd given it to him at the bar, in case something jarred his memory about Archer and Margot, or anything about that summer.

"Nathan left me a message," she said. "The day before he died. He wanted to meet up with me Friday night. He said he had something important to tell me about my sister's case."

A muscle in Irving's jaw twitched. He adjusted his tie, slipped on his jacket, and walked toward the front door.

Brett walked after him, matching his pace.

"We were supposed to meet at the Blue Whale Diner at eight-thirty," she continued. "I waited for him until around nine-thirty and then went home. As far as I know, he never showed. But we should probably send someone over to interview the diner staff."

He flicked her a furious glance, his nostrils flaring. "You think?"

"I wanted to tell you earlier," she said. "I tried, but we've all been so busy working this case and—"

"Stop," he interrupted her. "No excuses. This should have been the first thing you said to me on Saturday morning when we identified the body."

They left the building and stepped into the parking lot. Sun glinted off windshields. The trees edging the lot burned bright with fall foliage. A string of geese stretched across the scrubbed-clean blue sky headed south.

"We didn't know it was even a homicide until yesterday," she said. "So technically, I haven't done anything wrong."

Irving stopped on the sidewalk and turned to face her. "You interviewed Mary. You collected evidence." He let out an exasperated sigh and shook his head. "I can't have you on this case. You know that, right?"

"I can still help."

"Absolutely not. Nathan Andress was Archer French's cousin. You have history there. Even without that, you've just told me you had some kind of personal relationship with Nathan."

Crestwood was a small enough town that not having some kind of personal relationship with the people whose cases they handled was a rare occurrence. Brett wanted to believe she was a good enough cop not to let it affect how she conducted an investigation.

"It wasn't like that," she argued. "And anyway, Mary told me your wife used to babysit Nathan, so by definition, you had a personal relationship with him, too."

Irving held up his hand. "Nathan Andress had plans to meet up with you the night he was killed. Please tell me you can see how that is not the same as my wife babysitting him over two decades ago?" He pinched the bridge of his nose, inhaling deeply, then lowered his hand to his side. His voice was stern when he said, "This investigation is going to be complicated enough without your bias playing into it."

"I can be objective."

Irving laughed and stepped off the sidewalk, moving toward a row of pool cars parked near the building's front.

Brett continued to follow him. "The letters from French."

"What about them?"

"I really do think they could be important. What if French told Nathan something about Margot's death in those letters?"

"Or what if he was just lonely and wanted commissary money?" Irving reached the first car in the line and unlocked the door. "Look, Brett, I get that you're trying to be helpful, but if you stay on this case, you're going to end up doing more harm than good. Write up your interview with Mary, log whatever evidence you found in Nathan's room, and then go find another case to work."

As Brett was finishing her reports for the Andress case, Officer Nancy Fellowes appeared at the corner of her desk.

"Don't you look nice today?" Nancy smiled and plucked the sleeve of Brett's blazer.

Nancy Fellowes held the distinct honor of being the first female officer hired by the Crestwood PD. She'd started working Parking and Code Enforcement as a young recruit in the early 1970s and was still working Parking and Code Enforcement over ten years later. She wore pressed skirts and black nylons to the precinct every day, along with high-heeled, pointy-toed boots and a uniform shirt that strained around her large breasts. She wore her long blond hair pulled back in a prim bun and smelled faintly of lavender. She kept pictures of her husband and three teenage children on her desk. Her lipstick was never smudged. Nancy was the kind of female officer the men liked to have around—pretty and smiling, a hard worker who never asked for a promotion. She knew her place and was quite happy to stay there.

"The chief wants to see you in his office," she said, still smiling.

Her heels clopped loudly across the tile as she walked away.

Chief Henry Bascom was a man who wore his baldness with pride. He shaved what little hair he had growing on the sides and kept the dome slick and shined. He ran his hand over it as Brett entered his office, then gestured for her to have a seat. As if to make up for his lack of hair on top, he had grown a mustache, thick like Tom Selleck's, except Henry's was stark white and neatly trimmed at the edges.

"How are you settling in?" he asked.

"A few speed bumps," she said, "but nothing I can't handle."

"Good." He leaned his arms on his desk and folded his hands together. "And your grandmother? How is she?"

"We're still getting used to each other," Brett said.

Henry studied her a moment, then said, "I talked to her this morning."

"Oh yeah?" Even though Henry was her grandmother's friend, Brett didn't feel right telling him everything that was going on. Amma was a private person. If she wanted Henry to know her business, she could tell Henry herself.

"I called her up to find out if she wanted to have dinner with me next week." He paused, lifting one hand to tug on the end of his mustache. "She told me you're thinking of selling the cannery?"

"It's time," Brett said. "And we could use the extra money."

"No, that's good, that's good." He studied her a moment, then asked, "I think having you around is really going to be good for her.

Already I'm noticing a difference. She's much more herself these days. And I think it'll be good for you, too, if you want my honest opinion. People need people, isn't that what they say?"

Brett shifted in the chair, uncomfortable with this kind of familiarity from a boss.

If you need anything from me, he'd said on her first day, *anything at all, you just come let me know.*

But Brett doubted she would ever take Henry up on the offer. The other men on the squad already thought she was here not by her own merit but as a favor to the chief. She didn't want to be labeled a kiss-ass, too.

Henry cleared his throat and rearranged some papers on his desk. "Listen, the real reason I called you in here is because we had a new case come in this morning that I want you to handle." He lifted a thin manila folder from the stack. "A young woman believes she may have been sexually assaulted at a party."

He slid the folder across the desk. Brett took it and flipped it open. There wasn't much. A report taken by an Officer Harmon listed the girl's first and last name, age, and a brief summary of the complaint. The surname was familiar. Brett realized it was the same as her realtor's and vaguely recalled him mentioning he had a daughter. But the thing that stuck out most about the report was the girl's age. "Christ, Henry," Brett said, closing the folder. "She's only fourteen."

"Yes, it's a bit of a delicate situation, which is why I want you handling it." He rocked back in his chair, settling his hands over his stomach. "Plus, it won't be nearly as time-consuming as the homicide case you've been working with Irving."

She took a breath to tell Henry she'd been taken off the Andress case, but he spoke over her. "You'll be able to be home at a reasonable time with this one. No staying late or working weekends. Just work it when you can during your regular shift."

"I can handle difficult cases."

"I know you can, or I wouldn't have hired you." He flashed her a smile. "I don't want you taking on too much too soon, that's all. Besides, this one will do better with a feminine touch. She's still here. She's in room two, waiting for you to take a more detailed statement."

He rose from his desk and walked Brett out, patting her on the shoulder as they reached the door. "I raised two teenage girls myself. I know how they can be with their drama. Most likely, this will turn out to be nothing, and you'll have the paperwork finished and back on my desk by the end of shift. Just do your best."

As if Brett had ever done anything else.

CHAPTER 12

Interview Room Two was the nicest of the three options. The chairs had cushions. The lights didn't flicker. The heater worked. It smelled like Lysol, and the walls were decorated with ocean-themed watercolor paintings. A small window let in bright daylight and could be cracked open in the summer if it got too hot. It was the room detectives used to talk to family, witnesses, anyone they weren't looking to make squirm. Sometimes officers would eat their lunch in there, just for the peace and quiet of it.

When Brett pushed open the door, she found two girls huddled together on one side of the honey-oak table. One had long brown hair that swung loosely around her face. The other wore her white-blond hair in a short bob pinned behind her ears with pink barrettes. They stopped whispering when Brett entered the room.

"Elizabeth?" Brett sat in the chair across from them and laid a tape recorder and the folder holding the initial report on the table.

The girl with the longer, darker hair looked up. Her eyes were jewel-toned blue and rimmed with thick lashes. She looked nervous but not particularly distressed.

Brett smiled at her.

"I'm Detective Buchanan. I've been assigned to take a closer look at your complaint. If it's okay with you, I'd like to record our conversation?"

Elizabeth nodded. Brett pressed record, and the tape whirred to life.

The blonde clutched at Elizabeth's hand. "She didn't want to come in, but I made her. I told her we had to tell someone. She can't pretend it never happened."

"And what's your name?" Brett offered a gentle smile to this girl too.

"June. We're best friends." She gave Elizabeth's hand another squeeze.

"Were you at the party with Elizabeth?"

June nodded. "It was our first high school party."

"Did you see what happened?"

Elizabeth dipped her head to scowl at her lap. June's lower lip trembled, and she shook her head. "No, we...I was talking to some other friends. And Lizzie went to go get something to drink in the kitchen. I didn't see her after that for a long time until she came running down the stairs holding her shoes. She was crying, and I asked her what happened, but she just said she wanted to leave. So we did."

June's words spilled from her in a rush. Her leg bounced as she talked. Elizabeth held herself perfectly still with her eyes fixed on her lap.

"Okay, why don't we start from the beginning. Elizabeth, can you tell me what happened?"

"I already told that other officer everything," she said, her tone aloof, almost bored.

After leaving the chief's office, Brett had skimmed through Officer Harmon's bare-bones notes a second time. On Saturday night, mere hours after Nathan's body had been found on the beach, Elizabeth Trudeau, age fourteen, attended a party. She got drunk. She blacked out. She woke up in a dark room with her underwear missing and her shirt torn a little at the collar. She found her friend and left the party without talking to anyone else or calling the police. Brett had flipped the report over, but there was nothing written on the back, no other details about what happened after June and Elizabeth left the party.

She slipped the report from the folder now and pretended to skim it, then smiled at Elizabeth across the table. "Tell me about the party."

Elizabeth shrugged and rolled her eyes. "It was a party."

"So where did it take place? A friend's house?" She looked back and forth between the two girls, keeping her smile easy, her shoulders relaxed.

When neither girl responded, Brett shifted in her chair, tucking the report back into the folder and sliding it out of the way. She leaned her elbows on the table casually. "Listen, I don't care about the party, okay? So you went to a party, big deal. I went to parties when I was in high school too. Everyone does. They're supposed to be fun, right? You dance. You play spin the bottle. Eat some chips. Maybe you drink a little. So what? You're teenagers. It's the kind of stuff you're supposed to do at this age."

She kept smiling at them, hoping to break through their mistrust of her. She needed them to think of her as a friend, not an adult who'd get them in trouble for underage drinking. "I don't care about what happened at the party except for the part you already told Officer Harmon. About waking up in a dark room without your underwear? That's what I care about, okay, Elizabeth? Do you think you can help me out with that? Can you retrace your steps that night and help me figure out who might have hurt you?"

Elizabeth slouched lower in the chair and dropped her gaze to the floor. She seemed to be working over the words she wanted to say, but June broke the silence first. "The party was at the Whitmore Mansion. It's this old abandoned house out on Mountain View Road that my dad bought a few years ago. He keeps saying he's going to fix it up, but I don't know. There's always something wrong with the permits or whatever. Anyway, no one lives there. It's all fenced off and boarded up, but there's a hole around back where you can get through." She leaned over the table and, in a hushed voice, said, "It's haunted. Like with ghosts and stuff."

Brett took a notepad and a pencil from her pocket. Elizabeth stiffened at the sight of them, so she tucked the items away again and refocused her attention on June. "A haunted mansion, huh? That's pretty cool. Were you the one who invited people to come out?"

June shook her head. "My sister Marcie, she's a senior. She planned everything, and she's the one who invited us."

At the same time, Elizabeth answered, "We just heard about it through some kids at school."

The two girls exchanged a look, and Elizabeth added, "Her sister goes to our school. We overheard her talking about it with her friends, and we decided to go."

"We sort of invited ourselves," June said. Then with a grin that made her seem years younger, she added, "We were the only freshmen there."

Her grin faltered when she glanced at Elizabeth, who was scowling at her hands again.

Brett smiled back at her to keep her talking. "So, freshmen at a senior party. I bet all your other friends were jealous when they heard about that. Did you know everyone at the party, then? Were they all kids from school?"

"Mostly," Elizabeth muttered.

"But there were some we didn't know, too," June rushed in. "A lot of like, older kids? College-age? And some from Burlington High, I think."

"Did you talk to anyone you didn't know?" Brett asked.

Elizabeth shrugged. "I talked to a lot of people, yeah. I mean, it was a party. That's what you're supposed to do, right?"

"Did anyone seem to be paying special attention to you? Like did you notice anyone following you around the house? Or butting in when you were trying to talk to someone else?"

June started to say something but shrank from Elizabeth's angry glare.

"There wasn't anyone like that, no," Elizabeth said, scratching her thumbnail over a pen mark on the tabletop.

Brett studied the girl a moment. If she was lying, she was doing a damn good job at it.

Up to this point, Brett had asked simple questions, easing the girls into the conversation, trying to make them comfortable. Nothing accusatory, nothing about the upstairs room or what happened there in the dark. June was relaxed now, her eyes watching Brett closely, mimicking her body language. She smiled when Brett smiled, leaned forward when Brett leaned forward. She wanted to be helpful; that much was obvious. Elizabeth was still tense and defensive, but at least she was sitting back in her chair now, no longer looking for any opportunity to bolt.

As gently as she could, Brett moved the interview into more dangerous territory. "So you were drinking at this party, yes?"

Elizabeth's gaze snapped to Brett's. Panicked, wary. "I had one beer," she said. "That's it. I swear to God. One beer, and I didn't even finish it because it tasted like vomit."

"Someone put something in her drink," June said, rushing to defend her friend.

"You saw someone mess with her drink?"

June's lips twisted into a frown. "Well, no, but that's the only thing that makes sense. Because she doesn't remember what happened, and if she wasn't drugged, she would have remembered, wouldn't she? And when she came downstairs, she was acting so weird. Like slurring her speech and garbling her words all together so I couldn't make any sense of what she was trying to tell me. She could barely walk. I had to practically carry her home."

"I wasn't drunk." Elizabeth's voice pitched to a frenzy. "I mean not on purpose. I had one drink. Not even one. You can't get wasted from half a beer, can you?"

Her eyes darted between Brett and June. She wanted someone to reassure her, someone to tell her that what happened hadn't been her fault, that she hadn't done this to herself.

Brett leaned over the table, reaching her hand halfway. "Elizabeth." She waited until the girl was looking at her before continuing, "If you're telling me you had only half a beer, then I believe you."

She exhaled, and her shoulders slumped. She folded her arms around her stomach, fixing her gaze on the table again, frowning at some crack or smudge only she could see.

"Let's come back to that," Brett said, turning her attention once more to June, letting Elizabeth have a moment to collect herself again. "So you left the party, and then what happened?"

"We walked home," June said.

"How far is that?"

She shrugged. "Not far. A mile maybe."

"And Elizabeth stayed with you that night? She slept at your house?"

June nodded again. "My parents were in Seattle for the weekend."

"Have you told them? About the party? About what happened?"

June stared at her hands.

"What about you, Elizabeth? Have you told your parents anything?"

She shook her head. "I don't want them to get mad."

Brett spoke gently to her, with patience, "I'm sure once we tell them what happened—"

"Please, don't tell them," Elizabeth said. Then she scooted the chair back as if to leave. "You know what, never mind. This was a mistake. We shouldn't have come. Nothing happened at the party. I made it all up, okay? I'm sorry we wasted your time."

"Elizabeth..."

"Lizzie, don't." June tugged on her friend's arm, keeping her in the chair. "She won't tell your mom." She flicked her eyes to Brett. "You don't have to tell them, right?"

"Not if you don't want me to," Brett said. Eventually, the parents would need to be told what had happened to their daughter. Of course, they would. Right now, though, Brett just needed the truth. Even if that meant making promises she couldn't keep. "I just want to try and find out who hurt you, okay? I know this is difficult to talk about, but do your best. There's no rush. Just take your time and tell me what happened. Your parents don't have to know anything until you're ready for them to know. Why don't we go back to the party, okay? You had some beer that might have been drugged, and then what? Is that when you went upstairs?"

Elizabeth chewed on her lower lip for a second. She was still perched on the edge of the chair, tensed to run. June still gripped her arm, holding her down. She tenderly brushed a lock of hair from her friend's face. "Lizzie, please, she's just trying to help. Tell her what happened. Tell her what you told me."

A minute passed, and then Elizabeth nodded once, sharply, like she'd made up her mind. She breathed in deep, lifted her gaze once more to Brett, resolute this time. Beneath her fear, there was strength.

"I don't remember everything, just like, flashes. Like a flickering movie or something. There are all these jumps in time. I remember being on the staircase and looking down at everyone dancing. And then I remember opening a bunch of doors like I was looking for something, but I don't remember what I was looking for. Then there were hands, pushing against my mouth. And I couldn't breathe. I said, stop. I think I said stop or no or leave or something. I said something. And then there was this wolf, and he was clawing at me, tearing my clothes. And I just closed my eyes, I guess. Like if I couldn't see him, he would go away? The next thing I remember, I'm walking on the side of the road with June, and she's humming a Madonna song. What was it, June? What was the song?"

But Brett didn't give her a chance to answer. She held up one hand. "Wait, back up. A wolf?"

Elizabeth nodded. "I think it was a mask."

"Okay, do you remember anything else about this wolf? Can you tell me what else he was wearing?"

"I don't know. Black clothes, I guess. It was dark."

"Did he say anything to you?"

"I don't remember."

"Did he smell like anything, like cologne?"

"I don't know."

"Anything else? Anything at all that might help us identify him?"

Elizabeth thought for a second, then shook her head. Her voice trembled when she said, "I'm sorry. I...I..." She wiped at her eyes, glistening now with tears. "I told you everything I can remember. I don't know, I was trying to, I wanted to disappear, I guess? I went away somewhere. I let myself pretend it was just a dream. A nightmare."

She took a shaking breath.

June rubbed her back. "You're doing so great. You're so brave."

Elizabeth took another, deeper and more steadying breath and said, "I know it sounds stupid, but I didn't even realize anything bad had happened until I got to June's and had a chance to kind of come down from whatever." She bit the corner of her lip, then gestured to her lap. "It hurt down there, and when I went to the bathroom to check, I realized my underwear was gone. There was blood." Her voice hitched as she swallowed back a sob.

Brett's hands clenched under the table. She took a long, slow breath, then quietly asked, "Can you describe them for me? The underwear you were wearing that night?"

Elizabeth's voice was thin and on the verge of breaking when she answered. "There was a little red bow." She touched below her belly button where the top of her pants met her shirt, then she crumpled in on herself, burying her face in her hands.

June threw her arm around Elizabeth's shoulders and cradled her, making shushing sounds like a mother would to an upset child. When she looked at Brett, her eyes simmered with rage. "You believe her, don't you? You're going to help us? You're going to find the asshole who did this to her?"

Brett had worked with too many young women who'd found themselves in dark rooms with men who believed the word 'no' to be nothing more than a suggestion. Few of them had gotten justice. She knew she shouldn't promise anything to these girls. The odds of them finding the person who raped Elizabeth were small, the odds of prosecuting him even smaller. Still, she found herself turning off the tape recorder, then leaning over the table and grasping tight hold of Elizabeth's hand. She squeezed hard as if, with enough pressure, she could mend everything that had broken for this girl that terrible night.

Her voice was a rasping whisper. "I believe you, Elizabeth. And I'm going to do everything in my power to find this creep and lock him up for a long time, okay?"

The next part was the hardest part. Brett needed to collect whatever physical evidence she could, though she knew there wouldn't be much. It had been almost three days since the party, and Elizabeth admitted to having taken a shower at June's that night. Still, if there was even a trace of that bastard left somewhere on Elizabeth's body, Brett wanted it. June stayed by her friend through the whole terrible ordeal, clutching her hand and talking nonstop about soccer drills and a science teacher who nearly exploded the entire school during a chemistry experiment—anything to distract her. Brett wondered if Elizabeth knew how lucky she was to have a friend like June.

When it was over, Brett walked the girls out and told them to call her anytime, for any reason. She promised to be in touch soon. After the girls were gone, Brett returned to the interview room. She listened to the tape again, carefully taking notes for her report and trying to figure out her next steps. She needed to talk to more people who had been at that party, find out who was wearing a wolf mask. At some point, Brett found herself getting tired and hungry, her concentration waning. A quick glance at her watch told her that her shift was almost over. She'd come back to this later. For now, it was time to go home, get dinner started, find out how Amma did all day by herself. Brett gathered her notes and turned off the lights.

As she passed by Interview Room One, making her way back to her desk to grab her keys and jacket, the door flew open, and Danny Cyrus staggered into her. She grabbed on to him to keep from falling.

"Watch it." He shook her off and stormed toward the exit.

She stared after him, rubbing the sore spot on her arm where he'd run into her.

Irving came out of the interview room a few seconds later. His tie—pink flamingos dotting a purple background—was loosened. Sweat dampened the collar of his shirt.

"You're letting Danny go?" she asked.

Irving flipped through the pages of a notepad he was holding in his hands, then shrugged. "I don't have much of a choice. He has an alibi."

"So, what now?"

"That's not really your problem anymore, is it?" Without looking up from his notes, he brushed past her and walked toward the squad room.

CHAPTER 13

Brett heard the sails flapping as soon as she stepped out of the car. There wasn't much wind left by Tuesday evening. Yesterday's storm had blown east, leaving behind washed-blue skies and a light breeze that would hardly fill a kite. But Amma had taken the boat out anyway. Brett could see her in the distance, bobbing against a copper sea and watermelon pink sky.

The fourteen-foot wooden skiff was small enough for Amma to handle the rigging by herself, yet roomy enough to take a couple of friends for a picnic cruise if she wanted company. The boat was a sturdy little daysailer, robust in open water. Though, as far as Brett knew, Amma only ever sailed her around Sculpin Bay. Pop had bought the skiff for Amma on their fiftieth wedding anniversary. He'd named her *Anita Horizon*—Anita was Amma's first name— and they'd both had a good laugh over his cleverness.

It wasn't until Brett stepped onto the dock that she realized the *Anita Horizon* wasn't tacking. The sails flapped loose, continuing their racket, smacking the mast and hull like a woman shaking out wet laundry. Amma sat at the back of the boat, with one hand on the rudder, but from where Brett stood, it didn't look like she was trying to steer. It didn't look like she was doing much of anything but sitting and staring into the distance. A stark silhouette against the setting sun, Amma and the *Anita Horizon* looked like toys upon the vast expanse of water.

Brett cupped her hands around her mouth and shouted toward the boat, "Amma! Are you all right?"

Her voice was a foghorn blast that turned Amma's head. A second passed, the sails still flapping, then Amma lifted one hand and turned back around to watch the sunset.

"Amma?" Brett shouted again. "Do you need help?"

Amma and Pop had sailed together often during their marriage. Once, they cruised to Mexico after their only daughter, Brett's mother, left for college. They spent an entire year sailing from port to port, their skin turning wind-chapped and brown, their hair tangled with salt and seaweed. Amma knew how to sail, and she'd sailed plenty of times alone. She was a woman who loved the wind, water, and chasing the distant horizon, but Brett worried that it wasn't safe for her to be out there by herself anymore. She could forget how to tack, and the mainsail could fill too quickly, swinging the boom, tipping the boat. Or she could run aground in the many shallow places along the shoreline. Or she could simply get stuck, the way she appeared to be now.

A sliver of sun hovered above the ink-blot line of the sea. As soon as it disappeared, the light would vanish, and Amma would be swallowed up in shadows.

Brett trotted back up the dock and hurried to a house down the street, where she knew the neighbor kept his small fishing boat tied to his dock year-round. She pounded on the front door. A man with a huge white beard and a belly to match answered a few seconds later. Glasses were perched on the end of his nose. He held a book in one hand, his thumb pressed against the pages, keeping his place. She only really knew him as the man who lived next door.

Sometimes they exchanged waves when they rolled their garbage cans out to the street at the same time. Amma didn't have much to say about him. His name was Kenny, and he kept to himself. A bit of a hermit, Amma had said, quickly adding that those types of people make the best neighbors.

"I live next door," Brett said in case he'd forgotten.

"Yes, I know who you are."

"My grandmother seems to have gotten herself into a bit of trouble." She smiled, so he wouldn't panic. "Nothing too serious, but would you mind giving us a tow?"

Kenny was happy to help. It took him only a few minutes to grab his boots, a jacket, and the key to his boat. Before Brett even had time to think about what she was doing, they were on the water, bouncing over small waves, the motor roaring in her ears. Brett clung to the boat's handrail, fixing her gaze on the shoreline, trying not to get sick.

Margot was the one who'd liked the open water, always pleading with Pop and Amma to take her on their sailboat whenever the weather was fine. She'd stand against the railing, gripping tight to a rope, her body hanging over the waves, golden hair fluttering behind her, face tilted toward the sun. She'd laugh and gesture for Brett to join her, but it was all Brett could do to keep herself from barfing with each cresting wave. She'd spend entire trips with her back pressed against the cabin of the boat, knuckles white, double and triple-checking that the buckles on her vest were fastened.

Even years later, the old habit remained. Brett found herself reaching for a buckle that wasn't there. Her fingers grasped at the flaps of her windbreaker, tugging them tight though she knew the light nylon would be useless to save her if she went overboard.

Kenny downshifted as they approached the *Anita Horizon*, slowing to come up alongside her. Amma looked startled to see them and then annoyed. She flapped her hand, motioning them to move away.

They had to yell to be heard over the chaos of the flapping sails and the guttering engine.

"I'm fine!" Amma grabbed at a line that was flapping loose.

Brett couldn't tell which sail it was connected to, and it didn't seem like Amma knew either.

"You don't look fine!" Brett shouted at her grandmother. Then she pointed toward the vanishing sun. "It's almost dark!"

"I was on my way in!"

But the way she fumbled the ropes, it was clear she had no idea what she was doing.

"Kenny's going to tow you!" Brett shouted as the man leaned over the boat's hull to lash a rope to the *Anita Horizon's* bow fitting.

The whole way to the dock, Amma sat with her back to them, and her arms crossed over her chest. Kenny drove slowly. The *Anita Horizon* bobbed along behind like a stubborn, pouting duck.

As soon as they were within reach, Amma leaned over and grabbed the dock railing. With one hand, she steadied the sailboat. With the other, she lashed a rope around a large, metal cleat.

"Hang on a second, Amma," Brett called out. "Let me help you."

She rose too quickly, and the small fishing boat rocked and dipped beneath her. Brett lost her footing, stumbling a little. Kenny grabbed her elbow, steadying her again before helping her over the gunwale.

By the time Brett got to the sailboat, Amma was already out, standing on the dock, lashing a second rope to a second dock cleat, making sure the boat wouldn't slip its ties in a strong wind.

Brett tried to take the rope from her, but Amma shoved her away. "I don't need your help."

Amma gave the rope a hard tug to make sure it was secure, then she stalked toward the house without giving their neighbor so much as a wave or a nod in thanks.

Thinking now that she'd overreacted, that perhaps Amma

hadn't been in any trouble at all and could have made it back on her own, Brett gave Kenny an embarrassed shrug. "Thanks."

"Happy to help." Kenny unhitched the fishing boat from the *Anita Horizon* and motored away, sticking close to shore, fading into the evening shadows as he made his way back to his own dock.

Brett found Amma in the kitchen, slamming pans around, moving them from the stove to the cupboard only to pull them out of the cupboard again to set them on the stove.

"What are you doing?" Brett asked from the doorway.

"Making dinner."

Brett crossed to the stove and tried to take the saucepan from Amma.

"I told you, I don't need your help."

"Amma—"

"I can boil water. And I can damn well sail my own boat."

She'd never heard her grandmother cuss before. Amma dropped the saucepan onto the stove with a loud clatter. She spun away from Brett and stood staring out the window above the kitchen sink, with her hand gripping the cold water handle, though she didn't turn it on. She took deep, shuddering breaths, anger trembling her whole body.

"Amma. I'm here to help you. That's why I came. To help you. So let me." Brett brushed her grandmother's elbow.

Amma flinched as if Brett had pinched her. She pushed away from the sink, knocking Brett out of the way with the force of her motion. "I didn't ask you to come here, you know. I never asked for your help."

The pounding of her feet up the stairs shook the entire house.

———————————

Noises woke Brett in the middle of the night. First, the creak of stairs. Then, the opening of cupboards and a clattering sound as something plastic rolled across the floor. Then came the sound of the back door being opened.

Brett pulled on a sweatshirt and shuffled downstairs.

Earlier that night, Brett had eaten her dinner of grilled cheese and canned tomato soup alone in front of the television. She kept listening for Amma, expecting her to come back downstairs, but she never did. Brett had tapped on her grandmother's door on her way to bed but got no answer. Amma had either been asleep or pretending to be.

She was wide awake now, a midnight ghost, standing in front of a painting easel she'd set up on the back porch. With a large brush, she smeared large globs of black paint over a new canvas. Her hands worked quickly, almost manically, until there was not a single speck of white left visible. She dunked the large brush in a bucket of water and, from a small jar, picked a finer-tipped, soft-bristled brush. She squeezed white paint onto her palate and, working slowly now, carefully began dabbing stars onto the field of night.

Brett folded herself into a wicker chair and watched her grandmother's hand move deftly across the canvas. A flick, a flutter, the black sky came alive with nearly invisible specks of light. Amma bent over the left corner of the canvas and began to paint a slivered moon.

"This is how it feels," she said, making tiny strokes, adding a little yellow, a shimmer of pale blue. "Not every day, but more often than I want to admit even to myself." A gentle curve and the moon began to take shape. "It's like there's all this darkness. My memories get swallowed up in the blackest of nights, except for this small bit of light." She dabbed more paint onto the canvas. "This sliver of moon, these dots of stars, that I know are me. Or the me I used to be, and if I can just get close enough to them, I know I'll be able to see again. See myself again."

She lifted the brush and took a step back to examine the painting. Then she stepped forward again and, with a larger brush, added a wash of navy blue to the lower third of the canvas, turning the night into an ocean.

"I keep waiting for the sun to rise." She added the moon's reflection on the surface of the water. "But it never does. It just seems to be getting darker."

A final stroke of white, and she dropped the paintbrush into the bucket of water. She stared at the painting, tilting her head one way, then the other.

Then she turned toward Brett. "I'm sorry about what I said earlier. I'm glad you're here. You know I am. It's just, I never wanted this for you." She flung her hand at the painting. "I never wanted you to be stuck taking care of me."

"I'm not stuck. I'm here because I want to be here."

"I've always wanted more for you, that's all. After what happened with your sister, and then your poor mother. Life was always going to be hard for you, and I never wanted to be the one to make it harder. I just want you to be happy, Brett." Amma wiped her hands on her painting apron and began cleaning her brushes.

"I'm happy, Amma," Brett said, but the words came out sounding flat.

She was struck by how the ocean her grandmother painted seemed to ripple like the real one not even twenty feet away. Amma had taken painting classes for a few years through the community college, but mostly she was raw, natural talent. If she could still paint like this, Brett thought, then maybe things weren't so bad after all. But what would happen if that part of herself slipped into the darkness along with everything else?

"I think you should see another doctor," Brett said. "I think we should get a second opinion."

"I know you do." Amma cupped Brett's cheek in her hand. She

smelled like acrylic paint and salt. "Just give me more time, okay? That's all I need. A little more time."

Brett didn't know how much longer they could wait. But she nodded, agreeing because the sky above them and the one Amma had painted were filled with an infinity of stars.

Chapter 14

Clara knew she would marry Marshall when she was fifteen, the very first time they kissed. He'd taken her to see a movie. She thought it might have been *The Pink Panther*, but honestly, after all this time, it could have been anything. What she remembered was the dark of the theater, the flickering projector, Marshall's leg bumping against hers, her hand reaching for his, their fingers curling together. When the movie ended, neither of them got up to leave. The credits rolled. The music was a perfect soundtrack for what happened next.

Marshall leaned closer. He brushed his thumb along her jawline, drawing her face to his. He smelled faintly of licorice from the candy they'd been eating. His lips were soft and dry and lovely beyond anything she could have imagined. Her whole body responded to him, and she knew then that Marshall was her future. In a sticky-floored, discarded-popcorn theater with the film crackling to the end of the reel, and the acne-faced usher waving a flashlight in their faces, telling them to get the hell out, their life together started. As they ran out the exit doors, hands clutched, laughing, Clara thought she would never be happier than she was at that moment.

Then, five years later, Marshall got down on one knee at their favorite Italian bistro. She cried as she said yes, as he scooped her off her feet and twirled her in the air. They were so young. She would be twenty-one on their wedding day, barely, but that night with the candlelight and violin music going to her head, she was twenty, and all she could think was, what took you so long? Because she had been waiting for this day since the night of their first kiss. She would have married him right after high school if he'd asked, but Marshall had needed more time. To grow up and find himself. To try life without her.

Her mother cried at their wedding. His mother sat stoic and unmoved beside his father. *You're making a mistake,* Clara had overheard his mother whisper during the reception dinner. But Marshall shook his head. *You're wrong. Clara is the best thing that's ever happened to me. She loves me in a way no one else ever will.* They got married in a pretty little church at the top of a hill on the first Saturday of August with the bay sparkling in the distance and the trees flushed green. The whole world spun through with love and golden light.

They danced cheek to cheek until everyone else went home. When they were alone again, she in her wedding dress three months pregnant, her feet aching, he in his tux and a little drunk, with a love song playing softly through the speakers, he caught her staring. *Do I have something on my face?* He wiped his hand across his cheek. *You're perfect,* she said, tracing her eyes along the slope of his regal nose, the solid line of his jaw, his lips that would, from that day forward, only ever touch hers.

It was only much later after Marshall had fallen asleep, that Clara thought about her mother. She'd sat alone at the wedding, the seat beside her reserved for a man who had left them both decades ago for another life, another wife, another family. Clara was eight-years-old when her father packed a suitcase and moved to Ketchikan, Alaska with a retired stripper named Cherry. She hadn't seen him since. And he had never tried to contact Clara, either, never even sent so much as a birthday card. Her mother had dated a few men over the years, but none of them stuck. *I'm destined for loneliness*, she would say. And Clara couldn't help but think that everything could have been different if her mother had tried harder. If she hadn't given up so easily.

Love wasn't complicated. All it required was cultivation, sacrifice, and a heart unwilling to break.

As soon as Marshall got home from work, Clara would ask about Brett. She knew there was a perfectly reasonable explanation for why the two of them were coming out of his office together earlier this morning. Still, she had to ask. Just to be sure. As she waited, she distracted herself with the mindless task of laundry.

She grabbed a crumpled jean skirt from Elizabeth's basket and shook it out, checking the pockets. The skirt was acid-washed with rhinestone decorations on the back pockets and a hem that looked ripped. Clara thought it a hideous thing and too tight, but Elizabeth loved it. She would wear it every day if she could. Clara was about to toss the skirt into the washing machine when she saw the blood.

A dark spot on the back inside of the skirt—barely anything, the size of a quarter. Clara sprayed a stain remover on the fabric. She searched through the rest of Elizabeth's hamper, looking for underwear with blood stains to match but found none.

Clara had been embarrassed about her period when she was a teenager, too. What girl wasn't? For nearly all of the eighth grade, she'd stuffed her underwear with toilet paper, trying to keep blood from leaking through her skirts. Finally, her best friend had told her about sanitary napkins.

When Clara was a teenager, her mother had been impossible to talk to. She was always too busy or too depressed. Clara strived to be a different kind of mother to Elizabeth, a better mother. She tried her best to be approachable, supportive, and even-tempered. And yes, she loved her daughter fiercely. And maybe she was too suffocating with that love sometimes. But wasn't that better than Elizabeth wondering whether she'd ever been loved at all?

Clara thought she had proven herself to be the kind of mother a daughter could talk to about anything. Apparently not.

She grabbed a box of pads from under her bathroom sink and left them on Elizabeth's bed along with a note that read, *If you have any questions, please ask. I'm here for you whenever you're ready to talk. Love and kisses, Mom.*

She went back to sorting laundry.

Marshall got home around seven, a little later than usual. He came into the kitchen where Clara was chopping onions for spaghetti sauce, grabbed her waist, and spun her around. When he kissed her, he pressed his whole mouth to hers, seeking with his tongue. It reminded her of their first kiss. Fervent, devouring. It was the most enthusiastic he'd been with her in a while.

She allowed herself a moment of pleasure, then nudged him away and returned to chopping onions. "Where's Elizabeth?"

"She's not here?" Marshall loosened his tie and reached into the cupboard for two wine glasses. He uncorked a cabernet and poured them both a drink.

"You were supposed to pick her up from practice." She scooped the onions into the pan. They hit the oil sizzling.

"I did," Marshall said. "I tried. Coach said she didn't show up today."

Clara froze with the knife against the cutting board. When she'd found Lily in her crib last year, blue around the lips, not breathing, she'd called the ambulance right away. But it had been too late. Minutes, seconds even—this was all the time it took for everything she loved, her whole world, to be ripped from her arms.

"Hey." Marshall touched the back of her hand. A feather-light brush of his fingers, and yet it was enough to bring her back into her body.

She took a deep breath and moved a bell pepper onto the cutting board. The knife came down hard, the pepper obliterated by the sharpness of the blade.

"I'm sure she's fine," Marshall said. "She probably went to June's. I'll call over there and find out."

He moved toward the phone, but before he could pick up the receiver, the front door opened and slammed shut.

"Elizabeth?" Clara set the knife on the counter and wiped her hands on a towel.

Footsteps pounded up the stairs.

A few seconds later, Clara burst through Elizabeth's door without knocking. "Where were you? Your dad said you weren't at practice?"

Elizabeth stood staring down at the pads on her bed, a frown pinching her face. She picked up the box and turned it over, inspecting it a moment before tossing it onto her dresser with a disgusted curl of her lip. "What are those for?"

"I was doing your laundry this afternoon—"

"You went through my stuff?" Elizabeth whirled on her, a horrified look on her face.

"I sorted your dirty clothes. I'm sorry for doing you a favor." Clara's voice was edged in sarcasm. She crossed her arms over her chest.

She knew matching her daughter's attitude would only escalate their fight, but she couldn't help herself. Fear bunched at the base of her throat and trembled behind her eyes. She could feel Elizabeth pulling away from her and feared this was the beginning of a slow separating as she tested her boundaries into adulthood.

Already Elizabeth was keeping things from her. If she wasn't careful, Clara would know absolutely nothing about what went on in her daughter's life. She couldn't let that happen.

Parents were supposed to protect their children, even as their children pushed them away. They were supposed to set boundaries and keep their kids from giving in to their worst natures. She refused to be like her own mother, caught up in misery, so self-absorbed she hadn't seen Clara pulling away and falling apart. She hadn't noticed, or she hadn't cared—was there even a difference?

Fourteen years ago, the day Clara found out she was pregnant with Elizabeth, she'd vowed to be a better mother than her own. One who paid attention, who knew what kind of person her daughter was becoming.

Elizabeth threw her backpack onto the floor and sat on the edge of her bed. "What happened to you giving me more privacy?"

"You want to start washing your own clothes? Fine." Clara tossed her hands in the air, frustrated. With more cruelty than she intended, she added, "Next time you have your period, make sure you spray your skirts with stain remover right away, or you'll never get the blood out."

Elizabeth crumpled and buried her face in her hands, her shoulders shaking uncontrollably as she started to cry.

It wasn't the reaction Clara had expected. She stood a moment, uncertain. Marshall was still downstairs, finishing up dinner. If she called for him, he would be here in seconds to do what he did best, what he had done since Elizabeth was a baby—comfort, soothe, kiss away her hurts. Except for a teenage girl's churning emotional anxieties were a bit more complicated than the skinned knees that Marshall was used to. Whatever was going on with Elizabeth, she needed her mother now.

Clara sat on the bed and put her arm around her daughter's shoulders, drawing her close.

"Talk to me, sweetheart." Her tone was soft. Her anger vanished the second Elizabeth started crying. "Is it those girls at school? Are they still bothering you?"

Elizabeth shook her head.

"Then what is it? Why are you so upset?"

"I don't want to talk about it." She pulled away from Clara and laid down on her bed in the fetal position. Her sobbing had subsided to sniffles and shaking breaths.

Clara rubbed her back. "It might make you feel better."

She shook her head against the pillow.

Clara stretched out on the bed, tucking her body against Elizabeth's, cradling her in a way she hadn't for many years. When had her daughter, her tiny baby girl, grown so big? They were almost the same height. She smelled different too, like strawberry shampoo and a feral, teenage girl scent she'd forgotten about after all these years. Clara pressed her nose into Elizabeth's hair, searching for even the faintest scent of her once milky sweet baby. But her baby was practically grown now and smelled grown too.

"You know, sweetheart," she spoke in a whisper, "those girls who are mean to you at school are just doing that because they feel threatened by you. They see how special you are, and they're jealous of you. So don't pay them any attention, do you hear me? Don't give them any more of your energy. If they bother you again, I want you to come to me right away, okay? You don't have to handle any of this on your own."

She was quiet, hoping the silence would be enough to get Elizabeth to talk about what was really upsetting her. The swings of emotion she was having seemed too volatile to simply be because some girls at school were mean to her. Puberty could account for some of it, but Clara sensed there was more.

In the weeks following Lily's death, she and Marshall had watched Elizabeth closely, but she seemed to take the loss in stride.

She cried at the funeral, and once Clara had found her sitting in the nursery, hugging one of Lily's stuffed toys, but for the most part, she seemed to move through her grief quickly. She hadn't asked a lot of questions. She hadn't wallowed. She was sad for a little while, and then she wasn't. Or at least that's how it looked to Clara, who had trouble getting out of bed for months. But maybe Elizabeth wasn't done grieving. Perhaps she hadn't even started, and these past few days, this acting out, was related to her sorrow over losing her baby sister.

Clara stroked Elizabeth's hair, wanting to say something about Lily, something reassuring and wise, but she could not push the words past her own tangled knot of lingering grief.

From the bottom of the stairs, Marshall called up to them that dinner was ready.

Later that night, behind the closed door of their bedroom, as Marshall brushed his teeth and Clara rubbed lotion on her hands, she finally said the words she'd been holding on to all day. They bloomed hot in her chest, turning her voice hard-edged and sour. "I swung by the office this morning."

"Oh?" Marshall spat into the sink, rinsed, then turned off the light and came to join her in bed. He sat on the edge and removed his slippers. "When? I'm sorry I missed you."

"I saw you with her." She set the lotion on the nightstand and swung her feet under the covers.

He got in beside her, his brow pinched in confusion. "With who?"

"Brett."

"Oh, right." He punched air into his pillow, completely nonchalant, going about his nightly routine as if nothing at all was wrong. "She wants to sell her grandfather's cannery. We did a walk-through of the space today. It's a great piece of property. If I can find the right buyer, there's a real opportunity to develop it into condos or retail space. It would be nice to revive that area of the waterfront, don't you think?" He stopped fussing with his pillow and looked at her, his excitement fading. "What? What did I say?"

She shook her head. "It's nothing. It's great. I'm proud of you."

She rolled her back to him. The bed jostled as he got under the covers, then bounced again as he shifted his body against hers, drawing her in. "There's no reason to be jealous, Clara. She's a client. She came to me, asking for help."

"There are other realtors."

"But I'm the best. Isn't that what you're always telling me?" His hand moved along the slope of her hip as he kissed behind her ear. "Besides, that property could easily sell for upwards of a million dollars. That's a tidy commission that would be hard to turn down."

She rolled to face him, tucked her head under his chin, and pressed her hands to his chest. Maybe after the cannery sold, Brett would leave Crestwood. Clara could hope.

"You are the best." She tilted her head up to kiss him. "You'll sell it in no time."

"We'll see." He held her a while in silence, then shifted his arms a little to get more comfortable. "How worried should we be about Elizabeth?"

She'd sulked through dinner, eating a few bites before retreating to her bedroom, claiming she had homework to do. She'd turned down the ice cream Marshall brought her for a study break. She'd gone to bed without coming down to say goodnight the way she usually did.

"Something's wrong," Clara said.

"Those girls at school? We can talk to the principal again."

"I think it's more than that."

A long pause, and then he said, "It could be about Lily?"

The dark of their bedroom and the warmth of their bodies tangled under the covers cushioned the blow, but it still hurt to hear her dead daughter's name spoken out loud. She sucked in a breath, surprised by the words that slipped from her mouth, "Marshall, I'm scared."

He rubbed her back.

There was an intimacy to this moment. The shadows deepened. A sliver of moonlight played on the wall above their heads, and there was a feeling that they were two alone in the world, that the secrets they told here would stay here.

"You have no idea how hard it is to be a teenage girl." Her voice was barely a whisper. "The dangers that are out there, all the time, lurking around every corner. One wrong choice, and that's it. Your whole life is ruined. Something happens, and you can't come back from it. I'm trying so hard to keep her safe, but I—" The words choked her. She shook her head against his chest. "I'm so afraid something bad is going to happen."

"What do you mean? Like what?"

When she was Elizabeth's age, a girl had disappeared. A summer girl who flitted in and out of their lives, oblivious to the ripples she left behind. Margot Buchanan, Brett Buchanan's older sister, and the girl who almost ruined everything. After her body was found, parents locked their front doors at night, and kids stopped playing in the woods. That summer, everyone was scared another girl might be taken and killed. Clara had been afraid, too. She'd spent so many nights staring at the shadows growing on her walls, waiting for them to take the shape of her worst nightmares. She had never wanted her own daughter to feel that same kind of fear, the kind she still felt even after all this time.

"Whatever happens," she whispered. "We have to protect her. We have to keep her safe."

Marshall pulled her even closer. His chin brushed the top of her head, his chest rising, falling, steady, his hands firm, pressing the pieces together, holding her still. "We'll be fine, Clara," he hushed her. "She'll be fine. Nothing bad is going to happen. I'll make sure of it."

She wanted so badly to believe him, but they hadn't even been able to protect Lily. A baby, who hadn't gone anywhere without them, who had been asleep in her crib in the very next room with nothing but a thin wall between them when she died. How could they possibly hope to keep Elizabeth safe?

It was a long time before Clara fell asleep that night. When she finally did, it was Margot's voice she heard, calling to her from a dark woods, but it was her daughter she saw vanishing into shadowed trees.

Chapter 15

Brett called Crestwood High School the second she got to her desk on Wednesday morning. She spoke with a guidance counselor named Shep, and then with the principal, Ms. London. Neither was surprised to hear about Saturday night's party—kids will be kids, after all—but they were upset to learn about the assault. She arranged a meeting with them at the school later that afternoon, hoping they would let her interview a few students, June's sister specifically. She had five hours to kill until then. No new cases had come in overnight, and she was caught up on paperwork from older cases, so when Eli stopped by her desk and asked if she wanted to go for a ride, she said yes.

"Where are we going?"

He was dressed in plain clothes. Black pants, burgundy turtleneck, black windbreaker. His badge was clipped to his belt along with his gun and a set of handcuffs. He opened the door of an unmarked pool car for her and said, "Down to the docks to talk with Nathan's boss again."

Brett should have walked away right then. Irving didn't want her anywhere near the Andress case. She should have backed off, returned to her desk, and organized paper clips for the rest of the day. Instead, she got into the car and buckled her seatbelt. Technically she wasn't working the case. She had been invited to ride along as an observer. It was as good of a chance as any to get to know her colleagues and this town better, and if she happened to hear something interesting about the case, so be it. She promised herself she wouldn't interfere or handle evidence.

As Eli pulled out of the precinct parking lot, Brett asked, "How come Irving's sending you?"

He rolled his eyes. "You know, I was top of the list to make detective before you came along."

"I didn't steal your job," she protested.

"You kind of did." But when he said it, he grinned. "Look, no hard feelings. But Irving knows I'm good for this work. Besides, if I want the next spot, I have to keep my interview skills sharp. He got some info from Danny's interview yesterday that needs checking out. I volunteered. I don't know what it was like in the department you transferred from, if it was every man for himself or what, but here in Crestwood, we help each other out. If we see a thing that needs doing, we do it."

Before Crestwood, Brett had worked on the special unit that eventually brought down serial murderer Archer French. She was assigned early in the investigation, before any connection had been made between Margot's death and these other girls, and no one had any real idea what kind of monster they were hunting. The local cops were still scrambling to get their heads screwed on straight but calls were flooding into the tip line by the hundreds each day. So Brett was assigned to answer phones, take down whatever information she thought might be useful to the case, and bring those tips to the lead detectives. That was it. Sit at a phone bank twelve hours a day, sifting through tons of garbage, hoping to find something useful. And even though she was ignored by the other officers, shoved into a desk by the bathrooms, she felt helpful, necessary. Like she was a cog in a powerful machine. Like her work, however tedious, could make a difference to this case.

Except for every tip she brought to her superiors was ignored. The two girls, who called about a dark blue sedan parked outside of their sorority house for three nights in a row, were deemed paranoid and desperate for attention. The Oregon State soccer coach, who nearly got into a fistfight with a campus security guard after finding him lurking in the women's locker room, was a stuck-up bitch who needed to mind her own damn business. The ninety-year-old widow, who saw a man carrying a shovel into the woods across from her house, was blind and senile. Anyway, it was dark out, and she probably just saw a neighbor taking out the trash.

Brett had been on the unit for only a few weeks, attending daily briefings, when she met Jimmy, and it was Jimmy who started her thinking about Margot. He suggested that the Ophelia Killer, a name he'd come up with for his articles, was more prolific than the police believed. Up to that point, the police were working under the assumption that the Ophelia Killer had murdered five women. Jimmy claimed there were more.

Over several rounds of beers, Jimmy pressed Brett for information about the investigation. It didn't take them long to realize he knew more about the cases than she ever would. After meeting up a few more times, Brett finally told him about Margot. A few days later, Jimmy showed up at the bar with a copy of Margot's file. Brett didn't know how he'd done it, who owed him favors, but there it was. A thin folder with barely any information at all, but it was enough for them both to wonder if the Ophelia Killer was somehow connected.

But when they brought their suspicions to the detective in charge, pointing out the similarities between Margot and the other dead girls, they were brushed aside. *Girls died all the time*, he said, *that didn't mean the Ophelia Killer was killing every girl*. At some point, Jimmy became person of interest.

So with a hunch, a handful of witness statements, a rough sketch of a possible suspect, and a desire to clear his name, Jimmy had gone to Crestwood. While there, he interviewed half the town, finally finding his way to Mary Andress, who confirmed the suspect in the drawing looked an awful lot like her nephew Archer French. Archer French, who worked as a security guard at the Oregon State Campus. Archer French, who was a bit of a loner and a freak. Archer French, who drove a blue sedan. Archer French, who had been in Crestwood the summer Margot was killed.

But instead of letting Brett bring the information he'd uncovered to her superior officers and letting the police do their jobs, Jimmy had tried to be a hero. He'd confronted Archer French on his own. He was damn lucky he made it out of that madman's house alive.

When the special unit was disbanded, Brett was sent back to the Marion County Sheriff's department, where she naively assumed her work on the French case would be the turning point in her career. She'd hoped her superiors would recognize her contribution in bringing a murderer to justice and offer her a promotion. Instead, she found herself in the exact same place where she'd started—working as a patrol officer in the far reaches of the county, responding to welfare checks and domestic violence calls, serving eviction notices, and feeling stuck in a never-ending loop of mediocrity.

Maybe Crestwood was different. Maybe the men in this department could set aside their egos and allow her to be part of their boys' club, but she doubted it. Policing as a woman was a rigged game, and the rules were always changing.

―――――――――――――

"You do know that Irving pulled me off the case, right?" Brett asked Eli as he turned the car into the wharf parking lot.

"Yeah, I heard something about that." He shut off the engine. "He likes his cases clean, and he has a near-perfect close rate because of it, plus a good rep with the county prosecutor's office that he doesn't want ruined. So if he says you're off a case, he's probably got a good reason for it. But..." He popped the car door open, and the stench of fish guts blew into the cab. He grinned at her. "I won't tell if you don't."

The fish stench followed Brett and Eli into a single-wide trailer where Nathan's boss, Randy Borkowski, waited for them. He was a small man, squat and round, with thinning hair and bulging eyes. He sat behind a metal desk surrounded by stacks of papers and wrinkled maps. Another larger man stood slightly behind Randy near a pile of fishing buoys. This man was built like a football player with broad shoulders and large biceps. His head nearly touched the low ceiling. One of his eyes was ringed green and yellow from a fading bruise. He scowled through a thick red beard.

"Let's make this quick." Randy spread his hands over the top of the desk. "After you called, I pulled up Nathan's personnel file and took a closer look. He was working on the *Molly Brown*. Cole here's the captain." He gestured to the hulking fisherman. "Nathan hasn't always been the most reliable of employees, but we need all the help we can get. Not a lot of young men want to work on boats these days. They're all moving to Seattle or Vancouver for those fancy office jobs. But Nathan didn't mind getting his hands dirty, and he was strong, so we kept him on. Even if he was a pain in my ass."

"He liked to drink." Cole's voice was a graveling bark. "Showed up three sheets to the wind some days. Which case, we wouldn't let him on the boat. We'd set him up to do some work on the nets and gear out here on the docks until he sobered up. He didn't do a lot of talking, kept to himself. When he was sober, he was an asset. And when he wasn't..." He shrugged.

"Last Friday, how was his mood?" Eli asked. "Was he drunk when he came to work that day?"

"Nope," Cole answered. "He was out on the boat with me

all day. We worked a twelve-hour shift, came in around five or five-thirty."

"Was he acting funny? Scared or nervous?"

"He's always been a little jumpy. But no, not any more than usual."

Randy shuffled some papers on his desk and said, "There was a note in his file from about two weeks ago. Seems Cole counted Nathan absent on a day he was supposed to be working? Says here it was unauthorized?" He looked over his shoulder at Cole, whose scowl deepened as he thought a minute, then he snapped his fingers.

"Right, so. We usually start before sunrise, do some prep work on the boats before we head out. Nathan got to the docks on time that day, and he was sober, but as we were readying to cast off, he's nowhere to be found. I went up and down the docks looking for him, thinking he was taking a piss or something, but really worried he was sneaking a drink. I caught him with a flask in his jacket pocket once. On the boat. Nearly tossed him overboard, I was so angry. Tossed the flask over instead. Anyway, thought he might be up to no good. Sure enough, I come around the corner over by the mechanic's shop, and there he is talking to some kid. I was too far away to hear what they were saying, but neither seemed too happy. Nathan tried to give the kid something, an envelope maybe, but the kid kept pushing it back at him like he didn't want it. Kid stormed off after that. I thought Nathan would come on back to the boat, but instead, he got in his car and drove off. Boat couldn't wait any longer, so we went without him."

"How far away would you say you were?" Eli asked.

"Oh, about a hundred yards or so. I can show you exactly where it was."

Eli nodded, and the four of them walked out to the docks. Cole stood at the end of a pier, where the ramp sloped down to the boats. He pointed toward a large building on the other side of the parking lot, about a football field's distance from them.

"Yeah. They were right over there. Right where that lamppost is."

"The kid he was talking to," Eli said, "do you remember what he looked like?"

"Lanky. Probably a hundred pounds soaking wet. Clean-shaven, and like I said, he looked young. Wore all black, including a leather jacket that looked pretty expensive. Dark hair that could have done with a trim. I dunno. I guess I've seen him around places. I just don't know his name."

"You recognized him?"

"He's been out at Danny Cyrus's place a few times, but he just comes and talks to Danny for a minute, then leaves again. He never hangs around for very long."

"You and Danny are friends?" Eli asked.

"We know each other, yeah. We drink together sometimes."

"Were you out at his place last Friday night?"

The question seemed to surprise Cole, who opened his mouth, then quickly snapped it shut. His eyes narrowed, and he crossed his arms over his chest, turning suspicious and defensive. "What's that got to do with Nathan?"

Eli shrugged like it was no big deal and offered him a friendly smile. "Just trying to figure out where everyone was the night he died."

"Once he left the dock, I didn't see him."

"So, Nathan wasn't out at Danny's place on Friday night, then?" Eli asked in a way that sounded like he might already know the answer.

Cole's cheeks, what was visible above his beard, reddened.

"You did go out to Danny's on Friday, didn't you?" Eli pressed. "Just want to make sure we've got our facts straight."

Still tense, Cole nodded slowly. "Sure, I hung out with Danny and a few other guys on Friday night. We were goofing off in the woods, drinking and telling ghost stories and shit."

"This kid you saw with Nathan?" Eli asked. "Was he at Danny's on Friday with the rest of you?"

"If he was," Cole said, "I didn't see him."

Cole clammed up after that. Eli asked a few more questions but got nothing else out of him. It was clear he'd said everything he was going to say about Nathan and didn't think the rest of it was any of Eli's damn business. Eli thanked him and Randy for their time anyway and let them get back to work. On the way back to the car, Eli turned to Brett and asked if she didn't mind coming along for one more stop.

CHAPTER 16

From the wharf, Eli drove them out of town toward Lake Chastain. Through the thick wall of trees bordering the road, Brett caught glimpses of the North Cascades' ridged spine and a flicker of white in the far distance that might have been Mount Baker. Her thoughts flickered, too, trying to make sense of what Cole had told them.

"Yesterday, Irving said Danny had an alibi for the night Nathan was killed," she said.

"He does, but it's thin. Says he was hanging out in the forest with his drinking buddies. Cole Bozeman being one them."

"Let me guess. They were hanging out at the same spot we met up with him and Lincoln Byrne on Saturday afternoon?"

"Apparently."

"But even if Cole saw him there, it would have been easy enough for Danny to sneak away at some point," she said. "There are plenty of trails, lots of cover, with easy access to the road. He could have killed Nathan and gotten back there before anyone noticed he was even gone."

"Sure could have," Eli agreed.

He turned off the highway onto a different road than the one they'd taken Saturday. This one was paved to the end, where it widened into a turnout doubling as a driveway for a moss-covered cabin ringed by a rickety-looking front porch. Three hollow-eyed jack-o-lanterns sneered from the steps. Curtains were drawn over the windows. Eli took a gravel off-shoot to the left of the cabin and kept driving to a small meadow surrounded by regal fir trees. Set up on concrete blocks in the center was a trailer with a No Trespassing sign tacked to the door and a Confederate flag hanging off the edge of the metal awning. An ATV and a black and silver motorcycle were parked off to one side.

Eli had barely thrown the car in park when the trailer door slapped open, and Danny Cyrus stepped out onto the grass. One strap of his overalls was buttoned, the other hung loose like he'd thrown them on in a hurry. He was barefoot and holding a shotgun across his chest.

Brett reached for the gun in her shoulder holster, but Eli gestured for her to leave it. He rolled down the window. "You can put that thing away, Danny. We're just here to talk."

Danny glared through the windshield a moment as if deciding what he wanted to do. Even though Eli seemed to think he was harmless, Brett still kept her hand close to her gun. Another second, and then Danny lowered the shotgun and leaned it against the side of the trailer. It was still well within reach, but no longer an imminent threat. He patted his hands over his overalls before finally settling on the back pocket from which he pulled a pack of cigarettes and a lighter. He tipped out one of the cigarettes and cupped it to his mouth, lighting the end and blowing smoke toward the sky.

Eli got out of the car first. Brett, a few seconds after. She stood behind him with her hands firm on her hips, feeling the weight of her gun in its holster. She kept a close eye on Danny's hands, ready to pull her weapon if he made even the slightest, hostile twitch.

"At least you came to the front door this time," Danny said between puffs of a cigarette. "But I still ain't asking you inside."

"We can talk out here as good as in there," Eli said.

Danny sucked his cigarette one last time, then dropped the butt in the dirt, not bothering to snuff the ember.

"What'd ya bring her for?" His gaze shifted to Brett, eyes roaming the length of her before settling on her face. "I know who you are. You think you can hide behind that badge and those fancy clothes, but I never forget a face. Even if you are all grown up now. You here to ask me about your sister? 'Cause like I said back then, and like I'll say until the day I'm dead and buried, I had nothing to do with what happened to her. We had some good times that summer, but that's all we did. So if you came out here to stir things up for me again, you can get right back in that car and drive the fuck back out of here."

"We're not here to talk about Margot," Eli said.

Her name on his lips was an invocation that drew from the crisp autumn air a golden-haired girl, a bright-eyed nymph. Margot, sitting on the edge of the docks, kicking her feet in the water, spraying diamonds across the bluest of skies. Margot, head tilted back, laughing at everything and nothing all at once. Twenty years gone, dead more years than she'd been alive, and yet in the seconds it took for Eli to say her name, she was resurrected. Brett blinked away the images and returned her focus to Danny.

"We're here to ask you a few follow-up questions about Nathan," Eli said.

"I said all I'm going to say about it to that black cop who was harassing me yesterday." He crossed his arms over his chest and started tapping one foot.

"Do you know a kid about seventeen or eighteen, might still be in high school or recently graduated? Wears a lot of black? Nice leather jacket? Floppy hair?" Eli made a motion with his hand, dipping his fingers down his forehead.

Danny stopped tapping his foot. "I might. What do you want with him?"

"Just need his name, then we can go on and leave you alone."

"He in trouble or something?"

"Nope, we just need to talk with him like we're talking with you." Eli offered a tight-lipped smile.

Danny's mouth twitched. "Lotta kids around this town fit that description."

"And they all hang out with you?" Eli pressed.

"Who said anyone's hanging out with me?" His eyes narrowed.

"Come on, Danny, for once, can't you cooperate with us?"

A laugh exploded from his mouth. "Since when have I not been cooperating? I answer every single question you pigs ask me. It's not my fault you don't listen to any of my goddamned answers."

Eli widened his stance and matched Danny's defensive posture of arms crossed over chest. "Just tell us his name, Danny. We've got one witness saying this kid was an associate of yours and that he was fighting with Nathan a couple of weeks ago. Then we've got Nathan's own mother saying you threatened her with both a bat and a gun, that you were claiming Nathan owed you money. Now, I know you swear up and down you have an alibi for the night he died, but you and I both know alibis are easy to fake, so how about giving me something better than that?"

Danny rolled his tongue in his mouth but said nothing.

"Look," Eli said. "You're always going on about how you're one of the good guys, right? That you just happen to be in the wrong place at the wrong time and that us cops are out to make your life miserable. You're always going on about how you've never done a thing wrong in your whole sorry life. So prove it to us, Danny. Be one of the good guys today. Tell us who this kid is."

Danny glowered at Eli, and for a long stretch, Brett thought he'd turn and go back inside his trailer without saying a damn word. Then he twisted his head until his neck made a loud popping sound. He grimaced and said, "You know that kid whose in a punk rock band? They sometimes play down at the Pickled Onion? Zach?"

"Danforth?"

Danny nodded.

"I've seen him around," Eli said. "Who is he to you?"

Danny exhaled loudly and lifted his face to stare at the underside of the awning. Then he dipped his hand into his pocket and pulled out a second cigarette. He took his time to light it and take a drag before answering, "He's my brother-in-law's nephew. Which I guess makes him family to me, too."

"And?"

"And he sometimes does errands for me."

"Like what? Come on, Danny, stop dragging your feet."

"You said you just wanted a name."

"What errand was he running for you when he was talking to Nathan two weeks ago?"

Danny shrugged and said, "Like I told that black cop before, I loaned Nathan some money a while back. Don't ask me what it was for, because I don't know. People come to me when they need money, and I give it to them. I don't ask about their personal business. I gave him five thousand dollars, and he was supposed to pay me back a couple weeks ago. With interest, obviously."

"Obviously," Eli said with a tone of disgust.

"Hey, I'm not a charity." He turned his head and spat in the dirt. "Zach went to collect, but Nathan didn't have the money. Well, he had some of it, but I don't take installments."

"And when people don't pay you back?" Eli asked. "What happens then? You come in? Push them around a little? Maybe shove them off the end of a dock?"

"I'm not a monster," Danny snapped. Then he relaxed again, grinning in a way that made Brett's skin crawl. "Yes, I might do a little shakedown of my own every once in a while to make sure they aren't holding out on me. You wouldn't believe what people try to get away with if they think they can. But if putting a little fright in them still produces nothing, I simply extend the loan period. And add extra interest."

"So that's what you did with Nathan?" Eli asked. "You threatened him, then told him he had what? Another week? Two weeks?"

"Well, that's what I would have done," Danny said, swatting at a fly that had started buzzing around his head. "But someone killed him before I had the chance."

———————————

"What do you think?" Eli asked on the drive back into town.

Brett stared out the window at the trees sliced through with light, a stuttering row of trunks that blurred together as the car reached a certain speed. Finally, she said, "He's clearly lying about something, but I think he's telling the truth about Nathan."

She twisted to look at Eli. "But I mean, where is he getting that kind of money? Five thousand dollars? That's not nothing. And it sounds like he's giving out loans to more than one person. So, again. Where is that money coming from?"

Eli's jaw tensed in concentration. "I had the same question. He lives in a trailer on his brother-in-law's property."

"Rent-free, probably."

"And as far as I know, he hasn't been working. Not since the cannery closed."

"Drugs?" she suggested. "He might be dealing."

"That could explain it."

They passed the next few miles in silence, then Eli spoke up again, "He's a vet, you know. Served four years in Vietnam."

"Does he get any pension? Disability benefits?"

"I don't know. We can check, but even if he is getting anything, it wouldn't be enough to loan out."

They passed Ted's Tire Shop, then Shakey's Pizza, then the

roller rink, the buildings stacking tighter together the closer they got to downtown.

"Track down this Zachary kid," Brett said. "He'll probably have plenty to say once he realizes the trouble he's in." She glanced at her watch. "Can you drop me off at the high school? I'm running late for some interviews."

"No problem. It'll save me a trip." He turned off the highway onto the road that led to Crestwood High. "I've had a few run-ins with Zach Danforth over the past few years. Loitering, fighting, vandalism, petty theft. I've let him off with warnings up to this point, but he's the kind of trouble that's always looking for more. I had a feeling that's who Cole was describing, but I wanted to be sure before I picked him up. He's a senior at Crestwood. If he didn't cut class today, maybe I can grab him before someone tells him we're looking for him, and he disappears."

They walked into the front office together. Eli went up to the receptionist and spoke to her in a low voice about Zach's class schedule.

A man Brett guessed to be the school's guidance counselor stood from the chair he'd been waiting in outside the principal's office and shook her hand. He reintroduced himself, "You can call me Shep."

His voice was the same soothing bass as it had been on the phone earlier this morning. He wore his hair long and scruffy around his ears. His mustache needed to be combed, his bushy eyebrows needed a trim. His suit was too big for his narrow frame, his pants badly wrinkled. In a word, he was unkempt, and this Brett realized, was what made him the perfect person for this kind of job. He was approachable, more like an older brother or a cool uncle than a person of authority. He probably high-fived the jocks and winked at all the girls. The students would share their secrets with a man like Shep.

He held a short stack of manila folders against his side. "After we talked this morning, I pulled the school records for Elizabeth, as well as her friend June, and June's sister, Marcie. All three of them are straight-A students. Marcie's a senior. She's on the Honor Roll, works on the school newspaper and yearbook. June and Elizabeth play JV soccer. There are no disciplinary actions for June or Marcie."

"And Elizabeth?"

He handed her the folders. "Nothing until Monday when she was sent home for fighting with another girl."

Brett arched her eyebrows and flipped open the manila folder with Elizabeth's name written on the tab.

"It wasn't exactly a fight," Shep added. "A squabble, really. She dumped a can of soda pop over someone's head."

"Who was that?"

"Kimmy Darling."

Brett started to jot the name in her notebook, but Shep plucked at one of the folders. "I pulled her file too, but again, there's nothing very interesting. These girls..." He shook his head. "They aren't the ones I have to worry about around here. Not usually, anyway. Kimmy's a cheerleader. They're good kids most of the time. Keep their noses clean. Do their homework. Volunteer at animal shelters and things like that. I've known most of these girls since they were sixth graders. They don't seem like the type to get in this kind of trouble."

"Girls can change a lot at this age."

"Don't I know it." He grimaced and gestured toward the principal's closed office door. "She's waiting for you."

"Just give me a second, yeah?" She smoothed her jacket and brushed her fingers through her hair, then turned to thank Eli for the ride.

He was staring at her, gripping a piece of paper in one hand.

"You get what you need?" she asked.

He nodded and stuffed the paper in his pocket, then gestured for her to join him out in the hallway. When they were alone, he pressed close, his voice a rushed whisper. "Elizabeth? Elizabeth Trudeau? That's the assault case you're working on?"

To protect Elizabeth's privacy, she'd talked about the case during this morning's briefing without using her name.

"Yes." Brett was startled by Eli's sudden concern. "Why? Do you know her?"

He shook his head, then backed away. "I... Never mind. Jesus, Brett, she's a kid. You have to catch the asshole who did this to her. You can't let him get away with it."

"Why do you think I'm here?" His anger stirred hers, a feral, blood-and-splintered-bone feeling that she quickly tamped down. Right now, her focus needed to be on Elizabeth.

"If you need any help..." His gaze flicked toward the principal's office.

"I know where to find you."

———

Evangeline London, Effy for short, was a petite woman and younger than any principal Brett ever had growing up. She sat behind a large desk, her fingers folded together primly as she listened to Brett explain what she needed. "I think it's in Elizabeth's and the school's best interests to keep this as low profile as we can until we know more about what happened that night. No one's in trouble. Not yet. I just need to find out who was at this party, what they saw, if anyone knows who hurt Elizabeth."

"I agree." Principal London nodded once. "As long as I'm present during the interviews, then I have no problem pulling the girls from class to get to the bottom of this."

Brett worried the girls might not say as much with their principal listening in, but there really was no other choice. The girls were minors. It was either do it this way or get the parents involved.

"Who do you want to speak with first?" Principal London asked.

CHAPTER 17

"This is stupid." Kimmy Darling twisted a lock of long, blond hair around her finger. She cracked a wad of chewing gum between her teeth and rolled her eyes toward the ceiling. "She's the one who ruined my favorite jacket. I don't know why I'm the one getting in trouble."

"No one's in trouble," Brett reiterated. She'd already told her this at least three times.

Kimmy exhaled loudly and snapped her gum again. Brett resisted the urge to yank the pink wad from the girl's mouth. She crossed her legs, rested her notebook on her knee, and tapped the pen on the edge of the paper. "We just need to know if you saw Elizabeth at the party on Saturday?"

"I don't know about any party." Kimmy shrugged and narrowed her gaze on Principal London, who sat relaxed behind her desk with her hands resting in her lap. She looked like she was only half-listening.

"How much longer is this going to take?" Kimmy asked.

Principal London didn't flinch. "As long as it takes for you to answer Detective Buchanan's questions."

Kimmy sighed again and slouched in the chair, crossing her

arms over her chest. "If there even was a party on Saturday night, and I'm not saying there was, but let's say there was, Elizabeth wouldn't have been there."

"Why not?" Brett asked.

"Freshmen aren't allowed. It's, like, an unspoken rule? They ruin everything." She said it like she was stating something obvious.

"But she was there. So someone must have invited her."

"Well, it wasn't me."

"Did you see her there?"

"Why? What is she saying?"

"Did you see Elizabeth at the party?" Brett asked again.

Kimmy gave another harassed shrug. "No."

"Are you sure? You didn't see her the entire night?"

"I told you, no. All right? I didn't see her." She flipped her hair behind her shoulder. "She might have been there, but it's this huge house, right? There are, like, a ton of rooms and no electricity, but people bring flashlights and boom boxes so we can still dance. If I had seen her, I would have told her to leave. I probably would have dragged her out myself. But I didn't see her, okay? There. Am I done?" She leaned forward as if she was about to stand up.

"Just a few more questions," Brett said.

Kimmy sank back into the chair with a huff.

"Did you know everyone who attended this party? Were they all from Crestwood?"

"Pretty much." She inspected her nails, thinking, then added, "I guess there were a few people from other high schools, but like, still people we knew? Zach was checking people at the door, so no weirdos or nerds or anything crashed."

"Zach?" The name was coming up a lot today. "Does Zach have a last name?"

Kimmy puckered her lips and twisted her hair. "I don't know, probably. He's a senior. He's dating Marcie. Or he was. They're on-again, off-again. Anyway, I still don't understand why I'm here? We were just there to have some fun, you know? No one did anything illegal."

"You were trespassing," Brett pointed out.

"No, we weren't. Marcie's dad owns the place. She said she had his permission."

"And no one was drinking any alcohol?"

She shrugged but with less enthusiasm than before. "Elizabeth is kind of a drama queen. She likes attention. So whatever she's telling you happened, she's probably making the whole thing up, you know?"

"So this party," Brett said. "I heard it was a costume party?"

"Some people were wearing costumes, yeah, duh, it's like Halloween?"

"What costume did you wear?" Brett tried to sound interested.

Kimmy flashed a set of perfect white teeth and batted her eyelashes. "I was an angel."

"Do you know who was wearing a wolf mask?"

Kimmy's smile vanished. She lowered her gaze to her pink Converse with sparkling laces and uttered a meek-sounding, "No."

She was obviously lying. Brett leaned slightly forward in her chair. "This is important, Kimmy. I need to know who was wearing a wolf mask. So if you know who that was, I need you to tell me."

"Why? What did he do?" She snapped her mouth shut, realizing her mistake. Then she narrowed her gaze at Brett, her blue eyes hard as flint. "When are you going to arrest Elizabeth for vandalizing my car?"

The question caught Brett off-guard. "Excuse me?"

"Someone scratched 'cunt' into the hood when I was in class yesterday. My dad filed a police report, but I bet it was her."

"Why would she do something like that?"

"Like I said, she's a drama queen." A smile toyed at the corners of Kimmy's mouth. "Plus, she's crazy. She attacked me on Monday, out of the blue, for no reason. Principal London told you that, didn't she? Didn't you, Principal London?"

The principal said nothing.

Kimmy continued, "Elizabeth tried to say I was calling her names, but I wasn't. She's petty and jealous, and she's a liar. You can't believe a word that comes out of her mouth."

"You actually saw her vandalize your car?"

"No, but she wasn't at school yesterday, so she would have had plenty of opportunity." She folded her arms across her chest. "So, are you going to arrest her or what?"

Brett snapped her notebook closed and stuffed it into her jacket pocket. "Why don't you tell me who was wearing the wolf mask at the party, Kimmy, and then you can go back to class."

"I didn't see anyone wearing a wolf mask." Kimmy stared at Brett.

The clock hanging behind Principal London's desk ticked loudly.

Brett could see it in Kimmy's eyes, in the way she didn't blink, that she was lying and thought she was getting away with it. Let her get away with it, then. Brett counted to sixty to give Kimmy time to change her mind, then told her she was free to go. She didn't have time to play games with this brat. There were other people at that party, people who would be less of a pain in her ass.

A few minutes later, Marcie appeared in the doorway. She was a pretty girl with dark hair and light eyes, wearing a ragged jean jacket and faded ripped jeans with scuffed cowboy boots. She glanced warily at Brett before sitting down in the empty chair, where she chewed on the corner of her lip and twisted her fingers together in her lap, waiting for Brett to talk first. Her nails were painted sparkling silver. As Brett suspected she would, Marcie answered her questions in a soft voice and more readily than Kimmy did.

"Yes, I organized the party," she said. "I got permission from my dad to use the house. It was supposed to be this small gathering, you know, a few of my close friends. No more than like ten people, I swear. We were going to have a séance and gorge out on Halloween candy. But I guess word spread, and by the time I got there, the party was already raging. I tried to get people to go home. But no one listened to me."

"Was there alcohol?" Brett asked.

Marcie worried her lip, darted a glance at Principal London, then nodded. "But I didn't bring it. Zach did. He invited all the other people, too."

"Did you see Elizabeth at the party?"

"Yeah, and I freaked out because Lizzie and June have been connected at the hip since kindergarten. I knew if Lizzie was there, June would be too, but that I'd be the one in trouble if our parents ever found out. So I went looking for them. I couldn't make anyone else leave, but at least I could get June and Lizzie to go home."

"Did you find them?"

"Eventually. At some point, Lizzie went upstairs. No one was supposed to go upstairs, but she went. I saw her coming down. I don't know. She didn't look very good."

"What do you mean?"

"She was stumbling. Her hair was all messed up. I realized she'd been drinking, and then I knew I was in real trouble. I went to go get her, but June found her first, and when I saw they were leaving, I just let them go."

"You didn't go check to make sure they were okay?"

"What do you mean? Did something happen? Is that why I'm here? Did she—?" Her eyes grew wide, and her hands tightened to fists in her lap. "I saw Lizzie at school on Monday. She seemed fine. I don't understand. They came to the party, but they got home just fine. Am I in trouble because I didn't take them home?" Her gaze darted between Brett and the principal. Her lip was starting to bleed where she'd chewed too hard.

"You're not in trouble." Brett leaned over and squeezed Marcie's hand once, then let her go again. "Now, can you tell me...people were wearing costumes at this party, right?"

Marcie nodded, eager to help now, ready to answer every one of Brett's questions.

"Who wore the wolf mask?"

She thought a minute before squeaking out a name. "Zach Danforth."

Brett cursed silently in her head. "Are you sure?"

She nodded again, more vigorously. "We were...it was a couple's costume. I went as Little Red Riding Hood, and he was the Big Bad Wolf."

"You two are dating?"

"Not anymore." She stared at her hands a second, then added, "We broke up last week."

"But you still went as a couple to the party?"

Marcie shrugged. "Not as a couple. But neither of us wanted to come up with a new costume. I mean, we're still friends or whatever." Her eyes grew wide. Her lip trembled. "Did he do something to her?"

Brett leaned forward in her chair. "Why would you say that?"

Marcie shook her head and bit down on the corner of her lip.

"Do you have a reason to think he might hurt someone?"

Her cheeks flushed. Tears gathered in the corners of her eyes. Finally, she said, "Zach can be intense sometimes, that's all."

"What do you mean by intense?"

"I don't know. He doesn't care very much about other peoples' feelings. That's all I mean. He can be pretty selfish. Like if he wants something, he just takes it." Marcie shifted in the chair. Her eyes darted toward the clock. "I have an important test next period. I can't miss it."

Brett nodded and let her go. She had everything she needed now.

After Marcie left, Principal London leaned back in her chair and rubbed the bridge of her nose, sighing loudly. "These girls. They try my nerves."

Brett offered a sympathetic smile. "I don't remember being so difficult when I was that age."

"Oh, but we all had a little devil in us, didn't we?" Principal London said. "I used to hem my skirts so short I was always getting sent home to change. I lit my bra on fire once too, which almost burned down the whole school." She shook her head as if embarrassed by the antics of her younger self. "We survived, though. These girls will too." But there was doubt in her voice and worry in her eyes. "So, you think it was Zach who did this? What now? Will he be arrested?"

Brett wished it could be as simple as that, but since Zach was a person of interest in a murder case, she would have to coordinate with Irving first. Murders took priority. Always.

"We'll bring him in for questioning, yes," Brett said. "But then, I don't know. It depends on what he decides to tell us, I guess. Without any other witnesses, it will just be Elizabeth's statement against his. If he denies it, if he tries to say it was consensual, let's say, or that he wasn't the one in the room with her at all, then there won't be much we can do."

"He'll get away with it." Anger simmered in Effy's hazel eyes.

"They almost always do." Brett hated to say it, but hated even more that it was true.

Principal London sighed and shuffled some papers on her desk, then called her receptionist. After a few minutes of quiet back and forth, she hung up. "Not much of a surprise, but Zach didn't make it to school today."

"Does that happen a lot?" Brett asked.

"He has a history of delinquent behavior, yes," Principal London said. "He's been sent to my office more times than I have papers to file. He disrupts class, shows up late. His attendance record is scattershot. He's truant more days than he's here. He brought a knife to school last year, flashed it around at lunch, and made some poor freshman pee his pants. We've also found fake IDs in his locker on more than one occasion. He's been suspended a few times. Practically lives in detention, though he doesn't usually show up for that, either. D student on a good day. He'll be lucky if he graduates."

"His parents don't care about any of this?"

"He's basically on his own at his point. Single mother, but she's been sick for a long time. I think more often than not, he's the one taking care of her rather than the other way around. It's too bad, really. He's a smart kid. A lot of wasted potential there." She rose and showed Brett out. "If you need my help with anything else, don't hesitate to be in touch. I'll do what I can. They may drive me crazy, but these kids, they're like family to me."

It was only after she was standing in the parking lot that Brett remembered Eli had dropped her off, and she had no easy way to get back to the precinct where her car was parked. She stuffed her hands into her pockets and squinted toward the soccer field where a group of pony-tailed girls jogged in a circle. A whistle blew. The girls scattered. They were all so young and vulnerable. Brett couldn't tell one from the other, if Elizabeth was among them or not. She turned from their crackling, livewire energy, wanting nothing more at that moment than to go home, take a hot bath, drink a beer, and watch some stupid sitcom on television. She wanted to turn off her brain for a few hours and stop thinking about the many and terrible ways the world could wreck a girl. How so many were chewed up and spat out, and when Brett had a chance to do one small goddamn thing to make it right for one girl, she found her hands tied.

She was about to start walking the five miles to the precinct when Principal London came out of the school and, with an understanding smile spread across her face, walked over to where Brett was standing. "I'm heading across town to a doctor's appointment," she said. "Can I drop you off somewhere?"

CHAPTER 18

Clara came home from the grocery store to find Eli sitting on her front porch swing. He stood when she came up the steps and took both sacks from her, adjusting them to balance on his hips. She unlocked the door, and he followed her inside. He was dressed nice, and his hair was combed. She didn't at all like the worried look on his face.

"Why are you here, Eli?" she asked as she started to unpack the groceries.

"Marshall's still at work?" He grabbed an apple from one of the bags and sat down at the kitchen table.

"You know he is."

"What time does Elizabeth get home from school?"

She glanced at the stove clock. "She has soccer practice today."

"Good." He crunched into the apple. Juice sprayed everywhere.

Clara put the milk in the fridge. "I know you didn't come all the way over here to eat my apples and ask me about my family's schedule. So talk. What's going on?"

"Well." He inspected the half-eaten apple like he didn't quite know what it was. Then he said, "There's something I think you need to know. It's about Elizabeth. You're going to want to sit down for this one, Clare Bear."

When he finished talking, she sat a long time not moving. She stared at her hands, which were pressed down flat against the kitchen table, knuckles faded white. Her insides were shaking. She felt the tremors deep within herself, the very marrow of her bones emitting a high-frequency scream. But outside, she remained perfectly still, seemingly unaffected. Except for her hands—which gripped the table so hard that even if the world tilted sideways, she would not slide off.

"Are you sure?" She couldn't make her voice louder than a whisper.

He must have heard the name wrong. It was some other girl, not Elizabeth. Some other Crestwood High School freshman with long brown hair who had gotten herself into this mess. He was mistaken; that's all this was. But even as she tried to convince herself otherwise, she knew he was telling the truth.

"And you said this happened Saturday night?"

Eli nodded.

Elizabeth had told them she was spending the night at June's house. In the past, Clara would have called to check up on her, but she'd been trying to give her more independence. She thought of the next morning when Elizabeth came home wearing those strange sweatpants, looking tired like she hadn't slept at all. Clara hadn't pushed because Elizabeth was fourteen and, according to Marshall, entitled to privacy and secrets of her own. But this was the trouble with secrets, wasn't it?

Someone always got hurt.

Clara remembered the blood stain she'd found on Elizabeth's favorite skirt, and her grip on the tabletop tightened. Her daughter hadn't started her period at all. Her daughter had been assaulted at a party. And that blood was from the act, the violation. That blood was Clara's shame and her rage.

This was on her, as a mother. She should have done something to keep this terrible thing from happening. But what? If she had been paying more attention. If she hadn't agreed to give Elizabeth more space. A laugh bubbled up in her chest, but she shoved it down. *Don't worry*, Marshall had insisted. *Our girl is a smart girl, a good girl.* But that made it even worse, didn't it? If Elizabeth was a wicked creature, a girl with claws and teeth and a black heart, maybe she could have fought her way out.

The laugh leaked out of her in a whimper.

Eli stretched one hand across the table toward her. "So I take it she hasn't told you or Marshall yet?"

"No." It was difficult to talk, the words slow to form. "What should I do?"

"There's not much you can do," he said. "Let Brett finish her investigation. Maybe the guy will confess. Maybe there will be enough evidence to prosecute, but a lot of times, cases like this, they're he said-she said, and they die before they ever reach a courtroom."

"So whoever did this to her is going to get away with it? Go on with his life like nothing happened?"

"That might happen, yes," he said. "I want to be honest with you, Clare. So you won't be surprised later if that's how it plays out. But Brett, she's a good cop. A great one. If anyone can track this guy down and put his feet to the fire, it's her."

Clara curled her fingers, but her fists were useless in this fight. "I have to get dinner started."

She rose from the table, grabbed a knife from the block, laid the cutting board out on the counter, took an onion from one of the grocery bags, and cut it in half. The paper skin peeled away. Tears sprang to her eyes as she diced; she let them fall.

Eli sat another minute at the table before asking, "Do you want me to wait with you until Marshall gets home?"

"Thank you, Eli, but no. I'll be fine. I'm sure you have better things to do than babysit me."

She brought the knife down again and again. She was so focused on the blade, on the sound of it striking the wooden board, she didn't hear Eli leave.

When Elizabeth was a toddler, she suffered nightmares. In the middle of the night, she would wake screaming, a sound loud and desperate enough to wrench both Clara and Marshall from sleep. They would rush to her crib, thinking the worst, but always find her safe. Her little hands reaching to be picked up, which of course they did, lifting her, rocking her, soothing her until she settled back to sleep. Once she was quiet again, Marshall would go back to his own bed. But Clara always stayed, standing over the crib, watching the rise and fall of her baby's chest, wanting to be there in case she woke again gripped in terror.

She stood in the doorway to Elizabeth's bedroom now. In the dark of midnight, she watched the shape of her daughter underneath blankets, the smooth rise and fall of her shoulders as she slept.

The conversation that evening had gone much better than Clara had expected. She'd taken Marshall aside to allow him the space to move through his own emotions first without upsetting Elizabeth. From disbelief to shock to rage. He had slammed his fist against the wall when she told him, but not hard enough to break the plaster. He shook out his hand, wincing, then sat down on the bed and covered his face. He breathed in small ragged sips until he was calm again and ready to talk without shouting.

At first, Elizabeth was upset that they'd found out. "Who told you?"

"It doesn't matter." Clara reached for her, but she pulled away. "We love you so much, Elizabeth. We're on your side. What can we do to help you?"

"Whatever you need from us," Marshall said. "Whatever we can do to try and fix this."

"Do you know who it was? Tells us his name."

Eli hadn't given Clara very many details. Only that her daughter had been raped at a party. Only that the investigation was ongoing. Clara thought if she could pull the information out of Elizabeth, somehow she could fix this. She could set the world right again.

But Elizabeth curled into herself and shook her head. "I don't want to talk about it."

"Please," Clara insisted. "We can help."

"I just want to forget the whole thing." Her voice was so small and delicate, splintered through with cracks.

"You don't have to cover for him," Clara said, which upset Elizabeth even more.

Clara knew she'd said the wrong thing the moment the words were out of her mouth, but it was too late to take them back. Elizabeth completely withdrew from them then, saying she was tired and done talking about it. She had homework she needed to finish before bed.

Clara was about to go after her when Marshall put his hand on her arm. "Let her go."

She wrenched away from him, angry because wasn't that how they found themselves in this mess in the first place? Because he had said they needed to give her space? Look at what had happened when Clara wasn't there to protect them. Look at how quickly everything fell apart.

It had been raining on the day of Lily's funeral. Not real rain, but a gray smear, a mist that hung over everything, settling slick across the roads and seeping into the cracks. It was a mist Clara was familiar with, her whole life dampened by this same salt air, constant and corrosive, turning everything ragged and slippery.

That day, the weather fit perfectly with the somber mood of lowering a tiny casket into a tiny grave.

The doctor's words echoed in her head as the minister recited a prayer she would forget as soon as the service ended. *There was nothing you could have done differently. This wasn't your fault—nothing you could have done.*

Sudden Infant Death Syndrome, the doctors told them, and though Clara had heard the words before, they'd held no meaning to her then. Now they were words used to explain the unexplainable—how a perfectly healthy baby stops breathing. Her perfectly healthy baby dead for no reason, through no fault of her own. No one's fault. These things sometimes happen, and it's terrible, but there's nothing anyone could have done, so try not to think about it. Try to move on. But as they were driving home from the hospital, Clara clutching a blanket that still smelled like Lily, she thought of a million tiny moments that could have made a difference. A single, small choice might have changed the entire course of their lives and set them down a different path, one with a happier ending.

If Clara hadn't had that glass of wine before she'd let Lily nurse. If they'd done three minutes more tummy time. If she'd used the regular bath shampoo instead of the new bottle she'd brought home because it was a dollar cheaper. If she'd sung "Twinkle, Twinkle" instead of "Hush, Little Baby." God, that song was morbid. If she'd gotten up to check when she didn't hear her baby crying for a 2 AM feeding; if she hadn't rolled over with a shrug, thinking, *Finally, she's sleeping through the night. Finally.* But Clara had been so tired. Exhausted. And Elizabeth had started sleeping longer around this age, and so she stayed in bed and sank into a deep and tranquil sleep. And as she slept, her baby lay dying.

The doctor could say what he wanted, that no one knew why these things happened, why some babies die, and others live. *You couldn't have known*, he said. *You did everything right*, he said. Talk and talk all he wanted, Clara would never believe him. This was her fault; her past sins returned to haunt her.

Quietly, she shut Elizabeth's door and went downstairs to brew herself a cup of chamomile tea, hoping this would quiet her restless mind and allow her to sleep.

For far too long, she had relied on luck, even though she knew better. Good luck never lasts. She should have seen this coming. Lily, Elizabeth, they were only the beginning. She felt it then, standing in the dark kitchen, waiting for the kettle to boil—how easily everything could slip away from her, how quickly the threads might unravel.

CHAPTER 19

There were four holding cells in the basement of the Crestwood Precinct, and on Thursday morning when Brett arrived at work, all four were empty. She went upstairs to check the three interview rooms, but they were empty too.

She didn't understand. After Effy London dropped her off at the station yesterday afternoon, Brett had darted inside and confirmed with the front desk officer that Eli had brought a lanky, dark-haired kid in for an interview. According to the officer, the interview was still in session. Brett jotted Eli a quick message asking him to hold Zachary Danforth on suspicion of rape if they didn't decide to hold him for murder. She made it clear to the front desk officer that it was critical Eli got the note before he released the witness. The front desk officer nodded and promised he'd pass the message along. Then, because she could do nothing until Eli was done, she'd gone home. Let the kid sit in a jail cell for one night. It was less than he deserved. She'd deal with him in the morning.

Now it was morning, and Zach Danforth was nowhere to be found.

Brett hurried into the squad room, where she found Eli standing next to Irving's desk. The two men were deep in conversation. Eli had traded his street clothes for his patrol uniform. Irving was stiff in a mud-colored suit. A long-legged white crane with red plumage decorated his tie. Both men looked up when she approached. Eli's warm smile quickly fell away when he saw how agitated she was.

"You picked up Zach Danforth yesterday, didn't you?" she asked.

"Yep," Eli said. "Found him at the video arcade."

"Where is he now?" Brett glanced back at the interview rooms.

Eli's brow furrowed. He exchanged a look with Irving, who answered, "We cut him loose early this morning."

"What? Why?" Her voice pitched frantic, but she couldn't help it. She kept thinking of Elizabeth, alone in that dark, haunted mansion, a bass track thumping the floorboards. *I was trying to disappear*, she'd said. How alone she must have felt, how utterly abandoned.

"We need to bring him back in." She spun away from Irving's desk and marched toward her own, lifting the phone to have dispatch send an officer out to the school.

"Brett, wait." Eli chased after her. "What's going on?"

"Yes," she said to dispatch. "Zachary Danforth. If he's not at the high school, go by his house. And also check in at Lincoln Byrne's place. Yes, B-Y-R-N-E. It's urgent. Thank you."

She slammed the phone down and turned her attention to Eli. Irving had joined him at her desk. The two of them shoulder to shoulder, an unflinching wall.

"What is going on?" Irving asked.

"As of yesterday, Zachary Danforth is a suspect in my rape case," she explained.

Eli's cheeks paled. "What? You think Zach—?"

"It is a very strong possibility that, yes, Zach was the one who attacked Elizabeth."

Eli ran his hand down his face. Irving lowered his gaze to his tie, suddenly becoming very interested in making sure it was straight.

"And I would have picked him up yesterday as soon as I was

done with my interviews—" Her words were barbed, laced with anger that she was struggling to contain. "But since he was a person of interest in your case, I didn't want to get in your way."

"You should have called it in," Irving scolded her. "We could have held him for you."

"I did call it in!" She slammed her hands on the desk.

The office murmurs died down as everyone turned to look at her.

"Calm down, Brett," Eli said.

"Don't tell me to calm down. I have every right to be upset. I left a message with the front desk officer, who promised he'd pass it along to you."

Irving frowned but said nothing.

The officers in the squad room watched them. A few spoke behind their hands in whispers. One or two tried to pretend they weren't listening, but it was obvious by the lean of their bodies that they were as interested as those who were openly staring.

"Why don't we get some fresh air." Eli tried to take her elbow and guide her toward the exit, but she shook him off.

She lowered her voice, but anger still trembled beneath the surface. "What the hell happened, Eli?"

He stayed defensive. "I didn't get your message. That's what the hell happened. You think if I'd known, I would have let him go? If that punk hurt—" He took a deep breath. "Jesus Christ, Brett, I'm on your side here, okay?"

She softened toward him. Though her anger still simmered, it was no longer directed at Eli. "What's done is done."

"They'll pick him up again," he said, trying to sound reassuring.

Brett glanced at the phone, willing it to ring and for dispatch to be on the other end, telling her that they were bringing in Zach now.

"It could be a while," Irving said, turning to go back to his own desk. "Might as well try and focus on another case."

She had a few other investigations that needed attention, but this was the only one that mattered to her. The others were small in comparison, crimes against property, a missing bicycle, a vandalized fence. All of it could wait.

She walked to the front of the precinct, where the front desk officer worked. Eli tagged along with a guilty look on his face.

The front desk officer was a heavy-set, middle-aged man with a pinched mouth that, for some reason, made Brett think of a teddy bear. He was looking through a stack of take-out menus when she approached his desk. He blinked up at her, his polite smile falling away when he saw the look on her face.

"Do you remember when I asked you to give that message to Eli Miller yesterday?" she asked him. "The one about Zachary Danforth?"

"Zachary...Zachary..." He was obviously stalling for time.

"Eli was interviewing him," she said, "and I asked you to pass along a message?"

"Oh, right!" He snapped his fingers like the memory had just come to him. "A few minutes after you left, Officer Fellowes walked by. She was on her way into the squad room, so I gave her the note to put on his desk." He looked at her curiously. "Why?"

"I thought I made it clear that the note was important," she scolded. "I think I used the word 'critical?' I expected you to pass it on to Eli directly."

His face folded into a red and furious scowl. "Well, if it was so damn important, then I guess you should have gone in and given it to him yourself. Try to do something nice, and this is the thanks I get." He turned his back on her, still mumbling to himself.

Brett returned to the squad room.

Eli was right on her heels. "I told you I didn't get it."

Nancy wasn't at her desk. Brett asked if anyone had seen her. Everyone shrugged, acting like they had no damn idea who Nancy Fellowes was.

The phone on Brett's desk rang, and she rushed over to it. With

Eli breathing down her neck, she spoke to the dispatcher. When she hung up, she let out an exasperated breath and raked her hands through her hair.

"He wasn't at the school?" Eli asked.

"Or at home. They're sending someone to check at Lincoln and Danny's place, but knowing my luck, he won't be there either."

"They'll find him. There aren't that many places for him to hide."

"Tell me what happened," she said.

"What?"

"In the interview. Zach's the closest you've got to a murder suspect. What did he tell you that made you cut him loose?"

Eli glanced at Irving, who was deep in conversation with someone on the phone. "Let's talk outside."

She followed him to the parking lot.

Puffy white clouds raced across the expansive blue, rushing from the ocean to the mountains. A cool breeze nipped her cheeks. She tugged her jacket around her.

Eli stood with his arms crossed over his chest and stared at the road. "Zach confirmed what Danny already told us, that he was sent to collect on Nathan's loan, that Nathan only had half of the money, but promised he'd have the rest soon. Zach said he told Danny, and that was that. He didn't talk to Nathan again. He said he doesn't know Nathan that well, just that he borrowed money from Danny once and that he worked down at the docks."

"If Zach was collecting for Danny, he could have easily been the clean-up crew," Brett suggested. "Danny doesn't want to get his hands dirty, so he sends Zach to put a little fear into Nathan. Zach gets excited, goes a little too far with the threats?"

"Maybe, except Zach has the same alibi as Danny. He says he was out in the woods the night Nathan died, only he says they were doing more than drinking."

"Oh, really?"

"Apparently, Danny's running a fight club."

Brett laughed, but it was a hollow sound. "Of course he is."

"A bunch of guys meet in the woods every Friday and Saturday night to beat the shit out of each other. They've got bets going, obviously."

"Jesus," she breathed out the word.

"Danny handles the book and takes a large cut. Lincoln fights. Along with a lot of other local guys."

"Like Cole," she said, remembering the bruise around the boat captain's eye.

Eli nodded. "And some out-of-towners. Danny doesn't fight. He runs the thing. Zach helps. He collects money, takes bets, keeps an eye out to make sure no one cheats or makes side bets of their own. Zach's also one of the bouncers. He meets people at the top of the road and leads them down to the fight spot. It's a very exclusive club, apparently. They can't have everybody up there stomping through the trees and throwing punches. Neighbors wouldn't be too happy about that. So they try to keep it quiet. A couple dozen men at a time. A lottery to determine who gets to go and watch. They rotate fighters. It all sounds very organized."

"So Danny alibis Zach," she said. "And Zach alibis Danny. How convenient. How do we know they're not lying for each other?"

"Zach gave us a bunch of names of men who were also at the fight, men who saw both him and Danny. Irving's calling them up to confirm."

"He rolled over pretty fast for you, didn't he?"

Eli nodded. "He was definitely in a hurry to get out of here."

"Maybe he was afraid you'd start asking about the party." She sighed and shook her head, then gave Eli's uniform a once over. "So you're back out on patrol then?"

"Yep." He paused, then said, "I'll keep an eye out for Zach and grab him if I see him. But in case he's lying low, and we can't pick him up today, you should come by my parents' house tomorrow night."

He started acting suddenly shy. He tilted his head, staring at the sky, anywhere but her. His voice was awkward and fumbling. "We have this, like this Halloween party every year? It's sort of a costume party, but you don't have to dress up if you don't want to. Some people do. Anyway, it's a good time, usually. My mother hires the best caterers. There's bobbing for apples if you want. And a pumpkin carving contest. But mostly we just get drunk and dance and anyway, you should come? If you want. With me. I'll be there." He snuck a sidelong glance at her. "Odds are good Zach will be there, too."

She gave him a startled look. "Why would he be there?"

"I went over to my parents' house this morning. They were finalizing things, going over the caterer's list, and his name jumped out at me. He's going to be working as a server."

"You really think he's going to show up at a party where there are a bunch of cops?"

"It's not just cops." A small scowl tugged his mouth. "It's really not cops at all. I mean, I'll be there, and you, if you want to come. But it's mostly my parents' friends. He's a kid who needs the money. He'll show up."

"Yeah, okay, fine," she relented.

"You'll come?"

She cringed at the eagerness in his voice. "If we can't track him down between now and then."

"Yeah, right, cool." He hooked his thumbs in his belt and rocked back on his heels.

The silence stretched between them. Eventually, Eli stepped off the curb. "Okay, see you tomorrow then, if not before." He gave her a funny little half-wave and walked to his patrol car.

Brett wasn't ready to go back to the small squad room crowded with hot breath and the sweaty onion smell of men's bodies. She stood a few minutes, watching the clouds bunch and fold and drift away.

A car pulled into the parking lot, and a woman with shoulder-length, dishwater-blond hair that snapped in the breeze got out. The woman walked quickly toward the precinct, her long skirt twisting around her legs. Her eyes locked on to Brett as she came closer. Brett recognized her from a picture sitting on Marshall's desk at the Trudeau Realty office. Her mouth was set firm, and her brow was pinched, but she was clearly the same woman. Marshall's wife. Elizabeth's mother. Brett took a deep breath to prepare herself for what was coming next.

"You're Brett, right?" But she didn't wait for Brett to confirm or deny. She just rushed on, "You're the one in charge of my daughter's case?"

"I'm sorry, ma'am. Who are you?"

The woman's nose wrinkled in distaste. "Clara Trudeau. I'm Elizabeth's mother. Eli told me you are the one investigating her assault. Is that true or not?"

Brett clenched her hands at her side, her jaw tightening. This was why she hadn't said Elizabeth's name during the morning briefing. She hadn't been ready to deal with her parents yet. But now, no thanks to Eli, she was caught unprepared, scrambling to figure out how to calm the woman without violating the trust she'd built with Elizabeth.

"Yes," she finally said. "I'm handling your daughter's case."

"Have you found the bastard yet?"

"Excuse me?"

"Have you found the asshole who hurt my daughter?" Clara spat out the words, her whole body leaning toward Brett, tilting at such an angle, Brett worried she might tip over.

"The investigation is ongoing—"

"What exactly are you doing?"

"Ma'am?"

"What are you doing to track down this monster who rapes little girls?" Her voice cracked, and she pressed one hand to her chest. Her nails were painted pearl pink. The wedding ring on her finger was a simple gold band with a large center diamond.

"I can assure you, Mrs. Trudeau, I'm doing everything in my power to bring in the suspect."

"You know who did this? She told you?"

"I'm afraid I can't give you any details at this time."

"Of course you can. I'm her mother."

"Yes, and I'm sure this must be very frustrating—"

"Don't patronize me." She pressed her face close to Brett's. "Tell me who the fuck did this to my baby girl. I want his fucking name."

"My primary concern right now is protecting Elizabeth. I'm sure you understand better than anyone how delicate a situation this is. There are several different scenarios I'm looking into, and it might be a few days before I'm able to say for certain what happened."

"You know what happened. My daughter was raped. And you're doing jack-shit to find her rapist." She backed away, crossing her arms over her chest, her gaze roaming over Brett, taking the measure of her. She sniffed through her nose like she was disappointed by what she saw. "Of course, I shouldn't be surprised. Weakness runs in the family."

"What did you say?" Brett stared at the woman who was clearly and understandably emotional about what had happened to her daughter, who had perhaps gone off the deep end over it all. Eli was going to get an earful from her the next time she saw him. He could have at least told her what he'd done so she could have prepared herself for this.

The precinct door opened, and the front desk officer popped his head out. "Detective Buchanan? You have a call. It sounds urgent."

"One second," she said.

At the same time, Clara barked, "Can't you see she's busy?"

The front desk officer cleared his throat. "It's Officer Miller. Something about your grandmother?"

When Brett left the house that morning, Amma had been fine. In fact, she'd been downright chipper. She had started drinking two cups of ginkgo tea a day. She'd read somewhere that it could help with memory problems, and she was sure she was already feeling the benefits. *Ask me who the president is, Brett. No, wait, I'll tell you. It's Ronald Regan. Also, look, I put on the same color socks today.* They'd read the paper together over breakfast, something they hadn't done in weeks. Amma laughed at the comics. Brett scanned the classifieds to see how much other people were selling their sailboats for, in case they needed to sell the *Anita Horizon*. The way Amma was acting, though, maybe they wouldn't have to sell the boat after all. *I think I'll have lunch with the girls today,* Amma had said, referring to a group of friends from her country club that she'd been avoiding for months. Yes, everything had been fine, more than fine, when Brett had left for work.

Now she turned to Clara, trying not to sound panicked even though she was because, if nothing was wrong, Eli wouldn't be calling the station. She smiled calmly and said, "I'm sorry, Mrs. Trudeau. I'm afraid we'll have to continue this discussion another time."

Then she hurried into the precinct, leaving Clara standing open-mouthed and affronted in the parking lot, puffing on her own indignation.

Brett picked up the front desk phone and turned her back on the lurking officer in an attempt at privacy. "Eli?"

The first thing he said was, "She's safe."

Brett relaxed, but only for a second as she tried to make sense of what Eli said next. "I found her walking on the side of the highway. Out near the scrap metal yard? She didn't have a coat on. No shoes on either. She seemed lost. I pulled up next to her and asked her if I could give her a ride somewhere. She told me she was all right and that she was just looking for Margot."

He paused, and the silence was filled with the crackling of a bad connection.

"I managed to talk her into getting inside the car with me, and then I drove her home. She's safe," he repeated. "I'm still here with her, but I think you should come as soon as you can. I don't think she understands what's happening."

"Okay," Brett said. "Okay, thanks. I'm on my way."

She hung up the phone and hurried back into the squad room to grab her jacket and keys. She went out the back entrance, certain Mrs. Trudeau was still in the front parking lot waiting to ambush her again.

Amma sat on the edge of the bathtub as Brett washed her feet with warm water, soap, and a washcloth. The soles of her feet were black from dirt, and there were a few small cuts, but it could have been worse. So much worse.

"You could have been killed," Brett said, repeating what Eli had said to her when she'd arrived at the house twenty minutes after he'd called the precinct.

They'd stood on the front porch as he explained the semi-trucks rocketing past Amma as she teetered and weaved her way down the highway shoulder. A gust of wind from a passing truck almost knocked her into oncoming traffic. *She didn't know who I was*, he said, and the concerned expression on his face was the exact reason Brett hadn't wanted anyone to know what was going on with Amma. The pity and prying questions. *Is everything all right?* She'd told Eli it was nothing, just a side effect of new allergy medication. She asked him not to say anything to the chief, then sent him on his way, reminding him that he still had a suspect to chase down for her. Brett was in such a hurry to get him out of the house, she forgot to mention her run-in with Clara Trudeau. She'd deal with it later, she thought as she went inside to take care of Amma.

"Where were you going?" Brett squirted more soap onto the washcloth. The scent of lavender filled the room.

"Well..." Amma thought a minute as she tapped her fingers on the porcelain edge of the tub. "I was getting ready for lunch at the club, and I realized that I hadn't seen Margot in several hours. The house was quiet. Too quiet." Amma splashed her toes in the warm water gathering at the bottom of the tub. "So I went looking for her."

Brett washed the last of the dirt from Amma's feet, then turned off the faucet and reached for a towel.

"I can do that." Amma took the towel from Brett and began to dry her feet. "Did she make it home okay? Margot, I mean?"

The look on her face when she asked it was one of childish hope. Brett looked away when she answered, so she didn't have to watch her grandmother shatter all over again.

"Margot's dead, Amma. Remember?"

"What? When?" They were gasps more than words, splinters of sound that cut deep.

"She's been dead twenty years," Brett said the words slowly, so they had time to sink in. "The summer of 1964. She was murdered."

Amma was silent for a moment, staring at her feet, pale against the dark blue towel. She whispered, "Does your mother know? Someone should tell her."

But her words lacked enthusiasm, as if somewhere deep in the shadow places of her fading mind, she was remembering on her own that her daughter was dead too.

Brett gripped Amma's hand and squeezed it tight. "Amma, I'm sorry."

What she was sorry for, she couldn't say—all of it and none of it. Sorry Amma was forgetting, every day losing herself in small pieces. Sorry Brett couldn't protect her from this. Sorry, too, that she had to be the one to again deliver the terrible news about Margot, breaking her heart a second time, breaking it over and over. Sorry that she couldn't take it all back, bring the dead to life, return Amma to a world that was whole the way it was before she started losing everything.

Amma covered Brett's hand, so instead of holding her grandmother, her grandmother was holding her. She patted Brett gently. "We'll be fine." Then she let go, tucked her clean, dry feet into a pair of slippers, and stood up.

"You know, it's getting late, and I'm really feeling quite tired." She shuffled into the hallway, moving toward her bedroom. "So I think I'll turn in early tonight if that's all right with you. Be a dear and make sure the house is locked up and the lights are turned off before you go to bed, would you?"

"Sure thing, Amma," Brett said. She didn't have the heart to point out that it wasn't even noon yet, the sun still high and shining brightly through the windows.

CHAPTER 20

To call Eli's parents' residence a house would have been an under-statement. It was a mansion with two separate wings, gables, tur-rets, gargoyles, marble steps, and a sprawling, pillared front porch. When Brett pulled into the long driveway on Friday night, a valet took her keys, gave her a ticket, and drove her car around to the back of the house. With sinking dismay, she watched the taillights disappear. She was having second thoughts about coming.

She was worried about Amma, worried she'd wander off the way she had yesterday. Worried, too, about the way Amma had been shuffling around the house for the last twenty-four hours. She hadn't changed out of her pajamas. She hadn't brushed her hair or put on make-up. She swept through rooms like a ghost, with her nightgown fluttering around her ankles, not interested in any of her usual hobbies like painting or reading.

At some point this morning, Amma turned on the television and, by the time Brett was getting ready to leave for the Miller's party, she still hadn't moved from her spot on the couch. Brett told Amma where she was going, when she would be back, asked her if she needed anything. Amma flapped her hand and told her to go have fun. Brett hesitated in the doorway, wondering if she should stay. But she needed to talk to Zach, and Eli had promised her that he'd be at the party.

Standing in the Miller's driveway, Brett straightened her sweater, which she'd chosen for its autumnal brown and orange stripes, then ran her fingers through her hair. She'd make this quick. Get in, find Zach, get out. She lifted a brass door knocker shaped like a lion's head and pounded on the mahogany double doors. A few seconds passed, then the doors creaked open to reveal a butler who glowered at her a moment before sweeping his arm through the air and gesturing her inside.

As soon as Brett stepped into the ballroom, she realized her mistake. Everyone except her had come in costume. Tuxes and capes, top hats and elaborate walking sticks, sweeping ball gowns, glittering masks, feathers, elbow-length gloves, colorful make-up, and fancy wigs. Candelabras flickered at the perimeter of the room, and strings of lights looped across the ceiling, casting everyone in a magical glow. Waiters in white tuxes and red cummerbunds with matching red masks weaved through the room carrying trays of drinks and finger foods. The music from the string quartet was lively, and people danced in the center in a way that felt old-fashioned, yet somehow sensual. It was lovely and charming, and Brett was completely out of place. She backed toward the door, desperate to get outside again, away from the laughter and clinking glasses, the hidden faces, gazes flicking over her, casting judgment, finding her wanting.

Someone grabbed her elbow, spinning her around. A man smiled at her from behind a silver-and-white mask that had a nose hooked like a bird's beak. She recognized him when he spoke. "You came!"

She took in Eli's outfit, a burgundy velvet tuxedo jacket with lacy black cuffs and a high collar to match. Silver buttons glinted in the dim light. He wore the coat over a black shirt, and his pants were puffed like a pirate's. His shoes were shiny and decorated with a silver buckle.

"You told me not to dress up," she hissed.

"No, I told you, you didn't have to."

"Everyone else is."

He scanned the room. "First year that's happened." When he looked at her again, he was still smiling. "Don't look at me like that. It's true! Most years, only half the people dress up. I guess everyone really liked the theme." He waved one hand. "Masquerade."

Brett sighed, exasperated. "I'm going home."

"Wait, come with me." He grabbed her by the hand and wove her to the opposite side of the ballroom. "My mother always provides extra costumes. Just in case."

Inside a large closet, coats hung on racks alongside puffy-sleeved, taffeta dresses. Scarves and gloves spilled out of baskets on the floor. Another basket contained an assortment of masks. Eli took a midnight blue dress off the rack, then dug around in the basket of masks until he found one that shimmered blue and green and purple. Peacock feathers fanned the top. With a mischievous grin, he handed the mask and dress to her, then exited the closet. "I'll watch the door," he said and pulled it closed.

The dress was slippery, flowing over her body like water. The fabric was delicate, expensive, and decorated tastefully with small crystals around the hem and over the bodice. She had never worn anything as nice as this in her life. She smoothed the skirt, which was long enough to cover her clunky black shoes, then slipped the mask over her face. She folded her clothes in a neat pile and tucked them in the corner of the closet, then opened the door and stepped out.

Eli stared at her a moment too long.

"What?" she asked.

"You look beautiful."

Brett ran her fingers over the feathers of her mask. "I feel ridiculous."

A smile spread across his face. He pulled her through the crush of people crowding the center of the ballroom toward a waiter holding a tray filled with champagne. He grabbed two glasses and handed her one.

"Hey." She leaned close so he could hear her over the music. "Did you tell Clara Trudeau about my case?"

He clinked his glass against hers and tilted his head back to drink. Brett waited until he was looking at her again. "Eli. Did you tell Clara about Elizabeth?"

His smile faltered, but he pulled it tight again. "Want to dance?"

He plucked the still-full champagne glass from her hand and placed it on a nearby table, then tucked his arm around her waist and spun her onto the dance floor in a breathless rush. Brett tried to scan faces as they turned in circles, but the room was a blur, and the masks made it even harder to tell who was who.

"Where's Zach?" Her lips grazed Eli's earlobe.

Eli continued to twirl her, spinning her faster and faster and then suddenly bending her at the waist, dipping her low, and she couldn't help herself. She laughed. His smile brightened. He pulled her upright again, and they kept spinning together.

"How's your grandmother?" he asked.

"She's fine," Brett murmured against his chest. For a moment, she was swept up by the enchantment of it all. She gave herself over to Eli as he guided her in billowing circles, lost in the haunting melody of the string quartet, growing dizzy as the chandeliers spun to stars. Then she remembered why she was here in the first place, and she blinked the room straight again, stiffening in Eli's arms. "We really need to find Zach."

Eli sighed like he would rather talk about anything else, but then he brought his mouth close to her ear, his cheek warm against hers, and said, "I checked with the kitchen an hour ago. Zach is carrying the peach and prosciutto tray."

He spun her away from him and tipped his head toward a waiter offering a tray to a woman in a salmon-pink ball gown. The waiter was tall and lanky, with long dark hair. Eli spun Brett back into his chest, tightening his grip around her waist. "My parents will kill me if we make a scene."

"I can't let him walk out of here tonight without talking to him," she said.

"Be discreet. That's all I'm asking."

He lifted one hand and brushed his fingers over her hair. "You really do look beautiful, you know. The blue brings out the color in your eyes."

He spun her again and, this time, let go of her hand. When she glanced back at him, he had vanished into the crowd.

Brett wandered off the dance floor, inching closer to Zach, who had moved on to a different section of the room and a different set of hungry guests. The song changed to something slow and romantic. More couples started to dance. Brett followed Zach, staying a few feet behind him. He moved with surprising grace, bowing to offer food, then straightening again, lifting the tray high enough so it wouldn't get knocked from his hands by tipsy guests. When the tray was empty, Zach walked toward a closed wooden door that was nearly invisible between two large potted palms. Brett followed him into a hallway decorated with fleur-de-lis wallpaper.

Waiters moved back and forth from kitchen to ballroom, brushing past Brett as if she wasn't even there. The sounds of the party were muffled through the closed door behind her. From the swinging kitchen door at the opposite end came the clattering of plates and orders being shouted. Zach ducked out of the way of another waiter who was carrying a tray of champagne. He seemed to be in no hurry to get to the kitchen.

Brett caught up to him halfway down the hall. She grabbed his arm and pushed him through the closest doorway.

"Hey!" He cried out, trying to slip her grasp.

She shoved him inside the room and closed the door behind

her, then felt her hand along the wall looking for a light switch. The lights snapped on overhead, and Zach winced. He held his tray against his chest, like a shield. "What the hell?"

The room she'd pushed him into was some kind of game room, with a billiard table at one end and two pinball machines at the other. Board games and puzzles were stacked on a low shelf under the window.

Brett slid her mask to the top of her head so Zach could see her face. He gave no indication that he recognized her, so she said, "I'm a detective with the Crestwood Police. I need to ask you a few questions."

His eyes narrowed, and he laughed nervously. "Yeah, right. Where's your badge?"

"In the glove box of my car." She pulled two chairs out from under a card table and pointed at one. "Sit."

"I didn't do anything." But he did as she asked, perching tensely on the edge of one chair, while she sat in the other, directly in front of him, their knees almost touching.

"You can take off your mask if you want," Brett said.

He slipped it off his head but kept hold of it, teetering both the mask and tray on his lap. His eyes darted around the room, settling on nothing.

"This won't take long," she said. "And I appreciate your cooperation."

He shrugged one shoulder. "I told the other cops already, I didn't have anything to do with that dead guy."

"Zach, were you at the Whitmore Mansion last Saturday night?"

He thought a moment before answering. "Sure, there was a party. It wasn't a big deal or anything. Just a few friends hanging out, whatever."

"From what I heard, it was more than a few friends. It seems a lot of people showed up who shouldn't have been there?"

A frown tugged the corners of his mouth as he tried to figure out where she was going with this.

"People like Elizabeth Trudeau." She studied his reaction.

Tension spread across his shoulders. He blinked, once, twice, then said, "Elizabeth who?"

Brett shifted in her chair, crossing one leg over the other. The slit in the skirt of her dress went up to mid-thigh. Zach's eyes drifted to her bare leg, then back to her face. She let the silence stretch long before asking an entirely different question, "Did you wear a costume to the party, Zach?"

"A costume?" He looked confused. "Sure. Sort of. Everyone was dressed up."

"I bet you went as something badass. Did you go as something badass, Zach?" She uncrossed her leg and leaned her elbows on her knees.

His lips curved into a smile. "I was the Big Bad Wolf."

She smiled back. "I knew it. I knew it would be badass. What was it? A full suit or just some black face paint? A pair of ears?"

"I just wore black pants, a black shirt, my black leather jacket."

"And a mask?"

"Yeah, a wolf mask. Fangs and hair around the edge." He moved his hands around his face, demonstrating.

"Bad. Ass." She was still smiling at him when she asked, "Now what did you say your relationship with Elizabeth Trudeau was again? She's your girlfriend? Or were you two just hooking up?"

The color drained from his face. "What? No. Who told you that? Was it Marcie? Did she tell you I was dating Elizabeth?"

"So you do know Elizabeth?" Brett lifted her elbows off her knees, straightening the skirt, so it covered her legs again.

"No. I mean, yes, but not very well," he stumbled over the words. "I see her at school. She hangs around Marcie a lot, but we're not, I don't know her."

"But you saw her at the party? You talked to her?"

His eyes darted toward the door, and he started to get up from the chair. "I've got to get back to work. They won't pay me if they think I ditched."

"Sit. We're not done."

He dropped into the chair, his grip tightening around the tray.

"Zach, did you have sex with Elizabeth at the party on Saturday?"

She was done pretending to be nice, but she still needed his cooperation. If she called what had happened rape, he would shut down, get up and walk out of here. And she'd be back at square one trying to figure out how to get what she needed to send this case over to the county prosecutors' office to file charges.

He shook his head. "Who told you that?"

"Tell me what happened at the party, Zach. Between you and Elizabeth. I can help you, but only if you tell me the truth."

"Help me? With what? I didn't do anything. Nothing happened between me and Elizabeth." He was revving up again, his voice growing louder with each word. He stood from the chair.

"Sit down."

This time he ignored her. He angled his body to bolt out the door. She stood too, blocking his escape.

"Marcie's lying," he said. "Whatever she told you, it isn't true. I broke up with her, and she's still pissed about it. It'd be just like her to try and get back at me like this." He shook his head, like maybe this wasn't happening, and maybe if he blinked hard enough, Brett would disappear. "I didn't do anything to Elizabeth. Whatever Marcie might have told you, I didn't do it."

"You saw Elizabeth at the party, though," Brett pressed him. "You can at least admit that."

"Yes. She was there. I saw her."

"You talked to her?"

"I talked to a lot of people."

"Did you give her anything to drink?"

"It was self-serve," he said, rolling his eyes. "I know I'm waiting on people tonight, but that's only cause I'm getting paid."

"I'm going to ask you again, Zach. Did you and Elizabeth have sex on Saturday night?"

Defiant, Zach tipped up his chin. "No. I swear to God. She's a kid. I wouldn't do something like that even if she wanted to."

Brett studied his face for a second. He could have easily been lying as telling the truth, and she knew then, with a sinking in her gut, that this case was going nowhere. Not with Elizabeth saying one thing, Zach saying another, and no witnesses to confirm or deny either story. But that didn't mean Brett was giving up on it.

"I'd like you to come down to the station on Monday," she said.

"What for?"

"I'd like you to provide a formal statement and take a lie-detector test." She would also try to get a genetic sample from him, even though she knew it would probably just end up sitting on a shelf in the precinct basement with all the other dead-end cases.

He groaned and tugged his fingers through his hair. "What? Why? I told you I didn't do anything? I didn't touch her."

"Then you have nothing to worry about, do you?" She flashed him a smile. "If you're telling the truth, you'll pass the test with flying colors."

He ground his teeth together, then, with a resigned sigh, said, "Fine." He gestured toward the door. "Can I go back to work now?"

She followed him out of the room, turning off the lights behind them. In the hallway, Zach paused to slide his mask down over his face.

"Zach," she called out to him.

He turned toward her.

"I know how to find you now. Monday. Show up, or I'll write up a warrant for your arrest." She wouldn't, but she hoped the threat would be enough to get him to keep his promise.

He glared at her, then stormed toward the kitchen.

Brett turned to go back to the ballroom and nearly tripped over a woman standing in the hallway behind her. The woman was dressed in a simple cream-colored dress with glass beads sewn into the bodice. Her mask resembled a goat head. The entire mask was painted with a floral pattern, except the horns, which were ink black and glittered in the dim light. Her lipstick was crimson red, and Brett fixed on them as they moved around words of apology.

"I'm sorry. I didn't see you there." The woman pointed to the room Brett had just left. "Is that the restroom?"

"No, I'm afraid not."

"Oh. Well. Okay." The woman lifted her skirts and bustled away from Brett. She pushed through the door at the end of the hallway. Music and laughter swelled.

Brett gave herself another minute in the relative quiet of the hallway before she smoothed her dress, drew her mask down over her face, and went to find Eli.

Chapter 21

Clara hadn't heard everything that was said through the closed hallway door, but she'd heard enough.

When Marshall pointed out Brett from across the room a half an hour ago, the first thing Clara said was, "What is she even doing here? She should be working on Elizabeth's case."

Elizabeth was spending the night at June's house. Even though Clara had agreed to the arrangement, she had already snuck away twice to call and check on her daughter, who insisted she was fine. "We're not going to sneak out again, I promise," she said, and there was a beat of silence after that felt weighted with everything that had happened the last time Elizabeth slept over at June's. But Clara took a breath and tried to let it go. Elizabeth was safe.

Her anger surfaced again when she saw Brett drinking and dancing, wasting time when she should have been tracking down the bastard who'd robbed a young girl of her innocence.

"She's not a robot, Clara," Marshall said, guiding her around the dance floor. "She gets to take breaks."

"You should have seen the way she blew me off yesterday when I tried to talk to her about it." Clara grabbed a glass of champagne and tipped it to her mouth, gulping it in one swallow.

As Marshall twirled her around the dance floor, his firm hand pressed to the small of her back, she watched Brett, who wore a luxurious blue dress that glittered like the ocean at sunrise. Her mask was a tuft of fluttering feathers, shimmering in the candlelight. Eli said something to make her laugh, and her head tilted back, exposing a slender, pale neck. Then Eli and Brett separated. Eli moved toward a group of his parents' friends, and Brett followed one of the servers across the room, keeping her distance as if she didn't want him to notice. The server went through a door. Brett slipped quietly after him.

Clara broke from Marshall's grasp. "Ladies' room," she said, lifting her skirts and hurrying away.

She wasn't sure what she was planning, exactly. To finish the conversation that had been cut short in the parking lot of the precinct yesterday, maybe. To demand answers and action. Not this. Standing with her ear pressed to the door, Clara listened as Brett questioned the boy who'd raped Elizabeth. Of course, the boy denied everything. But what Clara didn't expect was for Brett to give him the benefit of the doubt and let him go. As if Elizabeth's version of events meant nothing.

The door swung open. Clara pressed herself against the wall. The boy who came out didn't give her even a passing glance. Without his mask, she recognized him. She moved to chase after him and ran straight into Brett.

"Oh, excuse me," Brett said. "I didn't see you there."

The mask was enough to keep her from recognizing Clara.

"I'm sorry." Clara made some excuse about looking for the restroom before spinning away and hurrying back to the ballroom. She circled, searching for Marshall, but he found her first, pressing his body against her back, his lips warm against the curve of her neck. "I've been looking everywhere for you."

The black feathers of his mask tickled her, raising goosebumps across her skin. She closed her eyes a moment, leaning into his strength. Then she turned to face him, whispering in his ear, "He's here."

"Who?" Marshall asked, brow furrowing.

"Do you remember that boy we saw talking to Elizabeth after her soccer game last week?" She looked around, but Zach was no-where to be seen.

Brett had reentered the room shortly after Clara and once again stood with Eli.

Marshall thought a minute and nodded. "Yeah. Vaguely, I guess."

"That's him. That's who hurt Elizabeth."

"What? How do you know that?" He scanned the room. "He's here?"

"He's one of the servers. I was looking for the restroom, and I overheard Brett talking to him. He's claiming he didn't do anything, though, that Elizabeth is lying. She's not going to arrest him."

His jaw tensed. "Point him out to me."

This time Clara spotted him. With his tray once again filled, he walked among the guests, offering them food. His mask was crooked, and as he reached to adjust it, a tremor ran through her whole body. Those fingers gripping Elizabeth, holding her still, forcing himself, forcing her quiet. Clara wanted to break every bone in his hand.

"There." She pointed. "Next to the ice sculpture."

Marshall shoved through the crowd toward the boy on the other side of the room.

She lifted her skirts and followed in his wake.

"Hey!" Marshall grabbed Zach's shoulder and spun the boy around.

Startled, Zach bobbled the tray. It went flying and crashed to the floor with a loud clang. Everyone stopped talking at once and turned to look. The violin kept playing, a thin and strangled sound in the quiet room. Distantly, Clara heard voices, someone calling out to Marshall, but her focus was on the boy in front of her. He had stubble on his chin and a startled look on his face that faded to a smirk as he looked Marshall up and down, measuring the size of him. He tilted his chin, sure and cocky. "What the hell's your problem, man?"

Marshall's fists clenched, and before Clara could do anything to stop him, he cocked his arm and punched Zach in the face.

A woman screamed. Zach's hand flew to his nose. Blood poured down his mouth and chin and dripped onto the front of his starched white shirt.

"What the hell?" His voice turned stuffy and nasal. "You broke my fucking nose. What the hell?"

Marshall shook out his hand. His face was pinched with pain, but he didn't back down. He shoved in close to Zach, spit flying from his mouth. "I'll break your fucking neck if you come anywhere near my daughter again. Do you hear me, you fucking prick? You touch Elizabeth, you breathe on her, you even so much as look at her, and I'll fucking break you in two."

Zach blinked, startled. Then his shoulders rolled back, and he seemed to be gathering himself, readying to lunge at Marshall. Hands grappled him from behind, and then Eli was there, pulling him away and guiding him to a nearby door. "Let's get you some ice for that."

When they got home an hour later, Clara ordered Marshall onto the couch. "Take off your tie."

She grabbed a beer from the fridge and a package of peas from the freezer, then sat down next to him and carefully lifted his hand to inspect his injuries. His knuckles were bruised and starting to swell. "Poor you," she said, wrapping a towel over the peas and gently settling them over his knuckles. She leaned against his shoulder, cradling his hurt hand in her lap.

With his uninjured hand, he opened the beer and took a long drink.

"Does it hurt much?" she asked.

"I'll be fine." Then he gave her a devilish grin. "I'd do it again in a heartbeat, you know."

"My hero." She kissed his cheek.

He sighed and leaned his head back on the couch, closing his eyes.

Clara hadn't even wanted to go to the Millers' stupid party. She hated being around all those rich people, hated pretending to like them because it was good for Marshall's business. This year especially, with everything that was happening to Elizabeth, Clara had wanted to stay home. But Marshall insisted, and now she was glad he had. Because even though they were the ones, not Zach, treated like criminals and ultimately escorted from the Millers' house. Even as Brett scolded Marshall—*You shouldn't have done that*. Even then, Clara had no regrets. Marshall had stood up for their daughter when no one else would.

Pride swelled in her chest as she pulled the peas off his hand and looked at the bruise again. "Can you move your fingers?"

He waved, then winced. "It hurts, but yeah."

So probably not broken, but his hand would be stiff and painful for a few days. Clara settled the frozen peas back over the swelling and looked at him. They were both still wearing their costumes, though their masks were gone—his dropped somewhere back at the party and hers sitting on the coffee table where she'd dropped it when they got home. She felt a little ridiculous, sitting around in her finery, but with the adrenaline rushing through her, it had been the last thing on her mind when they got home.

"What are we going to do?" She took a sip of his beer and handed it back.

He gave a half-hearted shrug. "What Brett told us to do, I suppose."

As they waited in the Millers' driveway for the valet to bring their car around, Brett had said that the case would be nearly impossible to prosecute without a confession. Especially since Elizabeth couldn't identify her attacker by anything other than the mask he was wearing. Especially since she'd been drinking and no one else had seen it happen. Then Brett told them something Clara wished she had never heard, something she wanted to go back and erase from her daughter's history. Elizabeth's attacker had not only violated her physically, but he'd also taken her underwear as some kind of sick prize.

But if Zach had the underwear, Clara had argued, wouldn't that be all the evidence they'd need to convict? So what were they waiting for? Search his house!

But no, Brett said, it wasn't as simple as that. They could ask Zach for permission to search his property, but if he didn't give it, they would need a warrant. And warrants, she said, were hard to get without physical evidence or a witness coming forward. Even if they got lucky and found the evidence they needed, did they really want Elizabeth to endure such a long and public trial with so little chance of conviction? And an even slimmer chance of a prison sentence? She said it like her hands were tied, and she wished the Trudeaus would drop the whole thing and forget it ever happened. Then she said that Zach was coming down to the station on Monday to give a statement, and after that, she'd have a better idea of what to do next. She told them the best thing they could do for their daughter right now was just be there for her. Leave Zach alone and let Brett do her damn job.

Which to Clara meant doing nothing, which meant letting a guilty man walk. She had watched Zach's face closely during the confrontation, and she was confident of his guilt, even if he'd told Brett otherwise. Clara had seen fear pass across his face when he'd heard Elizabeth's name. He was a good liar. Good enough to fool a cop, but not good enough to fool a mother.

The events of the evening played out in Clara's mind again. How quickly her husband had rushed across the ballroom, pushing aside anyone who dared stand in his way. His arm lifting, his biceps straining the suit fabric. The loud crack. How easily Zach's head snapped back.

Her husband, her protector.

She gently moved Marshall's injured hand out of the way and swung her leg over his lap, straddling him, unbuttoning the collar of his shirt. He seemed surprised and gently pushed her away, at first.

They had always been private about their love-making, preferring their bedroom to exotic locations like the kitchen counter and the top of the dryer. But tonight felt different. Tonight felt charged with electric energy, and Clara didn't want to bother moving to the bed. She wanted Marshall right here, no waiting.

Her lips brushed along his neck and, as if that was all the permission he needed, he set the beer on the side table and began fumbling with her dress. There were so many layers and tiny buttons down the back. After a few seconds laughing at each other's fumbled attempts, he finally unclasped the last button. Clara ripped the dress from her body and cast it aside in a lacey heap. She reached to remove the corset she'd worn to fit into the dress, but Marshall grabbed her arms and pulled them down by her side.

"Leave it." His voice was low and husky, thick with wanting.

She dipped her head and smiled, delighted that even after all this time, she could still turn him on. She reached to undo his belt buckle and pressed her lips to his.

———————————

Clara rolled to look at the clock on her nightstand. 2:03 AM. Beside her, Marshall snored softly. She slid out from under the covers, careful not to disturb him, and walked to their bedroom window that overlooked the street. Some sound had woken her, rattling cans and hushed voices, the rev of an engine, tires squealing away. But as she stood with her fingertips pressed to the cold glass, staring into the night, she saw nothing beyond her translucent reflection. She let the curtain drop over the window again, quietly dressed in a pair of jogging pants and one of Marshall's hooded sweatshirts, and went downstairs. She didn't bother turning on any of the lights. She knew this house like she knew her own body, which steps creaked, which table corners to avoid. Once in the living room, she slipped on tennis shoes and went out the front door.

She stood a moment, confronting the shadows, waiting for something to happen. Nothing did. Whatever or whoever had woken her, they were gone now. The stars were still out, and so was a large chunk of the moon. A perfect, clear October night, a terrible thing to waste. She was already awake, already outside. She started to walk.

When she reached the dock at Deadman's Point an hour later, she wasn't surprised. It was at least a three-mile walk, but of course, this was where her feet brought her. She sat at the end of the pier, removed her shoes, and dabbled her toes in the water. The cold burned and made her suck in a sharp breath. Even though it was tempting death to swim without a wetsuit, she still felt the desire to slip into the darkness and let the current take her where it willed. She swept her feet through the glinting reflections of the stars and moon above her, splintering them, destroying. Then she pulled her feet out of the water, re-laced her shoes, and walked home, her mind empty of every thought but one.

Zach would pay for what he'd done.

CHAPTER 22

Hoping to pull Amma from her funk, Brett suggested they take a walk downtown on Saturday morning to check out Crestwood's Annual Halloween Festival. Amma's mood improved the second they stepped outside. It was a beautiful day for an outdoor festival. The temperatures were cool enough that everyone was bundled in jackets and scarves, but they were lucky this year with sun and clear skies.

"At least it's not raining, right, Amma?" Brett pulled her toward Main Street, which bustled with color and noise.

Barricades had been set up to keep cars out. People in costumes wandered down the middle of the street and crowded the sidewalks. There were a lot of werewolves and vampires. A few witches, some fairies, and a smattering of princesses. There were more unique costumes, too, like an astronaut, a Mary Poppins, a pickle, a centaur, several famous musicians including Bowie and Prince, and an entire family dressed as the characters from *The Wizard of Oz*.

Amma scowled at a man dressed as Superman and asked, a little too loudly, "Why is that man wearing his underwear over his pants?" But then a man in stilts and a clown suit walked by, and Amma laughed, delighted and said, "I'm glad you talked me into this!"

Rock music blared from boom boxes on one end of the street, and a live bluegrass band clanged at the other end. There were face-painting booths, balloon animals, carnival games, everything dinging and ringing. Kids shrieked with delight as they chased one another through the crowd. The air was thick with the smell of barbecued meats and fried dough. People kept brushing against them, and it took all of Brett's effort to keep hold of Amma's elbow so they didn't get separated.

"What do you want to do first?" Brett shouted to be heard over the noise.

Amma tilted her head to one side and smiled like a little kid. "Eat cotton candy."

Brett handed a dollar to the pimple-faced kid working the booth. He passed back a cone of pink spun sugar and fifty cents in change. Brett pinched off a large bite for herself and gave Amma the rest. A few minutes later, her tongue dyed pink, Amma said, "One year they had a petting zoo. A small one with bunnies and goats and guinea pigs. I wonder if they're doing that again?"

"Let's go find out." Brett slipped her arm through Amma's elbow, and they wandered slowly down the street, pausing to watch a woman juggle three flaming sticks.

"My," Amma said, clutching one hand to her chest. "She certainly is brave, isn't she?"

Brett started to relax. She didn't have to think about work until Monday. And Amma was doing fine now, acting like her usual self again, and it seemed like they might both be able to let loose and have a little fun today. Then Brett saw Eli shoving through the crowd and her mood darkened again. Eli lifted his hand to wave at her.

She tried to duck from sight, but Amma had seen Eli, too, and dug in her heels. "There's that nice Miller boy," she said, dragging Brett toward him.

They met in the middle of the street. Eli was in his patrol

uniform, with a neon-yellow vest thrown over the top. He offered Amma a tentative smile. "How are you, Mrs. Wilson?"

"Fine, dear, fine. I was so sorry to miss your parents' party last night."

"They missed you, too. Don't worry, there's always next year." He shifted his gaze to Brett, jerking his head to one side. "Can I speak with you a minute?"

Brett clutched Amma's arm a little tighter, trying to come up with some excuse not to go with Eli, but Amma peeled away from her.

"You two go on." She made her way to a nearby bench, sat down on it, and crossed her ankles. "I'll be fine here."

She gave Brett a knowing look and turned her gaze on a group of children chasing each other in circles.

Brett walked with Eli a few steps away to talk in private while still staying in sight of Amma, who was being very obvious about her sneaking glances.

"I looked for you after the party last night," Eli said. "But you'd already gone."

"What happened to Zach was your fault, you know." Brett couldn't keep the anger from her voice. "You're lucky no one was seriously hurt."

Eli's jaw tensed, and his tone matched hers when he said, "Clara and Marshall have a right to know what is going on with their daughter."

"And Elizabeth has a right to her privacy," Brett snapped back. "She had a right to decide when and who she told about what happened."

"She's a child. She can't possibly know what's best for her."

"It's my case." Brett jabbed her finger into her chest. "Which means I'm the one who decides who knows what when. Marshall and Clara could have won Parents of the Year ten times in a row for all I care. It doesn't change the fact that Elizabeth wasn't ready.

It took a lot for her to come in and talk to me. Who knows if she'll trust me now? Did you ever stop to think how telling people might affect her? The gossip, the finger-pointing, the incessant questions from people who have no business getting involved. Not to mention how all of this is going to affect the case I was trying to build."

From the bench, Amma glared at Brett and made strange motions with her arms, which Brett interpreted as Amma telling her to be nice. Brett rolled her eyes and turned slightly, so Amma wasn't so much in her direct line of sight.

"Our chances for taking this case to trial were slim to begin with, but at least I'd convinced Zach to come down to the station and talk to me. Do you think he'll do that now? After nearly getting his nose broken? Do you think there's any chance at all he'll be interested in cooperating?"

"He said he's not going to press charges," Eli said, trying at reconciliation.

"Oh, good." Her voice was rough-edged sarcasm. "Let me just go find Elizabeth and tell her everything's going to be fine because the boy who raped her isn't going to press charges over a punch that never should have happened." She shook her head, disgusted. "Better yet, Eli, why don't you find her and tell her yourself."

"I'm sorry, okay? I thought I was doing the right thing." He touched her elbow, his hand lingering on her arm just above her elbow, an unspoken question in the brush of his fingertips, asking for her forgiveness.

She stepped back, breaking the connection, and glanced at the bench. It was empty. Amma was gone.

"Where is she?" Brett circled the bench, scanning the nearby crowd. "Amma!" She cupped her hands around her mouth and shouted for her again. "Amma!"

Brett grabbed a woman in a peach cardigan and spun her around, but it wasn't Amma. The startled stranger stumbled away.

"Brett?" Eli sounded confused. "Calm down. What's the big deal? She probably just got bored and went to get a cup of coffee or something."

The street was growing more and more crowded. So were the sidewalks. The parade was starting soon, but no one seemed to be paying any attention to the man trying to wrangle the participants into a straight line. Bodies rolled together, a shifting tide of faces, and none of them were Amma.

"Call on your radio," Brett said, pointing to the two-way clipped to Eli's belt. "She was just here. She couldn't have gone far."

She spun around again. Eli grabbed her by the elbow. "Brett. Stop. What is going on?"

She opened her mouth to tell him everything. Piece by piece, her grandmother was forgetting, regressing to a younger version of herself. She was like a child who needed to be watched constantly. It would be too easy for her to walk out onto the highway again, or for something worse to happen, something Brett couldn't bear thinking about.

Then Brett saw her, not even ten steps away, standing on the opposite side of the street near the Episcopal church.

Brett jerked from Eli's grasp and pointed. "She's there."

She hurried across the street before Amma had a chance to disappear again. As Brett got closer, she saw that Amma was talking to June and Elizabeth. Both girls were dressed like Madonna in mesh tank tops with black pleated skirts and lace fingerless gloves, thick black ribbons in their tousled hair. Elizabeth's mascara streaked down her cheeks, and her lipstick was smeared. She had a scrape on one knee. A small trickle of blood seeped down the front of her leg. As Brett reached them, Amma stepped forward and scooped Elizabeth into her arms in a suffocating embrace.

"You're going to be all right," she cooed. Then, noticing Brett, her expression turned to relief. "Oh, Brett, good. Your sister isn't feeling so well. We should take her home."

Brett peeled Amma away from Elizabeth.

Then Eli was there, too, in his neon yellow vest, asking if everyone was okay. He glanced between Amma and Elizabeth, the concern in his eyes unmistakable.

"Sorry," Brett said. "She just gets a little confused when she's tired."

"I'm not tired," Amma protested. "And I'm not confused. I'm worried about Margot."

She reached for Elizabeth again, but Brett pulled her away.

Eli stared at Amma for a moment. Brett could see the gears turning in his mind, the pieces falling into place. She wasn't sure how she would explain what was happening to her grandmother when she didn't fully understand it herself, but then Eli smiled. A patient, understanding smile. He threaded Amma's arm through his own with such tenderness, Brett wondered who in his family was sick.

He smiled at Amma, then at Brett. "Why don't you and I take a stroll around the fair, Mrs. Wilson? And let Brett talk to these girls alone."

Amma frowned, as if trying to decide, then nodded once and patted Eli's arm. "Yes, yes, that's just fine." She lowered her voice as she said, "Don't tell Frank, but I've always had a thing for a man in uniform."

Eli's smile widened as he turned and walked with her down Main Street, avoiding the more crowded sections, stopping to look at a display of necklaces before moving on to the next booth. With Amma in safe hands, Brett turned her attention to Elizabeth, who sniffled and brushed away tears. June stood close to her, shifting her weight on the balls of her feet, clearly anxious.

"Elizabeth." Brett touched the girl's shoulder.

She flinched. "I'm fine."

"Obviously, you're not." She gestured to her bloodied knees.

"These girls from school were trying to start something," June piped in.

Elizabeth shot her a glare.

"I'm on your side here," Brett said. "You can tell me what happened."

Elizabeth laughed, a brittle sound. "You promised we didn't have to tell my parents, and then you go behind my back and tell them anyway. So whose side are you really on?"

"I didn't tell them anything, Elizabeth, I swear." Technically, it was true. Technically, Clara Trudeau heard about the assault from Eli, not Brett. Brett hadn't given her any information beyond confirmation that she was investigating the complaint. Technically, she had kept her promise to Elizabeth. "I'm sorry they found out before you were ready to tell them, but you knew we had to tell them eventually, didn't you?"

"But not like this!" Elizabeth's voice pitched into despair. "I didn't want it to be like this, where everyone knows what happened. Now they're all saying it's my fault Zach's in trouble, that I'm a liar and a slut and that I'm going to ruin his life, and I should take it back and tell everyone I was lying, and it's not fair because I didn't—" She broke down into sobs.

June put her arm around her friend and glared at Brett. "Do something."

"Start over," Brett said. "Tell me exactly what happened."

Elizabeth sniffed loudly and explained that Kimmy Darling's parents were at the Millers' party last night and had witnessed the confrontation between Marshall and Zach. Kimmy's mom told Kimmy, and Kimmy told all the other girls, and then a few minutes ago by the dunk tank, they surrounded her and started pushing her and calling her names. "They shoved me to the ground and spat on me." Her voice was ragged as she shook her head. "I should have kept my stupid mouth shut. Zach's telling people he didn't do anything. That I lied about what happened at the party to get attention. Now everyone hates me."

June took her friend's hand. "Not me. I could never hate you."

This drew a fluttering smile from Elizabeth that didn't last.

She turned her dewy gaze on Brett. "You still believe me, don't you?"

"Yes, of course, I believe you."

But she knew it didn't matter, that they were just words. Empty, hollow words she could repeat every day for the rest of her life. It wouldn't change how Elizabeth saw herself in this new world where her own safety could not be guaranteed. Nor would it change the fact that Zach would walk away from this with no repercussions except a bloody nose.

"Where are your parents?" She scanned the crowd for Marshall or Clara.

"I don't know. Mom was here a minute ago." She looked around and shrugged, gesturing to the cut on her knee. "She went to go get a first aid kit or something."

"Well, I'm going to stay with you until she gets back, okay? Then we're going to come up with a plan for what to do next and how to get you through this. Because you will get through this."

Elizabeth nodded and sniffed, wet and ragged. June, still holding Elizabeth's hand, pointed toward the street. "The parade's starting."

Everyone in the parade wore a number pinned somewhere on their body. Some people twirled and spun and danced. Some handed out candy. Most just walked, smiling and waving. Everyone showed off their costumes. A flatbed truck led the way, blaring "Monster Mash" and Michael Jackson's "Thriller" on repeat as they wove down Main Street. The bass trembled the brick masonry of the buildings and rattled windows in their frames. Later, Brett would realize all this noise must have drowned out the first screams for help. It wasn't until she noticed a large group of people gathering near the caramel apple stand that she realized anything odd was happening at all.

The flatbed truck passed. The music grew noticeably quieter. The crowd around the caramel apple stand swelled. Then someone shouted, "Call an ambulance!"

"What's going on?" June arched on her tiptoes, trying to see over everyone's heads.

Brett looked up and down the street, but there weren't any other officers or medics or even parade volunteers rushing to respond to whatever was going on by the stand. She told the girls to stay put and pushed her way through the crowd. A glance over her shoulder told her that Elizabeth and June were right on her heels, but she didn't have time to send them away. She was close enough to the center of the commotion to finally see what was happening.

Marshall Trudeau kneeled on the asphalt beside a stretched-out figure in dark clothing. His pale blue shirt was rolled up at the sleeves. Both the shirt and his arms were covered in blood. A knife rested on the asphalt beside him. He leaned over the body on the ground, his hands pressed to the man's chest. He spun his head, searching the faces of the crowd surrounding him. His eyes were wild and terrified. Blood streaked down one cheek. His gaze caught hold of Brett, and a look of relief passed across his face.

"Help me!" he shouted at her. "I can't, I'm trying to stop the bleeding, but it won't, it won't stop. Please, help!"

Brett kneeled on the other side of Marshall. He had a jacket pressed to the man's chest, but blood had already soaked through and was sluicing between his fingers. Brett looked at the man's face for the first time, and alarm tightened her chest. The flop of dark hair over his forehead, the lean bone structure, and piercing blue eyes that looked back at her without really seeing anything. Zachary Danforth was alive, but with the amount of blood pooling the asphalt, Brett feared he was quickly running out of time. She repeated the call for an ambulance, then stripped off the sweater she was wearing and pressed it down over Marshall's hands.

Their eyes met when their hands touched, then he shifted his gaze behind her to where Elizabeth was clutching at June. The look of shock on her face was a mirror to the pale horror of her father's.

"It's not what you think," he gasped. "I didn't do this."

In the distance, sirens wailed.

CHAPTER 23

Headlights swept across the front window. Clara peeled back the curtain. A silver Jaguar pulled into the driveway, and Marshall got out from the passenger side. He leaned in to speak to the driver a moment, then shut the door and trudged toward the house as the Jaguar drove off.

Clara was at the front door to greet him. Marshall blinked at her for a second, as if uncertain she was real. Then he collapsed into her arms with a muffled sob. She held him tightly, stroking her hands over his back. He smelled of sweat, of something metallic and accusatory. The night air crept cool across her bare arms, and she shivered against him. He nudged her all the way inside, shut the door, and slipped off his shoes. They huddled together in the entryway, speaking in soft voices, careful not to wake Elizabeth, who slept curled on the couch.

"They let you go," Clara said.

He nodded, then pulled off his shirt, which was covered in someone else's blood. He peeled off his pants too, left them in a heap on the floor, and went upstairs. Clara carried his ruined clothes into the kitchen, where she stuffed them into the trash can, burying them deep beneath cellophane wrappers, coffee grounds, and eggshells. She washed her hands and went upstairs to talk to Marshall.

The shower was running, filling the bathroom with steam. Marshall's silhouette was visible through the curtain. He stood under the showerhead without moving, letting the water pour over him. A minute passed, then he reached for the soap and started to scrub.

Clara sat down on the toilet lid. "What happened?"

"I don't know." He spoke so quietly it was hard to hear him over the rushing water. "One minute, I was waiting in line to get a caramel apple, and the next, he was stumbling into me. I saw the knife in his hand first. I thought he was coming after me...I thought...." He exhaled shakily before continuing. "Then he collapsed. I guess instinct kicked in or something. I dropped down next to him and tried to stop the bleeding, but there was so much. God, Clara, I've never seen so much blood."

"And at the station?"

He shut off the water and reached around the curtain for a towel. "They asked me a few questions, then I told them I wanted a lawyer. I called Peter to come down, but it turned out I didn't even need him."

Peter Newmark was good friends with Marshall's father and one of the best and most expensive defense attorneys in the state.

"After they talked to some witnesses, they let me go," Marshall said.

"Because you didn't do it."

"Of course, I didn't." He rubbed the towel over his hair, then wrapped it around his waist, stepped out of the shower, and moved into the bedroom to get dressed.

Clara trailed after him and sat down on the bed.

"Where were you?" He asked the question with his back turned, but she could see the tension across his shoulders, how still he held himself waiting for her answer.

"When?"

He turned to face her. "Today. At the parade. When everything was happening."

"I was working at the cookie station, and then Elizabeth came over upset because those girls were bullying her again. She had a cut on her knee. I was busy taking care of her."

"I saw her," Marshall said. "Right before the ambulance came. She was with June. But you weren't there." He asked her again, "Where were you?"

"I went to the car to get a first aid kit. That must have been around the same time, but then I came back for her. Right after that, I was there with her."

"No, you weren't." Elizabeth's voice startled them both. She stood in the doorway with tousled hair and sleep-heavy eyes.

"How long have you been standing there?" Clara asked.

"You left to get something from the car, but you never came back for me," Elizabeth said. "Detective Buchanan took me down to the station with her after they arrested Dad, and later she brought me home. And you were already here. The car was in the driveway. When I came inside, you were upstairs. Taking a shower or something. I heard the water running."

Clara rose from the bed and took a step toward the door. Elizabeth tensed, and Clara backed off, stung by her daughter's mistrust. She glanced at Marshall, who looked too tired to be dealing with any of this right now.

She shook her head and turned back to Elizabeth, trying to explain. "Of course I came back for you, sweetheart. I came back to where I'd left you, but you weren't there anymore. So I walked around looking for you, but I guess you'd already gone off with Detective Buchanan? I don't know. Everything was chaos by then. There were so many people, and the police kept everyone back, and I couldn't see what was happening. I came home because I knew that's where you would come, too, eventually."

"Someone was stabbed, attacked in broad daylight." Elizabeth's voice grew loud. "And you didn't know where I was. And they arrested Dad. They took him away in handcuffs. And you just came home like it was no big deal? Like we would all be fine?"

"Well, we are fine," Clara pointed out. "Aren't we?"

"That's not the point!" Elizabeth's fists clenched at her side.

"Elizabeth." Marshall stepped in, his voice low and firm. "It's late, and everyone's emotions are running a little high. I think we should all try and get some sleep. We can talk about this in the morning."

He led Elizabeth to her bedroom, his soft voice a reassuring murmur through the walls.

Clara sank onto the end of her bed and buried her face in her hands. After a few minutes, the bedroom door clicked shut, and she lifted her head to find Marshall standing in front of her. He stared at her for a long time, a tempest of emotions passing over him. She was only now noticing how much he'd aged in the past year, every ache and worry forming a new line around his eyes, turning his hair gray. They had been through so much together, had survived so many things that would have crushed a lesser love.

"Clara," he breathed her name. He crouched in front of her, placed his hands on her knees, leaned and pressed his forehead to hers. "If something happened, I need you to tell me."

"What are you talking about? I told you what happened. Elizabeth was hurt. I went to go find a Band-Aid. Then everything got so chaotic, I lost her for a minute. It's fine. She's fine. You're fine. We're home now. Together. We're home and safe. That's what matters."

"I can call Peter. He'll come over. We can handle it, as long as we get out ahead of it first. I just need to know what you did."

"Marshall, stop it." She rose abruptly from the bed and pushed him away.

"He hurt our little girl, Clara." Marshall rose to his feet. "People will understand. Especially if he came at you first. He threatened you? Or he threatened her? You were doing what any mother would do. Protecting your child from a predator."

She dug her nails into her palms. "How could you even think that of me?"

"I won't be upset with you, Clara." He reached for her, but she stepped away.

"Stop saying my name like that."

"Like what?"

"Like I'm a child. You're talking down to me. And I don't know why you're saying these things to me, anyway, how you could think I'd even be capable of doing something like that."

"Maybe you didn't mean to?" he suggested, taking another step toward her. "Maybe you wanted to threaten him? Get him to back off? But he came at you, and you had no other choice?"

She shook her head.

"Clara." He cupped her face with his hand, stroked a thumb over her cheek. They were standing so close she could smell his shampoo, see the beginnings of a beard forming on his chin, the small freckle above his right eye that darkened in the sun every summer.

"No," she said and repeated it with more force. "No. I didn't."

She crumpled forward and buried her face against his chest.

He wrapped his arms around her. She felt his chin move across the top of her head as he nodded. "Okay, Clara, it's going to be okay."

They stood another few minutes, breathing in unison, then Marshall guided her to the bed. They fell asleep on top of the covers.

———————————

A few hours later, the phone next to their bed rang.

Marshall startled awake, flinging his arms and knocking Clara in the shoulder. He sat up, rubbing his eyes. "God's sake, what time is it?"

Blurry-eyed, blinking, Clara squinted at the alarm clock. "A little past three."

The room was dark, the house quiet. There were no cars on the road, no birds in the trees. No one was awake at this ungodly hour unless they were in trouble.

The phone rang a second time, and Marshall answered it. He spoke to someone in a gruff voice for a few minutes, then hung up, but instead of snuggling back in bed, he sat on the edge of the mattress with his shoulders slumped.

Clara brushed her fingers across the curve of his back. He shuddered and lifted his head. "That was Eli. Zach didn't make it. He died at the hospital."

He turned and looked at her, but there was no sorrow in his gaze, no fear, only relief.

"Maybe it's for the best," he whispered, and she nodded, agreeing, then opened her arms to him.

Chapter 24

Brett interviewed over a hundred people on Saturday afternoon, and all of them said some version of the same thing. Zach came stumbling out from the alleyway between Pip's Consignment Store and the laundromat, clutching his chest with one hand and holding a knife in the other. He was already stabbed and bleeding profusely by the time he crashed into Marshall waiting in line to buy a caramel apple.

Several other people confirmed that, yes, Marshall had been in line for at least fifteen minutes before Zach showed up. And too many more had seen him on Main Street before that, talking, glad-handing, passing out his business card. There was no possible way Marshall Trudeau could have stabbed Zachary Danforth.

More than exonerating Marshall, several witnesses called him a hero, saying that he stepped in to help as soon as Zach appeared. He got the boy down on the ground and put pressure on the wound right away, shouting for someone to call an ambulance. Certainly not the behavior of a murderer. Still, it had pained Brett to release Marshall last night. Even though it was the right thing to do, and it made sense, she had wanted it to be simple—an angry father exacting his revenge on his daughter's tormentor. But clearly, that's not what happened, and so she was back at square one.

She finished running a comb through her hair, dressed comfortably in loose-fitting slacks and a pastel blouse beneath a fitted blazer, then sat on the bed to lace her boots.

At yesterday's emergency briefing, the detective sergeant had officially put her in charge of the Danforth case. Not that Stan Harcourt had any faith in her abilities to do the job right. In front of the entire room, he'd said that he was watching her closely. If she so much as hiccupped wrong during an interview, he'd reassign the case to someone else.

When they'd released Marshall a little before midnight, Zach had still been alive. The hospital had called an hour later to tell her Zach had died in surgery. He'd suffered too much blood loss from over a dozen stab wounds to his chest and abdomen. Her assault with a deadly weapon case was now a murder investigation. Stan might very well use that as an excuse to pull her off the case. Until then, she had work to do. She'd assigned a few other detectives to help out with interviewing witnesses, but she wanted to be the one to talk to Zach's mother and search his room.

She slipped on her holster and buckled the gun inside. Then clipped her badge to her belt, smoothed the lapels of her blazer, and dabbed on a bit of lipstick.

Voices murmured downstairs. At first, Brett thought it was the television. The longer she listened, the more she realized it carried the cadence of conversation and that one of the voices belonged to Amma. The other was low and distinctly male.

Brett grabbed the rest of her things off the bed and made her way down to the kitchen.

A tri-colored beagle rushed her. Tongue lolling, tail wagging her whole body, Trixie barked once in delight and jumped on Brett's legs. Brett bent to pet the dog, then shifted her gaze to where Jimmy Eagan sat at the center island with his elbows propped on the counter. He grinned when he saw her and then rushed her with as much exuberance as Trixie had. He swept her up in a tight hug that felt so good, she almost started crying. Eventually, she pulled away from him.

"What are you doing here?"

She was genuinely baffled as to how her friend had found his way into her grandmother's kitchen. She hadn't spoken to him in a week, since last Sunday, and yet, as if he could read her mind, he had shown up right when she needed him most. Except, she knew Jimmy better than that. The only time he ever showed up somewhere unexpectedly was when he was chasing a good story.

"Seriously, Jimmy," she repeated. "Why are you here?"

He smiled and pointed at a pastry box sitting in front of him. "I brought croissants."

"He brought croissants," Amma repeated, clearly delighted by the gift.

Brett had been so busy over the past twenty-four hours working the Danforth case that she hadn't had a chance to check in with Amma about how she was feeling after yesterday's festival. She seemed like herself again, smiling at Jimmy as she poured a cup of coffee for Brett.

"You do know the way to a woman's heart, don't you?" Amma reached and patted Jimmy's cheek.

Jimmy winked at her. "Pastries have never let me down before. I didn't know which kind you liked best, Brett, so I brought a mix of chocolate and plain."

"There's jam in the fridge," Amma added.

"Sit." Jimmy patted the barstool next to his. "Indulge. Tell me what you're working on."

Brett shook her head. "I don't have time. This case—"

"Yes, this case," he interrupted her. "This case is why I'm here, actually. The croissants are too obviously a bribe," he said it like a confession. Then he smiled, so casually, with such charm. That smile was how he disarmed people and got them to talk even when they didn't want to. "I'm hoping you'll tell me all the gory details about what happened at this Halloween festival yesterday, so I can have a story on my editor's desk before we go to print tonight."

"Tragic," Amma muttered with a quick shake of her head.

"Come on, Bretty, help out an old friend?"

But Jimmy's smile rarely worked on her. Especially not when it involved her cases.

"No comment," she said tersely. She sipped the coffee Amma had made, then poured the rest into a thermos. "I'm glad you're here, though, even if under false pretenses. You and Trixie can hang out with Amma while I go work on this case. *My* case."

"I never lied." He pretended to look hurt. "The croissants are real. And I am here to see you."

"You're here because you want my help with this story."

"It's one reason." He gave her a meaningful look that made her cheeks flame.

She turned away from him and focused on Amma. "Do you need anything before I go? Will you be all right if I leave you here with Jimmy for a few hours?"

Amma reached down and gave Trixie a nibble of the croissant she'd been eating. "Don't make such a fuss over me, Brett. I'll be fine."

Thermos in hand, Brett hurried out the front door.

"Brett, wait." Jimmy caught her on the steps. He held out a croissant wrapped in a napkin. "At least take something for the road. Sounds like it's going to be a long day."

She took the croissant. "It's good to see you, Jimmy. Really, I'm glad you're here. And not just because you can babysit Amma for me. I'm sorry I'm rushing out on you like this."

His smile was real this time around. Not Jimmy the charmer and storyteller, but Jimmy the man she'd come to care deeply about since they first met seven years ago. Jimmy the man who worried about her and brought her croissants and said things like,

"You know I'm happy to help. And, come on, Bretty. There's no need to apologize. I get it. Evidence goes cold fast. People start to forget." He tilted his head, studying her a moment. "Go catch your bad guy, Detective."

Quickly, before she had a chance to second guess herself, Brett leaned forward and kissed him on the cheek. She didn't stick around to see his reaction. She turned and hurried to her car.

Jimmy called after her, "Whenever you're ready for a break, drinks are on me!"

Zachary Danforth lived with his mother in a trailer park on the outskirts of town. Tall fir trees ringed the park, shading the single and double wides, littering the roads and roofs with brown needles, turning everything sticky with sap. Brett picked her way around garden gnomes and overturned lawn chairs to knock on the single wide's front door. Wind chimes clattered in a light breeze. Inside, a dog yapped, and a woman shouted at it to shut the hell up. A few seconds later, the door opened, and a scarecrow blinked out at her from smoke-filled shadows.

Lindy Danforth was obviously drunk. Possibly even high. Her gaze was unfocused, the whites of her eyes streaked with red.

In a creaking voice, she asked, "You here about my boy?"

She pushed the door open and invited Brett inside.

A Chihuahua rushed from the kitchen, yapping ferociously, nipping at Brett's heels. Lindy shouted and kicked at the dog. The Chihuahua whimpered and, with its tail tucked, scampered to hide behind a recliner.

"That piece of shit belonged to Zach," Lindy muttered. "Now, what am I supposed to do with it? I can't take care of a dog."

She narrowed her gaze on Brett. "You going to find someone to take care of his dog?"

Lindy sank into the recliner. She was so skinny, she barely took up half the cushion. She folded her legs underneath her and wrapped a jade-colored afghan around her shoulders. A shiver ran through her. "It's too damn cold in here. All these blasted cracks in the windows. Zach promised he'd get 'em replaced next month. You gonna find someone to do that for me, too? Jesus Christ Almighty in Heaven." She fumbled her hand over the side table next to the chair until she found a half-smoked joint and a lighter. She lit up and asked, "Do you mind?"

The stench of marijuana filled the trailer.

"I get these terrible migraines. I know I should go see a doctor, but I can't afford it, so...home remedies." She lifted the joint to her lips and inhaled. "You ain't going to get me in trouble for this, are you? I mean, not after my son's been killed and all."

Brett waved smoke from her face. She could arrest Lindy for the drugs, but it would be a waste of her and everyone else's time. She made a mental note to send a social worker out as soon as possible, see about getting her some medical attention, maybe some rehab. For today, Brett's focus was on Zach and getting some damn answers. "Mrs. Danforth..."

"Please, I ain't been a missus since that good for nothing son-of-a-bitch up and left us when Zach was a boy. Lindy's what most people call me. That or hey, you." She chuckled to herself, then her eyelids drooped, and her head nodded to her chest as if she was having trouble staying awake.

"Lindy, I'd like you to tell me what you know about Zach's relationship with Danny Cyrus. Did you know he was working for Danny? That he was involved in illegal activity like gambling and organized fight clubs? Were you aware he brought a knife to school?"

"Zach was a good boy." Lindy jabbed the air with her finger. "Everyone's always trying to get him in trouble, trying to back him into a corner, saying he don't study hard enough, that he's always skipping classes, but you know that's just because he's bored. He's a smart kid, and they don't challenge him enough at that damn public school, but I can't afford private, so we're stuck with those idiots, and they don't know the first thing about what to do with a boy like Zach." She picked a fleck of something off her tongue and cooed to the dog behind the chair, coaxing the poor thing out from hiding, scooping it, and setting it in her lap. The dog trembled as she scratched its ears. "Danny took him under his wing, sure. He's been like a big brother, only ever been good to Zach. But Danny would never hurt him if that's what you're thinking. Zach made him too much money."

"And you were okay with that? With your son breaking the law?"

Lindy shrugged and stubbed out the joint in an ashtray. Her eyes drooped lower, her head sagged.

"Lindy," Brett said loudly.

The woman's head snapped up. She had dark hair like Zach's, but it was tangled and unwashed. She wore a ragged T-shirt with some kind of obscure rock band album cover printed on the front. Burn marks pocked the fabric where embers had fallen and smoldered. She squinted at Brett, a look of confusion on her face like she couldn't remember letting her into the house.

"Lindy, how did Zach act around girls at school? Did he ever bring home girlfriends?"

"Oh, all the girls loved Zach. He's so handsome, my boy, a real charmer." She smiled, and her eyes closed again, her voice turning lethargic. "They couldn't keep their hands off of him, but he's smart. My boy. Looks out for his future. Knows not to get any of those bitches pregnant, knows how that will ruin his future opportunities. My boy's smart. He's going to be a businessman someday. Going to own a boat. Going to sail us right on out of here. He's got his smarts from his momma, his looks from that no good son-of-a-bitch, but he knows how to use it. That's the difference. He knows that life's more than sleeping around and chasing pussy. It's about making something of yourself. That's what Zach's doing. He's making something of himself."

Brett sat quietly as the woman's head fell to her chest, and she started to softly snore. After a few minutes, Brett got up and walked around the trailer's living room and kitchen. The Chihuahua hopped off Lindy's lap and started yapping again. Brett gave the dog a piece of bacon she found stuck to a plate in the kitchen, and he stopped barking.

Zach's bedroom was easy to find. There were two to choose from, and she guessed correctly that his door was the one with a poster of The Clash taped to it. More posters of other rock and punk bands covered the walls inside his room. His bed was unmade, the sheets tangled. An electric guitar sat on a stand in one corner, an amp plugged in next to it. Model airplanes dangled on invisible wires from the ceiling.

The Chihuahua trotted over to a bean bag chair and clambered onto it, turning a circle, making a little divot for his small body in the fabric. The dog sighed and settled his head on his paws. His big, dark eyes followed Brett as she took pictures with a Polaroid camera she'd borrowed from the department. Zach's room wasn't a crime scene, but she was careful anyway, wearing gloves, making sure to get before and after shots, working the room from right to left.

She found what she was looking for under the bed. In the most obvious place. As if Zach wasn't even trying to hide it. She sat on the beige carpet, carefully opened the box, and snapped pictures of the contents before taking everything out for a closer look.

There was a small baggie of weed and a large manila envelope stuffed with pictures. Brett flipped through them quickly. Though she recognized several faces, including her detective sergeant Stan Harcourt and several councilmen, she wasn't exactly sure what she'd found. It looked as though Zach might have been collecting dirt on people. Husbands cheating on wives. Men in suits exchanging fat envelopes with people like Danny Cyrus and Lincoln Byrne. A few of the pictures were obviously from fight club nights. Brett pushed the photos aside to get to the contents underneath: three pairs of girls' underwear.

She picked up one pair, holding it carefully by the elastic band. A little red bow was sewn on to the front exactly how Elizabeth had described. She put it and the other two pairs of underwear into separate bags, labeling each with details of where and under what circumstances she'd found them. Not that she needed to be careful. There would never be a case brought in front of a jury where the chain of custody would matter. Anger gripped her. Anger at a mother's belligerent ignorance. Anger at a selfish boy who took what he wanted without asking. Anger at these other girls, unknown to her except for their blue polka dots and pink stripes, these other girls who had suffered before Elizabeth but said nothing. Anger at herself for not arresting Zach when she had the chance that night at Eli's parents' party. If she had, he'd still be alive.

She supposed his death could be considered a lopsided sort of justice. As wrong as it felt to her, as much as she would have preferred him to be sitting behind bars rather than dead in a cold storage locker, he couldn't hurt anyone else now. There was that, at least.

Brett gathered the evidence bags, along with the envelope of photographs, and taking one last Polaroid for good measure, walked out of the room. She stood over Lindy for a minute, watching her sleep. Part of her wanted to kick the woman awake and slap some answers out of her, but she knew Lindy wouldn't have them.

It was obvious Zach had been living his own life apart from his mother for a long time.

The Chihuahua followed Brett out of Zach's room. He stood by her ankles and blinked up at her, then his mouth parted in a clownish smile as his small, pink tongue flopped out, panting. Brett scooped up the little dog, juggling the weight of him with the evidence bags in her arms. As she left the trailer, Lindy snorted and turned over in the chair but kept sleeping.

Brett plopped the dog in the passenger seat and put the stuff she'd taken from Zach's room in the footwell. The dog sniffed a little, then turned a tight circle, curled his nose under his back paws, and let out a long sigh, settling in like he belonged here. He was tan with a white star on his nose. One ear was folded down, the other stood up straight. Looking at him in the daylight, he was actually kind of cute, in a pathetic street urchin sort of way.

"Crap," Brett muttered and started the car.

CHAPTER 25

"What the hell are you going to do with him?" Jimmy laughed and took the Chihuahua from Brett's arms to scratch under his chin.

Brett had been asking herself the same question all day as she brought the dog along with her to several afternoon interviews. The weather was cool enough that at least she could leave him in the car with the windows cracked. Every time she checked on him, he was standing on his hind legs, paws on the sill, his nose pressed to the window, fogging the glass, waiting for her return. When she eventually got back into the car, he gave her a single, perfunctory tail wag, then settled into that tightly curled ball again and fell asleep.

"What's his name?" Jimmy asked.

"I have no idea." She drank the last of her first beer and lifted her hand to the bartender to signal for another.

"You have to give him a name."

"I'm not keeping him."

"Then why the hell did you even take him?"

She stared at the dog whose eyes were half-closed in pleasure over Jimmy's attention. "He didn't belong there."

The bartender set two beers down on their table, even though Jimmy wasn't done drinking his first. He'd been too busy canoodling the dog to bother with drinking. The bartender, a middle-aged woman with red hair cut pixie short and tattoos up and down her arms, reached over and scratched the dog's head. She cooed like it was a baby, and Brett asked if she wanted to take him home.

The woman threw her head back and laughed, her hoop earrings rocking. "Oh, doll, I would love to, I really would, but my man's allergic."

She scratched the dog one more time and returned to the bar.

Brett sighed and sat back against the bench, taking her time with the second beer, picking at the paper label. Jimmy fed the dog a pretzel. Crumbs sprayed everywhere as the dog crunched on the snack.

"You like dogs," Brett said, more than hinting.

"Trixie gets too jealous." He shrugged like he was sorry, though she knew he wasn't. "Besides, I've been telling you to get a dog for months. And now one's just dropped into your lap. It's serendipity. Like it or not, he's your dog now, Bretty."

He passed the Chihuahua over the table. Brett settled the dog in her lap, stroking her fingers over its short but soft fur, wondering how the hell she was going to explain this to Amma. Not that Amma would mind. She liked dogs. The Chihuahua sighed and curled into a ball.

"So." Brett locked eyes with Jimmy across the table. "Are you going to tell me what you're really doing here? Because it can't possibly be to cover this story that's not even a story. Not really. Not by the *Oregonian's* standards."

"Sure it is." He counted the reasons off on his fingers. "It's topical. Stabbing takes place during a Halloween festival. And weird. Everyone's wearing costumes. And it's got a human interest angle. The victim is a high school kid."

"Who wasn't exactly a saint."

"Can I quote you on that?"

"No."

Jimmy laughed and shrugged. "Besides, two murders in a week? Two stabbings? That's the makings of a new serial murderer right there. And you know how well that sells papers."

"We don't know they're related."

"Yet." Jimmy leaned forward over the table, a familiar gleam in his eyes, like a predator on the hunt. "But clearly they could be?"

"I'm not talking about my case." She pretended to zip her lips and throw away an invisible key. The Chihuahua flicked his ears. "But why send you here to cover it? There are a dozen junior reporters your editor could have sent to cover this non-story, and he decides to send you?"

"I volunteered." Pink colored his cheeks.

"Oh yeah?"

"Well, it was an excuse to do more research for my book."

"Right. Your book."

"Plus, you know, I meant it the other night when I said I miss you." He grabbed his beer and drank until the bottle was empty. Then he grabbed the second one and tipped it to his lips.

Brett scanned the bar. For a Sunday night, the Pickled Onion was pretty lively. Several groups of people drank along the wall and at the bar itself. Couples sat tucked away in dark booths. Pool balls clacked together, and pinball machines plinked noisily in the back. Country music played from a speaker sitting on a chair near the bathrooms. The Pickled Onion was the kind of bar that had sticky floors and terrible food, but the drinks were cheap, and, for cops, the first one was always on the house, so it was the bar everyone came to. She saw Eli in the corner drinking with Marshall Trudeau and slouched lower in the booth, angling her face away, hoping they wouldn't notice her.

As if yesterday's festival stress wasn't enough, Danny Cyrus had filed a harassment complaint against her and Eli. Which was complete bullshit. They'd been doing their jobs when they went to talk to him at his trailer. But a complaint was still a complaint. Now Irving was pissed because he'd told Brett to stay away from the Andress case. And Stan was pissed because it meant extra paperwork. And the chief was pissed because she'd made him look bad. She hadn't talked to Eli about any of it yet. Not about the complaint. And not about what happened at the festival, with Amma mistaking Elizabeth as Margot. She certainly didn't want to talk about any of it now when she was half-drunk, holding a dog in her lap that she'd basically stolen from a victim's house.

Jimmy shot a glance in their direction, his eyebrows raised. "I take it you don't want me to go over and say hi?"

"So, how is your book coming along?"

He let her dodge the question. "The investigation into your sister's murder was crap."

"We figured that out a long time ago, Jimmy."

"No, I mean, I went back through the copy of the file I'm not supposed to have, you know, to refresh my memory for this book, and I forgot how bad it was. I remember when you and I met, when I started digging around in this case for the first time, I remember thinking how there was just so much missing. But looking at it again, after everything that's happened, it's like, did anyone even work it?"

"I'm sure Stan Harcourt did his best," she said, with a bitter laugh, thinking of her detective sergeant's sneering grin, his jaw working furiously around a wad of chewing gum. She'd come into the precinct three days last month to find him asleep at his desk in his corner office.

Brett lifted her beer, surprised, and a little disappointed to find it was already empty. She should slow down. Drink some water. Eat something. She grabbed a pretzel, and the dog lifted his head to beg. She broke off a piece and fed it to him.

"See? You're starting to like him already," Jimmy said, then kept talking about Margot's case. "The interviews were so half-assed. They didn't ask any of the right questions, or if they did, they didn't document it. They put so much energy into trying to prove Danny Cyrus did it that they didn't bother actually working the case from any other angle. It's no wonder Archer French flew under the radar for as long as he did. If I hadn't come along and started asking the right questions, who knows if we ever would have caught him."

"That's easy for you to say now," Brett said. "Hindsight being what it is."

"But this kind of stuff happens all the time, doesn't it? A cop works a case to fit his perp, not to find his perp. He'll include anything that proves his theory and toss out anything that doesn't. And then, by the time someone comes back around to take another look, all the good evidence is gone or degraded past the point of being useful. And then you're left trying to fill in the blanks with more blanks."

"Not every cop works an investigation that way," she said, the beer turning her edgy and defensive.

"No, but it happens more than it should." Jimmy laid his palms flat on the table. "And I can't help but think what else they might have missed? What else was overlooked?"

She sighed. "Stop beating around the bush, Jimmy. Say what you want to say."

"I just was thinking that if you're really sure about this gut feeling of yours, if you really think Archer wasn't involved—"

"I never said he wasn't involved," she interrupted. "I said I don't think he killed her."

"I'm trying to tell you that I think it could be worth taking another look." He reached his hand across the table and took hers, squeezing it gently. "I'm not saying we'll find anything new, I'm not even saying I agree with you on this whole French didn't do it scenario. I'm just saying, based on how the original investigation happened, it might not be a total waste of time. And I'm happy to do most of the legwork. You know how much people like talking to reporters, trying to get their fifteen minutes of fame. They say things to me that they'd never say to a cop. I'm happy to stick around a few days, re-interview people who lived in Crestwood that summer. They'll like me better now that I'm famous."

She swatted his hand away. "You're not famous."

"Almost." He grabbed her hand again. "I'm serious, Brett. You've got me curious now. Let me do some more snooping."

"You'd do that?"

"Of course I would."

"Why?"

"Because I want to get the story right."

"Archer's story. For your book." She started to withdraw her hand, but he tightened his grip on it.

"No, Brett. Your story. I want to get your story right. And Margot's. Her ending deserves something more than a 'probably' with a question mark."

They stared at each other across the table, and Brett found herself thinking about that night on the balcony before she left Portland. How she wouldn't mind kissing Jimmy again to see if it was as nice as she remembered, or if she had just told herself it was nice so many times she started to believe it. She leaned forward. Jimmy leaned closer, too.

"Hey, Brett." Eli dropped down into the booth with a tumbler of whiskey in one hand and scooted close enough their legs touched. "Good to see you again, Johnny, is it?"

"Jimmy," Brett said, letting go of Jimmy's hand and sliding as far from Eli as she could before she bumped into the wall. In her lap, the Chihuahua lifted his head at the jostling, then lowered it again after she stopped moving.

"Right. Jimmy." Eli flashed his teeth at them both. "So. Did you come back to our neck of the woods to stir up more trouble?"

"You two know each other?" Brett asked.

"Not really," Eli said, still grinning like he was about to take a bite out of something. "I never forget a face, though. He was up here a few years ago, snooping around the station, digging into everyone else's business."

"I was solving a cold case the rest of you had given up on," Jimmy said.

"Did you hear that, Brett?" Eli nudged her with his elbow. "Your old pal Jimmy here doesn't think we can do our jobs."

Brett was tired of their posturing, but when she tried to motion Eli to move so she could leave and get herself another drink, he ignored her.

"Oh, my apologies," Jimmy said, though he clearly wasn't sorry in the least. "I didn't realize you were a detective, too."

"I'm not," Eli corrected him. "I'm just a lowly beat cop who was on my way to making detective before your girl here took my spot."

"Eli, come on." Brett's voice was a low warning. "Don't do this."

"Do what? Tell the truth?" He turned his hard-edged grin onto her. His words slipped a little. His breath reeked of booze. "It's what happened, isn't it? You come waltzing in from nowhere, Chief's little pet project. The rest of us don't even stand a chance."

"That's not what happened, and you know it."

"Then why don't you tell me how it went down, huh? Remind me how I lost out on a promotion because I don't have a nice set of tits."

Jimmy stiffened and rose a little off the bench, but Brett shook her head, signaling him not to bother.

"You're drunk, Eli," she said.

"I'm cuckolded." Eli glared sharply at Jimmy before tilting his head back to drain the tumbler and signaling for another.

Marshall appeared at their table a few seconds later with an apologetic look on his face. "Sorry. I told him to leave you alone but—"

"But I told him that we should go introduce ourselves to Brett's friend. It's the neighborly thing to do, isn't it, Marsh?"

The bartender arrived to take their order, and Eli said, "Let me buy this round."

"I'm good." Jimmy gestured to his still half-full bottle.

"Yeah, me too." Brett shoved Eli out of the booth and gestured for Jimmy to come with her. "I've got an early day tomorrow."

Eli noticed the Chihuahua for the first time and tilted his head, his smile softening. "Who's that little guy? He's cute."

"This is, uh..." Brett looked down at the dog in her arms. His top lip was pulled back as he snarled in Eli's direction. "This is Pistol."

She scratched the dog under the chin. Pistol's tongue flicked out, soft and pink and wet.

"Goodnight, Eli. Marshall." Brett nodded at both men and left the bar, carrying the dog under her arm the whole way out.

Jimmy followed her.

They were getting into Brett's car when Marshall called out to her from the doorway of the bar. The neon lights from the sign turned his skin a rose color. "Can I talk to you a minute?"

Brett passed the dog over to Jimmy and walked to where Marshall was standing with a nervous smile playing on his lips. He stuffed his hands in his pockets and started to talk. "I wanted to thank you for taking care of Elizabeth yesterday. For making sure she got home safely, I mean, for not leaving her alone."

"Of course," Brett said. It had been a simple choice.

Marshall cleared his throat, obviously wanting to say something else. She waited quietly, knowing that sometimes all people needed was space and they'd easily find the words to fill it.

Sure enough, he started talking again, quieter this time and more reserved. "It's just all of this stuff with Elizabeth. It's got me thinking a lot about Margot."

Brett forced herself to relax, knowing that the second she put up her defenses, he'd stop talking. "Oh yeah? Anything in particular?"

He shook his head and scuffed his toe in the gravel. "No. It's just, she was about Elizabeth's age, you know?"

Brett nodded.

"Well, older, but still, I don't really think I realized how awful it must have been for you and for your parents. To lose her like that." His voice cracked. He took a second to gather himself again before continuing. "I loved her."

Brett was glad for the dark to hide her surprise. She remembered boys like Marshall and Eli hanging around her and Margot a lot that summer. But she never saw anything more than flirting, certainly nothing that would have qualified as a meaningful relationship. A childhood crush, maybe, but not love to be recalled in a shadow-filled parking lot two decades later.

"I mean, I thought I did at the time, anyway," Marshall rushed on with an uncomfortable laugh. "I don't know if we'd had longer together, if it would have lasted, or if it was just a summer fling or what. I don't know, but sometimes I think..." He waved his hand in front of his face like he was waving away a fly and laughed again, ducking his head, embarrassed. "Never mind, it's stupid. Forget I said any of that. I just wanted to tell you, you know, thank you for taking care of Elizabeth, and that I'm sorry. I wish...I don't know, I wish I could have done something back then to stop her from going into those woods, maybe, or, I just... I wish I could have been there for Margot the way you were here for my daughter yesterday."

He stepped forward and wrapped his arms around her in a stiff hug. He smelled faintly of smoke and beer and day-old cologne. She didn't hug him back, just waited for him to let go, then turned and walked to her car.

"What was that all about?" Jimmy asked.

Brett shook her head. Her mouth was dry, her heart thumping too hard. "I'm not entirely sure. He told me he was in love with Margot."

Jimmy craned his head to look out the back window, but Marshall had already disappeared inside the bar.

"I don't remember seeing anything in Margot's file about Marshall being interviewed." Brett twisted in her seat to face Jimmy. "Did you talk to him when you were here the first time?"

Jimmy shook his head. "No, but I guess that's who I'll be talking to next."

"Be careful." She glanced at the rearview mirror, certain she'd seen something moving in the shadows outside the bar. Now, there was only stillness.

"I'm always careful," Jimmy said.

"I'm serious." Brett drove in the direction of the motel where Jimmy was staying. "I don't know what I'd do if something happened to you."

"Aw, did you hear that?" He scratched behind the Chihuahua's ear. "I think she's starting to like me, too."

When she pulled into the motel parking lot, Jimmy asked her if she wanted to come inside. "I have a six-pack in the mini-fridge. We can raid the vending machine."

Hope glittered in his eyes.

"Goodnight, Jimmy," she said, taking the dog from him.

If he was disappointed, he didn't show it. He leaned and pecked her on the cheek.

After Jimmy let himself into his motel room, Brett sat another fifteen minutes in the parking lot, trying to figure out what her problem was. Jimmy was a nice guy, they got along, and she liked him. She liked him a lot, she realized. Then why not let herself be happy? Why not get out of the car, go and knock on his door? He'd let her inside. He'd be sweet.

She didn't deserve sweet.

Brett thought of the last time she saw Margot alive. They were sitting on the dock together, kicking their toes in the water. Margot stood suddenly and peeled off her sundress, her favorite green bikini underneath. *Watch me, Brett.* A leap, a graceful arc into the water. She stayed under so long that Brett almost ran for help, but as she was turning to go, Margot popped up again, laughing, gulping air, swimming back to the dock. The sound of voices approached, feet slapping the dock boards. Brett shouted at Margot, saying, *You promised you'd take me to the pool today. You promised.* Brett never swam in the bay. But Margot pulled her sundress on over her head, told her not to be a baby, told her not to tell Amma and Pop. *Don't worry, I'll be back before it gets dark.* But she wasn't. Brett tried to picture the faces of the kids her sister had run off with, but they were silhouettes in her memory, backlit against a burning orange sky.

Chapter 26

Clara broke another egg into the bowl, whipped a fork through the yolk, then added salt and pepper. The mixture sizzled when she poured it into a hot pan. She moved a spatula around the edges as the eggs cooked.

Marshall came downstairs with heavy feet. He shuffled into the kitchen and sat down at the table with a groan. "Is there coffee?"

She didn't need to look at him to know he was blurry-eyed, half-asleep, and probably hungover. The stench of beer and stale cigarette smoke wafted off him, along with the stench of another woman's perfume. She poured him a cup and handed it over with too much force. Coffee slopped over the rim onto his hand.

He hissed when the hot liquid touched his skin. "Watch it."

"Did you have fun last night?" She went back to scrambling eggs.

He groaned again.

"I have friends in this town, too, you know." She scraped the eggs onto a plate and slammed them down on the table in front of him.

He winced. "What's that supposed to mean?"

"Janelle Montgomery called me from the Pickled Onion. Said she saw you talking to Brett Buchanan. Said you left the bar with her."

"Janelle Montgomery needs to mind her own business." He shoveled eggs into his mouth.

"Were you with her last night, Marshall?" Clara stood over him with her arms crossed.

"I was at the bar with Eli." He reached for his coffee. "Brett was there with someone else, a friend of hers, but yes, I saw her. We talked."

"About what?"

"Nothing. I thanked her for taking care of Elizabeth the other day."

"And where did you go after?"

"Nowhere. Home."

He'd stumbled in close to four in the morning. Clara had only been pretending to sleep when he flopped into bed beside her.

"Bars close at two, don't they?"

He sighed and pinched the bridge of his nose. "Where is this coming from, Clara?"

"Where were you?" The question echoed flatly through the room.

He stared at her for a second before answering, "Eli and I were both too drunk to drive. We split a cab. We went by his place first, and I stayed for a few more drinks, then I walked home."

"Promise me you weren't with her?"

He gave her a hurt look and said, "Clara, please. I can't believe we're even having this conversation. But no, I promise, I wasn't with her."

She searched his face, wanting to believe him, but he had said the same thing to her twenty years ago. *Trust me, Clara, I love you, not her. Nothing happened. She's just a friend.* She had believed every word he said. And then, not even two days after that, she caught them up at Lover's Lookout, and later, he'd come to her apologizing. He hadn't meant it to go so far, but now that he had, he wanted to be with her—with Margot. Not with Clara. She had believed him, trusted him, and he had broken her heart. But that was years ago when they were still kids.

Marshall had come back to her, and he was still with her now, and she had to trust that commitment, trust him. They were completely different people with a completely different understanding of love and loyalty.

She took his hand and dropped into the chair beside him. "I'm sorry. I trust you, I do. I'm tired, that's all. It's been a stressful weekend."

"That might be the understatement of the year." He smiled at her, but the smile didn't reach his eyes.

She smiled back and got up to refill his coffee.

Elizabeth came into the kitchen with her backpack slung over one shoulder and her soccer bag over the other. She grabbed an apple and headed toward the door without saying a word to either of them.

"Elizabeth?" Clara called after her. "Did you remember your shin guards? They were hanging up in the laundry room. I don't want to get a call an hour before practice asking me to bring them to you."

"Actually... Dad, can you pick me up from practice today?" Elizabeth asked sweetly, one hand on the front door.

"Sure thing, sweetheart." Marshall looked at Clara and shrugged.

Clara sighed and let her go. The door slammed. A few minutes later, the bus rumbled past, shuddering the entire house.

"She'll come around," Marshall said. "Just give her some time."

Elizabeth had avoided her all weekend, leaving the room whenever Clara entered, hiding upstairs with her radio on, using Marshall as an intermediary. Clara could admit she'd made a mistake. She should have stayed at the festival, should have never left Elizabeth by herself the way she had, but at the time, Clara thought she was doing the right thing. Elizabeth was bleeding. She needed a Band-Aid. How was Clara supposed to predict what would come next?

Marshall brought his plate to the sink, then wrapped his arms around her waist, nuzzling his nose against the back of her neck. "You know how girls can be, so sensitive sometimes. She takes after her mother."

His voice was teasing and gentle, but she pushed him away, swatting him with a towel. "You stink."

He lifted his arm, sniffed, and made a face. Then he cupped Clara's chin in his hand. His expression was serious, his eyes searching hers. "Are you going to be okay today?"

"Why wouldn't I be?"

He studied her for another few seconds. "I don't know. Like you said, this whole weekend's been rough. I'm worried about you, that's all. You've been acting a little off. Jumpy or, I don't know, not yourself."

"I'm fine, Marshall. I told you, I'm tired." She turned away from him and busied herself at the sink, scrubbing plates before putting them in the dishwasher.

"I can stay home today if you want."

She shook her head. "You know how this town likes to talk. You need to get back to the office and show your face. Let people know you have nothing to hide."

He kissed her temple, then went upstairs to take a shower.

———

Yesterday morning Clara had spent two hours talking to a man who introduced himself as Detective Walker. He'd sat on her couch, drank her coffee, his voice a low drone as he asked questions about the Halloween festival and Zach's death.

What time did you get to the festival?

Who did you talk to?

What did you see?

Did you talk to Zach? Did you see Zach at all? Did you know he'd been stabbed?

Tell me again, where did you go after you left Elizabeth?

He jotted Clara's answers in a small notebook, seeming to be utterly bored with the whole interview. She answered his questions as thoroughly as she could. She got to the festival around ten to oversee the cookie decorating booth. She talked to a lot of people, but not to Zach. She hadn't seen Zach since the Miller's costume party the night before. If she had seen Zach, she would have avoided him. No, she didn't know he'd been stabbed. And no, she hadn't seen anything suspicious.

Detective Walker thanked her for speaking with him, then handed over his business card and told her to call if she thought of anything else.

After he was gone, Clara went into the bathroom and splashed her face with water. She'd gripped the edge of the sink, taking deeper and deeper breaths until her pulse returned to normal. Then she'd joined Marshall and Elizabeth in the kitchen where they were making nachos for dinner. Marshall had raised his eyebrows at her, a silent question—how did it go? She'd smiled at him. Fine, it was fine.

Everything would be fine.

Things would settle down again. Life would go back to normal.

Zachary Danforth had always been a troubled kid, the kind of kid who had no one and helped no one, whose story would have never turned out well even if he'd wanted it to. If not now, something like this would have happened eventually—a violent, untimely death was always going to be his end.

CHAPTER 27

At her desk on Monday morning, Brett flipped through the photographs she'd collected from Zach's room. She'd looked at them at least a dozen times in the past few hours, but rather than finding answers, she had only more questions. There were a number of powerful men in these pictures—city leaders and prominent businessmen, councilmembers, even a few cops, uniformed officers and brass alike. Upon closer examination, it was clear every one of them was participating in some kind of illicit activity. Buying drugs, hiring prostitutes, keeping company with known criminals. These photos were evidence enough to ruin a few careers should the wrong person get his hands on them, and sufficient motive for someone to want Zach dead.

Brett locked the photographs in her top desk drawer to look at again after getting coffee from the break room. She was thinking in circles but getting no closer to narrowing down a suspect. Zach had lost consciousness on the way to the hospital and remained unconscious until he died. The witness interviews had revealed nothing. Everyone saw Zach after he'd been stabbed, not before. There were no fingerprints on the knife. Brett was waiting to hear back from the medical examiners' office and the lab to see if they'd found anything interesting.

When she entered the break room, she found Officer Fellowes already measuring grounds into the filter. The other woman smiled at Brett as she poured water into the coffee maker.

"Heard it was a bit of a rough weekend around here," Nancy said. "Fresh pot will be ready in a few minutes."

The machine burbled and hissed as coffee streamed into the pot.

"I don't know how you do it." She leaned one hip against the counter, folding her arms over her chest and studying Brett.

"Do what?"

"Work with dead bodies and murder and all of that." A shudder rolled through her. "It's too gruesome for my tastes. And it's not really the type of work you can leave at the office, is it? Do you have kids?" She tilted her head to one side.

The coffee pot was half full. Brett willed it to brew faster. "No. I don't."

"Ah. That explains it. I couldn't imagine working with all that darkness and not having some of it rub off on me, you know?" She shook her head. Tiny diamond studs glittered in her earlobes. "Parking enforcement can be boring, but I'll take boring over bodies any day."

She laughed a little and pulled two mugs from the cupboard. She poured coffee into them both. "Cream? Sugar?"

"I can do it." Brett reached to take one of the mugs from Nancy.

She laughed again. "Right, sorry. I'm so used to taking care of the boys around here."

Brett stirred in a spoonful of sugar. "Can I ask you something?"

"Shoot." Nancy's smile never faltered. She sipped her coffee, which was nearly white for the amount of cream she'd added.

"The other day, the front desk officer gave you a message to give to Eli."

Her neatly shaped brows bunched together in confusion. "He did?"

"He told me he did."

Nancy thought for a moment and nodded. "Right, I remember. I left it on Eli's desk."

"Are you sure?"

The change was subtle. Nancy's eyes narrowed. Her shoulders lifted slightly, and her fingers tightened around the cup. Her voice turned razor-sharp when she said, "Of course I'm sure."

"He told me he never got it."

"Are you accusing me of something? Because if you are, just come out and say it. I'm a straight-talker. Always have been, always will be. I don't play games with people, and I don't like it when people play games with me."

"You left it on Eli's desk. You're sure? That's all I'm asking."

"And I told you, yes, I did. I dropped it in his inbox like Mike asked me to."

The two women stared at each other, the silence tense between them. Then Nancy said, "I have work to do," and brushed past Brett, leaving the break room as Eli was entering. She smiled at Eli but didn't stop to chat.

Eli poured himself a cup of coffee.

"Did you have fun last night?" Brett asked, taking her mug and moving toward the door.

"Brett, wait."

She paused and turned toward him. His hair was tousled, and there were dark bags under his eyes. Stubble shadowed his chin.

"I'm sorry," he said. "About last night. I was drunk."

"You were a dick."

"That too." He gave her a half-smile, one cheek dimpling. "Forgive me?"

She sighed and nodded. "Only because I owe you one for helping out with my grandmother. And because you're going to promise that you'll never pull that kind of shit with me ever again."

His cheeks flushed red.

"Right?"

"Right," he said meekly.

"Good. Now that we have an understanding. Is everything okay with you and Irving? He's not coming down on you too hard about this Danny bullshit, is he? I'll talk to him if he is. I'll tell him it was my idea to tag along on that interview."

"Don't bother. Danny's just rattling cages. It'll blow over." He frowned into his coffee mug and then looked back up at her. "Are you sure we're good? Because I really am sorry about what I said. I don't really think any of that—"

"Eli," she interrupted, holding up her hand to silence him. "We're good."

She took her coffee to drink at her desk.

———————

Two hours later, the medical examiner's office called.

"Are you sure?" Brett asked Charlie.

"I know that you and I are still getting to know each other, Detective," he said, "but how about I let you in on a little secret. The only time you'll ever get a phone call from me like this is when I'm sure. Damn sure. Take it to the bank sure. Stake my life on it sure. So, am I sure? You bet I'm sure. Never been more sure of anything except the day I said my wedding vows. I'll get the written report to you by the end of the day."

She thanked him and hung up.

———————

Irving was hunched over a pile of papers at his desk, which he quickly shuffled together and stuffed into a manila folder when

Brett approached. His tie today was forest green and covered in rows of dime-sized pheasants. He leaned back in his chair and waited for her to speak first.

"I just got off the phone with Charlie," she said. "The lab confirmed that the knife used to kill Zach Danforth is the same one that killed Nathan Andress."

He sat forward again. "Now that complicates things, doesn't it?"

"Zach's blood was all over the knife, obviously," she repeated what Charlie had told her. "But not just his. There was another blood type mixed in, and it matches Nathan's."

"So we have our murder weapon. And it looks like we'll be pooling resources." He rose from his chair. "We better update the sergeant."

She glanced across the room at Stan Harcourt's office. His door was closed, but a light was on inside. When she didn't move to follow Irving, he asked, "Is there something else?"

She took him back to her desk, removed the photographs from the drawer, and handed them over. He flipped through them, his frown deepening. Though he wasn't in any of the pictures, she could tell from his expression of surprise that he recognized a lot of faces. When he got to a picture of Stan Harcourt taking an envelope that looked to be stuffed with money from a man whose back was to the camera, he stopped.

"Where did you get these?" His voice was quiet.

"I did a preliminary search of Zach's room yesterday and found them in a box with some weed. And Elizabeth's underwear."

Irving's gaze snapped to her, then back down to the photographs. He flipped through them a second time, then stacked them together and rushed them to the detective sergeant's office. Brett chased after him, calling for him to wait, but he ignored her. He shoved the door open without knocking and dropped the photographs on the sergeant's desk. "What the hell is this, Stan?"

Stan looked up from his work, flustered and blinking stupidly.

He glowered at Brett, who hovered in the doorway, then reached for the photographs. He looked at the top one, the one of him taking money from someone in a dark alley, then set the stack down again and gestured for Brett to come inside. She stepped into the room and closed the door behind her with a quiet click.

Stan tapped one finger on the stack of photographs. "Does someone want to tell me where these came from?"

Irving glanced at Brett. She repeated to the sergeant what she'd already told Irving. When she finished talking, he shoved the photographs back into the envelope and then shoved the envelope into a desk drawer.

"What are you doing?" Brett demanded.

Stan's expression was unreadable as he took a pack of gum from the pocket of his shirt, unwrapped a stick, and folded it into his mouth. He chewed thoughtfully for a few seconds, then said, "What you're both going to do is this. You're going to forget you ever saw these pictures. You're going to pretend they never existed."

Brett sputtered in protest.

At the same time, Irving said, "Come on, Stan. Don't do this."

"This isn't anything you have to worry about anymore." He bared his teeth in a smile that looked more like a grimace as he waved them to leave his office. The chewing gum squished between his teeth, a sticky white glob that smelled faintly of mint.

Brett stood her ground. Irving stayed too.

"Those photos are evidence in a murder case," she explained.

Stan shrugged one shoulder. "Well, I guess you'll have to figure out how to investigate the case without them. You're a smart girl. I'm sure you can handle it."

"Stan, as of this morning, the cases are linked," Irving said and told him about the knife. "We're looking for the same guy, and chances are good he's in one of those photos. Zach was obviously in a position to ruffle a lot of powerful feathers."

"I said, leave it alone." Stan's voice was a warning.

"We need to bring Danny Cyrus back in," Brett said.

Stan's eyebrows shot up. "Absolutely not."

"He's our best link between Nathan and Zach."

"She's right." Irving backed her up. "Nathan owed Danny money. Zach worked for Danny. Zach and Nathan were seen together two weeks before he died. We need to reexamine that connection. Especially now that we know Zach was collecting dirt on every influential person in this town, including half our own force."

"Danny didn't kill Nathan or Zach." Stan sounded sure of it.

"Even if that's true, it wouldn't hurt to bring him in and ask a few more questions," Irving said.

Stan folded his hands over his desk. His jaw worked over that piece of gum as he talked. "Listen to me carefully—both of you. Danny Cyrus is working with us on a different case. He's been working as an informant for us for months. If you drag him in here a second time, you're going to fuck over this other thing we've been building. And I can assure you this other thing is much bigger than some two-bit, wannabe gangster getting stabbed."

"It's not just Zach—" Brett tried to argue, but Stan cut her off with a wave of his hand.

"Enough. This case with Danny has tentacles that run deep. We're working with multiple states and with Canada. And that's all I can tell you, but you get it, right? You need to steer clear of this. I can assure you neither Danny nor his crew had anything to do with Nathan or Zach's deaths. We've had our eyes on them every day since the investigation started. In addition to Danny feeding us info, we have officers working undercover. If Danny or anyone in his crew was connected to these murders, we'd know about it already. Besides, Zach was an asset to Danny. You're right that he knew a lot of things about a lot of people. But, I assure you, Zach is the last person Danny would want to turn up dead."

Brett shifted her gaze to Irving, gauging his reaction. He worked his lips between his teeth, and the muscles along his jaw were clenched tight. He didn't like what Stan was telling them any more than she did.

"And Nathan?" Irving asked, his tone detached.

Stan lifted his hands in a shrug. The gum cracked between his teeth. "He was nothing to them. A bottom feeder who owed Danny money. Dead, Danny gets nothing, right? See where I'm going with this?"

When neither of them said anything in response, Stan sighed, exasperated. "Ask the chief if you don't believe me. But don't go anywhere near Danny Cyrus. Do you understand me? He is off-limits. Him and his whole crew. Look somewhere else." He waved his hand at the door with more emphasis this time. "You're dismissed."

Irving spun on his heels and stormed out. Brett followed him.

"Do you have anything on your calendar right now?" he asked.

With the photographs gone and strict instructions from their sergeant not to pursue Danny Cyrus, Brett's case was stalled. She shook her head. "Not anymore."

"Good." Irving reached his desk and slipped on his windbreaker. "Grab your jacket and meet me in the parking lot."

"Where are we going?"

He pulled a heavy-duty pair of binoculars from his lower desk drawer and said, "I'm taking you birdwatching."

CHAPTER 28

Irving led Brett over two miles into the woods near Lake Chastain. He said nothing as they walked, except to point out various species of birds. Wrens and nuthatches, thrushes and sparrows. Once he stopped, tilted his head back, lifted the binoculars to his eyes, and said, "Last year I was lucky enough to spot a pileated woodpecker. He was right over there." He pointed in the distance. "Every time I come out here, I look for him, but I haven't seen him since. A once in a lifetime sighting was what that was." Whenever he spotted a bird of any kind, common or interesting, he would pause and make a mark in a small notebook he carried in his pocket.

When Brett left the office with Irving, she hadn't expected to be doing any actual birdwatching. At first, she was annoyed by having to thrash through tangled underbrush, cobwebs catching on her arms and face. Now that Stan had buried her only good lead, she had too much work to do to spend hours traipsing in the woods looking for varying shades of brown feathers. But the longer they walked, the more her anger dissipated, and she started to enjoy herself. It was a nice day, sunny, but not too warm. Crisp with the scent of autumn. After a while, immersed in the quiet task of spotting birds in the shadows, Brett could see how a person might find herself sucked into a hobby like this. It would be a good way to unwind at the end of a long workday and burn off some extra energy.

They climbed a small hill that was dotted with fir trees and scrub bushes. The vegetation at the top was sparse enough that it was possible to see for miles in any direction. Thin wisps of clouds drifted across the vast blue sky above them. Irving stopped next to a large stump and took off the small backpack he carried over his shoulder. He offered Brett some water. She drank deeply from the canteen. Tiny birds flitted through the branches of a nearby bush, picking at berries and hanging upside.

"Those are chestnut-backed chickadees." Irving made a note in his book. "Nothing too special, but they're fun to watch."

A shadow passed overhead, and Irving lifted his binoculars, tracking the path of a large black bird riding air currents. "This is the best spot to see raptors," he said, adding, "That right there is just your standard crow, though. Of course, if you ask me, there's nothing standard about crows. Fascinating birds, smarter than we give them credit for."

Brett sat on the stump that overlooked the rolling landscape, a patchwork quilt of trees and bare patches. Large sections had been logged, and holes in the canopy revealed smaller, natural meadows and glittering lakes. Where the light touched, the world was edged in copper and glinting.

Irving lowered his binoculars. "The thing about birdwatching is that you have to have patience. Sometimes I come out here, and I see maybe one bird if I'm lucky. Other times, it's like everywhere I look, there's something interesting. Osprey, sooty fox sparrows, belted kingfishers, loggerhead shrikes. Sometimes though, you have to know where they like to roost, where their nests are. You have to know which direction to point the binoculars." He took them off his neck and held them out to her. "Go on and give it a try."

She held the binoculars to her eyes, and Irving showed her how to adjust the focus. She swept slowly across the horizon, then up to the sky, trying to snag on some motion, some winged creature, but if there was a bird to find, she was looking in the wrong spot.

"Try over here." Irving touched the back of her hand, guiding the binoculars down and to the left.

At first, it was a blur of trees, branches overlapping, and then a break in the green, and she was staring at a meadow with flattened down grass. A tick to the right, and she found the fire road, the underbrush cut through with ATV tracks. It was the same meadow she'd stood in last week with Eli and Billy, the meadow Irving had sent her to investigate for noise disturbance.

Irving pushed her hand again, guiding the binoculars farther to the left, about ninety degrees south of the meadow. A chimney, a roof, a road. Then Danny's trailer came into focus. Brett sucked in a sharp breath and lowered the binoculars, lifting her eyes to Irving.

"I've been watching him for twenty years," he said. "Ever since your sister was killed."

"You were with Crestwood back then?" She made no attempt to hide her surprise. She'd known he'd been with the department for a long time, but she didn't remember seeing his name on any of the paperwork or reports in her sister's file. "Were you a detective?"

He shook his head. "I was a patrol officer, a few months out of the academy, but Stan put me on his team. For the experience, he said. Margot's case was the first murder I worked." He stared in the direction of Danny's trailer, though nothing but trees were visible without the binoculars. "To this day, I wonder if I should have pushed him to do more. He was so convinced Danny Cyrus had killed her—we were all so convinced—a lot got ignored." He sighed and shrugged. "What can I say? I wasn't even a year into the job, and Stan was my superior. I thought he knew what he was doing."

Brett lifted the binoculars again. Nothing moved in or around the trailer.

Irving continued. "Ever since your sister was killed, I've been doing my best to keep my eye on Danny, waiting for him to slip up, I guess, and show his true colors. Except for that fight club of his, though, he's...Well, as much as I can tell, he's living a damn monk's life."

Brett lowered the binoculars to stare at Irving. "You knew about the fights before Zach told us, didn't you?"

He nodded.

"Who else knows?

He shrugged. "Stan. A few of the old-timers, definitely. We don't mention it to the rookies unless we have to. Eli has no clue."

"And all of you who know, you just look the other way?" She shoved the binoculars at him. "Why am I surprised?"

She started to walk back down the hill toward their cars, but Irving stopped her with a gentle hand on her arm.

"I was the first to realize what was going on out here," he said. "It happened by accident, actually. I'd been coming up to this spot frequently during the day to check on Danny, but sometime last year, I came out for the first time at night. A friend in the birding community told me he'd spotted a long-eared owl nesting in one of those snags down there, and I wanted to try to see it for myself. I came at dusk. I didn't see the owl but noticed there was a lot of commotion happening in that clearing, so I stuck around to find out what was going on. I went straight to Stan with it after, but he told me to leave it alone, said everyone was consenting adults, that there were worse ways the boys of this town could be spending their time."

"So that disturbance call you sent me out on last week? You knew exactly what I was walking into. Why bother sending me at all?"

"I thought maybe if I sent a new face out there, someone who isn't friends with Stan Harcourt, someone Lincoln wasn't familiar with, then maybe it would put the scare in them, and they'd stop."

"Did it work?" she asked.

He squinted at the sky. "It's too early to tell, honestly, but they weren't at it over this last weekend, so maybe, yeah, it did work."

"Did you know about the ongoing undercover operation, too? That Danny's working with the cops?"

"No." Anger edged his voice.

They were quiet for a few minutes, then Brett said, "You don't always have to do what he tells you to do, you know. Stan, I mean. You can go above his head. Henry won't fire you."

Irving laughed like she'd said something stupid, then he said, "Stan saved my life once."

She raised her eyebrows in disbelief.

"It was during the early days of my career," he continued. "I was still on probation, and Stan was riding with me that night. We pulled this car over for a broken taillight. The driver wouldn't get out of the car. He was real belligerent about it. The next thing we know, he's whipping a gun out of nowhere, and I'm down on the ground with a bullet in my gut." His hand moved to his stomach, resting there a minute before finishing the story. "Stan moved fast. He got a med kit from the car, put pressure on the wound, and called for an ambulance, all within a few seconds. The driver was long gone by then, but Stan gave dispatch the license plate, and another patrol car pulled him over a few miles up the road and took him in without any trouble. Stan stayed with me, kept me conscious until the paramedics took over. If he hadn't been there, I would have bled out on the side of the road."

Brett stared at the ground, trying not to let him see that it didn't matter how many people Stan Harcourt saved—saving people didn't make him a good cop. It didn't mean he could be trusted either.

"Even if I didn't owe him my life, I owe him my career," Irving said. "Stan was the one person who fought for me to stay on the force when everyone else wanted me gone. Things were a lot different when I was coming up. Our sergeant at the time was a real...well, let's just say he didn't like me much. He undercut me at every turn, did everything he could to keep me from promoting. If I made even one tiny mistake, I was on desk duty for three weeks. Or worse, I was sent to work traffic. I was nearly fired a dozen times, but for Stan, who stepped in every time and took the blame for whatever the sergeant was accusing me of messing up. When that prick finally retired, Stan was promoted sergeant, which made things a lot easier for me. All those years, he looked out for me, and I looked out for him." He cleared his throat. "What I'm trying to say is Stan's not a bad cop. He just lost his way a bit. He's forgotten who it is we're supposed to be protecting. What he did back there, with the photographs, he shouldn't have done that. We've both got victims who deserve better than to be shoved in some desk drawer and forgotten. Nathan's family, Zach's. Elizabeth. She deserves better. But..." He paused and ran his hand behind his neck, like he knew what he was working up to say would piss Brett off. "But he's not entirely wrong."

Brett opened her mouth to argue, but Irving cut her off.

"What motive does Danny have for killing Nathan? Or Zach? One owed him money. The other worked hard to make him money. You don't kill the people bringing in the income you depend on to live."

"Maybe money wasn't the motive."

"I agree. Zach and Nathan were both stabbed multiple times. Nathan's autopsy report even indicates the stabbing continued after he was already dead. Whoever did that was angry," Irving said. "It was personal for them. These stabbings weren't self-defense or some kind of terrible accident. They were acts of rage."

"So what did Nathan and Zach do to make someone so angry?" She could think of something Zach had done, but from what they'd uncovered so far, Nathan didn't seem to be living the kind of life that would piss a lot of people off.

Irving cleared his throat. "I called the prison and confirmed that Nathan and Archer have indeed been writing to one another since July. They couldn't tell me what the letters said, only that they had outgoing and ingoing mail recorded between the two of them."

"No one reads the letters from death row inmates?"

"They do, but if there's nothing interesting, they let it through and forget about it."

"Archer was probably just asking for commissary money." She threw his words back at him. "Isn't that what you said?"

Irving sighed and ran his hand over his face. "You have every right to be pissed at me for brushing you off like that. I'm sorry, okay? But I think you might be right. There. Does that make you feel better? You were right."

She got no satisfaction hearing him say it.

"You don't think Archer French killed your sister, right?" he asked.

She shook her head. "No, I don't." And it was the first time she'd said it that she had full confidence in her answer, without even a sliver of doubt.

"But you think he might know who did? And you think he might have slipped some information to Nathan in those letters. That's what you were hinting at the other day, right?" He rolled his eyes toward the sky, where a large bird spun in slow circles. "Turkey vulture," he said, then continued where he'd left off. "So what if he did? What if Nathan knew something about Margot's death? What if he knew who really killed her? Because if it wasn't Archer, whoever did it has been walking around a free man for twenty years. And if Nathan started snooping around, and let's say, started asking questions, if he approached whoever killed Margot, if there was even a hint of threat to that freedom…" He spread his hands in the air, then snapped them into tight fists like he was breaking an invisible branch.

Brett's skin prickled with the feeling that they were circling close to the truth, but even if they were right and Nathan's death had something to do with Margot, they had no evidence. All of this was speculation.

"What about Zach?" she asked. "How does he fit? He wasn't alive when Margot was killed. He wasn't in contact with Archer as far as we know. His only connection to Nathan was through Danny."

Their eyes shifted over the treetops again in the direction of Danny's trailer.

"We have to talk to him," she said.

"If we so much as brush past him in the street, Stan will have us both suspended."

"He's the spider at the center of this web. Margot, Nathan, Zach—it all comes back to Danny."

"We can't go near him, Brett. Not unless we have some other kind of proof, something more than patched up guesswork. If we take this to Stan, he'll laugh us right out on our asses. Or worse."

"So, what then? We can't do nothing."

"First, we go into it with an open mind," he said. "We don't know Danny did anything yet. We're not going to make the same mistake Stan did twenty years ago."

"Then, what's your plan?"

"We start with Archer. We try to find out what he wrote to Nathan in those letters, what he knows. If he saw Danny kill Margot, if he provides a statement to that effect, I can take that back to Stan. He won't be able to shove evidence like that into his desk drawer."

Her heart hammered in her chest. Twenty years she had wondered, and now, in a matter of days, hours even, she might finally have the truth. She could see it in Irving's eyes, too, how Margot's death had weighed on him over the years. He'd been coming to this same overlook for over a decade with nothing to show for it. All that was about to change and all they had to do was convince Archer French to talk.

"I can drive down to the prison tomorrow," Brett offered.

"No," Irving said. "We need to do this the right way. I'll call and set up an appointment with his attorney."

"That will take too long," she argued. "I'm friends with a corrections officer down there. I can call in a favor. Besides, he might be more likely to talk to me than you."

"Because you're a woman."

"Because I'm Margot's sister."

"No," Irving repeated, more emphatically. "Let me handle this. If we're right, if this is related to your sister's case, it won't look good to have your fingerprints all over everything when it comes time to send it over to the county prosecutor's office. We don't want the defense arguing coercion or false testimony or whatever bullshit they'd conjure up to get our evidence thrown out."

He was right, even though she didn't want him to be.

"Look, I think you're a good cop," Irving said. "You're smart and persistent. You don't roll over easy. I think you're a great hire for the department."

She ducked her head, not wanting to show how pleased she was with his compliments. She was starting to like Irving, but accepting his praise felt like weakness, like something he could hold over her head one day.

"I look forward to working future cases with you, Brett," Irving continued. "I really do. But we both know you can't work this one. It's not fair to the case, and it wouldn't be fair to you. It's too personal. So I'm asking you to let me handle this. Can you do that? Will you trust me to bring this one in?"

It wasn't like she had any other choice.

She crossed her arms stubbornly over her chest, tilted her chin a little higher, and asked, "What am I supposed to do in the meantime?"

"Take up a hobby?" He held up his binoculars and offered her a sympathetic grin. "I've got an extra pair at home you can borrow if you want."

CHAPTER 29

Brett had just sat down to wait when the guard came to get her. He double-checked her ID, then buzzed them into the prison through another metal detector, looking bored with the whole thing. Passing into the cell block, he said, "You must have friends in high places. We don't normally allow same-day visits. Especially to prisoners like French."

A loud buzz echoed through the dimly lit hallway as the door slammed shut.

When Brett woke up Tuesday morning, she'd imagined the day playing out much differently. She and Jimmy had gone for an early run with the dogs by the water. Trixie chased alongside them, her hound legs muscular and quick, her tongue lolling in a grin, her tail slapping the air, her ears flapping out like sails. Pistol took his time, stopping to sniff at stones and shells, before rushing on little legs to catch up. They jogged all three miles down to Deadman's Point so Brett could show Jimmy where they believed Nathan's body had been dumped. He scanned the area, then said, "It's funny, isn't it? A different current, a different kind of tide, and you would have never found him. He'd still be down there, being picked apart by crabs."

On the jog home, Brett filled him in on her birdwatching adventure with Irving. She didn't tell him everything, just that they were looking into the Archer French angle again and hoping it would lead them anywhere but another dead-end. She said nothing of the photographs now locked in Stan's desk drawer, though she knew it was the kind of scoop he would love.

It had always been tricky with Jimmy, balancing the need for discretion on a case with their friendship. Sometimes it was useful having a reporter to feed information to, and sometimes Jimmy fed information back to her. Other times, the unspoken things sat heavy between them, filling her with loneliness. She wanted to talk to him. She wanted to tell him about her cases, ask for advice, get his opinion, but she couldn't trust him to keep her secrets. Especially not the kind of secret that might land on the front page.

They agreed to meet up for dinner that night. Jimmy had plans to talk to the editor at the *Tribune* and access the archives to find out if he could learn anything new for his book. Brett planned to spend the rest of the day at her desk, carefully re-reading the witness interviews from Saturday's Halloween festival to see if she'd missed anything. It was going to be a long day requiring multiple cups of coffee.

"Stay out of trouble," Brett told Jimmy as they parted.

"You know I won't."

But when Brett arrived at the precinct, Irving was waiting by her desk.

"I left four messages with Archer's attorney yesterday," he said, adjusting the end of his tie, which today was navy blue and dotted with small white doves. "No one called me back."

"We don't have time for this." Frustration edged her voice.

"I know," he said. "Which is why I called in a favor with that friend of yours in the corrections department."

She'd left Irving the man's number just in case.

"And?" she pressed him.

He looked at his watch. "It's a six-hour drive. If you leave now, you could be at the penitentiary by two."

"Me? But—"

"Archer agreed to a meeting," Irving interrupted her. "But only if you were the one who showed up. He won't talk to anyone else."

"So I'm going."

"If you want answers."

The guard led Brett into a small room with a bank of bulletproof windows and phones attached to the wall. She had been expecting to be able to do this in a private interview room, not in the visiting area where anyone could overhear. It was better than nothing, she supposed. The guard showed her to one of the booths. She sat down on the plastic chair to wait.

When Archer French was finally brought in through the door on the other side of the glass, a satisfied smile spread across his face. He was thinner than the last time she saw him at his trial. His shaved head accentuated the hard angles of his face. He looked older without the fine, blond curls softening around his collar. Archer sat in a chair on the other side of the glass. He tilted his head, studying her a moment. Her skin crawled under his ice-blue gaze, but she shoved the feeling aside, refusing to let him see how much being near him affected her.

With steady hands, she picked up the phone. Archer did the same.

His voice was smooth and friendly. "You are even prettier than your sister."

She didn't react. She was here for one reason and one reason only. She kept her voice curt and professional when she said, "Tell me about the letters you sent Nathan."

His smile faltered before returning, but there was a false charm to it, a thread of stiffness that tugged his shoulders back.

"It's a shame," he said, shaking his head. "Did you know that I had to read about his death in the newspaper? My own cousin. And no one bothered to come tell me personally. Nathan was a good kid. And Mary took me in when no one else wanted me. Neither of them deserves this."

Brett's grip on the receiver tightened. He wasn't wrong, but he'd shown no pity for the women he'd killed, and this inconsistency, this callous compartmentalizing, enraged her. She took a slow breath and returned her focus to getting the answers she needed. "Did you write to him first? Or was it the other way around?"

He leaned forward, resting his elbows on the laminate shelf in front of him. "You didn't drive all this way to talk about some boring old stack of letters, did you? Come now, Brett. I think we can talk about something a little more interesting than that."

"Nathan reached out to me before he died," she admitted to him. Archer looked intrigued. "Did he now?"

"He said he had something he needed to tell me about Margot." His eyes sparked when she said her sister's name. "Oh? Do tell."

"He was killed before we had a chance to talk."

"Too bad." He leaned back in his chair.

"Tell me what was in those letters. Did you say anything to him about Margot? About who killed her?"

"I miss the forest." He sighed when he said it, loud and longing. "I miss the trees and the way the sun comes through all dappled and thin. I miss the sound of the wind in the branches. There are so many places to hide in a forest, but I'm sure you already know that."

"Tell me what you wrote to Nathan."

His smile tightened, turning predatorily. "I am telling you."

"I don't have time for games." She pushed the chair back.

"I loved them, you know. Each and every one." He tapped his finger on the shelf. "I would never have left them in the forest to rot. I looked after them for as long as I could. I made them beautiful the way I made your sister beautiful."

Brett sank back down into the chair. "What do you mean, you made her beautiful?"

The corner of his mouth twitched. "I found her lying in the woods, abandoned. I found her, and I took her someplace safe, and I made her beautiful again." Another twitch of his lips, then he asked, "Did you know that cougars have been known to kill an animal to eat only its liver, leaving the rest behind? Wasteful, certainly, but not unexpected. Unlike humans, animals do not have a moral code. It's kill or be killed. Do what it takes to survive. They live and die by blood." He tugged on the phone cord then released it. "You can't cross into another's territory and expect to walk away without at least a few scratches."

Brett shook her head. "Enough with the riddles. Do you know who killed Margot or not?"

"I might." His eyes narrowed to hard slits. "But I'm not saying another word about it unless I get something in return."

Her whole body tensed at the thought of negotiating with someone who had caused so much suffering, who had so cruelly ended the lives of eleven women. Brett wanted to put her hand through the glass, tighten her fingers around his scrawny neck, and watch his lips turn blue. She wanted to knock the teeth from his grinning mouth. She wanted to give in and be the animal who survived.

Instead, she flexed her hand in her lap once, curled her fingers tight, and asked him what he wanted.

———————————

Brett didn't make Archer French any promises, but she didn't exactly tell him no, either. In the forty minutes they were together, he told her nothing useful, nothing Irving could bring to Stan as evidence. He swore up and down he had the information she wanted, though, and all she had to do to get it was secure him more yard time. The promise of one extra hour outside every day—that's all he was asking for—a little more time in the sun. An hour of yard time in exchange for the truth about Margot's death. Really, he pointed out, Brett was getting the better end of the deal. She'd tried telling him that it was the prison superintendent who granted yard time, that his request was beyond her level of authority, but he'd simply smiled at her, then gestured for the guard to take him back to his cell. There was nothing else for her to do but make the six-hour drive back to Crestwood.

Before she left, she used a payphone outside the prison to call Amma and let her know she was on her way home.

"Everything okay there?" Her words were weighted with concern.

"I'm fine, dear. Everything's fine," Amma insisted. "Drive safe, I'll see you soon."

There'd been no further episodes since the festival. Amma was even sleeping through the night again. No more midnight wanderings. No more waking Brett to find out if Margot had come home yet. Brett wasn't holding her breath that this normalcy would last forever, but it was nice to have a break.

After hanging up with Amma, Brett called Jimmy's motel room to cancel their dinner plans, but no one answered. It wouldn't be a bad thing if he showed up at the house, though. He could keep Amma company until Brett got back.

By the time she turned off the highway into Crestwood, it was after 10:00 PM. Except for the Pickled Onion and the movie theater, downtown was closed up for the night, the shop windows dark. Jimmy's car wasn't parked in Amma's driveway like Brett thought it would be and, when she let herself inside, Pistol was the only one who came to greet her. She scratched the dog's head as she took off her shoes.

A light was on in the kitchen.

"Amma?" Brett called softly.

Pistol danced around her feet. It took concentration not to step on him.

A stool scraped across the floor in the kitchen, and Amma appeared in the doorway. She was wrapped in her favorite purple robe, her face washed, and her hair pinned up for the night. She held a cup of tea in her hands. A look of relief spread across her face. "I've been worried sick about you. Where have you been?"

Brett tried not to show her disappointment. "I told you I was going down to Salem today, remember? I called a few hours ago?"

Amma's eyes shifted back and forth as she searched her memory. Frustration shadowed her face. Then she batted her hand in the air like it was nothing. "Yes, of course, you did. Don't listen to me. You know how my mind slips sometimes. Let me make you some tea."

She reached for the kettle, but Brett stopped her. "It's fine, Amma. I'm tired. I'm just going to go to bed." She paused on her way out of the room. "Did you and Jimmy have a nice dinner together tonight?"

A small frown tugged on her grandmother's lips, and her eyes darted with the same searching expression from earlier. "Jimmy? Was I supposed to meet him somewhere? Did I forget again?"

She smacked her hand on her forehead. "I have to start writing this stuff down."

"No, Amma, he was supposed to be coming over here for dinner. He didn't show up?"

"I haven't seen him since this morning when you two went for a run." She sounded uncertain.

It was possible, Brett supposed, that Jimmy had come over for dinner, and Amma had simply forgotten. But there were no signs of company, no dishes in the sink. And if Jimmy had shown up, he would have certainly stayed with Amma until Brett got home.

It wasn't like Jimmy to bail on plans he'd made. Then again, Brett had bailed first, so she couldn't really judge. She was tired from driving, too tired to worry about Jimmy. He probably just got caught up sorting through the *Tribune* archives. The story always came first for him.

Brett told Amma goodnight, then went upstairs. Pistol followed at her heels. In her room, she changed into pajamas. She stood a moment at the window staring over the black and shimmering bay. Seeing French had left her feeling bruised and brittle, and she had a feeling she would be tossing and turning all night, unable to sleep as she tried to figure out how to get French what he wanted.

She pulled the curtain over the window, dampening the moonlight, then crawled under the sheets. Pistol let out a sharp bark. Brett reached over and scooped him up onto the bed, where he turned a circle before settling in the crook of her knees.

For not the first time in the past year, Brett slid her hand over the empty spot beside her and thought of Jimmy, their kiss, his hands wrapping around her face, drawing her in. His lips finding hers so confidently in the dark. She wondered what it would be like to come home to someone at night, someone like Jimmy who loved her and wrapped his arms around her and made her feel, finally, safe. Then came the thought that always followed this one. How she wasn't sure it was even possible to feel safe in a world where men like Archer French existed.

CHAPTER 30

Clara stared at the man lying face down on her kitchen floor, then at the kettle of water in her hand. There was a smear of blood on the rounded metal bottom and splatter on the wood floor, but not much. And he was breathing.

He was still breathing. She clung to this fact, staring at the rise and fall of his ribs as the front door clicked open and Marshall called out to her. "Clara? Are you home?"

Then he was in the doorway behind her, inhaling sharply, exhaling a curse. She didn't dare turn and face him.

"What have you done?" his voice barely above a whisper.

Her hands began to shake. Then her whole body. She dropped the kettle. It clattered onto the floor at her feet.

Marshall came to her, grabbed her arms, pushed his face into hers. "Clara, look at me." His voice rose in anger. "What did you do?"

———————

The man had come to the house late on Tuesday afternoon. He rang the doorbell, introduced himself as Jimmy Eagan, smiled, and asked if he could come inside. There was something familiar about him, but Clara couldn't figure out where she knew him from. Then he said he had an appointment with Marshall, and she thought that must be it—he's one of Marshall's clients. She told him Marshall didn't usually get home until 6:00 PM, but Jimmy, still smiling, told her he didn't mind waiting. So she let him inside.

Clara did this to them, then. She opened the door wide and welcomed this stranger in. She said, "Can I get you something to drink?" And he said, "Coffee is fine." And she filled the kettle and turned on the stove, more than happy to accommodate one of Marshall's clients. In her mind, she gave the young man a wife and two kids. Because of his tweed jacket with elbow pads, the leather satchel he carried over one shoulder, and his fingers that were stained with ink, she imagined he was a teacher, or perhaps a college professor. He was looking for a starter home, something simple and functional, but quaint enough to impress his in-laws.

She smiled at him because he was smiling at her, and she didn't think anything was wrong until he said, "You grew up in Crestwood, didn't you?"

The way he asked it made her think he was here for more than a chat about the price of houses. But she answered him anyway. "I've lived here my whole life."

Then he asked, "You and Marshall? You went to school together? You were high school sweethearts for a while? That's what I heard, anyway."

And that's when she knew that he wasn't a father-husband looking for a house. That's when she remembered where she knew him from and realized the danger she was in. But she stayed calm, scooping coffee grounds into the filter and reaching into the fridge for milk.

"Yes, that's right. Marshall and I fell in love in high school," she said. "We've been in love ever since."

"But you weren't always together, right? I mean, that age, kids are always breaking up and making up." He was trying to be so nonchalant, so pleasant.

She turned to look at him, really look at him for the first time since he entered her house—since she let him in. "Who did you say you were again?"

"Jimmy." That smile was a fool's smile, a liar's smile, the smile of someone in the business of sticking his nose where it didn't belong.

"And you're working with my husband? You're buying a house from him?"

"Oh, no." A quick shake of his head. "I'm a reporter with the *Oregonian*."

It confirmed what Clara already knew in her gut. This was the same man who had come sniffing around years ago. She'd been lucky back then and clearly smarter, too. He'd been so focused on Archer French, he hadn't even noticed her. But now he was back and she had let him into her house. Now he was sitting at her kitchen table asking about her history with Marshall, and she could see quite clearly where all this was headed. She took a deep breath and turned her back on him to check the water boiling on the stove. The kettle rattled and hissed as the water grew hotter and hotter.

"I'm looking into the murder of a girl that took place around here over twenty years ago? Maybe you remember her? Margot Buchanan? She and your husband were close, weren't they? They were dating the summer she died, am I getting that right? I'm sorry. I don't mean to pry."

But of course, that's precisely what he meant to do.

That's when her hand wrapped around the black handle of the kettle.

———————————

"He was threatening me," she said to Marshall, who had let go of her and dropped to the floor beside the reporter.

Marshall pressed his fingers to the man's neck, checking for a pulse even though it was clear he was still breathing. A look of relief passed over his face, but this was quickly replaced by anger. "What happened?"

He rose to his feet, took a washcloth from a drawer, ran it under the faucet, then returned to the reporter and pressed it to the back of the man's head where the kettle had made contact.

"I told you," Clara said. "He was threatening me. He came into my home—"

"I invited him."

"Why would you do that?"

"He said he wanted to talk to me about Margot. That's why I'm home a little early."

"But why? Margot is ancient history. And why would you tell him to meet you here when you knew I was alone?" Her hands were still shaking. Her whole body rattling like the kettle on the stove, simmering to a boil.

"I was planning on being here when he got here, but I ran into some traffic." His brow pinched in a bewildered frown. "Please, Clara, tell me something that makes sense. Why is there an unconscious man lying on our kitchen floor?"

"He said..." She searched for something, anything, that would justify what she'd done. "He thinks you killed Margot."

Marshall's face paled, and he stopped fussing over the man. "He what?"

"He said he uncovered some new information, a new witness or something, someone who claims that they saw the two of you going into the woods that day. He wanted to know if you'd ever been violent with me. Or with Elizabeth." Her voice cracked.

The name of his daughter brought Marshall to his feet. He

stared at the reporter with a look of disgust, then he wiped his hand down his face and came to her, close enough that their faces were touching, breaths mingling. His thumb rolled over her wrist.

"I didn't kill Margot," he said. "I would never—"

"I know," she interrupted him.

He glanced over his shoulder at the man on their floor, then squeezed his eyes closed as if hoping when he reopened them, the man would be gone.

She had done this, forced him into this position. Her sins had followed her out from the woods, out from the shadows, and into her home. She had always been expecting this, though, hadn't she? Had always been expecting the truth of what she'd done to seep from the cracks in her lies. She knew what she was capable of, knew her own heart, how selfish and sharp-edged it was, knew she could—and would—do whatever it took to survive in this mean world. But Marshall, he was so gentle and kind, with the softest of hearts. She had always meant to keep him far away from things like this, far from these kinds of painful and necessary decisions.

She touched the back of his hand. "Elizabeth will be home from soccer practice soon. June's mother is dropping her off."

He looked lost, a younger version of himself. He wore the same expression he had the day Margot's body was found. Confusion, his spirit crushed as if he was losing pieces of himself with each breath he released. She had been there for him then, and she was here for him now, taking him in her arms, comforting him as best as she could. These kinds of losses were not insurmountable. She had been here before. She knew what came next.

"Clara." His voice was a rasping whisper, pleading with her. "What are we going to do?"

"Grab him under the arms." She crouched by the man's feet. On three, they lifted his body together.

CHAPTER 31

Brett left yet another message for Jimmy. "Where are you? Should I be worried? Please call me as soon as you get this."

She'd called his motel room five times already this morning, twice before she left home and three times from her desk at the precinct. She'd even talked to the front desk manager, who assured her that Jimmy had yet to check out. Not that Brett really thought he had. Jimmy would never leave without saying goodbye. Sure enough, the front desk manager confirmed he'd paid in advance for the room through next Sunday. Brett hung up and sat a minute, trying to decide what to do next.

Worry knotted in her chest, but she did her best to ignore it. Jimmy was a grown man who could take care of himself, and it wasn't her job to know where he was at all hours of the day. Right now, her focus needed to be on Archer French and the impossible task of convincing the superintendent to let a prisoner have one hour of extra yard time. She hoped Irving had some ideas for how to sweet talk the superintendent, but when she went looking for him, he wasn't at his desk or in the break room.

Brett circled the squad room, then went outside in case he'd gone for fresh air. It had rained overnight. The pavement was still damp, and the clouds lingered, soggy and ash-colored. The news was forecasting a very wet Halloween, with more rain coming in this afternoon and staying through the evening. Just in time to ruin trick-or-treating. It fit the town's mood, she supposed, which was still reeling from first Nathan's death, then Zach's. Two murders in two weeks. It had been only four days since Zach was stabbed at the festival downtown, and no one wanted to send their children out into the dark to knock on strangers' doors. Not with a killer still on the loose. Brett had a feeling the streets of Crestwood would be unusually quiet tonight.

As she turned to go back inside the precinct, a patrol car drove into the lot. It parked close to the building, and Eli got out, then went to open the backdoor. A very dirty and very wary beagle leaped from the car onto the pavement.

"Trixie?" Brett ran toward them. She lowered herself to the ground and beckoned for the dog to come.

Trixie approached timidly, with her tail tucked between her legs. Dried mud covered her flanks and burrs stuck in her fur. There was a large scratch across her nose, and her collar was missing. Otherwise, she seemed unhurt. She flicked her tongue out and licked Brett's cheek, then leaned her whole body into her leg and heaved a sigh. Brett scratched the dog's ears and cooed to her reassuringly.

"This is your friend's dog, isn't it?" Eli asked

"Why do you have her?" Brett glanced at Eli's patrol car. "Please tell me Jimmy's with you, too?"

Eli frowned and shook his head. "A man who lives out on the other side of Lake Chastain found her running loose on his property. He coaxed her into his barn with some hamburger, then called dispatch to send animal control. I recognized the description of her. I saw Jimmy walking her down at Egret's Park yesterday and remember thinking she was a good-looking dog. Since I was already out that way, I offered to bring her in."

He held his hand out to pet her, and though she wagged her tail half-heartedly, she didn't move from where she was pressed against Brett. "I thought it was strange for her to be out there by herself. Your friend doesn't seem like the kind of guy who would let his dog run loose."

"He's not." The anxiety she'd been pushing down all morning rose again.

"You think she could have slipped her collar and run off?"

Brett shook her head. She swallowed the knot in her throat and plucked a burr from behind Trixie's right ear. "I haven't heard from Jimmy since yesterday morning. I think something's wrong."

Eli's eyes narrowed with concern.

"It's possible he got caught up in a story," Brett said. "He does that sometimes when he's writing. Forgets to sleep, forgets to eat, forgets to check in. But he would never forget about Trixie. Never."

"Was he staying at the house with you?"

She shook her head. "He was at a motel downtown. I've left messages. Even drove past a few times, but he's never there."

"Maybe he went home?"

"Not without Trixie, he wouldn't." She scratched the dog's flanks, and Trixie leaned into her even more. "I have a bad feeling about this."

Eli hooked his thumbs in his belt. "I'm sure he's fine. Try not to worry. Maybe he went for a walk and got a little turned around. The woods out that way can be tricky if you're not used to them. I'm sure you'll hear from him soon, but look, I'm out on patrol all day. So I'm happy to keep an eye out for him."

It was something anyway. She nodded her thanks.

"What's he driving?" Eli asked.

She gave him a description of Jimmy's car, then watched him

climb back into his patrol car and drive off. When she turned and walked back into the precinct, Trixie followed close at her heels.

Brett made two more calls to the motel. Then one to the *Tribune*, where the receptionist confirmed Jimmy had stopped by yesterday morning and spent a few hours researching and talking to people. According to the receptionist, though, Jimmy had left the offices shortly before noon. Next, Brett called Amma, but Amma had heard nothing from Jimmy yet today.

"Everything okay?" she asked.

"I don't know," Brett said, not wanting her to worry. "Just, if he comes by, have him call me right away."

Brett peered under her desk where Trixie was curled around her feet, sleeping. She reached and stroked the dog's ear. Trixie blinked up at her with mournful brown eyes.

"You hungry, girl?"

She got a single tail thump in response.

Brett found a packet of hot dogs in the break room fridge, leftovers from a recent barbecue, and brought them back to her desk. Trixie gobbled up the bite-sized pieces Brett offered to her like she hadn't eaten in days.

"Where's Jimmy?" Brett muttered. "Huh, girl? Where's he hiding?"

Her tail thumped again at the sound of Brett's voice. She ate another bite of hot dog, her tongue sliming Brett's outstretched hand.

Brett sighed. "What am I going to do with you?"

"Buchanan!" Henry Bascom's voice bellowed through the squad room.

The chief stood in the doorway of his office, his face and cue ball head flushed crimson, his mouth a tight grimace beneath his bushy mustache. He'd never called her by her last name before.

"My office. Now." He pointed into the room behind him.

A few officers heckled her as she crossed the squad room.

"Uh oh, the little Princess is in trouble."

"Someone's gonna get a spanking."

She glared at them and took a breath, steadying herself. Trixie wriggled out from under the desk and followed her into the office.

Henry glared at the dog. "What the hell is this?" Then he shook his head. "You know what? Never mind. I don't want to know. Come in."

He closed the door and walked back to his desk. Irving and Stan Harcourt were already here, sitting next to each other in the only other chairs available, which meant Brett had to stand. Henry sank into his chair with a loud sigh. Trixie circled the room, sniffing the corners of filing cabinets and a potted plant, before returning to Brett and sitting down with a pitiful groan.

Irving flicked her and Trixie a glance, but she couldn't read his expression. Stan sat smug and smirking, with his skeleton fingers laced together in his lap. His tie was crooked. His jaw moved furiously around a piece of gum, pushing it from cheek to cheek.

Henry slicked his hand over his bald head and leaned forward on his desk. "Do you want to tell me where the hell you were yesterday?"

"Sir?" She stood with her hands folded carefully behind her back.

"I came looking for you at your desk, but you weren't there. Then Sergeant Harcourt gets a call this morning from a superintendent at the Oregon State Penitentiary, who says Archer French is acting up, and the next time we send an officer down to interview him, he'd prefer a few days' notice so they can properly prepare."

"I had to pretend I knew what he was talking about," Stan cut in. "Made me look like a damn fool."

"Chief, this is on me," Irving said before Brett could speak up. "I sent her down there."

"We were hoping to get some information from him about the Andress and Danforth cases," Brett added.

Stan snorted and shifted in his chair, jabbing his pointy elbows into the armrests. "I want the record to show I had no idea any of this was going on. No one ran anything by me."

Henry rolled his eyes. "Yes, Stan, you've made that quite clear. But it's your job to keep tabs on your detectives, isn't it? To know what they're doing and how an investigation is proceeding?"

Stan's mouth hinged open, then he sputtered and fumbled his hands over his pockets until he found a pack of gum. He unwrapped another piece and added it to the one already in his mouth.

Henry shifted his gaze to Brett. "Unless French suddenly turned Houdini, he's clearly not a person of interest."

"No," she said. "But he and Nathan Andress recently started writing letters back and forth, and we think French may have given Nathan information pertinent to our case."

Henry studied her a moment and tugged his mustache. "I'm afraid I don't understand. What information can French possibly have that would get two men killed?"

"He knows who killed my sister."

Silence filled the room, then Henry leaned back with a heavy sigh, flicking his gaze to the ceiling. "For the love of saints and hell's angels, Brett. Are you trying to get yourself fired?"

"Sir, I—"

"The Margot Buchanan case is closed," he said. "The man who killed her is in prison. I brought you on to this team to work new cases, not resurrect old ones."

"French says he didn't kill Margot."

Brett was tired of saying it, tired of defending a criminal, a man who had killed other women, even if he hadn't killed her sister. She didn't want to be on his side or grant him any favors. She wanted him to rot in his prison cell, and she wanted to never have to think about him or speak his name for as long as she lived. But Margot's killer still roamed free. Brett was more certain of this now after talking with French, and she wouldn't stop pushing for answers, even if it meant using French to get what she wanted.

She explained to Henry about the phone call from Nathan she got the day before his death, about her and Irving's working theory that Nathan and Zach's cases were related, that they might have known something about what happened to Margot, and that Danny seemed to be at the center of it all. To prove all of this, they needed to know what Archer French had written in his letters to Nathan.

Stan interrupted her explanation with a snorting laugh, the wad of gum nearly flying out of his mouth. "You can't be serious. I told you already, Danny has nothing to do with Nathan or Zach. This is a wild goose chase, and we all know it. That bastard French killed Margot, and now he's screwing with the both of you just for shits and giggles."

"How would you know, Stan?" Irving asked quietly.

"Excuse me?" Stan stopped chewing. His cheeks flamed bright red.

"Your initial investigation wasn't exactly..." Irving took a moment, trying to choose his words carefully. "Well, I'm sorry to say it, but it wasn't exactly thorough."

"Are you kidding me with this bullshit?" Spit flew from his mouth. "I worked my ass off for that case."

"And yet you let more than a decade go by without making any arrests."

Stan rose from the chair and jabbed a finger across Henry's desk. "You're just going to let him sit there and talk to me like that?" Then he turned his anger on Irving. "After everything I've done for you? I've had your back since the beginning, and now you're going to climb up on some goddamn high horse and criticize me."

"Stan, come on, don't overreact," Irving said. "It was a tough case."

"Damn right, it was a tough case."

"But you let a few things slide, that's all I'm saying, and it wouldn't hurt to go back through and take a closer look to make sure we didn't miss anything."

Stan's eyes narrowed to thin slits. He made smacking sounds with his gum as he talked, his jaw working faster with each word. "I can't fucking believe this. You've had over a decade to revisit the Buchanan case if you'd really wanted to, and as many years to undercut me with your own investigation. If you really thought I fucked up that case, why wait until now to say something, huh? What's changed?" His eyes flicked to Brett, and his lip curled in disgust. "A few months? That's all it takes for you to turn traitor?"

"Stan," Irving said, anger rising in his voice.

But Stan brushed him aside. "I hope you're at least getting something from her in return."

The innuendo settled ugly between them, but before Brett or Irving or anyone could respond, Stan stormed out. Over his shoulder, he said, "Don't expect any more favors from me, Irv. You made your bed, now you're gonna lie in it."

After he was gone, Henry exhaled loudly and smoothed his hand over his head again. "Are you sure about this? You don't have any other leads?"

"This is the best we have," Irving said.

"You know Danny's working with us on another case, right?" Henry asked.

"Stan told us."

Henry scratched his mustache and cursed quietly under his breath. "Right. Okay. Do whatever it is you need to do to get these cases closed. I'm sick and tired of hearing about them. I'll tell our guys in Danny's crew to keep their eyes and ears open. If they hear anything interesting, you'll be the first to know."

Irving stood to leave.

"Brett, hang back, please," Henry said.

Irving hesitated in the doorway, but Henry dismissed him with a wave.

"Close the door," Henry said after he left.

Brett did as she was told.

She stood in front of Henry's desk, waiting for him to say something. Trixie still sat on the floor next to her feet. She was chewing her tail.

Henry studied Brett for several seconds, his expression that of a disappointed father. After what felt like a painfully long amount of time, he leaned his hands on the desk. "Do you know why I was looking for you yesterday?"

"No, sir."

"You were gone quite a while. What? Ten, twelve hours? It's a long drive to Salem and back."

She nodded but said nothing.

"Did you even think about your grandmother before you left?"

"Sir?" The change in topic surprised her. She thought she was going to get a lecture about her poor use of time, or wasting department resources, or going over her supervisor's head to investigate a shaky lead, not get his thoughts on her personal life.

"You left her alone all day," he said.

"She's an adult."

"She called me a panic. She said you were missing, that she hadn't seen you in hours and she had no idea where you were. She wanted me to send out a search party."

Brett stared down at Trixie. The dog looked up at her with worried eyes. Brett shifted her gaze back to Henry. "I told her where I was going before I left."

"How bad is it?" Henry asked.

When she didn't answer, he said, "I know dementia when I see it, Brett. I'm not stupid." He sighed and leaned back in his chair. "Do you know why I offered you a detective position here?"

Brett didn't want to answer. She could see where this was headed, but he was waiting for her to say something, so she did. "I assume it's because you needed another detective, and I'm a damn good cop with a lot to offer this department."

"I offered you this position because I knew it was the only way you'd agree to living in Crestwood. You wouldn't move here without a job, but, of course, you wouldn't take just any job. From the way your grandmother talks about you, I knew you'd only say yes to a detective spot, so I gave you a detective spot. Honestly, no, we don't need another detective. But it's such a small thing, a title that means very little. I just needed to get you here." His chair creaked as he shifted slightly forward. "Anita needs someone looking after her. That someone should be you."

Brett's mouth went dry. "I am looking after her."

"Are you?" He tilted his head. The fluorescent lights glinted off the sweat of his brow. His smile was cutting as he spread his hands over his desk again and said, "Look, I get that you want to make a good impression here. I can appreciate that. But we have a lot of good officers doing a lot of good work. What I need from you is to make sure Anita is safe. And you can't do that if you're running all over the place, leaving her alone at the house for hours on end."

Brett heard Henry's words as an incessant hum at the back of her head. She was doing the best she could with her grandmother. She was trying. Sure, there'd been a few hiccups, but she was handling it. And nothing terrible had happened. Yet.

"Eli told me he picked Anita up off the side of the highway the other day." Henry's voice burst into her thoughts again. "He said she almost got herself killed out there."

Brett silently cursed Eli for telling Henry when she'd specifically asked him not to.

"You should have come told me the minute something like that happened."

"She wasn't hurt."

"Yeah, thanks to Eli." Henry sighed. "Brett, let me help. I want to help."

"How?" She heard the anger rising in her voice but did nothing to tame it. At her feet, Trixie whined. "Amma doesn't think there's anything wrong with her. She refuses to see a doctor. She won't even let me help her. But if you think you can do something different, please, do it. I'd love to see what you come up with."

"I care about your grandmother, Brett," Henry said, matching her tone. "Frank was like a father to me, you understand? He'd kill me if he knew I wasn't looking after her the way he would. He'd want both of us to be doing whatever we could to take care of her and make sure she's happy and safe. Right now, I think that the best thing would be for you to be home at a reasonable time so you can keep an eye on things. I think you need to start setting up a routine that she can rely on."

"I'm already doing that. She knows where I am at all times and when I'm coming back. She knows how to find me if she needs me. I can work my cases and take care of her. I've been doing it for the last four months without any problems."

He lifted his eyebrows. "After what happened yesterday, I'm not sure that's true anymore. There's no way you can look after Anita properly and be three hundred miles away from her." He shuffled some paperwork and cleared his throat. "Irving can handle these murder investigations just fine without you. I want you on burglaries, warrants, typing up reports. Basically, I want you at your desk, and when you're not at your desk, I want you at home."

"You can't be serious." Just when she was getting close to finding answers, he was benching her. "Yesterday was a fluke, a one-time trip."

He stiffened in his chair, then folded his hands on his desk. "I think the words you're looking for are 'yes' and 'sir.'" He softened again, rounding his shoulders into a slight hunch, his tone changing too as if he was offering her a favor. "Listen, why don't you go ahead and take the rest of today off, too, okay? Go home early. We've got all the shift coverage we need for tonight."

A glance at her watch told her it was barely three o'clock. Her shift didn't end until six, which was plenty of time to help Irving figure out this Archer French situation. She started to argue, but Henry cut her off with a sweep of his hand and pointed at the door.

"Thank you, Detective," he said, his voice edged with disdain. "I appreciate your cooperation. Oh, and get that dog out of my precinct, please. She stinks."

CHAPTER 32

Brett drove circles around town for an hour looking for Jimmy, his car, any sign of him. Trixie rode in the passenger seat with her head hanging out the open window, nose twitching the air, but she proved useless as a search dog.

Before leaving the station, Brett had filled Irving in on her conversation with Archer French the day before, and he'd promised to handle it. She'd hovered at his desk a few more minutes while he called the prison. After several 'yeahs' and 'uh-huhs' and 'okay, thanks,' he hung up. "Apparently, the superintendent has gone home for the day. They'll have him call me first thing tomorrow morning."

So that was that. French wasn't saying a damn thing until he got his extra yard time, which might never happen if they couldn't convince the superintendent to bend the rules.

Frustrated and not ready to go home, Brett drove slowly through the industrial part of town, double-checking alleyways and open warehouse doors. At some point, she called Eli on the radio. He told her he hadn't found Jimmy yet, but he was still keeping an eye out. "He'll turn up," he said, trying to sound reassuring.

She'd looked everywhere she could think to look. Eli was looking, too. There really wasn't anything else she could do for Jimmy but wait and hope he turned up soon with a damn good explanation for where he'd been the past two days.

After stopping by the grocery store for candy and dog treats, Brett finally went home. Pistol greeted her and Trixie at the door with excited barks and a wagging tail. She gave each dog a biscuit, and they took off, chasing circles around each other.

Amma appeared in the kitchen doorway, looking flustered. "Whose dogs are these?" She twisted her fingers and fretted as the dogs darted through her legs. "You know your sister's allergic." Then she said, "You're home early."

"Amma, did you talk to Henry yesterday?"

She thought a minute, then nodded. "Yes, I think so."

Pistol ran into the kitchen, scratched at the french door, then returned to the living room and pleaded up at Brett.

"When was the last time you let him outside?" Brett asked.

"Outside?" Amma looked baffled. "Won't they run away?"

Brett went into the kitchen and opened the back door. Trixie and Pistol darted down the porch steps. They peed in the grass, then began to sniff. Brett called the dogs, and they followed her to the beach. They stuck close, wandering a few feet away from her to inspect a patch of grass or nose a broken clamshell, before returning with gentle bumps against her leg.

She walked with the dogs for almost an hour. Wind buffeted from the bay, tugging on her hair. Wisps of clouds darkened to black, gathering in ever thicker layers over the water, swirling more menacing each minute. Her pace quickened as the wind grew fiercer and colder. She whistled for the dogs to hurry. The first raindrops started to fall as they reached the house.

The dogs were quite a bit calmer now. Brett gave Trixie a quick bath to get the worst of the mud off her fur. She inspected her for other injuries besides the cut on her nose but found none. After that, she scooped food into two bowls. She'd bought a small bag of kibble for Pistol the day after she brought the dog home, but if she was going to be taking care of Trixie, too, she'd need to get more food tomorrow. She hoped Jimmy would be back by then.

Brett was scrubbing a pile of dirty dishes when the doorbell rang. The dogs started to bark and howl. Brett wiped her hands on a towel. The doorbell rang a second time, and the dogs barked louder. A thump sounded from upstairs, where Amma had retreated after dinner.

"I got it!" Brett pushed the dogs back with her foot as she cracked open the front door.

"Trick-or-treat!" Three young children grinned at her from behind plastic masks and face paint. They held up pillowcases and stared at her empty hands.

"Oh. Right. One second."

She grabbed the bowl of candy sitting on the table near the door and tossed handfuls into each pillowcase. Once they were gone, she shut the front door and looked down to find the dogs staring at her expectantly.

"What?"

Trixie wagged her tail. Pistol cocked his head to one side, which exaggerated his already crooked ear.

There was another thump from upstairs and a scraping sound.

Brett glanced at the ceiling. "Amma?"

More scraping, like furniture was being moved, then a clattering sound, like something had spilled. Brett bounded up the stairs, the dogs at her heels. The hatch to the attic was open, the ladder hanging down.

"Amma? Are you up there?" Brett climbed up, hoping she wouldn't find Amma with the BB gun again. She'd hidden it in her grandfather's office after the last time.

"Yes, dear, I'm fine. I'm sorry about all the noise. I was feeling nostalgic. I wanted to look at some old pictures, but there are just so many boxes up here. I don't know what Frank was thinking, keeping all this stuff when he knew I wouldn't be able to do a damn thing with it after he was gone." Amma hardly ever cursed.

Brett poked her head into the attic. Amma sat on the floor in a mess of photographs and old cameras. It was the same mess Brett had made the day they found Nathan's body on the beach. She hadn't had a chance to climb back up here and finish putting it all away. Amma picked up a photograph and smiled at it. Her cheeks were damp with tears.

"Are you all right? Are you hurt?" Brett clambered closer to Amma.

She brushed her hand over her cheeks. "Oh, I'm fine. Just remembering. Look." She held the picture out for Brett. "Wasn't your mother beautiful?"

It was a photograph of her parents' wedding. Her mother in a satin dress with long sleeves and a scalloped collar. Her father in a simple, three-piece suit. Amma and Pop stood on either side of them. Her mother looked happy. Her father did, too. It was hard for Brett to remember her parents being anything but shattered. Margot's death had laid waste to their lives and their marriage. Whatever love they'd had for each other in the beginning had not been enough to keep them from falling apart after Margot died. And whatever love they'd had for Brett had not been enough, either, apparently. Her father abandoned his family to start a new one, not even a year after Margot's murder. Her mother had gotten drunk and crashed her car into a highway barrier five years later, preferring her own death to a life without her eldest daughter. Brett was nineteen when she buried her mother. Amma and Pop had been at her side then, too, the same way they'd been at her side when Margot died. Amma stoic and straight-backed, dabbing at her silent tears with a handkerchief. Pop had broken, though, collapsing onto a chair as his only daughter was lowered into the earth. He wept loudly, his face lifted to the clouds, and Brett had been embarrassed by his outburst. Now she understood how much courage it must have taken to express his feelings so openly.

Amma stared at the wedding photograph for another few seconds, her eyes clouded with sorrow. She dropped it back into the box and said, "Time flies over us, but leaves its shadow behind." Her smile was thin and trembling. "Nathanial Hawthorne said that, I think."

They sat a few more minutes together, quietly looking through the rest of the photographs. Amma offered commentary on a few.

"This was your grandfather's first boat."

"That's your second cousin Esmerelda. She was a lovely ballet dancer when she was young."

"I think this was when your grandfather and I went to Paris. Yes, look, right there, you can see the Eiffel Tower in the background."

"Oh, and this was our Grand Canyon trip. I was pregnant with your mother, and your grandfather didn't get enough ice for the cooler, and all our food spoiled, and I threw up because of the smell." She laughed. "I was miserable the entire time, but you know, looking back on it, I can't help but think, it wasn't so bad. We were so young and in love and your grandfather—" She pressed her hand to her chest in a swoon. "So handsome, that man."

Her smile faded. "You know what's funny. I can't remember where I put my car keys some mornings, or what that thingy in the kitchen is called with the metal and the handle and the sharp edges that slivers the cheese. I wake up sometimes in the middle of the night, thinking Frank is in bed next to me. I can feel the weight of him, but when I slide my hand over the sheet, it's cold and flat. I forget some days that he's dead. But then I come up here, and I see these pictures, and it's like all of this happened just yesterday. I remember it so vividly."

Brett flipped through a stack of photos featuring Pop and his fishing buddies. She recognized a younger Henry Bascom among the faces, bald even back then, but his mustache was dark, and he was about twenty pounds skinnier. Her humiliation at his earlier reprimand returned, and she shoved the picture aside.

Amma picked it up and her smile widened again. "Look at Henry. So young here." Her gaze shifted to Brett. "Henry knows about me, doesn't he? About my..." She tapped a finger to her temple.

Brett nodded. "I'm sorry, Amma. I didn't tell him."

"Henry's a smart man," she said, that soft smile still tugging on her lips. "Maybe it will be better for you. For me, too. Ever since Frank died, Henry's tried to be there for me. He checks in on me, makes sure I have what I need and that I'm not lonely. Even when I push him away, he keeps coming back. I think it's good that he knows. Good for everyone."

Dust drifted through the spray of light cast by the bare bulb hanging overhead.

"Are you lonely, Amma?" Brett asked.

"Not anymore, I'm not." Amma brushed her thumb over Brett's cheek. Then she scooped up another stack of pictures and flipped through them before returning them to the box.

She looked happy reminiscing, surrounded by old memories and pictures of people she had cared deeply about for many years, people who were long gone. Brett couldn't imagine what it must be like for her, how terrifying to have the memories of your life stutter and disappear, to watch the faces of your loved ones fade into blankness, to lose the very things which defined your sense of self. To grasp for some part of who you used to be, only to find the air in front of you empty. Brett was still angry with Henry, but maybe he wasn't wrong. What Amma needed most was support from the people she loved. What she needed were people she could count on to be there for her, people who would show up when she was no longer able to show up for herself.

"Oh, here's one of you," Amma said, growing excited. "This looks like it was taken outside of the cannery. I wonder if Frank even knew you were there."

Brett took the picture from her and studied it. Pop had clearly been trying to take a picture of a fishing trawler. The way the sun glinted off the rigging made the whole thing feel magical. It could have been a postcard. *Wish You Were Here.* But it was a figure near the right edge that Amma was pointing to.

A young woman ran past the boat with her back to the camera. She held her hands away from her body like she was sweeping the wind toward her. One foot was lifted, the photographer caught her mid-step. Her blond hair blew sideways in the wind. A bit of yarn was braided through one side. The light on her was golden, too, her skin kissed by a sinking copper sun. She wore a sleeveless sundress that looked white in this picture, but Brett knew it was yellow, pale lemon with orange and red flowers dotted all over it.

"This isn't me." Her finger stroked the blond tresses.

"Are you sure?" Amma took the picture back and held it close to her face, blinking and squinting. "I could swear it's you. Oh, no, you're right." She lowered the picture again. Sadness clouded her eyes. "Do you remember how Pop took you girls to see that James Bond movie three times that summer?"

Brett nodded, even though the memory was muddled for her, the edges blurred by time. She wondered if this was what it was like for Amma when she struggled to remember.

"You were always eating ice cream. I remember that. Your mouth and fingers were so sticky with sugar. And Margot's bikini. That pretty emerald green that matched her eyes. Her hair was so long, she was always sitting on it." A smile teased the corners of her mouth then vanished as her tone shifted, turning bleak. "I remember other things, too. Things that aren't so pleasant. Like the look on your mother's face when they came and told us the news. Sometimes I wish I could choose what to forget and what to hold on to." A shudder ran through Amma's shoulders. "Your father blamed Frank and me for what happened. He said we let you girls run wild, that it was our responsibility to set boundaries. But you were so happy doing what you wanted to do, making your own rules. Now that I've had some time to think about it, though, I worry he might have been right. You can't let girls run free like that and not expect trouble."

She handed the photograph back to Brett. "You keep it. It's a nice picture of her."

Amma began to gather the rest of the photographs into a pile.

"I can clean this up later," Brett said, but Amma insisted.

Once everything was returned to the box, Amma rocked back on her heels and said, "You know, it's okay to want more for your life, Brett. It's okay to move on. It's not good for you to be always reliving the past, regretting a tragedy over which you had absolutely no control. You were a child. You're not responsible for her death."

A lump formed in Brett's throat as she stared at the picture of her sister, frozen forever in this snapshot of a moment. "There's still so much I don't understand about what happened that summer, Amma. I need answers."

"And will that change anything? Will getting those answers finally make you happy?"

Before Brett could respond, the doorbell rang.

Amma swiveled her head toward the sound.

"More trick-or-treaters," Brett reassured her.

Amma smiled. "Well, I guess we should go down there and give them something sweet before they egg the house."

Brett helped Amma out of the attic, then folded the ladder and closed the hatch.

As they went downstairs, she slipped the photograph of Margot into her back pocket.

———————

Brett knew when she pulled into Irving's driveway that it was too late to drop in on him like this, but she wouldn't be able to sleep until she knew for sure. She would have come earlier, except Amma insisted on passing out candy to trick-or-treaters, and Brett couldn't leave her alone for fear she'd end up giving out raisins or thumbtacks instead. By the time their doorbell stopped ringing, it was almost 10:00 PM. Brett got Amma settled in bed, then grabbed her keys and jacket and drove across town.

Irving answered the door wrapped in a plush navy blue bathrobe, wearing a pair of duck slippers on his feet. He blinked at her, clearly baffled as to why she'd be standing on his front porch this late at night.

"Trick-or-treat?" She smiled nervously.

"You do know what time it is, right?"

From inside the house, a woman's voice called out, "Irv? Who is it?"

"No one. Go back to bed, sweetheart." He started to close the front door. "Goodnight, Brett. I'll see you at the office tomorrow."

"Irving, wait." She stuck her foot in the gap. "Amma and I found something in the attic tonight."

She pulled the picture from her pocket and handed it to him. He frowned, tilting it to catch the light.

"It's Margot," Brett explained. "That's the same dress she was wearing the day she went missing."

CHAPTER 33

Irving shook his head, still frowning at the picture Brett had handed him. "I'm not sure I understand."

"Look at the date on the back."

He turned it over. Stamped on the white backing was a date. September 14, 1964. One month after Margot was found dead. It was the date the photograph had been developed, not the date it had been taken. But Brett remembered Margot buying the dress she wore in the picture earlier that summer before they drove up to Amma and Pop's. She found it on clearance, but even then, to be able to afford it, she'd had to do extra chores and babysit the neighbor's kid a couple of times. She'd had a big fight with Dad over it because the skirt was too short, and there were no sleeves, just thin straps. But she'd worn it anyway, partly, Brett thought, to spite him. Pop had taken this picture that same summer, and Brett was confident, the very day Margot went missing. The dress and the sandals, the shimmering charm bracelet on her right hand, and the pink and green yarn braided into a chunk of her hair. Brett had braided that yarn for her the day she went missing. On the dock, the morning sun hot against their tanned skin, she'd twisted the threads up with

Margot's golden tresses. In turn, Margot had twisted yellow and blue into Brett's brown hair.

Her fingers lifted, twirling the hair near her temple. "This photograph was taken the day she went missing. I'm sure of it."

Irving turned the picture back over to study the image of Margot on the pier. "The sun's starting to set," he said, and his expression changed as he realized what it meant for the case. "She went missing later than we thought."

Brett nodded. All this time, she thought she'd been the last one to see Margot when she left Amma and Pop's house around ten. All this time, the police investigated under the assumption that Margot went into the woods sometime in the morning. But here was proof she had still been in town, alive and well, much later in the afternoon.

"Why didn't your grandfather say anything about seeing her back then?" Irving asked.

"I don't think he even noticed her when he took the picture. His focus wasn't on her. She must have darted by right as he was snapping the shot."

"But when he developed these, he must have noticed her then, in the background. He should have brought this to our attention."

Brett shook her head. She couldn't speak for her grandfather, and he wasn't here to explain himself. "We know now, though, and now we can take another look at the interviews, right? The alibis. You asked people where they were in the morning, didn't you?"

"Of course we did." He sounded annoyed that she would even ask.

"Who was unaccounted for?"

"Just Danny."

"Who else did you interview?"

Irving thought a moment, a frown tugging on his lips. "We didn't have a lot of leads, but Stan did talk to a few kids who'd been hanging out with your sister that summer. Let's see. Eli, for one."

"Our Eli?" Brett interrupted, her cheeks warming when she said it. "Officer Miller, I mean."

He nodded. "And Marshall Trudeau. Stan talked to both of them, briefly."

"He told me he was in love with her," Brett said, and then clarified, "Marshall did. The other night at the Pickled Onion. But I don't remember seeing his interview in the file."

Irving pursed his lips, and she realized her mistake telling him she'd seen the file when she shouldn't have, but a lecture from Irving was the least of her worries right now.

He shook his head, apparently deciding to let it go. "The boys didn't know anything," he said. "Danny told us to take a closer look at them. He said Margot had been spending a lot of time with them that summer. But Eli's father was a city councilman on the fast track to becoming mayor. And Marshall's father owned half the property in this town. They threatened to bog us down in red tape if we so much as hinted their boys were persons of interest. So, Stan, he did what he could. I had barely any interview experience, seeing I was still so new to the job, but he let me sit in. Watch and learn, he said. We talked to Marshall and Eli with lawyers in the room, which meant Stan didn't get much from them. I guess whatever he got, he didn't think it was worth writing down." He thought a minute, then continued, "If I remember right, Marshall was working at the country club pool as a lifeguard. Eli said he was playing golf with his father all morning. They had airtight alibis. Everyone did."

"Except Danny," Brett said.

He nodded. "Except Danny."

"But now we know Margot didn't go missing until later that day. Which changes everything, doesn't it? Who might have had the opportunity? I know, I'm rushing ahead, I just want to get a jump on this while we have the chance."

"Brett, it's late." Irving handed the picture back to her with an apologetic look, then glanced over his shoulder as if listening for his wife.

"Yes, but—"

"Nothing's going to get done tonight. Go home and get some sleep. Bring the picture with you to the office tomorrow, and we'll figure out what to do next." He stepped back into his house and closed the door.

The lock clicked. The porch light snapped off, and Brett was left standing in the dark.

———————————

It was nearing midnight, and downtown Crestwood was quiet. The kids who had come out for trick-or-treating earlier had filled their bags with candy and all gone home. Main Street was empty. Brett's Beetle was the only car along the entire mile-long stretch.

As she drew close to the place where Zach Danforth had lain dying, she slowed. Over the past few days, a memorial had appeared on the sidewalk. People had left the usual things, candles and flowers, stuffed animals and balloons, and less usual things like guitar picks, a Clash poster, and a bong. Posters with Zach's face and words like, "We Miss You," "RIP Zach," "Gone but not Forgotten," hung on lampposts and the walls of nearby buildings.

The shadows near the memorial shifted, and two figures separated from the dark. One kicked over an unlit candle, bouncing it into the street. Another tore down a poster and ripped it to pieces. Brett parked and approached the girls quietly. Elizabeth wore her hair in a long braid down her back. June had on a knit cap, but it sat crooked on her head, her blond hair jutting out at crude angles. They were too focused on their frenzied destruction to notice her. Elizabeth picked up a teddy bear and tried to tear off its head, but the stitching stayed. She dropped it onto the sidewalk and ground the heel of her boot into the soft stuffing instead.

Brett cleared her throat.

The girls were startled by her sudden appearance. Instantly, their tough acts vanished. They cowered together in the dark.

"Do your parents know you're out this late?" Brett asked.

Elizabeth and June exchanged a look.

"I'll take that as a no. Okay, come on, let's get you home." She guided them to her car.

The girls huddled in the backseat and spoke in whispers too quiet for Brett to hear what they were saying. She glanced in the rearview mirror. Elizabeth glared back at her and slouched low in the seat. Between the chaos of Zach's murder on Saturday, the ensuing investigation, and worrying over Jimmy's sudden disappearance, Brett realized she hadn't had a chance to check in with Elizabeth. She hadn't yet told her about finding the underwear in Zach's bedroom, confirming he had been the one who attacked her at the party, though there wasn't much else Brett could do for her now that Zach was dead.

"It's okay to be angry," she said, darting her gaze between Elizabeth in the backseat and the road ahead. "For a little while, it's okay to let yourself be mad. You have every right. But don't let him ruin the rest of your life, okay? Don't let him have that power over you forever."

Elizabeth turned her face to the window. Orange light from street lamps sputtered through the glass, twisting shadows across her pale cheeks. June shifted closer to her friend, slipping her arm through Elizabeth's elbow.

Probably Brett was saying the exact wrong thing, but she didn't care. The last thing she wanted was for Elizabeth to live the rest of her life defined by one single, terrible moment at a high school party. She didn't want the pain Zach had inflicted on her to be a scar that never faded. Life was expansive, days piled on top of days, and Elizabeth was young. She had plenty of time to become someone greater than the worst moment of her life.

"You don't even have to think about him ever again if you don't want to," Brett said.

Elizabeth's gaze again found hers in the mirror. "Did you find out who killed him?"

"Not yet. We're still narrowing down suspects."

"Well, when you finally do figure it out, thank whoever did it for me, okay?" Her voice was flat. She lowered her head against the seat and closed her eyes.

June gave Elizabeth a worried look, then she faced forward, her expression stern. When Brett caught her gaze in the mirror, June tensed her jaw, anger evident in the flush of her cheeks.

"We're not apologizing for wrecking his stupid memorial," she said.

Brett drove through an empty intersection. "I never asked you to."

———————————

Brett dropped June off first, then drove to Elizabeth's house. As soon as she pulled the car into the driveway, the front door opened and Marshall rushed out. Elizabeth got out of the car and slouched up the walkway. Marshall hugged her, then pulled away. There was anger in his voice when he said, "I thought you were spending the night at June's."

He looked over Elizabeth's shoulder to where Brett was getting out of the car. "Is everything okay?" Then he turned to his daughter. "What did you do? Are you in trouble?"

"Everything's fine," Brett said. "I found her and June hanging out downtown and offered them a ride home."

"Thank you." Marshall hugged Elizabeth again and pushed her toward the house. "Go to your room."

When Elizabeth was inside, Marshall turned back to Brett. "I don't know what I'm going to do with her." He exhaled loudly and rubbed his temples. The words were obviously difficult for him to say, like he was trying to figure out how everything had come apart for his family like this, so quickly, without warning. "Ever since that boy, she's changed, you know? This whole thing has changed her, and I don't know how to fix it. How to fix her."

"I'm not sure you can."

He squinted at the sky. The rain had stopped, but the clouds were still layered thick. No stars were visible beyond the darkness churning.

"All you can do is be there for her," Brett said. "Make sure she has someone in her life she can trust. Someone she can count on. She'll find her way through."

He nodded and offered her a faint smile. "Thanks for bringing her home."

He turned to go back inside, but she stopped him. "Marshall? Can I ask you something?"

"About the cannery sale? Sorry, things have been so hectic." He laughed nervously. "Well, you know how it is. I'll have a listing ready for you to look over next week, I hope. I mean, that's if you still want me to handle the sale?"

"Oh, no." Brett had forgotten about the cannery. "I mean, yes, that's fine, you can still handle the sale, but no, what I wanted to ask you isn't about the cannery. It's about Margot."

His expression tightened. He twisted his wedding band around his finger. "Margot?"

"Yes. I was digging around in Amma's attic tonight, and I uncovered some new information. About what time she went missing."

He flicked his eyes toward the house, then back at her. "Okay."

He kept twisting his wedding band.

"It seems she went missing later than we thought, sometime in the early evening rather than in the morning. Do you remember where you were that afternoon? What you were doing?"

He swallowed hard and squinted at his feet. His toe scraped against the asphalt as he thought for a second, then he lifted his face again and frowned. "The afternoon, huh? I guess, I mean, it was so long ago, but that summer I worked a lot. I was a lifeguard and swim instructor at the country club in the mornings. Then most afternoons, I worked with Eli as a caddy on the golf course, or we went and grabbed burgers and hung out on the beach or at the batting cages, or we'd go out to the drive-in theater. I guess that's probably where I was that day, too. On the golf course." He swept his hand through his hair and shook his head. "But like I said, it was a long time ago."

Brett glanced at the house. "Is Clara home?"

"She's asleep." His words were clipped short, and he took a step back toward the house, moving away from her, drawing their conversation to a close. "Look, I should go back inside. Check to make sure Elizabeth's okay. But, um, but thanks again for bringing her home. I'm sorry if she was any trouble."

"No trouble at all."

Marshall disappeared inside the house. In the front window, a curtain twitched, and a shadow fluttered as someone moved away from the glass.

Chapter 34

"Clara." Marshall's hushed voice reached for her in the dark. "What are we going to do? We can't leave him out there."

She rolled toward him and settled her hand on his chest. His heart was beating as fast as if he'd just come back from a run.

She had been expecting this conversation. Waiting for it ever since Brett dropped Elizabeth off at the house, ever since Marshall stood on the porch talking to her, pretending everything was fine when nothing was.

When the car first pulled into the driveway, Marshall nearly had a heart attack. Wide-eyed with panic, he'd turned to Clara, and she'd done her best to reassure him. Stay calm. Act normal. Everything will be fine. He shook his head because he didn't know what normal was anymore, not after what they'd done. What she'd made him do. They don't know, she'd told him. If they knew, it would be more than Brett pulling up in her ruby red Beetle. It would be squads of lights and sirens and men in black boots with guns. If they knew, their daughter wouldn't be climbing out of the back of the car, acting like nothing was wrong.

Clara had almost gone outside to deal with Elizabeth herself, couldn't believe that, once again, her daughter had broken the rules and found herself in trouble. But she'd stopped herself at the door and turned to Marshall instead. She wiped the sweat from his brow, straightened his shirt, and sent him out to talk to Brett because, for them to survive this, she needed him to see how easy it was to lie.

In the dark, his hand found hers, clutching tight, as if she was the buoy that could save him from drowning.

"We have to let him go," he said. "We have to go to the police and apologize and say we made a mistake. They'll go easy on us. We haven't done anything, we haven't—" He choked on the rest of it, his failed attempts to rationalize.

Because up to this point, what had they really done wrong? Besides attacking a man, kidnapping him, keeping him locked in an abandoned hunting cabin in the middle of the forest—the sarcastic voice in her head wouldn't shut up. On the other hand, they'd left him with water and a baloney sandwich and a blanket and a bucket to shit in, and up to this point, they could still take it all back. Couldn't they? They could explain away their actions as panic, as fear, as temporary insanity. Marshall thought they could.

He didn't know the rest of the story, the house of lies Clara had built, how quickly it could all come crashing down around them. She didn't know how much Jimmy knew, only that it was enough to be dangerous. He was the crack in the foundation that could ruin everything.

She should have taken care of him already. The longer they waited, the more likely someone would find him. But she didn't want to do it in front of Marshall. Killing would break him, she knew, in a way it wouldn't—hadn't—broken her. She had needed Marshall's help to carry Jimmy out of the house, though, and stuff him in the trunk of his own car. Marshall had driven the family sedan, and she'd driven Jimmy's car, ten miles through town, to an old hunting cabin near Lake Chastain that Clara knew hadn't been used in years. That damn dog howled in her ear the whole way. When they got there, they dragged the still unconscious man inside the cabin and dumped him on the floor, padlocking the door behind them. The dog escaped from the car during the shuffle. She'd tried to grab it, but the dog had wriggled free of its collar and disappeared into the trees in a white flash of fur. *Let her go*, Marshall had said. They dumped Jimmy's car on an overgrown fire road and drove back to the house together.

She had planned to come back later without Marshall to do what needed to be done to keep them safe. Except Marshall hadn't left her side in the past twenty-four hours, since they got back from the hunting cabin. He clung to her, worrying and fretting. She tried to get him to go into the office, to act normal, but he gestured to his sweat-drenched shirt—*Does this look normal to you?*

In front of Elizabeth, he plastered on a fake smile and did his best to act like nothing was wrong. As soon as Elizabeth left for school, he started panicking again, desperate for some solution other than the most obvious one.

She had hoped he would make peace with the situation on his own, come to accept the reality of what must be done, and allow her to do it. Instead, he kept circling around the idea that if they just let Jimmy go, everything could go back to the way it was before. But that wasn't how things like this worked, and they were running out of time.

"We have to kill him," she whispered the words, testing them, testing her husband, saying out loud what she had been hinting at, holding her breath to see how they landed.

Marshall stiffened and tried to pull his hand away from hers, but she grabbed hold, refusing to let go. He always had such a tender heart, so soft and kind.

A few months before they started dating, she and Marshall were paired up in anatomy class to dissect a rabbit. Marshall had picked up the scalpel first, thinking because he was the man, he should make the first cut, but he couldn't do it. So Clara had taken the knife from him, quietly, without anyone noticing. It was an easy thing. The scalpel felt good in her hand, natural. It was—if she could admit this—exciting to slit the rabbit from chin to groin, revealing the inner workings, the tissue, bones, and organs. He'd stared at her with a mix of admiration and gratitude and maybe a bit of fear. What she remembered most about that day, though, was thinking how easily she could fall in love with a boy like Marshall, a boy so gentle he couldn't even skin an already dead thing. She believed that a boy like that would keep her safe from hurt, too. How young she'd been, how naïve. The world was pain, she'd learned. So you do whatever it takes to survive. You make your skin tougher, you become the one doing the hurting, rather than being hurt, and you find your power in that.

Just as he'd needed her all those years ago, he needed her now, and she would be there for him, the way she'd always been there for him. She would do the hard things that needed doing so he didn't have to. Because she loved him, she would hold the knife.

"You don't have to do anything." She squeezed his hand. "I'll take care of it."

"You can't be serious." He rolled to face her.

"I'll handle everything. You don't have to worry or think about it. You just have to...you have to say nothing. That's it, that's all I'm asking. Keep quiet, pretend none of this ever happened. You never saw him. You never spoke to him. You don't know anything about it. Okay? That's all you have to do, say nothing, and we'll be okay."

He sat up, throwing the blankets off of them both. He curled over his knees and dug his hands into his hair. "I don't understand. Why can't we just go to the police?"

"We'll go to jail." She rubbed his back.

"If we tell them he attacked you, they'll understand."

"They won't," she said, adding quietly, "Marshall, please, think of Elizabeth."

He groaned and buried his face in his hands.

"We have to do this for her," she said. "Think of what will happen if she finds out. What will happen to her if we both go to jail. Think of how that will ruin her life. What she'll think of us, of you. We can't let that happen. We have to protect her. From all of this."

He shook his head harder, refusing to hear her. She understood his denial, his desire to wake up from what surely must be a nightmare—she really did understand. That didn't change the fact that they had only one option, a choice that had been made for them the second Jimmy stepped into their house.

He sucked in a deep breath and released it all at once. "We're good people. They know us. Eli." He twisted his head toward the phone. "Eli will know what to do."

Clara scrambled, clamping her hand over his, jerking him away from the phone. "No."

He looked at her, stunned. He got up from the bed and started to pace. "How can you be so nonchalant about this? You're talking about killing a man. Killing a person, Clara. A person. A living, breathing—I don't understand how you can sit there and be so calm about any of this."

She kneeled on the bed, watching him walk back and forth, his hands flinging the air.

"This isn't supposed to be happening. How did this happen?" He stopped and turned toward her, his whole body rigid. "Outside, on the porch tonight, Brett told me, she asked about Margot. She asked me where I was the day she went missing." He shook his head like he was trying to shake the words loose. "But it wasn't the same time that they asked me about before. She asked me where I was in the afternoon. Not in the morning. She didn't go missing in the morning." He grew quiet.

A sliver of moonlight came through the curtains where they didn't quite meet, and in his face, she saw the full gravity of the situation pressing on him. She watched as the pieces clicked together to form a new and terrible picture of his wife. The woman he'd trusted for his entire life, now someone he could barely stand to look at. She'd worked so hard to keep this monstrous part of herself hidden, and all for nothing. She was going to lose him anyway.

"What did you do?" He came toward her and grabbed her arms.

"You're hurting me."

"What did you do?" He shook her. "Tell me."

"Keep your voice down. You'll wake Elizabeth."

"What happened to Margot? Did you hurt her? Did you...?" He choked on the words and flung her away, returned to the window, pushed aside the curtain, and stood with his head pressed to the glass.

She rose from the bed and crossed to where he was standing. She touched his arm. He flinched away from her.

"You came to me that afternoon." His voice was a rasping whisper cutting the shadows. "You were covered in blood. You said it was yours. You said..." He took a slow breath. "You said you had tried to hurt yourself. That you were upset because I'd broken up with you. Because we'd... You couldn't stand the thought of living without me." He whirled and grabbed her wrist, lifting it to his face even though it was too dark to see much more than her pale skin. "You had cuts on your arms. I saw them. I cleaned them and taped you up. I wanted to take you to the hospital, but you wouldn't let me. You said you were too embarrassed. That you didn't want to get in trouble." His thumb ran over the soft underside of her arm, and he drew her closer, lifting one hand to cup her face. "What really happened? Please, tell me the truth. I won't be mad. I just want to know. I need to know."

"I did what I had to do to protect you," she said. "To protect us."

"What do you mean? What did you need to protect me from?"

"From her." Clara leaned into him, but even as she did, she felt him stiffen and pull away. "She didn't love you. Not like I did. Like I do. She was using you to get back at Danny and make him jealous. She was going to dump you. She told me. She was going to break your heart. I couldn't let her do that. You deserved better than her."

"Clara..." He held her at arm's length. "Please tell me you're not saying what I think you're saying."

For so long, she had pushed it all down, buried deep the sins of her childhood. A single moment that changed everything. Like what happened downstairs with Jimmy. Her hand finding something heavy to grip and swing.

Clara hadn't set out to kill Margot. She'd sent Margot a note, pretending to be Marshall, and lured her out to a secluded section of the forest. She hadn't known exactly what she would do when Margot showed up, only that she wanted to humiliate her, hurt her the way Clara had been hurt, make her feel the same pain she'd felt when she saw Marshall and Margot in the car kissing. She'd wanted Margot to suffer, that was all. Maybe shove her to the ground, tear her favorite dress to pieces, push her into the river, but then the rock was in her hand, and Margot was dead, and after, it made a perfect sort of sense. Killing Margot, the thing she should have been most ashamed of, the thing that should have ruined her, was the very thing that saved her.

What would her life have been like without Marshall? Who would she have become? She didn't like thinking about it. Losing Marshall meant losing Elizabeth and the short time she had with Lily, meant losing this home, this beautiful life, the security and safety of love. Losing Marshall meant losing everything. So no, she had no regrets about what happened in the woods that summer. She would do it again in a heartbeat.

"Please, try and understand."

He shook his head and backed away. "How could you do it? How could you?"

"It was an accident." Which was the truth, despite everything else that came after.

"I'm calling the police." He stepped toward the phone.

She blocked him. "Don't. Please let me explain."

He backed away again, his face etched in fear.

"I'm not going to hurt you. I would never..." Clara clutched her hands tight together, holding them against her stomach. "Everything I've done, I did for you. For Elizabeth. To keep you safe and make your life better."

"How did killing Margot make my life better?" His voice trembled, rage and sorrow mixing together.

"You came back to me," she said.

He made a sound like he was choking and reached his hand, grasping for something to hold on to. Clara tried to offer her support, but he pushed her away and fell onto the bed instead, bending double and clutching his stomach.

"This isn't what I wanted. I don't... I'm done, Clara. This is over. I'm calling the police, and we're going to tell them everything." He reached again for the phone.

"You're a part of this now, too," she said.

He held the receiver to his ear but didn't dial.

"You helped me get Jimmy into that shed."

"I did what you told me to."

"You did what you needed to protect this family."

"No." His fingers tightened around the phone.

"I didn't threaten you, did I? I didn't force you to do anything. You helped me because you knew it was the only choice we had."

"No, it wasn't. I don't know why I helped you. I shouldn't have, I..." Marshall shook his head like he was flinging away her words.

"But you did help me," she repeated. "And I think it's because a part of you has known all along. About Margot. About me."

"No," he repeated, his voice a harsh whisper.

"Part of you was relieved that she was gone, admit it."

"Stop."

"Relieved that you didn't have to deal with her drama anymore."

"Clara—"

"Go on then, call the police." She waved her hand in the air like she was giving up. "Tell them whatever you want. Tell them your version, and I'll tell them mine, and we'll see who they end up believing."

"Is that a threat?"

"Look at you, that's all I'm saying. Look at you and then look at me." She gestured first to him, a nearly six-foot-tall man in reasonably good shape, and then to herself, at five foot six inches, pudgy around the middle. "Who looks more capable of knocking out a full-grown man and carrying him out of here? Who looks more capable of violence?" She paused a moment to let her words sink in, then said, "We did this together. We did this to protect our family. Our daughter. If you call the police now, who will be there to look after Elizabeth when the dust finally settles?"

With a ragged sigh, he returned the receiver to its cradle and sank onto the bed.

Clara dropped to the carpet at his feet and clutched both of his knees. "Look at me, Marshall. Look at me."

He searched her face, his eyes darting and wild.

"We can figure this out, but we have to stick together," she said. "You have to trust me."

"I don't even know you." His anger lanced through her.

"Don't say that. You do know me. I'm still me. I haven't changed."

But that was the problem, wasn't it? If she was behaving abnormally, irrationally, he could perhaps forgive her. His gaze was one of revulsion like he couldn't stand the sight of her.

"What else don't I know?" he asked. "What else have you been keeping from me?"

She started to rise to her feet, but he grabbed both her wrists and held her down. Her heart fluttered at the strength in his grip, how easy it would be for him to break her.

"Zach," he said.

A single name, a questioning look.

"Did you kill him, too?"

She nodded, and a convulsion rocked him. He flung her away. She crawled back to him.

"You wanted me to." She grasped for his hands.

"What?" He reared away from her.

"At the party. When you hit him, you said you wanted to kill him."

"Those were just words. I didn't actually want him dead. I would have never..." He stood, for a moment towering over her, staring with obvious pity. Clara didn't want his pity; she wanted his loyalty. She wanted him to keep his promises. They were a family. For better or worse. He was supposed to be on her side, sheltering her, not pushing her out, turning his back on her when she needed him most.

"Do you not see the difference?" he said softly. "You can't kill people because you're angry or because they hurt you. Tell me you know that."

She glared up at him defiantly, saying nothing.

His eyes closed for a long moment. When he opened them again, Clara knew it was over.

"I want you to leave," he said.

"Don't do this," she said. "Please, don't send me away. I need you." She grabbed on to him. He peeled her fingers back and stepped out of reach.

"I love you, Marshall, and I know you love me. I know you do. Please don't do this. Don't ruin us."

She could apologize, and maybe that would fix everything. Except she wasn't sorry. She would never be sorry. Everything she'd ever done had been for him, for Elizabeth, their family. She wouldn't apologize for loving them the only way she'd known how—fiercely, with her whole being. It was easy to say you'd do anything for love, but she had done it. She had killed for them, and she would kill again in a heartbeat if she had to. Because of her, Marshall had a beautiful life and two beautiful daughters. Because of her, the monster who'd hurt Elizabeth had gotten exactly what he'd deserved. But now, the very things she'd done to keep them together were tearing them apart.

She sank to her knees on the floor and dug her fingers into the carpet, clinging to hope that Marshall would change his mind. He would return to her, choose her, accept her as she was, as she had always been. He had come back to her before; he would come back to her now.

Then came the sound of letting go. His feet brushed softly across the carpet as he moved toward the bedroom door. "I'm taking Elizabeth to my parents' tonight. In the morning, I'm calling the police."

But in his words, she heard one final act of love. He was giving her time to disappear.

CHAPTER 35

Trixie wouldn't stop barking. Loud and persistent, the barks echoed through the entire house. Brett flung the blankets off her legs and blinked at her watch lying on the nightstand. The numbers blurred together before settling again. It was almost 7:00 AM. Gray light trickled through the window curtains. Trixie was still barking. Pistol joined in. Bass and soprano, a low rumble followed by a shrill yap. Brett pulled a sweatshirt over her head and hurried downstairs.

Amma peeked her head around her bedroom door. "What's all the racket about?"

"Quiet!" Brett scolded the dogs, but they ignored her.

Trixie scratched at the back door. Pistol pranced around the beagle and then pranced around Brett's feet, nearly tripping her.

Brett scooped Pistol into her arms. "What has gotten into the two of you?"

Through the glass, movement caught her eye. There was a man on the beach, facing the water. In the early morning light, he seemed to be made of little more than shadows, but then he turned and started to walk toward the house.

Brett cried out in surprise and relief. She flung open the door.

Trixie burst through first and ran toward Jimmy, who laughed as he squatted and opened his arms to her.

Brett ran after her with Pistol still clutched in her arms. "Jimmy!"

Trixie was all wiggle and hop, throwing herself against her owner in wild gestures of love. Jimmy reached to hold on to her, petting her, reassuring her. "I'm here. I'm right here. It's okay, Trix. Good girl." The beagle rolled over, exposing her belly.

When Brett reached Jimmy, she set Pistol on the ground. The Chihuahua sniffed Jimmy to make sure he was all right, then wandered off to sniff the grass.

Jimmy rose to his feet, teetering a little before steadying himself. He looked like he'd had a rough two days. There were dark circles under his eyes and scruff on his chin. His clothes were dirty and torn. He reeked of sweat. The only visible injury, though, was a walnut-sized bump on his right temple, a bruise spreading purple around it. A smear of dried blood streaked down the side of his face.

"You found her." He smiled down at Trixie. "I was worried they'd done something. I was worried they'd hurt her. Thank God she's all right. How did you find her?"

"Damn it, Jimmy!" Brett scolded him. "Forget Trixie for a second. Where the hell have you been?"

She brushed her fingers over the bump on his head. Jimmy flinched from her touch, in obvious pain.

"I'm fine," he said.

"You're not fine."

His smile widened. "Aww, Bretty, if I didn't know any better, I'd say you missed me."

Brett wrapped her arm around his waist and helped him toward the house. "You idiot. Come inside and tell me what happened to you."

Even though Jimmy protested, saying he didn't need to see a doctor, Brett insisted on taking him to the hospital anyway. On the drive there, she listened with growing alarm as Jimmy told her where he'd been for the past two days.

"I set up a time to come by and talk to Marshall, but when I got to the house, Clara was there alone. I started asking her some questions. About Margot. About her husband. About their relationship that summer."

"I told you not to go looking for trouble."

He shrugged. "Next thing I know, I wake up to find myself locked in a tiny cabin in the woods, and it's dark, and I've got this killer headache." He touched his temple.

He couldn't remember very well what happened in between, or even how he'd gotten hurt in the first place, but he did remember enough for Brett to draw her own conclusions. Clara's shoulders going tense when he said Margot's name. Hearing Marshall and Clara arguing outside the cabin. Clara throwing him a blanket, a sandwich, and a canteen of water from a darkened doorway. Her cold stare when he asked about Trixie.

"I thought I was going to die out there." A shudder ran through his shoulders.

"But how did you escape?" Brett asked.

Jimmy shook his head, looking bewildered for the first time since showing up on the beach. "There was only one window, but it was boarded up, so I just kept trying the door, even though I knew it was locked. I kept going over and rattling the knob. I tried kicking it open, but that hurt me more than the door. Then early this morning, I don't know what time, but it was still dark. I'd been asleep, I guess, but I heard a noise. And when I tried again, the door opened. Just like that. The door opened, and I walked out."

"You walked out."

"I walked out." He laughed in wonder. "I didn't really know

where I was other than in a forest somewhere near Crestwood, or at least, I hoped that's where I was. I wandered in circles for a while, then I got lucky and found a road, and I followed that for a long time. Then, as the sun started to come up, I started to recognize things, and somehow I found my way to the beach, and I just kept walking along the beach until I found you. I don't know, I probably should have gone straight to the police station or found a payphone or something, but I kept thinking I had to get to you. I kept saying your name over and over in my head, Find Brett, find Brett. It's the only thing that kept me going."

They were parked in front of the hospital. Brett turned in her seat to stare at Jimmy in disbelief. She had come much too close to losing him forever.

He grinned at her. "What? Stop looking at me like that."

"Like what? I'm not looking at you like anything."

He reached across the center console and squeezed her hand. "Let's get this over with, and then I want you to tell me what I've missed being locked up for two days. Because I can see it on your face. Everything's changed, hasn't it?"

———

While Jimmy was being checked out by the emergency room doctor, Brett found a payphone in the lobby and called the precinct. It rang so many times, she almost hung up. Finally, someone answered. The voice was gruff and out of breath. "Crestwood PD."

"Irving?"

"Yes, speaking. Who's this?"

"It's Brett. Listen, we need to send a car to pick up Clara and Marshall Trudeau as soon as possible." She explained as quickly as she could about finding Jimmy on the beach this morning, how he'd been asking questions about Margot when Clara attacked him, how she and Marshall had locked him in a hunting cabin for almost two days, how he certainly would have died out there if not for a miracle.

Irving whistled softly through the phone. "Well, that might explain the message I got this morning then. Marshall claims to have information about Margot's death, but he's saying he'll only speak with you about it."

"Where is he now?" She twisted the phone cord around her hand.

"At his parents' house." Irving rattled off directions.

"What about Clara?" she asked. "Is she there too?"

"I don't think so," Irving said. "But Eli is."

"Why?"

"Not in an official capacity, I don't think," he added quickly. "As a friend, I guess."

"Okay," she said, trying not to assume the worst, that Eli was somehow involved in all of this too. Then she asked Irving to send a car to Clara's house, in case she wasn't with Marshall.

"I'll go myself," he said. "Hopefully, I can get some information out of her before she asks for a lawyer."

"Let the chief know what's going on, too, okay? I'll be in touch with him as soon as I find out what the hell Marshall has to say for himself about all of this. Jesus Christ." She rubbed her eyes, exhausted already and her day had barely even begun.

"Brett..." Irving hesitated, then rushed on. "I just, I don't want you to get your hopes up here. It might not be what we think it is."

She hung up and returned to the waiting room. A few minutes later, Jimmy appeared with a bit of gauze on his forehead and a half-empty bottle of apple juice. After running a few tests, the doctor had cleaned his head wound and given him the all-clear to go home. He was bruised up pretty bad, a little dehydrated, and had suffered a mild concussion, but he would live.

They stopped by the motel on the way home so Jimmy could grab a change of clothes, then Brett dropped him off at the house.

"You sure about this?" she asked, leaning over to look at him through the open car window. "I can send someone to pick him up. He can stay in a cell overnight. Whatever he has to say to me can wait until tomorrow."

Jimmy laughed. "Bullshit, Bretty, you know it can't. I'll be fine. All I want to do is take a hot shower, eat a good meal, and fall asleep watching TV on the couch. I don't need you here for any of that. Well, maybe the hot shower part."

His grin was playful, but she could see his own exhaustion trembling beneath the surface. The last two days had nearly broken him. Before she could say anything, he patted the top of the car and said, "I'll still be here when this is all over. You can take care of me as much as you want then, I promise."

He turned away from her and limped toward the house.

Marshall's parents lived a few miles outside of town on sprawling acreage. A large ranch house and an even larger set of stables sat in the middle of rolling pasture land surrounded by white picket fences, dotted with thoroughbreds and apple trees. As Brett turned her car into the driveway, she saw Elizabeth standing on one of the split-rail fences, leaning over it to pet and feed a jet black horse. At the sound of the tires crunching in the gravel, Elizabeth looked around. She stared at Brett's car as it got closer to the house but stayed where she was on the fence, her elbows hooked over the top railing, her cowboy boots planted firmly on the lower one.

Brett parked in the circular driveway and walked to the front door, where Eli stood waiting for her. He was dressed in plain clothes, jeans and a well-fitted T-shirt. His expression was grim when he asked, "Did your friend, Jimmy, did he get home okay?"

She took a step back from him, her hands automatically reaching for the handcuffs she'd brought with her. "You knew about this?"

"Easy." Eli held his hands up. "I just found out this morning, same as you."

She exhaled, letting some but not all of the tension release from her shoulders. Her thoughts raced ahead of her. She realized she no longer cared who knew what when; she just wanted answers. About Margot. About that summer.

"Marshall called me an hour ago," Eli continued. "He told me what he'd done to Jimmy. He said he had other things he needed to confess too, but he wants immunity first."

"That's not how this works, Eli, and you know it."

"I tried to tell him that."

"I can arrest him right now. Is that what he wants? I have enough to charge him with kidnapping and attempted murder."

Eli grimaced. "He's trying to do the right thing, Brett. Give him a chance."

Too little, too late, was what she wanted to say. Instead, she bit down on her cheek and followed Eli to a plant-filled sunporch at the back of the house. Marshall sat on a wicker chair, staring out over the expansive property and the stables behind the house. Elizabeth was visible from this room, walking along the fence line. The jet black horse followed her, tossing its mane.

Marshall kept his eyes on his daughter even as Eli and Brett entered the room and sat down on a wicker loveseat placed at a right angle from the chair.

"Tell me something, Brett," Marshall said. "Do you think you can ever really know a person? Like really, deeply know them, a down-to-the-very-core kind of knowing?"

He settled his gaze on Brett a moment, studying her. A smile teased his lips, then fell away again as he looked back out the window. "I thought I knew my wife."

"Tell me what happened, Marshall. Start from the beginning."

"I don't want to go to prison," he said and wiped his hand over his mouth, shaking his head. "I can't do that to Elizabeth."

Outside, the girl was running, her hands flying out to catch the air. The horse ran alongside her, tossing its head.

Eli leaned forward on the loveseat and touched his friend's knee. "Marshall, Elizabeth will never be left alone, and you know that. She's got your parents, and Geana, and me."

"And June," Marshall said.

Eli nodded. "Tell Brett what you know. It'll feel good to get it all out. And we'll do what we can to keep you from prison. We'll talk to the prosecutor, see if there can be some leniency for cooperation. We can't make any guarantees, but we'll try, right, Brett?"

She flicked him a withering glance and then to Marshall said, "No promises, but if you tell us what happened, we can put in a good word for you."

He nodded and kept nodding, and for a moment, she didn't think he was going to say a damn thing, then he ran his palms over the tops of his thighs, cleared his throat, and said, "Clara killed Margot."

The words hit her full force in the chest, sucking the breath from her. She tried to stifle her surprise, but the gasp was already out, hovering in the air between them.

Marshall looked at her, tilting his head in a curious way. "I was surprised, too. All these years, I've been living with a stranger. A murderer. A liar." He flipped his hands over and stared at his palms.

"How long have you known?" Brett asked, and then swiveled her head to glare at Eli. "And you? I bet you're going to sit there and tell me you didn't know about this either?"

Eli's mouth hung open. He looked just as shocked as she did. He shook his head and started to protest, but Marshall spoke over him. "Eli had nothing to do with any of this. I swear on my life he didn't. I didn't even know about Margot until last night when Clara and I were arguing about what to do with that reporter, with your friend."

"Jimmy." Brett could barely push his name past her clenched teeth.

"Yeah. We were arguing about him. And I was thinking about what you told me when you dropped off Elizabeth, about Margot going missing in the afternoon, not in the morning like we all thought. And I couldn't stop thinking about that day, the day Margot went missing. Clara came over to my house that afternoon, and she was all cut up and shaking. When I asked her what happened, she told me she'd tried to hurt herself, and at the time, no one even knew Margot was gone, and even after, I didn't think..." He let out a low moan and buried his face in his hands. "I believed Clara. I believed her about everything because that's what you do, isn't it? You believe the people you love."

"She told you she killed Margot?" The words scraped her throat dry.

"She told me it was an accident." In his voice was the desperate need to believe his wife, even after her betrayal, knowing all he knew now. "But then she told me she killed Zach, too. Because of what he'd done to Elizabeth. And after what happened with Jimmy..." He swallowed, the sound loud in the quiet room. "I came home and found him lying on my kitchen floor. I thought he was dead." He laughed, a brittle stutter. "She said he attacked her. And I believed her about that, too, but that was before I knew about Margot and Zach. So I did what she told me to do, I helped her move him. We drove him to a hunting cabin in the middle of the forest, I don't even know how she knew it was there, but I did what she asked me to do because I believed her. I thought it was an accident, and I didn't want her getting in trouble. I didn't want either of us getting in trouble."

His gaze moved out the window, searching for his daughter, but Elizabeth was nowhere to be seen. He looked heartbroken as he shifted his gaze back to his hands. "But now I know who she is, what she's done. I shouldn't have done it. I should have stopped her. If I had known..." The rest of the words broke off in a muffled sob.

"What about Nathan Andress?" Brett asked.

Marshall's brow furrowed.

"Do you think Clara might have killed him, too?" she pressed.

"I don't know." He squeezed his eyes shut. "Before, I would have said no, absolutely not. Clara is a good person with a good heart. But now, I have no idea who that woman I married is. A monster capable of anything, I suppose."

And it was starting to make a terrible kind of sense. Clara loved Marshall first. But Marshall fell in love with Margot. And that day in the woods, in a fit of jealous rage, Clara killed the girl she perceived as a threat. Clara killed Margot. But there were so many things Brett still didn't know. Why did Margot go out into the woods in the first place? Had Clara lured her there, or was it merely happenstance? An accident like Marshall claimed, or something far more sinister? And how did Archer find them? What had he seen?

She imagined Archer crouched in the shadows, in one of the forest's many hidden places, watching as Clara and Margot argued, as Clara struck Margot down, as Margot never got back up and Clara fled. And after Clara was gone, Archer gathered Margot up, covered her in flowers, made her beautiful in his own twisted way. Her death stirred in him dark desires from which he would never be able to turn away.

There was still so much Brett needed to know about that day, so much only Clara could tell her. She clenched her fists in her lap, thinking of the woman who had spent the past twenty years walking around Crestwood free, raising a family, happy and unburdened by the decisions she'd made. Did she feel any guilt at all for the lives she'd ruined?

Twenty years Brett had pushed down her grief. It rose now, a cold wave breaking over her, drowning out Marshall's explanations, the roar of her grief louder than his pitiful excuses.

She'd heard enough.

She stood from the loveseat and reached for the handcuffs clipped to her belt. "I'm going to have to bring you down to the station."

"You're arresting me?" His gaze swung wildly to Eli. "You said—"

"You admitted to keeping a man prisoner in the woods," she cut him off.

"I let him go," Marshall protested. "That has to mean something, doesn't it? I get it. We all make choices in this life, and we have to live with the consequences of those choices. But I'm trying to make things right. I've told you everything you wanted to know, haven't I? I'm cooperating."

He might not have done the killing, but in Brett's mind, he was no better than Clara. He had kept her secrets, for all these years, for his own selfish reasons. To share a house, a bed, a life with a monster and claim to not have known, to not have even the smallest inkling of an idea—Brett didn't believe it. Some part of Marshall knew and had known all along. Some small kernel of doubt lived inside him, but he was too much of a coward to let it grow, to hold it to the light and reveal what was hidden there. He hadn't wanted to know, and so he had looked the other way. For this, he was guilty. For this, Brett would never forgive him.

She stood resolute, waiting for him to get up and go with her. His gaze darted between her and Eli, panicked, and then his whole body sagged, and finally, he nodded. "Fine, I'll go, but not in handcuffs. I'll go of my own free will. Because it's the right thing to do."

She scoffed at him but hooked the cuffs back on her belt and gestured him to his feet.

"And just..." He took a long, slow breath. "Please, can I say goodbye to Elizabeth first?"

Brett allowed it, though not to make Marshall feel better. She didn't give a damn about his feelings, but she thought Elizabeth deserved a chance to hear the truth straight from her father. Nothing would be the same for her after today. The rest of her life would be defined by this—before and after she found out what kind of people her parents were—but at least she wouldn't spend half her life wondering the way Brett had. Knowing couldn't change what happened, but it did give Elizabeth a chance to grieve the wreckage of her old life and perhaps build something new from the rubble.

CHAPTER 36

The sky was a bruised and knotted cloud. The bay churned, brewing another storm. The tide swelled, and waves crashed against the rocks. Clara closed her eyes, gritted her teeth, and slipped into the cold water for one final swim. The ocean against her bare skin burned, and for a brief second, she wished for her wetsuit, though of course, the wetsuit would keep her from doing the very thing she'd come to do—slip under the waves and disappear.

Last night after Marshall left, taking Elizabeth with him, Clara had been all motion.

She pulled clothes at random from her closet and stuffed them into the suitcase. What do you pack when you don't know where you're going? Or who you will be when you get there? From the can on top of the fridge, she grabbed a wad of emergency spending money and tucked it into her wallet. Then she dug her passport from the metal box that was collecting dust under the bed. She wasn't sure where she would end up. Far. Away. Somewhere no one knew her face, which was a lot of places.

Already her chest ached with yawning loneliness at the idea of stretched out days with nothing to do and no one to love. She would have to find a job. She would have to change her name. She would have to change her hair and everything about herself. But one thing she would never do was build herself another family. She would never replace the people she loved most who had once loved her. She would never even try.

She went into Elizabeth's room and stood breathing in the scent of her daughter—dryer sheets and strawberry lip gloss. She cataloged every inch—the music posters and soccer trophies, the pictures and books, the dangle of ribbons from the ceiling fan. When she was miles from here and alone, she wanted to remember every detail.

On the dresser sat a framed picture, the only one they'd ever taken together as a family of four. Clara picked it up and rubbed her finger over the glass. It was a few days after they brought Lily home from the hospital. They went for a picnic by the bay. The water sparkled blue in the background. Marshall had his arm around Elizabeth, her smile full and bright. Clara held Lily, swaddled in a pink elephant blanket, her tiny fists shooting into the air. They looked happy. They looked like a family with love and time enough to spare.

Clara sank to the floor and curled herself around the picture.

If she could cry, she thought, if in this moment tears dampened her cheeks, then she would know that she wasn't a complete lost cause. She would know that there was still a piece of her self worth fighting for, some gentle part worth saving. And if there was a part of her worth saving, maybe she could do what Marshall wanted her to do and turn herself over to the police. Perhaps she could find redemption. She waited, counted the seconds, the minutes, watched the shadows shift on the wall. The tears never came.

She was packed, and part of her whispered in a furious and terrified voice to go, go, go. But there was another voice too, one that whispered gently for her to stay. This was her life, her home, her family, and it wasn't fair that she was being asked to leave it all behind. Right when they needed her most.

Another few minutes, she kept telling herself. She had until morning, until the sun came up at least. Marshall had promised her. Another few minutes wouldn't hurt. It was less than an hour's drive to the Canadian border and vast stretches of nothing and no one after that. It wouldn't take long for her to disappear. So these few and desperate moments could be spared, and she clung to them, sifting through every good memory of her life with Marshall.

Their first date, their first kiss, their wedding, buying this house. The birth of their first daughter, the way he sang her to sleep at night, the time at the county fair when he won them the largest stuffed bear Clara had ever seen. The night Clara told him she was pregnant again, which was unexpected certainly, but he'd been so happy. She remembered the look on his face, how he promised her forever. She remembered, too, the last time they made love a few days ago, though she hadn't realized then that it would be the last time. She missed this life so much already, and she wasn't even gone yet.

She knew she should be grateful for the years she did have. More than she ever imagined she'd get. That day twenty years ago, when she walked out of the woods covered in blood and scratches, her whole body trembling, she thought her life was over. Instead, it was just starting, and it had been a beautiful one. Until Nathan Andress ruined it.

She thought of that night at Deadman's Point. Two weeks ago now, though she remembered it clearly enough it could have been yesterday. How pathetic he'd been, how stupid. Somehow he'd known the truth about Margot. The details of how he found out didn't matter to Clara. What mattered was he knew. He knew what she was capable of, knew she had killed once before, and still, he pushed his luck. He'd already come to her once demanding money in exchange for his silence. That first time, she'd given him every-thing he'd asked for, anything to get him to go away. But he kept pushing. He threatened her a second time, and it was then she understood that no matter how much she paid him, he would always demand more. To keep her secrets from getting out, she would need to do something she hadn't done in twenty years. Something she never thought she'd do again for as long as she lived. It was his own damn fault. He got too greedy.

Clara shuddered and shoved aside the memory of the knife cutting deep, the blood on her hands. Tonight she wanted only the beautiful moments in her life, the joy-filled ones that she had always tried so hard to cherish because she knew, hadn't she? In the back of her mind, she knew that one day her luck would run out.

At some point, adrift in the warm memories of her old life, she fell asleep on the floor of her daughter's bedroom curled around the smiling faces of her beautiful family. She hadn't meant to. And when she woke, dawn cracked the windows, spreading eerie gray light through the house, and fear gripped her and sent her leaping to her feet and into her bedroom where she'd left the suitcase. But as she grabbed it, a new thought came to her, one that felt better than running, one that seemed easier to bear.

She had gotten into her car and driven, not north to the Canadian border, but west toward the ocean.

She tried to relax into the crush, the hiss, the cold, tried to give herself over to the waves, but her reflex was to keep her head above water, to bob with the roll and splash, to keep breathing. She started shivering. If she was going to do this, she needed to do it now or swim back to shore and get on with the rest.

When the next swell came, she dived under, pushed deeper, floated there in the dark, hovering in a nowhere place, in an emptiness that filled her. She held her breath until her lungs hurt. This was harder than she thought it would be. All she had to do was open her mouth and let the ocean flood in.

They would find her body washed up a few days from now, the way they'd found Nathan's. Or maybe they wouldn't. Maybe the ocean would cooperate this time, and she would drift on a dark tide, pulled out to sea, never to be seen again. Either way, it would be over. Marshall would tell them everything. They would have their answers, and this act of drowning could be her final act, her kindness, and her redemption.

She tried. She forced her mouth open. Water rushed in. She sputtered, coughed. The water kept coming. Relax, she tried to relax and let it fill her, but her legs kicked, thrashing despite herself, and her arms propelled her to the surface, her head breaking free. She coughed, gagged, took a breath. Her arms moved slowly, keeping her afloat. She stared toward the horizon where the islands should be. They were hidden behind a dark bank of clouds, thunderheads moving toward land.

She turned and swam back to the dock.

———————————————

That should have been it. Clara should have gotten in her car then, driven north without stopping until she was a face no one recognized, a woman without a past. A woman with nothing and no one to return to. She checked her rearview mirror. There were no cars on the road but hers, and maybe it was the salt drying on her skin, the cold ocean still icing her blood, but she felt invincible. No one could touch her unless she let them.

She drove to the cemetery at the edge of town. Her feet carried her through the wet grass to the granite gravestone engraved with her daughter's name and the too-short time she was alive. Clara stared down at it, and the stone stared back, indifferent.

She pressed her hand to the cold marker. She whispered good-bye, whispered she was sorry, whispered she wished things had been different. A loosening in her chest and she was one step closer to leaving. But first, she had to see Elizabeth. What kind of mother would she be if she left without saying goodbye to her babies? She knew she wouldn't be able to explain, not in any way that mattered, but she didn't want to disappear from her daughter's life the way her father had disappeared from her own. She didn't want to leave her daughter wondering. Elizabeth deserved better than that. And if Marshall wouldn't let her talk to Elizabeth, she could at least see her one last time, memorize the shape of her face, the flecks in her eyes, the freckle patterns across her nose.

She recognized Brett's Beetle in the driveway as soon as she crested the hill. Eli's green Jeep was parked there, too, next to Marshall's car. Clara pulled off to one side of the road and watched for a few minutes, her heart pounding hard in her chest. Marshall had kept his word. He'd waited until morning, but even now, he was betraying her. Her grip on the steering wheel tightened as the house's front door opened and out stepped Eli, followed by Marshall, followed by Brett. He wasn't in handcuffs, and this hurt her more, that he would go so willingly.

Marshall got into Eli's Jeep, and the two men drove in the opposite direction of Clara, not noticing her there at all. Brett paused outside her car, her hand on the door. She said something, and Elizabeth appeared around the corner of the house.

Her hair was a mess, flying all over the place, but Clara had never seen her daughter look more beautiful. Her daughter. Her flesh and blood and every good thing in this life, brushing tears from her cheeks, then taking a step forward and folding herself into Brett's open arms. Bile rose in Clara's throat. She held perfectly still, the rage in her chest coiling and uncoiling. Yet another Buchanan sister taking what didn't belong to her.

Clara turned the car around and sped back to Crestwood with a new plan.

Cowards ran. Prey ran. Clara was neither of these things.

There were only so many places to hide in this world, only so many roads to sneak down. Eventually, the net would pull tighter. Eventually, they would come for her. They would catch her and punish her for what she'd done, and she would resign herself to that fate. But until that day came, she was still in control. She could decide, and she was not going to stand by and watch Brett poison her daughter against her, the way Margot had tried to poison Marshall. She would not let the Buchanan sisters take everything from her.

Not without taking something of theirs in return.

CHAPTER 37

No one knew where to find Clara Trudeau.

Irving told Brett that he'd gone to the house, but Clara hadn't been there. Her car was gone. The front door left unlocked. The bedroom closet had been in disarray, clothes strewn everywhere.

"We need to consider the possibility that she's on the run," Irving said.

Marshall claimed the reason he hadn't immediately called the police after Clara's confession was that he'd been in shock and needed time to process. He was afraid for his daughter's life and for his own. His first priority had been getting away from his murderer wife. By the time he'd calmed down enough to think straight, the sun was starting to come up.

But all Brett could think was that he'd done it on purpose. By waiting so long to tell them, he'd given Clara hours, a half a day or more even, to escape.

Once they understood what they were dealing with, Irving sent out a bulletin to state and county agencies as well as border patrol. Then he tracked down Clara's mother and confirmed with her that she hadn't seen or heard from her daughter in almost a week. Not since the Halloween festival and Marshall's arrest.

"She's worried sick," Irving reported back to Brett. "Says she'll let us know right away if she hears anything from her." He hesitated and added, "I asked her about the day Margot disappeared."

"And?"

A scowl furrowed his brow. "She seemed confused at first, but when I told her that Margot went missing later in the day than originally thought, she kind of just collapsed. She was shaking and crying. Eventually, I got her to calm down long enough to tell me why. Apparently, Clara was working at the grocery store that summer. Geana got her a job part-time stocking shelves. She was supposed to work from four to eight that day but didn't show up, and when Geana called the house, no one answered. When she got home later that evening, she found Clara sick in bed. Clara claimed she'd been throwing up and could hardly move from the pain."

"And Geana believed her."

"She had no reason not to," Irving said. "Plus, according to Geana, she was sick. She was pale and shivering and hot to the touch."

"What about cuts? Bruises? Anything to suggest she'd been involved in a fight?"

Irving shook his head. "She doesn't remember seeing anything like that."

On a hunch, Brett asked Marshall to draw her a map of where the hunting cabin was, and she sent an officer out to check, but the place was empty. There were signs of Jimmy's captivity, though, and the officer found Jimmy's car abandoned a few hundred yards away on an overgrown fire road. Marshall had led them to the right place, then. It was just Brett's hunch that was wrong.

Clara wasn't stupid. Once she realized the careful lies she'd crafted over the past twenty years were coming undone, she certainly wouldn't stick around Crestwood for long. Brett could only hope they'd learned the truth soon enough to catch her before she vanished for good. County, state, and border agents had a description of Clara's car as well as her driver's license photo. There wasn't anything Brett could do now but wait and see how this played out. They'd either get lucky, or they wouldn't.

In the precinct break room, Brett poured herself a cup of stale coffee. Irving intercepted her before she reached her desk.

He plucked the cup from her hands and shook his head when she tried to take it back. "Go home, Brett. You've done all you can. You've got every cop in the state out looking for her. If she's still here, she'll turn up. And if she's not, there's no point spinning yourself in circles, is there? Might as well get some rest while you have the chance. The prosecutor's office is sending someone over early tomorrow to figure out what they want to do about Marshall. You're going to want to be here for that."

"Even if I did go home, I wouldn't be able to sleep. Not while she's still out there." She snapped her fingers. "What about roadblocks? We haven't done that yet. We could set them up on some of the major highways going in and out of town."

"It wouldn't hurt to ask. Henry hasn't left yet." He pointed at the chief's office, the window glowing warmly in the twilight haze of the squad room.

Brett tapped on the door and entered.

Henry hung up the phone. Before she could get a word out, he said, "I'm worried about your grandmother. I've been trying to reach her for the last hour, but she's not answering the phone."

The news surprised her. It was nearly seven, around the time Amma typically had dinner. If she was at home, she would have answered. Brett supposed Jimmy might have taken Amma out to one of the restaurants in town, but that didn't seem likely considering what he'd suffered the past two days and how exhausted he'd seemed when she'd dropped him off earlier. Maybe the phone was just disconnected. It had happened before. Amma, tired of telemarketers, unplugged the cord from the wall. It had stayed that way for days before Brett finally noticed. Or maybe she'd wandered off again, and Jimmy had gone looking for her.

"I'm sure she's fine." Brett pushed aside a growing sense of unease. "I was about to head home anyway. I just wanted to ask about roadblocks."

Henry looked confused.

"For Clara Trudeau."

"Right, yes, I'll call State Patrol and see if they can get something set up." Henry reached for the phone.

Brett didn't hang around to see what happened. She hurried from Henry's office to grab her jacket and keys.

"Call me when you find her!" Henry shouted at her back.

The house on Bayshore Drive was a blazing beacon in the dark. Light spilled from every window. Amma's car was parked in the driveway, unmoved from where it had been parked when Brett left this morning. She swung open the front door and scraped her boots on the welcome mat, calling out that she was home. Upstairs, Trixie started to bark. The sound was muffled like she was locked in one of the bedrooms.

"Amma? Jimmy? Hello?" Brett moved through the living room into the kitchen.

On the stovetop, a pot of water had boiled down to nothing and was beginning to smoke. Brett flicked off the burner. A package of unopened pasta sat on the counter next to the stove. A pile of unchopped lettuce wilted on the cutting board.

"Is anyone here? Jimmy? Amma?" She rushed through the house, checking all the rooms. Upstairs, she found Trixie and Pistol shut inside the guestroom. The dogs rushed her, delighted to see a friendly face. "Where is everyone?" she asked them and got only tail wags in response.

Back downstairs, she opened the french doors, and the dogs ran out, chasing each other around the grass. Brett called for Amma and Jimmy again. Her voice echoed in the dark. Waves splashed against Amma's sailboat, still tied to the dock. She squinted into the shadows, scanning the beach for any signs of her grandmother, but seeing no one. Trixie had made her way down to the boathouse, where she scratched at the door whining. Brett whistled both dogs back inside and called Henry.

"I'll send a car over," he said, panic in his voice.

"Just wait a few more minutes, Henry, please."

"Brett, if she's wandered off—"

"I can find her," she insisted. "Listen, Clara needs to be our top priority. I don't want anyone pulled from that search if we can help it. Amma and Jimmy probably went out for a walk. I'm sure they'll be back any minute." But even as she said it, she knew Jimmy would never go for a walk without Trixie.

Henry exhaled loudly and said, "One hour. That's all you get." His tone was stern now, decided. "If you haven't found her by then, I'm sending a car over to help."

"Fine," Brett said and hung up.

She removed her shoulder holster and gun, setting both on the counter, alongside her badge and handcuffs, then rubbed at a knot twisting in her neck.

Pistol wound circles around her feet. Trixie stood by the backdoor, staring out into the night. Brett dug in a drawer for a flashlight and went outside again, leaving the dogs behind. Her feet whispered through the damp lawn.

"Amma?" she called out again as she moved toward the boathouse.

A light flickered across the small window, and a shadow moved inside. Relief rushed through her, followed quickly by something that felt like fear. Her hand reflexively reached for her gun, only to remember she'd left it in the house.

"Amma?" Her voice was too loud in the quiet stillness. "Is that you?"

Brett hesitated when no one answered, torn between going back for her weapon and continuing forward unarmed. If it was her grandmother, rummaging through the detritus of her life with Pop, Brett didn't want to give her a heart attack by running in with her gun drawn. Then again, nothing about what she'd found so far—the dogs locked in the bedroom, the pot nearly in flames on the stove—made her feel confident that Amma was safe.

Before Brett could make a decision, a ragged scream pierced the dark.

Chapter 38

Brett didn't think. She just ran. Onto the dock, crashing through the door of the boathouse, screaming Amma's name. She stopped short just inside the threshold. In the beam of the flashlight, her worst fears were revealed.

Amma sat on a wooden stool in the center of the room, shivering from cold or fear or both. Her hands in her lap were bound with rope. A red bandana had been shoved into her mouth as a gag. Beside her stood Clara Trudeau, a knife pressed to the soft curve of Amma's neck.

"Nice of you to join us," she said. "I wouldn't come any closer, though, if I were you."

"Put the knife down, Clara." Brett lifted both hands to show she wasn't a threat. The flashlight beam swept the rafters. "Let's talk this through. We can work something out. But you have to put down the knife. Kick it over to me," she said, "and let's go inside and have a real conversation about all of this."

"Shut up."

Brett recognized the knife as one from a set she'd gotten for Amma and Pop a few Christmases ago. Clara gripped the handle tightly, but if Brett could get close enough, she thought she might be able to disarm her.

She shuffled a step closer, but Clara tensed, then shook her head and pushed the blade right up against Amma's skin. "Don't even think about it."

Amma whimpered. Brett tried to offer her a reassuring smile, but all she could manage was a brittle grimace.

"Look, Clara," she tried again. "I can help you, okay? I'm on your side here. Just tell me what you want."

Clara tilted her head and studied Brett in the dim moonlight filtering through the boathouse's single window. "You're just like her, you know. You manipulate people like she did. Do you think I'm stupid? She thought I was stupid." Then she laughed, a single sharp note. "You can't give me what I want anyway. No one can."

"Try me," Brett said.

Clara's eyes narrowed to hard slits, and a shudder ran across her shoulders. Her words were thick with sadness when she said, "I want to start over."

"Okay," Brett said. "Okay, you can do that. I can help you do that. All you have to do is drop the knife and come with me to the station. Turn yourself in."

A sad smile teased Clara's lips. She shook her head. "I can't change the things I've done. I can't go back. You know I can't."

"No, but you can go forward," Brett insisted. "You still have a chance to make this right." When Clara still didn't move, Brett added, "Think about Elizabeth."

She flinched at the sound of her daughter's name. The blade nicked Amma's skin, and Amma gave a muffled cry and pulled back sharply. A trickle of blood appeared on her throat. Brett almost lunged at Clara right then, but she held herself still. She'd found a crack to chip away at, and so she pressed on.

"I know how much you love her. Elizabeth's lucky to have a mother like you, you know, a mother who would sacrifice so much. You would do anything for her, wouldn't you?"

Clara's lower lip trembled. She nodded.

"So do this now," Brett said, reaching her hand into the space between them. "Give me the knife. Show Elizabeth that her mother's not a monster, that there is still good in you."

Her sad smile returned. "I'm not sure there was ever a time in my life when I was good."

"Clara. Give me the knife."

Brett saw when Clara decided to give up. The change was subtle. Her shoulders sagged. She lowered the blade and stepped away from Amma. One hand swiped furtively at her cheek. Brett stepped forward to take the knife, and it all should have been over in that moment.

Outside, a dock board creaked. Clara tensed. Her gaze shifted over Brett's shoulder. Someone stepped into the doorway, and a long shadow stretched across the boathouse floor. Brett could feel the atmosphere shift, how Clara was once again retreating into the darkest parts of herself. Whatever chance Brett had of bringing this night to a peaceful end was gone. She didn't have much time. In that brief second when Clara was distracted, Brett lunged.

She grabbed Clara's wrist and shoved her toward the back of the boathouse. They stumbled over crab nets and a pile of sails before falling to the floor. Clara dropped the knife. Brett scrabbled to find it. Clara grabbed her ankle and pulled her back.

"Don't move!" Jimmy's voice boomed through the small space.

"Jimmy! Get Amma out of here!" Brett grappled with Clara, who was climbing on top of her, clawing at her face and eyes.

"I said, don't move! I have a gun!"

Clara hesitated. Brett took the opportunity to swing her elbow and clock the other woman hard in the jaw. Clara grunted and fell back against a pile of traps, circular metal cages tied with ropes and buoys that reeked of brine and seaweed.

"Jimmy." Brett rose to her feet and held out her hand. "Give that to me. Then take Amma and get her the hell out of here."

Amma struggled a moment, rocking before finally standing to her feet. Her legs weren't tied, only her hands, but she was trembling hard, which made walking difficult. She teetered a few steps toward Jimmy, who reached out to her and, at the same time, lowered the gun. Brett grabbed for it, but before she could get her hands around the grip, she was hit from behind by something heavy that reeked of fish. She spilled forward, knocking into Jimmy, who stumbled against Amma. In his attempt to keep the older woman from falling, Jimmy dropped the gun on the floor. Then, in his attempt to pick it back up while keeping Amma close, he kicked it into the shadows on the other side of the boathouse.

"Shit!" Jimmy cursed, shoving Amma toward the door before diving after the gun.

Brett struggled to get out from under a tangled mess of ropes and crab traps. Finally, she flung the gear off and leaped to her feet. But she was too late. Clara had found the gun first, and she was pointing it straight at Jimmy.

"No!" Brett shouted.

The explosion inside the tiny room left Brett's ears ringing. Jimmy cried out and dropped to the floor, clutching his leg. Brett rushed to where he'd fallen and dropped down next to him. He moaned and cursed. "Fuck! She shot me!"

He was bleeding from his right upper thigh, and Brett worried the bullet might have hit an artery. Jimmy was still conscious, which was a good sign, but the sooner she slowed the bleeding, the better. She whipped off her belt, wrapped it around his leg, and cinched tight. Jimmy screamed louder. Then his scream faded to a whimpering groan, and his eyes fluttered like he was about to pass out. She smacked him gently across the face.

"Don't you dare, Jimmy," she said. "Stay with me, okay? Stay right here."

As she worked on slowing the bleeding, she glanced over her shoulder. Clara had taken the gun and run off. Amma was gone, too.

"I'm sorry," Jimmy said, his teeth clenched with pain.

Blood slicked her hands and pooled on the floor. Too much blood. She checked the wound. It was still bleeding, though less than before. She smiled at him so he wouldn't see how worried she was. "You have nothing to be sorry about."

"I was only gone a few minutes," he said. "I just wanted to get the rest of my stuff from the motel room, that's all. I wanted my notebook. I wanted to get it all down, all the—" He hissed in pain. "I thought she'd be okay. I told her to stay inside and keep the door locked."

She wrapped his hand around one end of the belt. "Hold it like this. Don't give it any slack. Keep it as tight as you can, even when you get tired, okay? Jimmy, okay?"

He nodded. "Yeah, okay."

"I need you to stay alive."

"I love you, too, Brett," he said with a grimace.

She left him there and, praying Amma had made her way up to the house to call for help, went to find Clara.

It didn't take long. Clara had made it only as far as the end of the dock where Amma's sailboat was tied. She was bent over, struggling to unwind the ropes from the dock cleat.

"Clara, stop," Brett called out to her softly.

Clara straightened and whirled around, gun raised and pointed at Brett.

Brett froze, her breath catching in her chest as she tried not to think about dying. What would happen to Amma? Who would feed Pistol? Who would tell Jimmy that she had loved him, too, from the very beginning, the very first day when he walked into that bar and bought her a basket of fries? She knew it would hurt but hoped it would be over fast and that Margot would be waiting for her on the other side.

Seconds stretched to what felt like an eternity, but Clara still didn't shoot. Slowly she lowered the gun, though she kept both hands wrapped around the grip, her finger on the trigger.

"All of them deserved it, you know," she whispered hoarsely. "They were terrible, selfish people. Every single one of them. Even your sister. I did what I had to do to protect myself and to protect my family. Don't tell me you wouldn't have done the same."

Brett shook her head, but she couldn't get any words to come out of her mouth.

For an instant, remorse flickered across Clara's face. Then her hard defiance returned. "I'm going," she said. "If you try to stop me, I will shoot you. Don't make me shoot you."

She crouched by the rope. With her eyes still fixed on Brett, and one hand holding the gun at the ready, she reached to untangle the boat from the dock.

A shadow separated itself from the boathouse, and before Brett could react, Amma had launched herself at Clara. The force was enough to send both women toppling over the short dock railing and into the water with a thunderous splash.

Brett ran to where they'd gone in. The two women were tangled up in one another. Amma, whose hands were still tied, thrashed and managed to kick away from Clara, knocking her in the face with a wild flail of her legs. Clara choked on a mouthful of water and swam away, coughing and fighting to keep her head above water.

Brett called to Amma and stretched out her hand. "Grab on! Swim toward me!"

But the kick had been a powerful one and had sent Amma spinning into a set of waves that pushed roughly toward shore. She struggled to keep her head above water, but the current was too strong, and she was dragged under.

Brett worked her boots off her feet and peeled off her jacket. She scanned the spot where Amma had disappeared, saw a flood of air bubbles pop the surface, and dove in next to them.

The water was ice cold, and the current tugged on her, trying to drag her out even deeper. Brett flailed a moment, then sucked in a breath and dove under, flinging her hands from side to side, feeling for Amma. Salt burned her eyes. Her lungs ached. She came up for air, then dove back under, the waves tumbling her, roiling her stomach.

This time her hands brushed over something. Instinctively, Brett drew back, terrified by the idea of what might be swimming in the dark beside her. Then she lunged forward again, reaching for whatever it was she'd felt before. Her fingers tangled in softness, the hem of a shirt. She tightened her grip and kicked to the surface. Her head broke first, and she breathed in deep. Pulling hard, she yanked Amma's head from the water.

Amma floated limply in Brett's arms. Brett couldn't tell if she was breathing. She ripped the gag from her mouth and shouted at her but got no response. Wrapping one arm around her grandmother to keep her head above water, she used the other to stroke as hard as she could toward shore. It wasn't far. Less than twenty feet, but it felt like she swam the entirety of the Pacific Ocean. Small waves spat them out onto the pebbled beach. Brett stumbled forward, dragging Amma from the greedy ocean. She laid her grandmother down and pumped her hands on her chest. Amma coughed and sputtered. Brett turned her over as she vomited saltwater onto the rocks.

She was breathing, gasping and coughing, but breathing. Her eyes fluttered open, and seeing Brett, she offered a small, victorious smile.

Brett tore at the ropes around Amma's wrists until she was free. Amma started to shiver. Brett, too, was chattering hard, her bones rattling from the cold. She left Amma on the beach and ran back to the dock to grab her jacket.

Up on the road, a car door slammed, and someone called her name.

"Irving!" she shouted, then stood and waved her hands over her head. "We're down here! Call an ambulance!"

She draped her jacket over Amma and swept a hand over her forehead. "You're going to be all right. You're going to be fine."

Amma nodded. She was still smiling, though her teeth chattered hard. Brett couldn't tell if the moonlight was making her lips look so gray or if it was from the cold.

Irving appeared on the beach, panting from his rush to get down to them. He stared at Amma, at Brett, both of them dripping and shivering. "What the hell happened?"

"Jimmy's in the boathouse with a gunshot wound to the leg," Brett explained as quickly as she could. "Amma's showing signs of hypothermia. They both need the hospital. I have to go back in."

"You what?"

But she was already racing toward the water again. "Clara!" she shouted over her shoulder at him. "She's still out there!"

She splashed in up to her knees, then dove forward into the rolling waves, taking long strokes, kicking hard to get back to where she saw Clara start to go under. Her shivering lessened as she swam, but she could feel her hands and feet going numb. She knew that she didn't have long before she got too cold, and it became dangerous for her to stay in the water.

When she reached the spot, she slowed, treading water, and scanned for any sign of Clara. A flicker of white, a hand raised, clawing for something to hold on to, or a body, floating face down, anything to suggest there was still a chance to drag her to shore and make her answer for the lives she'd ruined. Anything to indicate she wasn't dead at the bottom of the bay, waiting to be tossed ashore or dragged out to the ocean to be picked apart by sturgeon and crabs. But there were only the waves and the tide and her own splashing arms, only the dark swirling water beneath her, a bottomless void she did not have the strength to swim through.

For several minutes she thrashed. Diving and surfacing, diving and surfacing, searching for Clara, stretching her arms into the darkness, feeling with her fingers, but finding nothing.

Thanks to Marshall, she had answers, enough to close three

cases, but that felt like nothing. A hollow victory in the face of her losses. She wanted to know what exactly had happened the day Margot died, every damn detail. The words that were said, if Margot put up a fight or if she had tried to run. If her death had been quick. If she'd suffered. And why, and why, and why? With every stroke of her arm, every kick of her leg, the word thrust through Brett. Why Margot? Why Nathan? Why Zach? Why anyone? But the longer she swam in circles, the more she stopped caring about the reasons behind Clara's choices. All her anger, frustration, and grief twisted into a tight knot until why was replaced with good and good and good. This is what she deserved—the ocean could have her rotten soul.

In the distance, the night lit up with wailing sirens. Faintly above that, she heard Irving shouting at her from somewhere, telling her to swim back, but she had passed the point of rational thinking. She treaded water and stared out over the vast empty space of the ocean, unable to tell where the water ended and the sky began. She felt herself sinking under, but she no longer had the strength to fight against it.

A hand grabbed the collar of her shirt and hauled her from the water. Her back scraped against a wooden railing, and she was tossed like a fish onto the boards. She hadn't realized she'd floated so close to the dock. She would have struggled, would have fought to stay in the water and keep searching, but she had nothing left. The cold and the effort had left her empty and numb.

"Brett." Irving's voice sounded miles away rather than right here beside her, throwing a blanket around her shoulders. "Are you with me?"

She huddled in a ball, shivering.

"It's over," he said, rubbing one hand over her back for comfort or warmth or both. "She's gone. You did the best you could, okay? Listen to me. You did the best you could."

He stayed with her until the paramedics came.

Chapter 39

Two Whatcom County sheriff boats cruised the shoreline outside Amma's house. Brett stood on the dock, watching them. Divers donned their gear and slipped into the water with barely a ripple. They were farther out today than they'd been all week, having exhausted the area closest to shore.

Five days of searching. Five days coming up empty-handed.

The water temperature hovered near fifty degrees, too cold for anyone to survive for more than an hour or two. And the current was strong enough to sweep a body far out to sea, farther than the boats and divers were willing to search. But the tide had carried Nathan ashore, lifting him from the deep to expose Clara's secrets, and Brett didn't think it was too much to hope that this same tide might pull Clara in as well. The longer the search dragged on, the more that hope dimmed.

The sheriff's department was doing them a favor, searching like this. Henry hadn't even wanted to ask. *She's dead, Brett. You saw her go under, and she never came back up. What more do you want?* She wanted a body. She wanted to know this was over. Really over. So she'd pleaded with him until finally Henry caved and placed the call to the sheriff asking for a couple of boats and extra manpower. But searching cost money, and the deputies had their own jobs to get back to. Today was the last time they'd go out on the water, the last chance for Brett's luck to change.

She turned her gaze toward the road, empty now, though the first day of searching had been a circus. Amma's yard had been taped off again, and bystanders pressed against the perimeter, trying to get a good look at the boats in the water. Some brought chairs and coolers of beer and spent the whole day watching the divers. The *Tribune* sent reporters with cameras and obnoxious questions. Seattle's KING5 even sent a crew. But after a few days of finding only trash at the bottom of the ocean, the crowds went home. Even the officers she'd recruited the first two days to comb the beaches, in hopes Clara would have washed up at some point, stopped coming. Brett didn't blame them. The weather had been terrible all week. Rainy and windy and damn cold. Ice-breath, teeth-chattering cold. She understood not wanting to be outside in this kind of chill working over an empty beach, freezing your ass off for nothing.

Brett dug her hands in her pockets and buried her chin into the collar of her coat, trying to stop her shivering. Ever since Irving had pulled her from the water, she'd been unable to shake the bone-deep ache of near-hypothermia. Hot showers, multiple cups of coffee, sitting in front of the heater, blankets piled on top of her—nothing warmed her. She was thinking about taking a vacation. California or Florida. Fiji. Hawaii. Someplace where she could lie in the sun all day.

She glanced at the house where Amma stood silhouetted against the glass of the french doors. Pistol, that crooked-eared clown, pranced beside her.

They'd gotten lucky. Amma had spent only one night in the hospital, for monitoring. She had a few bruises and cuts but no lasting problems from her near-drowning. She'd actually found the whole thing to be quite exhilarating—her words—and had taken to reciting the events in great detail to anyone who would listen.

Brett had stayed at her grandmother's bedside the entire night. Even after the doctors told her to go home, she stayed, watching her grandmother sleep. Her thoughts were a prayer as she watched the rise and fall of Amma's chest—alive, alive, alive.

In the middle of the night, Amma's eyes had fluttered open. "Where am I?"

"The hospital," Brett reminded her. "You almost died."

But Amma swatted gently at her. "I did not. I knew exactly what I was doing when I pushed that bitch into the water."

"Amma..." Brett laughed at her grandmother's crass language.

She squeezed Brett's hand. "I'm so sorry. None of this would have happened if I hadn't let her into the house."

"It's not your fault."

"No, it is. Jimmy told me to keep the door locked. He told me what Clara and Marshall had done to him, and I..." Her gaze drifted over Brett's shoulder to the window. "I forgot. When I saw her on the porch, I thought I must have invited her over." A shudder ran through Amma's body, frail beneath the hospital sheets. "You almost lost him because of me. You almost lost both of us."

"We're fine, Amma." Brett bent and kissed her forehead. "We're all going to be just fine."

Amma's eyes started to droop shut. Just when it seemed like she'd fallen asleep again, she whispered, "I talked to the doctor when you were out getting coffee. They gave me the name of a neurologist in Seattle. He's supposed to be the best." She tapped a piece of paper lying on the bedside table. "I told them to write it down for you. In case I forgot. You know how I'm always forgetting." Her words faded as she drifted to sleep.

Brett tucked the slip of paper in her pocket.

The next day, Amma was discharged.

They had an appointment to see the neurologist in December. Until then, they were home again and had slipped into a quiet routine. Amma painted in the mornings when Brett was at work and the light was best. When she could manage it, Brett came home for lunch, and they took Pistol on a walk. Then Amma would nap or read in the afternoons. In the evenings, they watched television together. When Amma was feeling particularly energetic, they played board games. Amma sometimes forgot where she left her shoes. She sometimes asked Brett when Frank was coming home. She'd stopped complaining about the noises in the attic, though. Whatever she'd heard scratching around up there in October seemed to have moved on, but Brett left the traps set, just in case. She wasn't sure how long this calm would last, but for now, she was grateful for it.

Amma retreated into the house again. Pistol stayed by the door, though, nose pressed to the glass.

Brett had stopped by Lindy Danforth's trailer last night, intending to give the Chihuahua back to the woman. It had been wrong of her to take the dog in the first place. Lindy had been surprised to see them both. She'd reached to take the dog but then pulled back, shaking her head. *He's better off with you*, she'd said. Out of guilt or a sense of fairness, Brett had pulled twenty dollars from her wallet and offered it to Lindy. The woman hesitated only a second before snatching the bill from her fingers and slamming the trailer door shut.

"Guess you're stuck with me," Brett had said to the dog. Tail wagging, Pistol had licked her face.

A car pulled up to the curb, and Pistol started barking, his yips muffled by the glass doors. Irving got out of the car, holding two Styrofoam coffee cups in each hand. He walked down to the dock and offered Brett one of the cups.

"Thanks." She took a sip, grateful for the brief second of warmth.

They stood in silence, drinking their coffees and watching the divers work.

After a while, Irving glanced at the house. "How's Anita today?"

"She's fine," Brett said. "She keeps hinting that she wants to take the boat out."

Irving raised his eyebrows. "Awfully cold for sailing, isn't it?"

"I keep telling her that." Brett smiled. "But she says sailing is for all seasons as long as the wind is blowing."

Irving grunted a laugh and shook his head. "Don't let her talk you into it. What about your friend Jimmy? Is he still around?"

Instead of the usual button-down shirt and patterned tie, Irving was wearing a casual dark green polo. Brett found herself missing the birds.

"He and Trixie drove back to Portland after breakfast," she said.

The bullet had missed every major artery in Jimmy's leg and done no damage to the bone. A quick surgery to remove the slug, a few stitches, and with the help of a cane, pain killers, and sheer stubbornness, Jimmy was up and walking in two days.

This morning as she helped carry his suitcase to the car, with Trixie weaving between their legs, he'd offered to stay in Crestwood. Permanently.

"I'll move here for you," he'd said, and she told him that was the codeine talking. "I didn't take any today," he'd said, and then, "Bretty, I'm serious. Say the words, and I'll stay."

She had tried a few times, practicing the words in her head—*I love you, Jimmy. Yes, please stay. Stay here for me. Be with me.* But they stuck in her throat whenever she tried to say them out loud, and she couldn't tell if it was because she didn't love him enough or because she loved him too much.

There was nothing for him here. Seeing him shot, nearly bleeding out on the floor of the boathouse, Brett realized that she would never be able to give Jimmy Eagan the life or the love he deserved. She would forever be holding him at arm's length, afraid of this—afraid of losing him forever. It was better, kinder, to let him go now before he got too attached.

She'd given him a quick hug goodbye but felt him lingering, holding her tighter, giving her time to change her mind. She pulled away first. "Call me when you get there." And then he was gone. The last she saw of him was a hand darting out the window in a quick wave before he turned onto the highway and drove south.

"How many more times are you going to come out here?" Irving asked.

"This is the last," she said.

"And then what?"

She shrugged. "And then we write her off as shark bait, I guess."

They stared over the water. Waves lapped the pebbled shore. Without a body, it all felt so unfinished.

Brett gestured to a small dark bird with gray and white markings bobbing off the far end of the dock. "What kind is that?"

Irving squinted at it. "Hard to say for sure without my binoculars, but it looks like a Pacific Loon. They nest around tundra lakes up north during the summer but spend their winters here. It's rare to see one alone like that. Last year, there were thousands."

They watched the bird paddle in lazy circles. Without warning, it stretched up from the water, extended its wings, and flapped wildly, running across the water's surface a significant distance before taking flight.

Irving gave a satisfied grunt, then turned to Brett and said, "I know it's not exactly the ending you wanted, but it is an ending."

He left her standing on the dock and walked back to his car.

As the sun sank, the county sheriff's boats took a final circle around the harbor and roared south, back to the mooring dock where the crew would unpack their gear and head to the bar for drinks. The search for Clara Trudeau was officially over.

Brett sighed and turned to go back inside the house, but a figure standing on a small hill on the other side of the road drew her attention. The view of Sculpin Bay from that spot was expansive, and neighbors would often walk up to enjoy the sunset or watch for whales. This evening, Elizabeth stood alone, eyes scanning the horizon. She wore a puffy green jacket and a pink wool hat pulled low over her ears. Her face was wrapped in a striped neon scarf. When Brett arrived at the top of the hill, Elizabeth scooted over, making room for her on the flat patch of grass.

Twice this week, Brett had stopped by the Trudeau's ranch house to try and talk to Elizabeth, but she'd been turned away at the door. Her grandparents said Elizabeth wasn't ready to speak to anyone, let alone the cop who arrested her father.

Elizabeth turned to her now, anger sparking in her eyes and burning her cheeks red. "Did she really do what they're saying she did? Did my mother really kill all those people?"

Brett nodded. The girl had been lied to her entire life. It was about damn time someone told her the truth.

"And Zach? Was it because of me?" Here her voice trembled. "Did she kill him because of what he did to me?"

The simple answer was yes. Clara had killed Zach because of what he'd done, but it was also far more complicated than that, and Elizabeth certainly wasn't to blame.

"Your mother made her own choices that had nothing to do with you," Brett said. "You did the right thing coming forward after what happened to you at the party. Don't ever let anyone tell you otherwise."

Elizabeth bit her lip and stared down at her feet.

Brett continued, "I know this is a lot for you to take in, and it's going to be a long time, I think, before you start to feel anything resembling normal again. But you will, I promise you that. You might be all kinds of broken right now, but give it time, and it'll start to hurt less. You'll find a way to live with this. You'll find a way to move on. And Elizabeth. Elizabeth, look at me."

She lifted her head.

"Anytime you need to talk. Anytime you have questions, or just need someone to scream at, or someone to be silent with. I'm here. I want you to know that, okay? You're not alone." She brushed her fingers across the back of Elizabeth's arm.

Elizabeth recoiled from her and cast her gaze across the churning sea. "She's a good swimmer, you know. She's been swimming her whole life."

"The water's cold," Brett said. "Even a strong swimmer would have trouble."

"So, you think she's dead?" There was no tremble in her voice now, and she didn't wait for Brett's answer. Her words were sharp-edged when she said, "I hope she is."

Brett said nothing, allowing the silence to swell between them. Down on the water, seagulls bobbed on white-capped waves, their silhouettes stark against the copper horizon.

"Do you know what's going to happen with my dad?" Elizabeth asked. "Every time I ask my grandparents, they tell me not to worry about it. That he'll be home soon."

"His attorney is working with the prosecutor on a plea deal," Brett told her. "They're charging him with false imprisonment and accessory after the fact. If he continues to cooperate, he might only have to pay a fine and serve probation for a few months. But you should prepare yourself for the possibility that he might have to serve some prison time."

Elizabeth shook her head hard like she was trying to shake

out every painful feeling swirling inside her. She squeezed her eyes shut, then opened them again, wrapped her arms around her chest, holding herself together. "She made him do all that. He would have never done it by himself, you know. He was trying to protect me from her."

"He might have been trying to protect you, but he still has free will. He made his own choices too," Brett pointed out. "He knew what the consequences could be."

The muscle in Elizabeth's jaw tensed. "Do you really think he knew? About what she'd done? Do you think he knew this whole time what she was capable of?"

"He says he didn't."

"But how could he not have known?"

"Did you know?"

A shuddering breath, a gulp, and then she shook her head. "She was just, she was my mom, you know? That's it. She was overprotective sometimes and got mad at me when I left the toothpaste cap off and did this annoying thing where she would hum whenever she was at a red light. But she was my mom. She took care of me. She loved me. I think. I mean, she must have. But I don't...How could she do what she did?" Elizabeth turned tearful eyes onto Brett. "Is it that easy? To kill another person?"

Brett wanted to tell her that killing was the hardest thing in the world, that taking another person's life changed you irreparably, that Clara had been broken in a way most people weren't. But she knew that wasn't the entire truth. Every person was capable, everyone a flicker of uncontrolled rage away from taking another's life. Given the chance, Brett would have killed Clara without hesitation if doing so meant Margot got to live.

"I don't want to end up like her." Elizabeth tossed the words toward the ocean like a prayer.

"You won't," Brett tried to sound reassuring.

Elizabeth clutched her hand against the base of her sternum for a moment, with her fingers curled in a fist like she was holding something precious. She turned toward Brett again, a haunted look in her eyes.

"I thought about it, too. About hurting Zach. About taking a knife and..." She sucked in a sharp breath, pinched her lips together a moment before finishing. "How does that make me any different from her?"

Without waiting for an answer, Elizabeth spun away and marched down the hill. Brett let her go.

Amma's house—her house now, too, Brett realized—glowed invitingly at the bottom of the hill. Brett knew when she finally went back inside, there would be a hot bowl of soup and a cozy pair of socks waiting for her. And later, Pistol would curl up beside her in bed with a tiny sigh of contentment, and she would burrow beneath the covers until sleep overtook her. And in the morning, the sun would rise, and she would rise with it. But for now, she stayed on the hill, gazing out across the smudged aluminum of Sculpin Bay.

The shadows lengthened as the sun dipped low, and the sky bruised purple. Waves tumbled rocks one over another as the tide tried to devour the land. A few minutes passed, and then the moon appeared high above her, stitching a slender silver thread over an ocean that never stilled. Her breath made white puffs in the dark.

There had been a moment in the water when Brett thought she had found Clara. She heard a splash and lunged toward the sound, but her hands grasped nothing. She felt something brush against her leg, but when she turned, she found herself alone in the cold and endless dark, on the verge of drowning. Then Irving pulled her to safety.

There was a slim chance that Clara had gotten away. That she swam to some shadowed beach, pulled herself from the water, and disappeared into the night. Even now, she could be in a new town, with a new name, building herself a new life.

But Brett had been in the water that night, too. She'd felt for herself the power of the tide, the ravenous way it pulled you under, and she knew in her heart that Clara Trudeau was lost to the deep. Only the ocean could tell her secrets now.

ACKNOWLEDGEMENTS

I couldn't do any of this without support from readers like you. Knowing you're excited about reading my books, keeps me excited about writing them. Thank you for loving books as much as I do!

Special thanks are also owed to the following people.

Alisa Callos: who suggested the beach house writing retreat where the seed for this book was planted, who also reads many of my messy drafts and is excellent at double-checking the nitty-gritty details I often overlook.

Caroline Starr Rose: who lets me emote all over her and then kindly reminds me to keep going, whose gentle nudges and daily check-ins keep me grounded and optimistic.

Carrie La Seur: who came in late to the game but whose insightful feedback changed everything.

Julia Kenny: who helped shape this book from the beginning and gave her blessing when I decided to blaze my own trail for a while.

Nathan Andress: who lent me his name and promised not to get mad.

Caitlin Doughty: who got me out of the house when I thought I'd be stuck in a rut forever and continues to be there for me whenever I need to freak out.

My sweet friends and family who are constantly telling me not to be so hard on myself. Thank you for cheering me on with the big and small stuff—I would probably quit if not for your voices in my head.

Finally, kisses and unflagging devotion to Ryan, a man who continues to prove himself to be my biggest fan. He is the reason I have space and time to create. He is also the reason I don't starve. More than that, he is the reason this book exists as something other than a file on my computer. Because when I thought I was done, he took my hand and said, What have we got to lose? Thank you for being willing to step out into the unknown with me.

ABOUT THE AUTHOR

VALERIE GEARY is the author of *Everything We Lost* and *Crooked River*, a finalist for the Oregon Book Award. She lives in the Pacific Northwest with her husband where they enjoy hiking favorite trails and discovering new ones together.

Want to go behind-the-scenes with the author, receive exclusive content, pre-order information, reading recommendations, and more?

Sign up for Valerie Geary's monthly newsletter at:

valeriegeary.com

CPSIA information can be obtained
at www.ICGtesting.com
Printed in the USA
LVHW051448090521
686924LV00001B/72

9 781954 815001